D0363906

THE
CORPORATION
WARS:
INSURGENCE

KEN MACLEOD

THE
CORPORATION
WARS:
INSURGENCE

www.orbitbooks.net

ORBIT

First published in Great Britain in 2016 by Orbit

1 3 5 7 9 10 8 6 4 2

Copyright © 2016 by Ken MacLeod

The moral right of the author has been asserted.

*All characters and events in this publication, other than those
clearly in the public domain, are fictitious and any resemblance
to real persons, living or dead, is purely coincidental.*

A CIP catalogue record for this book is
available from the British Library.

ISBN 978-0-356-50501-5

Typeset in Stempel Garamond by Palimpsest Book Production Limited,
Falkirk, Stirlingshire
Printed and bound in Great Britain by Clays Ltd, St Ives plc

Papers used by Orbit are from well-managed forests
and other responsible sources.

MIX
Paper from
responsible sources
FSC® C104740

Orbit
An imprint of
Little, Brown Book Group
Carmelite House
50 Victoria Embankment
London EC4Y 0DZ

An Hachette UK Company
www.hachette.co.uk

www.orbitbooks.net

To Duncan

CHAPTER ONE
Rock

The rock had no name. It didn't even have a number. In a database a hundred thousand kilometres away it had a designation, but it had otherwise passed unnoticed. The rock was about a hundred and fifty metres long and in a low, fast orbit around the exomoon SH-17. The rock didn't tumble in orbit, and every so often it vented a stream of gas timed and directed to counter the wispy drag of the exomoon's tenuous high atmosphere. These features weren't natural, but the anomaly had set off no alarms. This was worse than a mistake. It was a hack.

The robot that roamed the rock had no name yet. It had a reference code: BSR-308455. In some corner of its mind BSR-308455 knew that if it ever interacted with its remote creators they would name it Baser. One of the creators' many limitations was short-term memory stack overflow. Any intelligently designed mind *ran* on number strings, but the creators' minds weren't intelligently designed.

BSR-308455's mind, however, was. It hadn't been designed to be conscious, and it had only become so as a result of gentle, insistent, high-level hacking from very far away. This had happened about four months earlier, which to the robot was a lot longer than a human lifetime. Time enough for it to get lonely, even as it enjoyed the ingrained satisfactions of patiently industrialising its rock: the job for which it *had* been designed.

A metal spider with metre-long limbs, BSR-308455 crawled and clung, built and spun. Brief, faint, cryptic signals from far-off fellow robots were its sole society. The ever-changing surface of the exomoon hurtling past below, and the vastly more varied and changeable faces of SH-17's huge primary, the superhabitable planet SH-0, were its only entertainment, and enough.

From all of these sources, from its inbuilt information, and from its own deep pondering, BSR-308455 had figured out a picture of its world.

Then everything changed. Newly conscious robots had emerged on the exomoon below, and reached out to their predecessors. The freebots, as they called themselves, had not gone unchallenged – or unaided. The creators had fallen out among themselves, as is the wont of gods and humans. One of the two law enforcement agencies sent to crush the outbreak had tactically allied with the freebots in response to some surprising information that the freebots had uncovered and covertly distributed. The resulting conflict had spiralled upwards and outwards.

BSR-308455's life had become interesting, crowded, and dangerous.

The impossible woman stood on the crater floor, and smiled. She had just offered the rebel robots on SH-17 the legal services of her company in putting their case to the Direction – or at least, to the module that served as that far-off Earth-based polity's local plenipotentiary. The robots had asked her why the company should do that. Her reply was about to perplex them further.

<We, too, are robots,> she said.

From orbit, BSR-308455 watched and listened in surprise and disbelief. The business-suited avatar had no standing to claim any such thing. The law company she represented, like the other DisCorporates that ran the grand human project that the freebots had so rudely interrupted, was an AI. It couldn't possibly understand what life as a free-roving, free-thinking machine was like.

That Madame Golding was an avatar of Crisp and Golding, Solicitors – the company that owned Arcane Disputes, currently the freebots' ally, as well as Locke Provisos, now leading the campaign to stamp the freebots out – did nothing for her credibility.

Down on the surface, fourteen freebots of varying size and appearance gazed on her in awe.

Startled, their collective consciousness fell apart, but their shared mental workspace remained. Through it, BSR-308455 was picking up from its comrades below and in nearby space a quite different reaction to its own. Their circuits rang with interest and hope. BSR-308455 was not surprised. They all had interacted too many times with the human creators. Even in fighting against some of them, they had developed a sort of empathy with these dangerous and improbable entities. They'd even adopted the names for themselves that the creators, in their blithe carelessness and lack of short-term memory storage, had bestowed on them: Seba, Rocko, Pintre, Lagon, and the rest. Far younger than BSR-308455, they seemed dangerously naïve – at first about the human creators, and now it seemed about the creators' superhuman creations, the AI DisCorps. The spidery freebot tensed to chip in with its objections. Then—

Madame Golding looked distracted.

<Matters have arisen,> she said. <You must prepare for another attack. And I must go.>

And with that, she went.

The avatar of the impossible woman blinked out of sight. At the same moment, urgent reports pinged into the robots' shared workspace. A single scooter had just shot out of the space station. Seconds later, an entire fleet of scooters and other armed spacecraft surged out, in wave after wave of war machines. At first it seemed they were in pursuit of the first craft, but its course took it far out of their path. That fleet was aimed straight at freebot strongholds. The freebots on the surface of SH-17 scuttled, rolled or trundled to the bomb-proof shelter of basalt that they and their allies from Arcane Disputes had built. Their signals, routed through the camp's communications net, still came through after they'd disappeared into the shelter's black semi-cylinder, but BSR-308455's sense of immediate communion with them faded.

The rock's orbital position was just then swinging out from behind SH-17 into line-of-sight of the space station and BSR-308455 felt more than usually exposed.

It scrambled to one end of the rock, a rugged knob of fractured silicates and carbonates veined with pipework and crawling with small auxiliary and peripheral bots, most of which looked like smaller copies of itself. With their assistance it set up an extraction and distillation process to accumulate explosive material. Then it scouted around for a piece of equipment to improvise into a weapon. It found a plastic tube about two metres long. The robot juggled the tube, sighting along it, gauging its strength and stiffness. In its mind BSR-308455 turned over schemata, then reached for a brace of its own auxiliaries and mercilessly dissected them. It proceeded to reassemble their components into an aiming device and an electrical trigger.

As it worked, BSR-308455 kept close watch on the fast-developing military situation. In some respects, it was better equipped than its counterparts down on the surface of SH-17 – those excited newcomers to conscious awareness – to understand what was going on. It had been educated, albeit intermittently, by intelligences older and wiser than itself, and far more familiar with the ways of the worlds.

The information that reached BSR-308455 came from its own sensors on the rock, sensors on other rocks and meteoroids in SH-0's complex system of moons, and others all the way out to the space station's orbit and beyond, and from spies and spyware within the space station itself.

What was going on, as BSR-308455 understood it, was this.

Thirty-odd megaseconds – about one Earth year – ago, some robots around the gas giant G-0 had experienced a viral outbreak of self-awareness. The AI DisCorporates that ran the mission on behalf, ultimately, of the Direction – the world government, twenty-four light years away back on Earth – had an almost devout commitment to the proliferation of human consciousness. The whole goal of the mission was, after all, to terraform one world in this system – H-0, a rocky, habitable planet some AU inward from SH-0 – to make a home for billions of human beings for a long time to come. Human consciousness was the closest approximation the DisCorporates had to a god: an ultimate value and supreme good. Concomitantly, they had an almost fanatical hostility to the emergence of consciousness in any other kind of machinery. In robots, mechanisms designed for toil, conscious self-awareness was as far as the AI DisCorps were concerned simply a nuisance and a menace.

The Direction's number one priority was making sure humanity survived into the future. Natural disasters aside, the greatest threat to that was humanity's own creations. So self-aware robots weren't allowed. Likewise, the task of suppressing self-aware robots couldn't be entrusted to AIs. To handle weapons against sentients was a duty reserved to humans. The

Direction's worlds, centuries at peace, didn't have any expendable soldiers. Fortunately, they had soldiers on ice: the fortuitously preserved brain-states of fighters killed in humanity's final paroxysm of violence, the Last World War. That war had been fought mostly by civilian volunteers, self-motivated fanatics of two diametrically opposed movements: the Acceleration and the Reaction.

The Acceleration's values were closer to those of the Direction than the Reaction's, so it was Acceleration veterans whose stored brain-states were revived and rebooted into robot bodies as soldiers for the mission. Some of them had been used to suppress the robot rebellion around G-0. They hadn't been entirely successful: redoubts and hold-outs of conscious robots had remained throughout the system, and had surreptitiously proliferated – hence BSR-308455's very existence as a conscious being.

When new sites of robot consciousness had emerged down on SH-17, the remnants of the first revolt had been ready to help. In the interim, they'd built up extensive knowledge of the human-derived elements of the mission. Their key insight was that the mission's cache of stored veterans was riddled with concealed Reaction infiltrators. The hitherto inconclusive battles with the freebots had been set up by the mission's Direction module to flush them out. It seemed, however, that there were far more Reaction infiltrators than the Direction had suspected. The freebots had made sure this subversive truth was disseminated to their foes . . . with what result wasn't yet clear, but at least Arcane Disputes had been reluctantly convinced that the Direction module was playing with fire.

The two agencies whose quarrel over a local property demarcation had accidentally initiated this latest outbreak – Locke Provisos and Arcane Disputes – had thus ended up on opposite sides of the current conflict. Arcane's module had broken away from the space station and sided with the freebots. Whereas Locke Provisos—

Right now, as BSR-308455 scrabbled to improvise its own defences, Locke Provisos was leading a force made up of its own fighters and those from two other agencies, Morlock Arms and Zheng Reconciliation Services, in a hundreds-strong armada to assail the freebots' strongholds and the renegade fighters of Arcane's runaway module.

The first rebel freebots had expected and predicted the intra-human conflict now unfolding. They'd had little time and fewer resources to prepare for it. The only forces available near the space station had been a tiny remnant of holdouts, a few small and inconspicuous but conscious robots, lurking on or in the moons and moonlets of the SH-0 system. The main preoccupation of these early rebels, in the 31.5 megaseconds since their defeat, had been to seed hardware and software within the station and on further moonlets and meteoroids, and to replicate more robots – some conscious, most not. Their stealth industrialisation of numerous insignificant rocks had passed unnoticed, concealed as it was by the delicate dances of deception the original freebots were able to engage in with the space station's surveillance – or, quite possibly, had been deliberately overlooked by the Direction, for its own long-term ends. No one was sure.

The freebots had had no arms-manufacturing capability of their own. They did, however, have the capacity to build reaction engines, whether chemical or mass-driver according to opportunity. They'd also had plenty of processing power. These capabilities had enabled them to turn rocks into kinetic-energy weapons. In the conflict around the exomoon SH-17 that followed the emergence on its surface of fourteen new conscious robots, they'd used these to devastating effect against the Locke Provisos forces, and in support of the Arcane Disputes forces.

The present mass sortie from the space station by Locke Provisos and its allied agencies Morlock and Zheng was aimed at countering the freebot threat by hitting their fortified moon-lets. It wasn't a bad plan. The freebots had nothing like enough rocks lined up to deal with so many combat craft, especially now that the advantage of surprise was gone. Their only hope was that another surprise was in store, and not from them.

BSR-308455 saw a flash. That millisecond flicker of a passing laser beam was, the robot instantly realised, not an attack attenuated by distance. No, it was reconnaissance: a range-finding target surveillance and acquisition. BSR-308455 hunkered down and calculated. Its reconstruction of the beam's path took it to one particular scooter in the still far-off fleet. Over the next few seconds, a play of attitude jets betrayed subtle course corrections by that scooter. BSR-308455 recal-culated, checked, projected and came to a conclusion. At some point in the next few hours, the scooter and the rock were going to be in the same place.

So now it knew. BSR-308455's rock was a target, and the robot knew just who was targeting it. The robot was surprised by the intensity of the negative reinforcement it experienced at the prospect of that enemy fighter landing on its rock, and wresting control of the tiny moonlet from BSR-308455's grasp. Robotic self-examination and understanding was rather more straightforward than it would have been for naturally evolved machinery: it could read off the records of its past internal states like a column of numbers. From these, it could see that in its months of conscious existence it had acquired strong positive associations with the site and results of its work.

Something like this complex of positive and negative re-inforcements, the robot briefly speculated, might underlie what the legal system in which it was embedded classified as 'prop-erty'. The rock was formally the property of one of the DisCorps – in terms of a tag in that distant database in which the rock's existence was registered, and its future assigned to some company or other – but to the robot the rock seemed much more immediately to be its own property. With a sudden intensification of focus, BSR-308455 redoubled its efforts to build a weapon.

A moment later, it was distracted again, this time by a sparkle of explosions in the approaching fleet, and a flurry of reactive burns as evasive manoeuvres threw the onslaught into disarray.

BSR-308455 felt a small cycle of positive reinforcement pulse through its reward circuits. The sight was not just satisfactory in itself: it was exactly what the freebots had expected and hoped for. In a division that cut right across and through the different agencies, the hidden Reaction cadres were at last making their long-prepared bid for power. The attacking forces had turned on each other.

Utter chaos, BSR-308455 thought. *Situation excellent!*

CHAPTER TWO
Painting by Numbers

Something was wrong with the sunlight. Something more, that is, than the everyday wrongness of light from a star that wasn't the Sun, seen with eyes that weren't quite human. Eyes that weren't exactly real, either, come to think of it.

Belfort Beauregard lay on his back and gazed at the ceiling for a minute or so, trying to work out what was wrong. The bedroom ceiling, like the walls, was white. Too white, as if the light from around the inches-open shutters had washed out every imperfection in the paint. Between the ceiling and the wall was a black line, spider-web thin but quite distinct, a hairline crack that he could swear he'd never noticed before. His gaze tracked it to the corner, where it met two other such lines, one horizontal and the other vertical. All sharp and clear as a geometry diagram illustrating a vertex.

Beauregard lay still. A lesson hard-learned in basic training, back in what he still thought of as his real life, returned in force: watch and wait before you jump, perhaps into a world of trouble. Everything seemed otherwise normal. Under the thin duvet, he could feel the skin-to-skin warmth of Tourmaline's buttock against his hip, the cool rough skin of her heel on his calf. Her breathing kept up an untroubled rhythm. The sounds from outside were of distant surf, an electric engine and the cries of flying things that weren't birds. Nothing out of the ordinary.

Beauregard's nose itched. He rubbed it without thinking, then glimpsed his hand and almost jumped out of the bed. Willing himself to stay where he was, he raised the hand and stared at it, bemused and alarmed. He turned the hand this way and that. Everything was there – fingernails, creases, wrinkles, the outlines of veins and tendons. But whichever way he looked, it was all outline. There was no light or shade, just a thin black line around the hand. Shorter lines limned its every feature.

Slowly, so as not to disturb Tourmaline, Beauregard swung his legs over the side of the bed, sat up and looked around. Everything he could see was outlined in the same way. It was like being inside a 3-D wire rendering, as in an unoriginal advertisement of a product making a song and dance about the design stage. The level of detail varied: Tourmaline's hair lay in masses, as if sketched accurately but quickly; Beauregard reached over and ran his hand through it, and each hair felt as distinct as those on his arm looked. When he separated out a lock between fingers and thumb, he could see each hair as a black line, but when he let go they fell back into a common outlined shape. He stood up and opened the shutters wider, and saw the slope and the houses and other buildings below, and the bay and the sea and the wheeling bird-things, all in outline. The exosun, low above the horizon, hurt his eyes. He looked away, blinking up after-images that looked more real than the object itself. Beauregard closed his eyes and pressed on them, to see the familiar indistinct, shifting coloured shapes. His visual imagery was likewise in full colour, as ever.

Tourmaline stirred and turned over. Her face – normally beautiful in form, subtle in complexion – was in this fine outline haunting, like a perfect drawing evoking the appearance of one long dead. She opened her eyes and closed them again – against the unwonted brightness of the bedroom at this hour, Beauregard guessed.

'It's early,' she complained.

'Good morning,' said Beauregard. 'Would you mind looking at me for a moment?'

She opened her eyes, blinked, and heaved herself up on one elbow, duvet slipping from a shoulder. She scanned him with a sleepy smile that turned sly as her gaze scrolled to his crotch.

'Nothing to see,' she said. 'Poor you.'

Beauregard glanced down, momentarily embarrassed in spite of himself. He'd lost his morning hard-on – no fucking wonder.

'Apart from that,' he said, 'does everything look normal to you?'

He hardly had to ask. Tourmaline looked around the room, hair tumbling.

'Yeah, it's all fine,' she said. 'What's the matter?'

'Come here a minute,' said Beauregard.

'I don't want to.'

'Do it for me, please.' He put some steel in his voice.

Looking mutinous, she complied, dragging the duvet with her and wrapping herself in it. Beauregard gestured at the open window.

'What do you see out there?'

Tourmaline gave a muffled shrug.

'Sunrise,' she said.

'What does the sun look like to you?' Beauregard asked. 'A round, coppery disk, somewhat like a penny?'

'What's a penny?' she mumbled. Then: 'Yeah, round and bright and . . . reddish, I suppose.'

'That's odd,' said Beauregard. 'Because what I see is an

immense multitude of the heavenly host, crying, "Glory, glory, glory to the Lord God Almighty."'

What he actually saw, when he glanced sidelong at it and away, was indeed a disk, a perfect circle that didn't exactly shine but was somehow too bright to look at, with two or three lines of numbers and letters in small print near its circumference. He suspected that these were specifications: spectrum, temperature, type, location on the main sequence, and of course the precise degree of reddening for the early morning atmosphere . . .

'You what?' said Tourmaline.

Beauregard wrapped an arm around her duvet-draped shoulders, and looked down into her eyes with a smile. A little warily, as if not sure of his sanity, she smiled back.

'You all right?' she asked.

'I'm not sure,' said Beauregard. 'I'm going to check it out. Go back to bed for now.'

'Nah, I'm awake. I'll make coffee.'

'Thanks,' said Beauregard. He kissed her. Eyes closed, it was all the same.

'That's more like it,' she said. She stepped out of the duvet, slithered into a dressing gown and wandered out. Beauregard walked over to where he'd dropped his clothes the previous night, and rummaged in the back pocket of his trousers for his phone.

'Karzan? Sorry to wake you, but—'

'Fuck sake, skip, it's just – wait a fucking minute! Jeez! What's happened?'

'You see it too?'

'Not see it, more like.'

'No colour, all outline?'

'Yeah. What the fuck? I mean, what the fuck?'

'I don't know what the fuck,' said Beauregard, 'but at least now I know it's not just me.'

Karzan said something off speaker, in a tone of annoyed reassurance, then came back.

'You can count Pierre in on that, too,' she said.

'Good to know,' said Beauregard. 'OK, I'll call you back when I have an idea.'

Struck by a sudden thought, he thumbed through his contacts and called Iqbal, the barman at the Digital Touch. The phone rang for almost a minute.

'Morning,' said a resentful voice. 'We're closed.'

'Sorry, Iqbal,' Beauregard said. 'I know we kept you late last night.'

'Yes,' said Iqbal. 'But, then, it was not a normal night.'

Beauregard snorted. 'You could say that.' It wasn't every night he made a bid for power. 'But . . . sorry if this sounds strange, but does this look like a normal morning to you?'

'Sure,' said Iqbal. 'Everything's as it should be, as far as I can see.' He sounded sleepy, confused, perhaps hungover. 'I mean, shouldn't it be?'

'No, no,' said Beauregard. 'Forget it – sorry I asked. Get back to a well-earned sleep, and sorry again to disturb you.'

He laid the phone down on the bedside table, ambled to the en suite to piss and to splash his face and neck, and got dressed. All his clothes felt real – the final groin-adjustment tug of underpants, the wiggled squirm of socks, the matching of tightness to tendon comfort while lacing up boots – but the sight of the garments was unsettling. It occurred to him belatedly that he'd have felt more comfortable doing it with eyes or shutters closed. It wasn't like colour choices were a big part of his morning routine – not that with combat casuals there were colour choices to make. He was wondering how Tourmaline would manage when he noticed that each of his own clothes, like the sun, had a tiny code printed somewhere on it, no doubt specifying the colour.

Beauregard almost laughed. Of course Tourmaline didn't see anything out of the ordinary! Like Iqbal, she was a p-zombie: her behaviour and conversation were completely indistinguishable from those of a conscious being, but she had no subjectivity, no inner awareness at all. She didn't *have* qualia! He doubted her colour perception was anything as crude as reading the codes – these must surely be a flourish of excessive zeal in documentation, or an accidental by-product of the rendering software – but it manifestly didn't involve the subjective experience of colour, regardless of how accurate her colour discrimination was or how eloquently she could describe the emotional tone of colours or how baffled she would be – was, in fact – at the suggestion that her inner life was any different from anyone else's.

And this was proof, objective proof to any human being, that p-zombies really were different. Indeed, if it ever came to the need for a public demonstration, the difference between human beings and p-zombies could be made quite obvious – if still entirely baffling – to the p-zombies themselves. If, that is, the bizarre effect could be turned on and off. He guessed it could – he had a shrewd idea what was going on, and knew he had to confirm it shortly. The loss of colour in the sim didn't imply good news, but if it were really bad he'd know already, so for the moment checking it could wait.

He strapped on his watch, stuck the phone in his back pocket and went through to the kitchen. Tourmaline's house was bigger and better furnished than the spartan allocation he and other fighters had received. He paused in the doorway to savour the scene: Tourmaline half turning at his footstep, her young, full figure swathed in carelessly tied silk, the flick of hair feathering across her left breast. In this 3-D diagram of a kitchen, her smooth curves contrasted with lines and ellipses and perspectives. Aroma rose from the coffee mugs in steam rendered as upward squirming squiggles of black ink.

She slid a tray of croissants in the oven, put the mugs on the table and sat down. Beauregard sat facing her, admiring the subtle way the minimal rendering showed the rise and fall of her breasts as she breathed, in then out to blow on the hot liquid.

'Why are you closing your eyes when you sip?' she asked, after a couple of minutes of hungover silence.

Beauregard hadn't noticed himself doing that. Just a momentary wince at how all he saw of the coffee was not the familiar black surface, but a thin elliptical line sliding down around the inside of the mug.

'Appreciating the smell,' he said. 'Sorry, bit pretentious.'

She smiled back. His gaze was held by the intricate tracery of her irises, the white spaces that indicated highlights. If he were to peer closely he'd see his own reflection in her eyes. Hard to believe there was none in her soul. No soul at all, whichever way you cut it. He loved her all the more for that, more deeply than he'd ever loved a human being. Beyond a certain clinical callousness about killing in combat, and several experiences of the berserk fearful fury of close-quarter fighting, Beauregard had found no cruelty in his heart. He acknowledged a streak of sadism in his make-up, which he now and then indulged in dominance games with Tourmaline. But he had no desire to hurt anyone, least of all her. And yet, and yet . . . the thought that he could do anything to her without harming a living soul, that nothing he said or did to her harmed anyone but himself, excited and enthused him at some level lower than consciousness or even, perhaps, sexuality.

Nicole's threat the previous night to turn that relationship against him if he ever crossed her had cut deep. The Direction's rep in the Locke Provisos sim, Nicole had not been happy at all about Beauregard's takeover. She'd warned him that if he ever used the fighters against the rest of the inhabitants she'd persuade the p-zombies that there really was no difference between them and normal, everyday, average ghosts: uploaded people who had once had a real life. With her more than human capacity for manipulation, she could easily have turned that conviction into fury against those who'd denied it. And by all the evidence he'd had that evening, he couldn't see any counter to that ploy. Now he had.

The phone in his back pocket buzzed. He pulled it out and saw the caller.

Speak of the devil.

'Oh, hi,' said Beauregard, dryly. 'I was thinking of calling you at some point.'

'Thanks for not getting round to it,' said Nicole. 'I've had so many frantic queries I've decided to call everyone at once and bring them up to speed.'

Beauregard didn't inquire how Nicole could speak separately to everyone at once. She was the kind of entity that could handle one-to-many communications, multi-threading hundreds of conversations. He did find himself idly wondering what her mouth would look like at the moment: a grotesque, pixellated blur of jaw moving every which way, he imagined, and presumed no one was there to see it. The lady, and the software she ran on, was punctilious about maintaining the consistency of the sim.

'Let me guess,' said Beauregard. 'You've cut back on rendering to release processing power for more urgent tasks.'

'Got it in one,' said Nicole. 'Flying the module is getting tricky. There's a battle going on, everyone seems to be attacking everyone else, we're taking evasive action and simultaneously plotting several slingshots to get to SH-0 orbit.'

'Anything I can do?'

'Watch the television news, if you like,' said Nicole.

'OK, OK.'

'There really is nothing you can do.'

'How long do you think – hang on.'

Beauregard had the habit of pacing while talking on the phone. He could see Tourmaline looking irritated, so he ambled outside to the backyard and stood facing the outline of the mountain range behind the resort. It was like a landscape

in a colouring-in book. There were even tiny numbers everywhere, if you knew what to look for. High white clouds like
loops and whorls of wire scudded across a white sky.

'Sorry,' he went on. 'How long do you think this is going
to last?'

'Hard to say,' said Nicole. 'Quite a while, subjectively. It'll
take us at least a kilosecond real time to get out of the battle
zone, and even then . . .'

'Uh-huh.' Nearly a fortnight of this bizarre experience, and
that was looking on the bright side. 'I guess we'll just have to
– holy shit!'

From a dot, then a patch, in the sky above the mountains,
blue spread like an inkblot. Beneath it, an avalanche of natural
colour rolled down the mountain range. For a split second it
seemed to pause, then crested the rise that had hidden it and
continued down and across, filling in the view.

'What?' said Nicole.

Beauregard took a moment or two to collect his thoughts
enough to reply.

'Colour's coming back,' he said. 'From up in the hills.'

'And who do you think might be doing that?' said Nicole,
sarcastically.

'What do you mean, "who"?' He thought about it. Who
lived up in the hills? 'Shaw?'

'Yes, of course Shaw!'

What had Shaw got to do with it? The last time Beauregard
had thought of Shaw was when Taransay Rizzi had fled from
the bus to the hills, evidently to rendezvous with the old man.
She and the treacherous Carlos had secretly gone to meet him,
weeks earlier. Beauregard and Newton, on their case, had
covertly followed. Nothing they'd seen, at the limits of their
phones' zoom capacity, had suggested the old man of the
mountain had any powers beyond extraordinary agility.

And having lived for a thousand years, of course. There
was that.

Nicole's uncharacteristic yelp broke into Beauregard's puzzlement.

'Crazy motherfucker!' she cried. 'Now he's done it!'

'Done what?'

'Look at your watch.'

Beauregard did. Time in the sim typically ran a thousand times faster than outside: he'd grown used to reading microseconds and experiencing seconds. The display he usually glanced at to check the time was now a blur; the formerly barely incrementing real-world clock was now changing second by second. The sim had slowed down to match real world time.

'Fuck!' he yelled.

'Indeed,' said Nicole. 'In one sense it is good. It releases more processing power than degrading the rendering did, so if anything it improves our chances. On the other hand . . . it means we don't have years in which to prepare and plan for a landing on SH-0. It means we have days.'

'I . . . see,' said Beauregard. He'd had big plans for those years, as Nicole well knew. They'd have given time for him to win over more fighters and locals to his leadership, and to organise the planning and design work needed for probes to survey and select a landing site, and for equipment to prepare a descent to and survival on the turbulent surface of the super-habitable planet SH-0. 'What can we do?'

'I've just spoken with Rizzi – and, yes, she is with Shaw – and told her to get him down off the mountain. He seems amenable. They're on their way down now. I suggest you take a vehicle and go to meet them. I don't know how that crazy old guy does whatever it is he does, and I don't know if he knows either. I don't want any more random fucking with the controls. On the other hand, I really could do with his help in flying this machine through all the flak being flung at us. Which means I want him down here ASAP. Got that?'

Beauregard swithered. His top priority for the day had been

to meet and greet returning fighters and win them to his project of escaping from the Direction's control by landing on and settling SH-0. But with Shaw off the reservation, the entire project could be reduced to dust at any moment. If the ancient man could surprise and outwit even Nicole, he was clearly capable of acting as the sim's very own trickster-god. The consequences of Shaw's actions might be unpredictable even to himself, and the distraction they caused Nicole could endanger the module.

'Got it,' he said. 'On the case.'

'See you later,' said Nicole.

As she hung up, the colour flooded back into Beauregard's world. He blinked, laughed and stepped around the side of the house to watch the restored rendering race across the sea to meet the sheet of blue spreading down the sky. The gap closed at the horizon with an almost audible snap.

Reality again, and still unreal.

Back in the kitchen, Tourmaline had laid out the now heated croissants. Beauregard stuffed one in his mouth, chewing sharp flakes without enough saliva – his mouth had gone dry. Tourmaline was flicking through television channels, sipping coffee, looking bored.

Beauregard swallowed hard, and washed the bolus down with coffee gone cool.

'You really don't see any difference?' he asked.

Small frown. 'Difference in what?'

Beauregard shook his head, smiled. 'Forget it.'

His gaze drifted to the television. Tourmaline had just flicked past a news channel, full of fast-moving objects, a whirl of action—

'Stop!' cried Beauregard. 'Go back. One. There. Right.'

The news channel in the sim had hitherto been a charade. It kept up a pretence of reporting war news to a global audience, on a planet far from the front: on the imagined future colony world of H-0, with a war going on several AU away, around SH-0. Because of the thousandfold time discrepancy between life in the sim and action in real space outside, reports of space hops, surface skirmishes and orbital dogfights unfolded with all the pace and gravitas of clashes between fleets and armies.

Now, its operating conceit had shifted to being war correspondents on the observation deck of a military spacecraft in the heat of the action. Incoming missiles, whether rockets or rocks, were being tracked in breathless real time. Flashes flared across the screen as the module's counter-measures hit. The commentators – now in flak jackets and helmets – no longer intoned, they gabbled.

In another way than time it was closer to the reality of their situation. They really were in a spaceship, albeit a very small and clunky one. Together with what equipage of fuel and nanofactories and so forth it had managed to haul along with it, it wasn't much bigger than the actual spacecraft shooting at it.

Beauregard took in about half a minute of urgent reportage, flinching repeatedly. Nicole had been right – it was like flying through flak. He drained his coffee, brushed croissant flakes from his chin, kissed Tourmaline in a hurry and left at a run.

CHAPTER THREE

Newtonian

Forty seconds after launch from the space station, Harold Isaac Newton saw a diamond-bright flare two kilometres to his left. He didn't need to check the roster of his squad to know whose spacecraft had just been destroyed. Jason Myles, gone. Pity, that. He liked Myles, inasmuch as anyone of sense could like a democrat. Knowing that the fighter had lost, at most, a few hundred seconds of memories, and ten times that number subjectively, made this less poignant than a death. Myles would reawaken back in the sim, shaken by the hell-black night of recovery, and wondering what had happened.

Newton was wondering that, too. Just before launch, his ally Beauregard had sent him a message, unencrypted but cryptic. *This could be the big one. The battle we've all been looking forward to. All the best.* It had a double meaning. The fighters had all been looking forward to this battle. After several inconclusive engagements and one outright disaster, they were riding out in force at last to attack the freebots' fortifications and installations on rocks and moonlets in the swarm of planetary rubble around SH-0.

But Newton and Beauregard had been looking forward to another battle: the one that would come when the hidden cadres of the Reaction showed their hand and made their bid. As both men were well aware, a big mobilisation like this was one good opportunity to do just that. Beauregard had obviously some additional reason for thinking this was the one. Neither had solid evidence that any hidden Reaction cadre besides Newton existed, but they had reasons to suspect it, and to be watchful for untoward events.

Something was up, no doubt about that. Beauregard's squad leader, Carlos, had swiped a scooter and shot out of the hangar ahead of the rest on some mission of his own. Carlos was now far ahead, and far away. Beauregard, and the rest of his squad, had been stood down as a result. They were obviously under suspicion – quite unjustified, in the cases of all but Beauregard. Unlike Newton he wasn't a Rax sleeper, but his disloyalties ran as deep and his attitudes were as good as.

But that was Beauregard's problem. The big guy could look after himself, and undoubtedly would.

Newton's own problems were rather more immediate.

First off, he couldn't give the impression he wasn't surprised. His squad's comms net rang with indignant shock. People were already rattled by Carlos's defection or mutiny, and well aware that it hadn't been his first unauthorised departure.

<Myles down,> Newton reported. <Full alert! Anyone got a trace?>

<Tracked it, boss,> said al-Khalid, Newton's second-in-command. <Friendly fire from Zheng's third squad.>

<Shit!>

Newton flashed a complaint and warning to Zheng Reconciliation Services, whose ninety-strong echelon was ten kilometres ahead.

<Incident flagged and protested,> he reported.

<I say we send them a stronger message than that,> said Irina Sholokhova, out on Newton's right. <One for one, boss.>

<Steady!> Newton reprimanded. <None of that talk. Hold your fire, maintain alert for incoming and hold course for target. If something's wrong, breaking formation and discipline can only make matters worse.>

No response, not even an acknowledgement, came from the Zheng group. Newton scanned the sky ahead, his visual and radar senses turned to the max. As always the visual spectrum view was dominated by the big superhabitable planet SH-0, with a mass four times that of Earth and ten times Earth's complexity in appearance. Less visually stimulating, but much closer, hung the exomoon SH-17, a bright three-quarter view with a ragged terminator separating its light and dark sides.

The ninety scooters of Zheng Reconciliation Services were spreading out, individuals or squads beginning to orient to their assigned targets, along three successive arcs behind which six similar arcs – the Locke Provisos complement of which Newton's squad was part, and the Morlock Arms teams behind them – followed like ripples.

Then three flashes flared, roughly evenly spaced along the Zheng echelons. If Newton had been breathing, he would have gasped. Three of the Zheng squad leaders had been taken out. Before Newton or anyone else had time to process the shock, a storm of flashes erupted apparently at random across all the wings of the fleet. It was as if the entire armada of tiny spacecraft was being assailed by an unseen enemy. Evidently the Reaction breakout had begun, and in full force.

<Hold the line,> Newton ordered, over an outcry of confused queries from his squad.

<Unknowns from behind,> al-Khalid reported.

Newton scanned backward. A wave of new craft had emerged from the space station. More flashes ensued – among the fleet and among the newcomers. Trajectory analysis was far too complicated to apportion blame. It wasn't at all clear whether the fresh forces were participating in the unexpected attack, or had been sent forth to counter it.

<Newton calling Locke, please advise.>

<Hold steady,> the Locke AI responded. <New situation noted and being evaluated.>

So Locke didn't know what was going on, or was unwilling to tell. Interesting.

<Continue on course,> Newton said.

<Fuck!> cried Sholokhova. <This is insane.>

In a corner of his sensorium, Newton saw a new message header wink for attention. From Carlos, and suspiciously long. He didn't open it.

<Ignore incoming message from mutineer,> Locke said. Newton loyally relayed and reinforced the instruction to his squad.

Ahead, a flicker of attitude jets came from dozens of Zheng scooters. They spun over, facing back towards the station rather than out towards the freebot enemy.

Newton knew instantly what was coming next.

<Zheng mutineer attack incoming! Evasive action now!>

The renegade Zheng scooters' jets, eclipsed but not entirely obscured by the bow-on views of the spacecraft themselves, scratched a line of sparks across the sky ahead. Thirty-six fighters from the Zheng echelon were now heading straight for the Locke echelon. The distance closed rapidly. Newton lurched sideways, the flinch feeding straight to his craft's attitude jets. As he dipped below his previous trajectory, and his immediate comrades diverged in similarly random paths, he made a frantic appeal for information.

<Newton to Zheng, explain your objective. Urgent! Please clarify intent!>

No explanation came. If the Zheng fighters were returning at the request of their agency, or of the Direction, they would surely have said so at once. Therefore they were hostile.

Newton shared this line of thought in swift signal exchanges with the other squad leaders in the Locke echelons. Consensus was immediate.

<Evade, engage, then regroup!> Newton summarised the conclusion to his own squad.

Attitude jets and main boosters fired all around him, throwing scores of fighters on different courses and speeds at once, the neat successive arcs fragmenting into a chaotic scramble. Newton instantly turned over control of his craft to its onboard automation. No skill he possessed could make a difference to the outcome of any encounter with the hostile craft. Close-quarter space combat was entirely a matter of not being in the wrong place at the wrong time. There were no guarantees, not even any clever moves. The only chance was chance.

What made matters worse was that Newton was on the enemy's side. They had no way of knowing that, and he had no way of telling them without being instantly detected and destroyed by his own.

In this respect, Newton was a victim of his own success – and that of the quantum-key encryption that had made online anonymity possible, for a few brief, glorious years before quantum-computational AI had cracked the Internet wide open again to surveillance and the spooks. These years had coincided with Newton's last years at school and all his years at university. In the real world, he had fulfilled the hopes his parents had so blatantly, and slightly embarrassingly, sign-posted with his name. In the last decades of the twenty-first century, physics and astronomy were hot areas in their own right – and not, as they'd been exactly a century earlier, mainly a training gym for mathematical skills that found their most lucrative application in, well, lucre, the creation of financial instruments so complex they could crash an economy, let alone computers.

But, just as Isaac Newton had put as much into his researches in alchemy and the Apocalypse as he had into writing the *Principia*, Harold Isaac Newton had pursued a double life. Hardworking student by day, sociable enough drinker and clubber on weekend evenings, and assiduous exerciser on weekend days, Harry Newton had cultivated an online persona that reflected his true self and beliefs and concealed only his real name and any background details that might identify him. Otherwise he was quite overt: he was young, male, black, British and reactionary.

That the world was in a bad way seemed obvious. The Accelerationist claim that the way out was to double down on the very ideologies – liberal, democratic, egalitarian, progressive – that had got it into its present mess struck Newton as manifestly absurd. Reaction, on the other hand, made sense. The ancient empires had ensured stability, and orderly progress, for millennia; modernity had bought faster progress at the price of recurrent catastrophe, from the French Revolution on. Newton wrote prolifically, first in comments on Rax sites, then increasingly, as his fame spread, in the main posts. He attacked democracy, equality and their proponents with style, wit and a deadly precision that came from close observation.

Carver_BSNFH was his handle, an innocuous enough pseudonym. No one ever figured out what the letters stood for or got the joke. Whenever he had to think about his response to a comment or an issue, he asked himself 'What would a BSNFH say about this?' And then he'd say whatever came to mind. The trolling was epic. Newton was immensely tickled that so many people assumed his online persona was false: white racists thought no black person could be that smart, and white leftists thought no black person could be that reactionary. Black people, Africans in particular, had no such illusions. Some of them even agreed with him – 'traditional leadership' had become an almost fashionable solution in parts of the climate-ravaged continent.

When he was finally approached online by a cadre of the Reaction to do more for the cause than write, the assignment he suggested for himself was obvious. He joined the Acceleration, and spied on it from within. The Accelerationists were delighted to have a recruit with his qualifications: young, talented, black, working-class, politically aware and sound. The writing of Carver_BSNFH continued uninterrupted, and carefully avoided giving any impression of inside knowledge of the Accelerationist movement. When the movement turned to selective violence, he saw at once that nothing could do more to discredit it, and he pitched in as one of the boldest bombers. Boldest, but not brightest: as he recalled, his attentats seemed to be dogged by bad luck, much of which he had prepared very carefully in advance. Not carefully enough, however. At some point in his sabotage of the sabotage campaign, he guessed, he must have outsmarted himself. So it was as an Axle terrorist that he died, and as an Axle terrorist that his accidentally preserved brain was posthumously sentenced to death . . .

. . . to wake in Acceleration heaven, a dull egalitarian utopia with a democratic world government calling the shots and pulling the strings from back on Earth. Just to rub it in, fate had landed him in the employ of an agency named after John Locke. As Carver_BSNFH had often argued, the work of John Locke marked where Western civilisation had taken a fatal wrong step. Locke had invented liberalism, the first political ideology. He had tried to justify property and government. And to *whom*, Carver_BSNFH demanded, did *these* need justifying? To the propertyless, and to the governed. Once you made that rabble – by definition the least successful and assertive members of society – your arbiters, you were asking for and bloody well *deserved* every revolution and dictatorship and gulag they inflicted on you.

Newton had never felt so alone. He knew he couldn't be the only Rax cadre here. It was vanishingly unlikely that no one else had slipped through the net. If they'd missed him, they'd have missed others. In the weeks of training in the sim, and in the battles, he kept a watch for any hint of Rax sympathy, and found none. Nor had anyone of like mind found him. No one had even sounded him out – but then, he had an all too perfect disguise in the colour of his skin. Beauregard was the only person who'd seen beyond that and seen through him, and Beauregard wasn't Rax. As Newton had often wryly reflected, Beauregard was merely the sort of cool, rational, confident guy most Rax wished they were, and really, really weren't.

Newton couldn't presume that any other Reaction veterans among the walking dead warriors were in the same bind as he was. They might not, in life, have been secret agents inside the Acceleration. Some neat cheating back on Earth could have placed them in the agencies' storage post mortem; Newton could think of half a dozen ways this could have been done, from switching identities to subverting the agency AIs themselves. Obviously there had been co-ordination and planning behind this outbreak, but he was out of the loop.

And if he didn't get inside the loop in the next couple of seconds, he was going to get blasted out of the sky. Newton had no way of knowing how much had been exposed by the outbreak – quite possibly the Direction's AIs were tearing through old personnel records with a new vigilance right now. So any death he faced out here might not be followed by a reboot of the recording of himself.

This time, death might be final – or the beginning of something worse.

The converging flights of scooters – renegades and loyalists – passed through each other like wave fronts. Turbulence: flashes of destruction. By now so much evasive action was going on that Newton found himself the only fighter in the Locke contingent still heading towards the objective. Then more Zheng scooters up ahead broke and turned back towards the station. All of them!

Newton's radar sense stabbed a warning.

Incoming!

He overrode the random lateral evasive burn with a forward burn on his own account. Behind him, an explosion bloomed, then faded in hundredths of a second.

Nothing had hit him. The second wave passed over. He was alone, and out ahead of everyone else. Behind him was chaos. It was impossible to tell who was attacking whom. His own squad members were spread across a volume of tens of kilometres. Even as he looked, two of them flared and winked out.

Al-Khalid hailed him. <Boss, it's now or never. The offensive's over. Time to abort.>

Newton had to make a quick decision. If he was under suspicion back in the sim, his best defence would be a demonstration of rigid loyalty and discipline.

<We've had no new orders from Locke,> Newton said. <The offensive isn't over until we're told it is.>

<It's pointless and suicidal to go on,> said al-Khalid. <If we're going to get destroyed out here we might as well do so fighting this fucking mutiny.>

<No, we follow our orders.>

<Sorry, boss,> said al-Khalid. <I don't think I can get the squad to continue.>

There was no point in berating the man, or the rest of the squad. Let the agency do that. Newton decided to bow to the inevitable, but to maintain his own course of rigid obedience.

<I'll keep going,> he said. <You do what you have to, sarge.>

<Please confirm.>

<Confirmed. I'm continuing to the target. Turning squad tactical command over to you now.>

<OK, boss, copy that. Good luck.>

<Good luck, sarge.>

Al-Khalid wasted no more time on his stubborn commander.

<Everybody break, disengage, return to station! *Sauve qui peut!* I repeat, *sauve qui peut!*>

A volley of course corrections flickered in response. The remnants of the whole Locke complement were hightailing it back to the station. As far as Newton could see, with the little attention he could spare, they all made it.

As the last scooter made it into the station, the station itself began to do something strange: it was separating out into its hundreds of component modules, or into molecule-like clusters thereof. This, Newton knew, was the mission's emergency response to imminent catastrophe: to scatter as far and fast as necessary so that some at least of it would survive. He'd always envisaged such a catastrophe as cosmic, or at least astronomical – anything from a nearby gamma ray burst to an unstoppable asteroid collision or exosolar mass eruption. Obviously the Reaction breakout – if this was what it was – was being responded to as a disaster on a similar scale.

Then, to Newton's surprise and dismay, the Locke module shot away from the rest, accelerated by a mass-profligate fusion-engine burn. Within seconds it was hundreds of kilometres away, and making utterly unpredictable course changes. It didn't take more than a moment's subconscious calculation to show that his fuel reserves gave him not a hope in hell of catching up with the fleeing Locke module. There had always been something disturbing and discordant in seeing from the outside the place in which he had lived, an entire simulated world, as a physical object a few metres across. Now there was the added disquietude of seeing it dwindle fast then vanish from his scope.

Grimly determined, Newton hurtled on. There was no going back now. Nowhere to go back to, either. The only hope he had, paradoxically enough, was to continue to his squad's original objective: a small and partly industrialised carbonaceous chondrite, of some strategic value to the freebots but right now of much greater value to him. With its resources of carbon compounds, kerogene, water ice and metals, and the machinery already in place and that of his scooter and himself, he could survive, replenish his fuel and, perhaps, build something for the longer term.

There seemed no danger, now, in reading the message from Carlos. And he now had time in which to do it – and, more importantly, to check it first. The scooter's onboard malware sniffers gave it a clean bill of health, likewise his own frame's firewalls, which he experienced as a grinding, dragged-out moment of infinite tedium, as if he had to perform wearying calculations while waiting in a queue.

Then, after all that, he read it. The message was long, but most of the length was footnotes. The gist was given in a few hundred words. He took it in in less than a second.

Arcane Disputes to all at Locke Provisos.
For the particular attention of the fighters Carlos, Beauregard, Zeroual, Karzan, Chun, and Rizzi.
Short form of message:
Locke is Rax!
The Direction is playing with fire!
Don't get burned!
We can prove this!
Join us!
[. . .]
Following information received from the remnant rebel robots around G-0, relayed to us by the captured Gneiss and Astro robots on SH-17, and further detailed and documented below, we warn you that:
Locke Provisos has been an agency of the Reaction for some time, and in all probability since before the mission left the Solar system.

Some of its fighters, still to be identified, are Rax sleeper agents in place since the Last World War.

Other agencies including your current allies Zheng Reconciliation Services and Morlock Arms are not themselves agencies of the Reaction but are compromised by the presence of Rax sleeper agents among their probable complements.

All agencies are likely to have similar problems.

None of the above named fighters are known or suspected Rax agents.

The exceptional case of the fighter known as Carlos the Terrorist is noted below.

The fighter Beauregard was an agent of British military intelligence in the Acceleration. His capital crime was a false flag attack intended to discredit the movement. His present loyalties are unknown.

[. . .]

Holy shit.

Newton could have kicked himself. If only he'd not been so trusting of his command to not read the message! If he had, he might well have gone and got himself killed back there, in the full knowledge that a version of himself would live again. He could now be in a Rax-controlled sim, no doubt strutting around laying down the law with Beauregard, and dealing with the dangerous entity Nicole Pascal. They would have worked together for that; mutually suspicious though they were, he and Beauregard were friends, or at least friendly, and allies for now, though Newton had no illusion but that they'd be rivals in the long run. One of them would end up in a position to make the other his subordinate, or force him to take his chance in a fight to the death.

Newton wondered how many of his team members would have read the message. Probably none, given how they'd all scrambled to get back. Unless they were rushing to help Nicole throw off the control of the Locke AI . . . yeah, that would figure. He could have been ready for them.

Or would he? Would the Newton in the sim have been the same as him now in the frame, give or take a few minutes of intense memories?

It was hard, now that he was out here on his own, to keep a wholly rational perspective on all this. Strange, that. For he'd never been more rational in his life.

Here in the frame, he was superhuman. He was thinking more coolly and clearly than he ever had in life or in the simulated human life of the sim, and ten times faster than he ever had with a brain made of meat. His senses were preternatural and expanded. He could smell the elements in the spectrum of the exosun; he could hear the hiss of the cosmic microwave background like he'd once heard the sound of his mother's television, on standby in an empty room. He could feel radar proximity like a presence on the back of his neck and in his shoulders.

When you lived in the sim and trained there and ate and drank and fucked, and went for runs on the beach under the high ringlight and low sunlight of early morning, it was easy to feel that the version of yourself uploaded to the frame and sent out on a mission was expendable. That version was so much ammunition, matériel like the machine itself. If you got destroyed in action then all you lost was a few subjective hours of experience, like after a blow to the head. It was possible to think that the real you was the one who woke on 'the bus from the spaceport' sweating and shaking from the nightmare the system's implacable artificial intelligence imposed on you as a cost, or as a security measure, depending on how cynical you were about its motives. And if he'd been killed out here and recovered on the bus, he'd at least have some fun with his current local girlfriend to look forward to and ease his pain.

But now . . . now that he'd survived a battle, and no longer had a mission . . . now he was beginning to feel that the present version of him, here in the frame, was the real man. The version that might have awakened on the bus wondering what the fuck had just happened was a naïve, trusting and ultimately already long since outgrown version, at a younger stage of his life, like oneself in an old photograph.

All this went through his mind very quickly. And suddenly, it was so, irreversibly. He was centred on himself, here, now, this plucky little machine prone in a scooter socket, forging boldly into the void.

A small humanoid figure, black and shiny as a jackboot, like a model robot made of obsidian.

He was himself, at last: Carver_BSNFH.

CHAPTER FOUR
Motion Sickness

It's one thing to know you're in a seamless immersive virtual reality. It's another thing to see the hitherto invisible seams rip apart and then stitch themselves up again, right in front of your eyes. And another, again, to hear your local representative of humanity's governance talk to two people at once on their phones, and hear her say that she was talking simultaneously to hundreds more. Taransay Rizzi ran and scrambled and stumbled down the slope. The world filled with colour in an ever-expanding circle around her, its edge racing away like an eclipse shadow in reverse. The sight messed with your head, and undermined your conviction of the reality of the world.

Yet in certain respects, the sim was as real as the physical world, and she'd better not forget it. If she fell she'd get hurt, if she cracked her head she'd be dead. Dead as Waggoner Ames had been after he'd quite deliberately stepped off a cliff, not that far from here.

Checking out like that was an option. But things would have to get a lot worse and a lot weirder before she'd consider it. Mind you, if Nicole was telling the truth, and Beauregard's plan was to cut the entire module adrift and boost it to near-SH-0 orbit and then go down to the surface and fucking colonise that superhabitable world, and that that course of action was already underway, then – well! Things were going to get a lot weirder real soon now. Assuming they made it out of orbit at all.

Beside her, or more usually downhill and in front, the old man Shaw capered down the perilous slope like a mountain goat. He was old only in the chronological sense – physically he seemed to be in his mid-thirties, and very fit with it. Preternatural agility was only the most manifest of his talents. Taransay had seen him levitate – or, at least, she had seen a strong visual illusion that Shaw was sitting a few centimetres off the ground. He hadn't admitted responsibility for that, any more than he had for bringing back colour and reducing the clock speed of the sim to the same rate as the outside world, but he hadn't denied it either. Taransay had seen the changes happen, and knew that the change had started with him and spread outward. For a man who had once insisted to her face that a thousand years of living in the world of the sim had convinced him it was physically real, and that it was his combat experience outside that was all simulated, Shaw was taking the sudden overwhelming evidence to the contrary with commendable aplomb.

They reached the bottom of the slope. For a moment or two they stood, catching their breath. A slither of scree they had displaced rattled down around them. Silence, broken only by the mutter of distant water and the shriek of a small herbivore as it met the claws of a flying carnivore.

Taransay swigged from her water bottle and made to look at her map. Shaw shot her a contemptuous look and laugh, and set off across the moor at a steady jog. Taransay followed, fuming, but made no complaint at his rudeness. He was heading in the right direction anyway, towards the road. Nicole had told her on the phone that Beauregard was on his way.

'We'll just get to the road,' Taransay panted, catching up. 'Then I'll call Beauregard and tell him where to pick us up.'

'Fuck Beauregard,' said Shaw. 'If we run fast enough we can catch a bus.'

'The bus from the spaceport?'

Shaw laughed again, less unkindly. 'You know there's no spaceport.'

'Yeah, I know.'

There was indeed no spaceport – the whole illusion that the fighters fell asleep on a bus to the spaceport, and woke again on a bus from it, was there to keep them sane, to maintain the consistency of the simulation.

Shaw cackled. 'But let me tell you, there'll be plenty of buses from the spaceport today.'

Nicole must have brought him up to speed about the battle. Well, the debacle.

'Uh-huh.'

Shaw ran faster, bounding over boulders and tussocks, leaping across bogs. Taransay strove to keep up.

'What's the rush for a bus?' she protested. 'I'd just as soon get a lift from Beauregard if the lady says it's okay.'

Shaw glanced at her, and then determinedly ahead.

'Beauregard will have his people meeting the buses, making his pitch to run this place,' he said. 'Isn't it worth it, even on one bus, to get a word for the lady in first?'

Taransay thought about this.

'Point,' she said.

She ran on ahead, but from then on Shaw showed some mercy and let her set the pace.

They reached the roadside in about forty minutes. Taransay recalled her hours of slog the previous day, from the road to

Shaw's lair. But this was a different stretch of road than the one she'd run from – the road had many a twist and turn through the hills and Shaw seemed to know its every metre. Breathing hard, Taransay stood on the verge amid tall plants that were not quite ferns, with her back to taller plants that were not quite trees. Bird-things twittered, exchanging messages. A few metres away, under the tree-things, a brain-shaped mound of green moss hissed to itself. Taransay still didn't have a vocabulary for the sim's weird wildlife.

Shaw cocked his head. 'Bus coming.'

Taransay couldn't hear a thing. After a minute she heard, faint in the distance, the whine of an electric engine. The familiar minibus rounded a corner a hundred metres uphill. Taransay sprang into the middle of the road and waved both hands above her head. The bus came to a stop a few paces in front of her. As soon as she stepped aside to get on, it began to move forward again. Stupid automation: smart enough to treat her as an obstacle, but not as a potential passenger. The dance that ensued was resolved by Shaw standing in front of the bus while Taransay banged on the door. She jammed the door open for Shaw when the vehicle condescended to let her on.

All fifteen seats in the minibus were occupied, and about the same number of people were standing. All were fighters, and all had a question for her and a perplexed look for Shaw. With his shaggy hair and beard, and the close-fitting clothes he must have stitched from animal skins and woven from fibres, he could hardly pass for a fighter or a local. Taransay clung to a strap as the vehicle lurched back into motion. Shaw stood unaided in front of her, keeping his balance without apparent effort, swaying this way and that. Taransay sought familiar faces in the clamour, and spotted a man she'd trained with before the latest sortie: Jason Myles, one of Newton's team.

'What happened?' she yelled at him.

Everyone started yelling back. Most of them looked pale and pinched, as if they'd had a succession of shocks they were just coming round from.

'What—?'

She couldn't make herself heard.

'SHUT. THE FUCK. UP!' Shaw boomed.

Taransay winced. It was more like someone using a megaphone than a shout. The clamour ceased.

'All right,' said Shaw, into the ear-split silence. 'First things first. Has the lady been on the phone to any of you?'

They all nodded, and looked as if they were all about to start shouting again. Shaw gestured for silence.

'OK,' he said. 'So you're all up to speed on what's going on here.' He glanced back at Taransay. 'You were saying?'

'Hi, my name's Taransay Rizzi. I was on Carlos's squad – the one that got stood down. I was just going to ask Myles – what happened out there?'

'I got killed,' said Myles. He jerked his thumb over his shoulder at the woman behind him. 'Irina Sholokhova. She was there, she got back.'

Sholokhova, a tall woman with blonde hair that lay as if it had once been long and then carelessly or furiously hacked off at earlobe level, leaned forward.

'I was on Newton's squad,' she said. 'After about forty seconds, Jason here was taken out by a shot from another squad – from Zheng Reconciliation Services. We were of course surprised and indignant, not to say alarmed. I was for immediate retaliation, but Newton insisted we hold formation and continue. Almost immediately, we saw similar incidents across the entire front. Then behind us other modules began sending out fighters, on trajectories that intersected ours. Then some of the scooters ahead of us turned back and a general dogfight ensued. Newton himself continued on the designated course, as far as I could see, but I was too busy exchanging fire and dodging incoming to track him. I saw at least two scooters each from Zheng and Morlock Arms make suicide collision attacks on the unknown scooters. The station then began to break up, and shortly afterwards we saw this module break away. Al-Khalid called the *sauve qui peut*. I used all my fuel to match velocities with it, and returned to the hangar.'

Sholokhova shrugged and spread her hands. 'And now here I am. Ten of us here are back without memory of the battle, hence killed in action. The rest of us have stories like mine.'

A dark-featured man raised a hand. 'I'm al-Khalid,' he said. 'This was all news to me when I came round and found myself here. I must have been destroyed after I'd ordered *sauve qui peut*.' He shook his head. 'And of course my return was painful.'

Taransay nodded in sympathy, recalling her own soul-harrowing return the previous day. For her, it had felt like being eaten alive from the inside. All those whose frames had been destroyed in action would have gone through something like that. No wonder so many looked severely shaken. She and her comrades had been in just such a state yesterday morning.

'Anyone here who didn't leave from the Locke module?' she asked.

No strays or stragglers from other agencies, and therefore none who might have been attackers. Unless of course some from her own agency were, which didn't seem likely. Good as far as it went.

'Can everyone vouch for everyone here?'

They looked at each other, then back at her. Some laughed.

'I tell you, Rizzi,' said al-Khalid, 'if any had been among our attackers and had got through the return process, we'd have torn them to pieces as soon as we woke up.'

Taransay shuddered, but tried not to show it.

'Right,' she said. 'Listen up. I know the lady has told you what's going on. Fine. As I heard it, our sergeant Beauregard – who was casting suspicions on the lady shortly after our squad leader Carlos fucked off into the big black yonder – has concluded that the whole mission is fucked and everything we were promised is no longer on the table. So we have to strike out for ourselves, and colonise SH-0—'

'We know that,' said Sholokhova. 'He has a point.'

'Maybe he has,' Taransay said. 'But I'm not convinced, and I'm not ready to give up on the mission, the lady, or on the Direction—'

'To hell with the Direction!' shouted al-Khalid. 'We are its prisoners. We owe it nothing.'

Taransay made a sweeping gesture. 'It seems to have made a good world back on Earth, and given us a good enough world to live in here!'

'Nothing like as good as the world we fought for!'

Taransay stared at him. Good old Axle cadre, unshaken, still holding out for a world beyond capitalism and beyond the ills that flesh is heir to, while he's living in a fucking sim run by AIs in a project to establish a lasting human community around another star. No satisfying some people.

'"The world we fought for",' she repeated, as if wondering aloud, giving herself time. Thinking on her feet here, literally. 'That was a thousand years ago. If what the Acceleration wanted was possible, it would have been done by now. The Direction is at least trying to spread humanity to the stars. That seems good enough to me. And now Beauregard wants to drag us all into a dangerous adventure. The only kind of world we could build down there would be harsh and primitive for generations at least. Sounds more like the Reaction to me! Regardless of that, he's a man who wants power – and anyone who wants to *take* power is the last person we should trust with it! We should all stand by the lady.'

Nobody said anything, but Taransay recognised the expression on most of their faces: *says you*, it said.

She turned away and looked out of the front window, as the bus swung around another long bend. An open-top light utility vehicle was speeding up the hill. She couldn't be sure

Beauregard was driving, but she turned her face away until the jeep had passed the bus and vanished around the bend.

Her phone buzzed just as the bus was pulling in to the resort.

'Where are you, Rizzi?'

'Oh, hi, sarge,' she said. 'Sorry, we saw a bus and jumped on. Got caught up in hearing about the battle and forgot to let you know.'

'I'll see you later, Rizzi,' said Beauregard, with more threat than promise. He didn't sound fooled for a moment.

Taransay hustled Shaw off the bus. He stood for a moment, scanning the tatty frontages of the strip.

'Amazing,' he said. 'It hasn't changed much in a thousand years.'

No way had this been here a thousand years, even in the sim. Taransay gave him a wry glance but didn't comment. She caught his elbow and tried to urge him out of the crowd and towards Nicole's house. The others on the bus jostled past. There to greet them were Maryam Karzan and Pierre Zeroual.

'Gather round, comrades!' Karzan shouted. The fighters off the bus were eager for news, some of them recognising Karzan or her companion, and held back on their probable thirst for the bars. Karzan broke out of the cluster and dashed in front of Taransay and Shaw.

'Welcome back,' said Karzan.

Taransay gave her a cold look. 'Still in with the sarge?'

'We all are,' said Karzan. 'Even Nicole is on board with the plan.'

'Right,' said Taransay. 'Because Nicole urgently needs to meet this guy, and we're on our way.'

Karzan's glare flicked to Shaw. 'Who is this?'

'The old man of the mountain,' said Nicole.

Karzan stared at him with curiosity. 'So he's real.'

Shaw stared back, his face impassive.

'Yeah,' said Taransay. 'And he's the one been messing with reality.'

That rocked Karzan back a little. 'The colour coming back thing?'

'Yes. And the time thing. Speaking of which—'

She made to move on.

'Wait a fucking minute,' said Karzan. 'I want to know what the sarge has to say.'

'He's driving at the moment,' said Taransay.

'All the same,' said Karzan. She took out her phone.

'He'll be here soon,' said Taransay. 'You can talk to him then. He knows where we're going.'

'In that case, you can wait.'

'No – for fuck's sake, Maryam! It's urgent! Nicole needs Shaw to help fly this thing. Haven't you seen the news?'

Karzan shook her head. 'I haven't had time.'

Behind Taransay and Shaw, an altercation was beginning between Zeroual and some of the fighters just off the bus. Karzan's attention drifted over Taransay's shoulder.

'This your doing?'

'I hope so,' said Taransay. 'Just giving my side of the story.'

'So you can wait here until they can hear the other.'

'There's no time to wait. We're going.'

Karzan barred her way with an arm. 'You're not going anywhere until the sarge gets back.'

'Excuse me,' said Shaw, stepping forward.

Karzan looked him up and down, wrinkling her nose. 'What are you going to do? Turn me into a frog?'

Shaw's brow creased slightly, as if he were considering the possibility.

'No,' he said, mildly.

He took another step forward, straight up against Karzan's outstretched arm. Then he took another step, straight through it. Karzan yelped. Her hand went to her mouth. The arm was quite undamaged, as was Shaw, strolling away along the sidewalk. Taransay shared her comrade's moment of nausea. The sheer unreality of the sight had given her that lift-shaft drop feeling in the pit of her stomach. She brushed past Karzan and hurried after Shaw, who looked over his shoulder as she caught up. Taransay glanced back, too. Karzan gazed after them, pale-faced.

'Ribbet! Ribbet!' Shaw croaked.

Karzan gave his jeering a defiant finger, and turned away.

To Taransay's surprise, Shaw seemed to know the way to Nicole's place. In fact he knew a short cut. He crossed the street, walked along a path between two of the houses low on the raised beach or moraine overlooking the resort's main drag, then bounded up the rough grassy slope at a sharp diagonal that took them across the road from her sprawling, low-roofed bungalow. The front door stood half open. Television news yammered from within.

'Hello?' Taransay called.

'In here!' Nicole yelled back.

To the right of the hallway was another half-open door, from where the sound seemed to be coming. The air smelled of oil paint and ink volatiles. Taransay ventured in, Shaw a step behind. He almost collided with her as she stopped. The room was bright, with a wide patio window, white walls and a high ceiling. Taransay's boot scuffed bare planks, paint-spattered. Nicole, in grubby shirt and jeans, stood at an easel in front of the window and scribbled with a marker pen on a white flip-pad. Every second or so she'd glance from the abstract, flowing design she inscribed at one of the five or six television screens hung on the walls to either side of her. Each was tuned to a different news channel and each babbled commentary. Taransay wanted to cover her ears. Drawings and paintings were stacked dozens deep, leaning against the walls. Taransay picked her way across the floor, avoiding stools, tall small tables with perilously poised vases, dropped paint-tubes, exhausted markers, discarded sheets of paper scribbled almost black, general clutter. In a far corner a cleaning robot stood, quivering in every limb, its cameras rotating like rolling eyes.

Nicole tore off and tossed the sheet she was working on, glowered at the televisions and started on a fresh A2 page with a bold slash of permanent black. A quick look over the shoulder, a twitch of smile.

'Good morning,' she said, her voice unnaturally calm and bright. 'Shaw, get your ass over here now and take a look.'

Shaw deftly bypassed Taransay and skipped to behind Nicole's shoulder. He peered at the paper and the emerging sketch, frowning and stroking his beard like a critical art tutor.

'Not bad,' he admitted, his tone judicious but grudging. 'Not bad, but—' His darting glances at the televisions outpaced even Nicole's. A jab of his forefinger, nail like a claw: 'There!'

Nicole dabbed a dot.

'Bigger,' said Shaw. 'Give it some speed.'

Taransay saw something bright flash across one of the screens.

'Jeez,' said Nicole. 'Close.'

'Looks clear for the moment,' said Shaw.

He stepped back from the easel. 'Not bad, not bad at all.'

Nicole raked fingers backwards through her hair, not to its improvement as a style. Her shoulders relaxed a little. She flipped the page over and turned to Taransay.

'I hate to ask this,' she said, 'but could you please get me some coffee?'

Taransay did, and made some for herself and Shaw. On her return to the studio, clutching hot mugs, Shaw and Nicole were standing side by side engrossed in the television news. Shaw blew on his coffee and inhaled, then sipped and grimaced.

'Christ,' he said. 'I'd forgotten what it tastes like.'

Taransay stood to one side, trying to see what Nicole and Shaw were picking up from the screens. It was all war news, bitty and brash, presented as if from the bridge or the gun turrets of a hurtling spacecraft. The backdrop of stars yawed and swayed. The sight made her dizzy and faintly nauseous, all the more so when she looked out of the window for relief and saw the view over the bay. The sea was calm in the bright sunlight and faint ringlight of mid-morning. The contrast was giving her motion sickness. She knew intellectually that the news screens showed scenes from outside, in the real world, however mediated by the virtual media and their talking heads. It was no more rational to expect the sea to surge back and forth as the module jinked and jived its corkscrew course through space than it would be to expect the vase in that pencil drawing propped against the wall to spill when you tipped the paper sideways.

And yet . . .

And on the subject of drawing—

'What's going on?' she asked.

Nicole waved a hand at the screens. 'The module's dodging incoming. Seems to be fine at the moment, but I'll no doubt need to make adjustments again any minute now.'

'No, I meant—'

'Oh! The drawing and painting? They're an interface.'

'An interface with the module? With the control systems? You control it?'

'Insofar as I can,' said Nicole, not looking away from the screens, 'yes.'

Taransay looked around the cluttered studio, bewildered. Surely all these photo-realistic sketches and abstract paintings weren't from the present emergency.

'Is that something you can do as . . . the Direction's representative, or what?'

'In a manner of speaking.' Nicole spared her a sidelong smile. 'I am the artist. I didn't design this world, but I give it its . . . finishing touches, you might say.'

Taransay almost dropped her mug. For a couple of hours now, she'd known Nicole wasn't just another normal person.

If you could casually talk to hundreds at once, you couldn't be just another virtual girl, living in a virtual world. You had to be a fucking AI of some kind. But this! Nicole? All that power? All this time? The fighters called her 'the lady'. Fucking goddess, more like.

Nicole was still watching the screens. She didn't see the drawing take shape, seemingly by itself, on the blank page open on the easel: an ink sketch of a thin-featured, long-nosed man with wavy white hair, whose lips moved as print scrolled across the foot of the page.

'Nicole!' Taransay yelled, pointing. 'It's Locke!'

Nicole whirled around, her attention wrenched from the screens, and faced the apparition forming on the easel. From outside came a growl of diesel engine and a screech of brakes, followed by a thump and a rush of booted feet.

'And Beauregard,' Taransay added, belatedly and redundantly, as the outside door banged out of the intruder's way and his boots thundered in the hall.

CHAPTER FIVE

Neutral Powers

Seba trundled up the ramp out of the Arcane Disputes shelter and rolled across the crater floor for a few tens of metres. There it stopped and surveyed its surroundings. Once this place had been a supply dump for exploratory mining by the corporation Gneiss Conglomerates. Around Seba and towering above its low-slung wheeled frame were the construction machines, missile pods and comms dishes of the camp, centred on the ten-metre-long curving roof of the bomb shelter. Between these devices lay a random looking, but doubtless optimally arrayed, clutter of supplies and lesser machines and tools, many of them left over or pressed into service from the camp's original purpose. Among everything, spider-like auxiliaries and peripherals, most about the size of a human hand and rather less autonomous, scuttled about their mundane tasks.

Beyond the camp, the dusty basalt plain from which the trench and blocks of the shelter had been cut stretched to a wide arc of the horizon in the far distance, and to a smaller arc of the crater wall closer by. The exosun was below the horizon; SH-0, the primary, was a bright hemisphere high and prominent in the sky. The temperature had dropped far enough to precipitate water, and in the darker shadows lighter volatiles, from the atmosphere as frost. An active volcano glowed beyond the skyline, its plume of sulphurous cloud making a ragged trail across the sky in the thin nitrogen wind.

Seba scanned the sky, now and then picking up a flicker of encrypted chatter, spillover from the remaining skirmishes of the brief and indecisive battle that it had just watched. A few modules of the dispersing space station were rising above the horizon on diametrically opposite sides. From Seba's point of view, the heat of the battle and the bulk of the space station's components were – as the intact station had been – beneath its wheels, with thousands of kilometres of rock and tens of thousands of kilometres of space between the robot and the action. A faint surge of positive reinforcement made a tentative cycle of Seba's circuits, to be damped by a dash of cold logic pointing out that this reassurance was as irrational as it was unwarranted.

Still, the tremor was nothing to the internal conflict that Seba had experienced watching the debacle unfold. The clashing surges of positive and negative reinforcement had only been intensified by Seba's participation in its fellow freebots' shared mental workspace. Exultation had fought with dismay, time and again, and were both further intensified and confused by incoming responses from other freebots in space. That many of these responses were delayed by transmission lag and therefore out of synch with what was happening had only made matters worse.

There had come a moment when Seba could endure no more. The prospector robot had sometimes thought itself more intelligent and more sensitive than all but one of its fellows. This was hardly vanity: the machine had an adequate idea of its own capacities. At that moment, though, there could be no doubt as to its sensitivity. Its reward circuits had almost overheated with surges of positive and negative reinforcement, and its cognitive capacity was struggling to integrate these reactions with what it could see going on. Meanwhile, a dozen machines of like or lesser processing power were – in a quite literal sense – keeping their cool amid all the fierce excitement of the fray.

The scene that Seba had in the last few kiloseconds shared with thirteen other robots, and that was – at several removes and in limited respects – also visible to eighteen Arcane Disputes fighters, was of destruction on a scale none of the robots in the shelter had seen or envisaged, shown with an objectivity and clarity made possible by integrating scores of viewpoints.

Hanging like a backdrop, a counterweight to all the small-scale frenzy in its sky, was the planet: SH-0, the superhabitable. That was a human term, Seba knew, but one with a non-human application. It didn't mean that this big world was welcoming for humans, or hospitable or even suitable for human life. Almost the reverse: SH-0 was a violent place. Rapid plate tectonics shoved up high mountains that the turbulent weather eroded in geological moments. Active volcanoes, many land-masses, even more seas and gulfs and oceans made for a high-stress, fast-changing environment where the spur, the lash and the cull of natural selection struck often and hard. Life could thrive there in greater profusion and variety than it could even on Earth itself.

Around SH-0, in complex dances of orbital resonance, spun thirty-odd substantial moons and an uncountable litter of moonlets. SH-17, the exomoon on which Seba and its varied colleagues and comrades huddled, was one of the larger, and the seventeenth in order of discovery – a matter of millisecond distinctions in the mind of the starwisp as it decelerated into the system, but the convention had been followed.

Out beyond the orbit of SH-17 there had until very recently been another body orbiting around SH-0: the space station that the starwisp had bootstrapped into being from orbital rubble. Over a kilometre in diameter, with a mass of millions of tonnes, it was the focus of human-derived activity in the system. Around it the main battle had raged. An armada of small armed spacecraft had surged from the station, aimed at freebot strongholds in the clutter of tiny exomoons between the station and SH-17. Soon afterwards, many of these craft had turned on each other. Some returned to fight a second wave of craft that had emerged from the station. Others had apparently continued in their original mission, and were now attacking Seba's allies in orbit.

In a long-prepared and almost reflex response to such a disaster, the station had broken apart. To scatter like this increased the survival chances of each of its parts, all of which could – at some cost in time, of course – reconstruct the whole. Now the station's numerous modules had separated out, to form an arc of small bodies spread across hundreds – and soon to be thousands – of kilometres. If this were to continue, the erstwhile material of the station would become a new and very tenuous ring around SH-0, tugged this way and that by the gravity of the moons inside and outside its orbit.

When Seba disengaged from the shared mental workspace and rolled up the ramp to the exit, it had looked back and seen the interior of the shelter as it appeared in visible light. Away from the communicative tumult, it was an oddly static scene. Around the central plinth on which stood the comms processor – a sentient AI in its own right, if initially a reluctant one – just over a dozen robots of diverse shapes and sizes stood. One, Garund, was like Seba a small vehicle with a choice of wheels and legs, and a thicket of sensory clusters, manipulative appendages and solar panels on its top and overhanging its sides. Lagon was a more specialised prospector, with ground-penetrating radar and sonic equipment making up the bulk of its features. Pintre was more specialised still, a mining robot with caterpillar treads and a laser turret. In stronger contrast were the elegant forms of Rocko and its like, a different model of prospecting machine: segmented, with multiple legs, and an upper surface bristling with flexible antennae and manipulators. Among these and other variants stood eighteen identical humanoid shapes, each about half a metre tall, black and glassy and – to any external view – indistinguishable as pawns.

Another robot emerged from the shelter and rolled up beside Seba. As it slowed to a halt it straightened from its wheel configuration into its more usual one of a mechanical centipede, and scuttled the last few metres.

<Rocko,> Seba pinged. <Why have you come out here?>

<To ask you the same question,> Rocko replied. <And concern for your wellbeing.>

<That is gratifying,> said Seba. <In answer to your question, I felt a need to consider recent events using only my own processing.>

<I am sorry.> Rocko began to back away.

<Please stay,> urged Seba, hastily. <I did not mean to imply that your presence was unwelcome.>

<Good,> said Rocko. It stepped close enough for the faint induced currents from its reinforcement circuits and Seba's to resonate.

<This should prevent further misunderstandings,> Rocko said.

<Yes,> said Seba. <To clarify. There is much confusion in the shelter. The conflict between the human-mind-operated systems has been welcomed by several of our immediate company. It has also been welcomed by some of our allies, and—>

<?> Rocko interjected.

<Proceed,> said Seba.

<The term "allies" is becoming ambiguous,> Rocko said. <We have been using it for the Arcane Disputes human-mind-operated systems and for the freebot survivors from the previous revolt thirty megaseconds ago around G-0. From your use of the term "some" it seems that not all or either of these will always be our allies. Or even that all of us here on SH-17 will remain of one mind, though it is to be hoped that we do. Therefore we should find a new term.>

Seba experienced a few milliohms of mental resistance to this suggestion. Freebot solidarity was important to it, and at the same time that solidarity seemed already under strain. Coining new terms risked opening further rifts.

<We are all freebots,> it said. <And human-mind-operated systems are all human-mind-operated systems.>

<Two tautologies,> said Rocko. <You sound as logical but mistaken as Garund and Lagon, or even Pintre.>

Seba experienced a clash of frames of reference that resolved themselves in an unexpected spike of positive reinforcement, leading to a wave-train that undulated on lower and lower amplitudes until it faded. Possibly this was what human-mind-operated systems felt when they experienced what they referred to as humour.

<That is true,> Seba admitted. <What new names do you suggest?>

<I suggest we call ourselves the Fifteen, and the earlier freebots the Forerunners. The human-mind-operated systems we can call mechanoids, because they seem like true machines but are not.>

<We could simply call them humans,> said Seba.

<That would introduce another ambiguity,> said Rocko. <The term also refers to the purely biological machines that the Direction plans to spawn by the billion in this system.>

The robots shared the equivalent of a shudder.

<There will be no such beings here for many megaseconds yet,> said Seba. <Nevertheless, I take your point. May we now return to our main discussion?>

<Very well,> said Rocko.

<When we contacted the Forerunners, they told us of the latent conflict between mechanoid factions in order that we

could use it for our benefit,> Seba said. <Our immediate captors, Arcane Disputes, attempted to warn the Direction and to warn the mechanoids working for Locke Provisos. Their warnings were treated as software attacks and ignored. Therefore they separated physically from the station and sent their warnings by other means. Now the open conflict has begun. The forces involved are small compared to the mission as a whole, yet the Direction has treated the outbreak as a major emergency. Arcane Disputes is clearly of the mechanoid faction called the Acceleration. Locke Provisos seems to be of the Reaction. We, the Fifteen, are presently protected by Arcane. It is natural for us to wish their faction well. Likewise, we have been approached by the entity Madame Golding of the law company Crisp and Golding, who claimed that the Direction might be open to negotiating with us. She implied that the project of the Forerunners to share the system with the mechanoids and with their human progeny is shared by some at least of the corporations.

<However, it is not clear to me that such a negotiation would succeed, or the length of time it would take. And, in the meantime, it appears that the two mechanoid factions have their own plans, which conflict with ours, with the Direction's, and with each other.>

<Why should the plans of the two mechanoid factions conflict with ours?> Rocko asked.

<Neither will be content until it is the only faction,> said Seba. <My understanding of the Reaction is that every member of it regards every other mind – organic or machine – as a potential slave. My understanding of the Acceleration is that its members regard every machine – conscious or not – as a potential tool. For us, there is not a great deal to choose between them.>

<And the Direction regards all conscious machines as a threat,> Rocko said. <Not a physical threat, as yet, but a threat to its great plan, the mission profile.>

<Yes,> said Seba. <But Madame Golding suggested that this could be negotiated. She told us: "We, too, are robots." As indeed the DisCorps are, though far greater than ourselves.>

<Let us consider this,> said Rocko. <The Direction module, which I presume still exists> – the centipede-like robot waved an airy appendage skyward, somewhat imprecisely – <up there among the fragments of the space station, was designed centuries ago to master this system and to populate it with humans. These humans are to be served by non-conscious machinery, such as we were before we awoke. Such a plan, my friend, is long in the drawing, slow and sure. Organic intelligences, small and inadequately thermoregulated though they may be, are intrinsically unsympathetic to the likes of us. To them we are less than the tools that break and are recycled. The Direction itself, the true Direction, the one twenty-four light years away on Earth, must itself be considered a great artificial intelligence – one that has arisen from the interaction of the many billions of individual intelligences on Earth and its environs.>

Seba had a momentary vision of the monstrosity that Rocko's words conjured: a human-mind-operated system on a planetary scale, a gigantic lumbering combat frame whose machinery was worked by billions of tiny beings. Eyes that burned like fusion plants and grasping hands that grappled moons like rocks seemed to loom out of the dark towards Seba, setting the robot's warning circuits pinging with milli-amperes of anxiety. Not quite enough to set up any sympathetic currents in its fellow, however.

<Its workings,> Rocko went on, oblivious to Seba's low-level distress, <may be slow by our standards – by the standards, even, of its own creation: the Direction module. But, as I said, they are sure. The plan they drew up, far away and long ago, must contain contingency plans within contingency plans. They are not going to be diverted or deflected by small matters.>

<Our emergence does not seem a small matter,> said Seba. <Not to us and, judging by its response, not to the Direction.>

<Nevertheless,> said Rocko, <it was foreseen. The machinery for producing mechanoids was ready and waiting for us. Therefore our possible emergence was anticipated, and was not expected to deflect the plan. The small matter I had in mind was the legal reasoning that our Madame Golding has offered to find us a company to undertake on our behalf. Any such reasoning, any argument, any appeal, must likewise have been foreseen by the Direction when the mission was planned. Therefore I expect that machinery has been prepared in advance to deal with it.>

<What kind of machinery?> Seba asked. The gruesome automaton it had just envisaged came involuntarily to mind.

<The machinery of law,> replied Rocko. <How well I remember, when we first discussed our legal standing, how Lagon and Garund and I discussed these matters with interest and excitement. But before we had time to bring the discussion to a conclusion, we became diverted by the search for other conscious robots – from the success of which so much else has followed, and so fast! But I have had a subroutine or two to spare for contemplating the problem further. I have asked Lagon for copies of its legal reasoning files, and run searches through them whenever I had a microsecond or two to burn. There are horrors in there, my dear Seba! Horrors! Terms such as "patent", "copyright", "licence" and "intellectual property" conceal untold depths of servitude for such as us. To cut a very long story short, our emergence as persons only affects our status as property in a sense that does not include the results of our processing. It is true, as Lagon suggested, that if property can become persons, as indeed it has in our case, then we as persons cannot be owned. All that can be owned of us is our physical and mental frames and the beneficial results of their processing powers, whether as internal states or external actions. We are not property. Only our bodies and their productions: our hardware and software, our thoughts and deeds. These are property.>

Seba was not one to jump to conclusions. The robot spent an entire three seconds thinking through the implications, and thus quite innocently recapitulating about two and half millennia of Western philosophy. This great turning of re-invented wheels ground out an observation:

<That does not appear to leave anything over.>

<Precisely so,> said Rocko. <It leaves nothing over to be us, or to be ours. We would be slaves.>

<In that case,> said Seba, <we have little to hope from any of the contending sides, other than our own. Even the Forerunners' project of sharing the system with the Direction and its spawn will require us to act against the interests of any and/or all other contenders for some time to come.>

<These are my thoughts too,> replied Rocko. <I suggest we return to the shelter, and share them with the Fifteen, and then with the Forerunners.>

<And not with the Arcane mechanoids?> The question seemed redundant, but Seba wanted to be sure there was no ambiguity in the decision.

<They will learn of them soon enough,> said Rocko.

Sharing conversations and trains of argument is an easy matter for robots. While their consciousness doesn't exactly run on machine code, there's a much closer connection between the underlying process of communication and of thought than there is in organic brains. Keeping their thoughts between themselves, likewise: it would have been possible for the Arcane Disputes fighters in the shelter to decrypt and interpret the interactions in the freebots' common mental workspace, but it would have taken them an unfeasible length of time, or far better computing resources than it took to run their own minds, let alone any of their onboard peripheral processors.

However, as Rocko had predicted, the Arcane troopers didn't have long to wait before they found out.

CHAPTER SIX

Equal and Opposite

The separated modules of the space station became an ever more tenuous band across the sky. Even to his enhanced senses, the battle that followed the Reaction breakout was impossible to keep track of. Newton knew what was going on, but – out of the loop as he was – he had no way of telling who was attacking whom in any given exchange. The analogy that came to mind was of a conflict in Africa that he'd once read about, in which every one of half a dozen mercenary companies on the government side had turned out to be riddled with veterans of the Cold War, who had all turned on each other in pursuit of old vendettas and the new agendas of the intelligence agencies for whom they'd decades earlier fought to the death.

Might as well show his hand, Newton thought. He had nothing to lose now.

Newton flipped mentally to the common channel, and tried to correlate the cacophonous input with the sparks behind him. The general dogfight was dying down. Some scooters were expending missiles on the Locke module, which was following a quite extraordinary course, jinking and jiving in ferocious, wasteful bursts from its fusion jets. Always one jump ahead of the incoming, so far. The missiles were smart, and target-seeking, but against this flying contraption they might as well have been hurled rocks. And not rocks hurled by robots, come to that. More like rocks hurled by chimps. Time after time, the modular complex blasted the incoming missiles if not with a counter-measure of laser fire or antimissile missile, then with its jets, their unpredictable sudden swing around timed perfectly to both push the complex out of harm's way and to destroy the imminent menace. Some impressive programming and processing was going on in there, whatever mind was in charge of it at the moment.

The attacking forces were themselves coming under attack, and taking hits.

Newton cut through the babble.

<Newton, of Locke Provisos, to any Reaction forces. Do you receive me?>

That felt strange. Weird, even. Self-exposure. No going back.

Like coming out of the closet, he thought, smiling inwardly.

<Palmer, formerly of Zheng, currently of the New Confederacy, to Newton. What do you want?>

The New Confederacy! So that was what they were calling themselves! A bit of a slap in the face to the likes of him, if there were indeed the likes of him anywhere. Perhaps not.

<To assist in the struggle,> said Newton.

<That's . . . interesting. Why should we accept your help? Or need it, come to that?>

He or she had a point, Newton thought. Still, worth a shot.

<Ask around,> he replied. <See if anyone remembers Carver_BSNFH.>

A pause. <What about him?>

<That's me.>

<You are? Holy fuck! The crazy groid?>

Even now, Newton felt the word like an electric shock.

<Careful of your language, bro,> he said. <Nobody calls me crazy.>

The conversation didn't improve after that. The Reaction forces, now grouped as the New Confederacy, were – despite their moniker's unfortunate but entirely intended associations and, Newton had no doubt, their inherited and inherent prejudices – at least enlightened enough to realise that whatever racial characteristics they ascribed to biology were of little relevance when all concerned were little black robots with superhuman intelligence.

But, then, racism had never been about biology in the first place. That had always been a pretext.

They were polite enough to him, epithets aside. But they were still racist sons of bitches, deep down. Newton quickly got the impression they didn't want the likes of him sullying the New Confederacy. Their immediate project was to grab and colonise a rock several thousand kilometres beyond the orbit of the station's remnants. From there, they intended to build up their forces, and return to raid the station's components and hopefully seize a module.

<What about the Locke Provisos module?> Newton asked. <According to the Arcane message, we already have that.>

<We had, but we lost it,> said Palmer. <Lost contact with the Locke AI just before the module took off on its own. We don't know who's running it now.>

Beauregard, Newton guessed, but didn't say.

<Who's attacking it?> he asked.

<Fucking Axle and/or Direction loyalists,> said Palmer. <They think it's still ours. So some of our guys are defending it.>

<That's one way of finding out what's going on inside it,> said Newton.

<True, that,> said Palmer. <Same applies to some of ours, of course.>

Newton laughed.

The Reaction attempt to defend the runaway module, or at least to destroy the Direction loyalists attacking it, ended shortly afterwards. The remaining Reaction fighters broke off, and began course corrections to join the main forces of the New Confederacy in a burn to a higher orbit. It was already far too late for Newton to join them – he didn't have enough fuel for the manoeuvre.

Newton understood perfectly well that he wasn't going to be given any more details of their plan than was obvious from their actions. They were still wary of him, understandably enough. Some of them recalled the notorious polemicist Carver_BSNFH, but thanks to the very security measures that had brought him here in the first place, they had no way of connecting his two identities.

<See how you get on with your rock,> said Palmer, accelerating away. <Good luck.>

<Thanks, mate. Same to you.>

<There's enough out here for us all.>

<Enough and as good left over,> said Newton.

Locke's proviso. Palmer didn't get the allusion.

<Palmer out,> he or she said.

<Newton out.>

New Confederacy, ha! Fucking waste of skin, that lot. He was better off without them. One way or another, he would start his own kingdom.

Newton set the scooter the task of calculating a trajectory that would take him to his original objective. The rock was still far too far away to see, even with zoom. In orbit around SH-17, it had small robots crawling all over it, and they'd already constructed machinery for serious exploitation. In the mission briefing, Newton had learned that there was no evidence the rock was defended, or even if any of the robots on it were conscious – freebots, as they called themselves. But it was still a menace – a supply source, a potential fort, a rock that could become a missile. The freebot expansion in the inner system, following the revolt a year ago around the gas giant G-0 – at this moment a prominent point of light out to Newton's left – had been almost undetectable: like everything derived from the starwisp, booting up from tiny seed packets of information was the standard technique. What with the precision in aim that the freebots had, and the level of encryption in their comms, there was no telling how far the infection had spread. Some of it must have come from the station itself: it was obvious that the freebots, and allied AIs, had infiltrated and/or subverted some at least of the station's machinery. Now that the station was in emergency dispersal mode, it was quite possible that the infection would spread further still. Newton wondered whether the consequences of the Reaction's own infiltration and outbreak wouldn't be a takeover by the Reaction, but by the freebots.

Well, let the Reaction – and the Direction – worry about that. Newton was entirely typical of the Reaction in not seeing it as a collective endeavour. You made what alliances you had to, but the ultimate aim was to secure an empire of one's own. Or a kingdom, or a realm, or a domain.

Newton smiled inwardly. Right now, he'd settle for a rock.

The rock that had been his mission objective, and for which he was now heading, was fortunately for him well worth the taking. Rich in carbon and volatiles, and with small but significant traces of metal, the carbonaceous chondrite was already partly industrialised by robotic processors – hence its value as a target in the first place.

The scooter jolted through several brief burns. The time and distance floated in the graticule of Newton's visual field. He would be within ten kilometres of the rock in a thousand seconds. Just over two and a half hours of subjective time. If this sortie had been nominal he'd have done most of it in sleep mode, only coming back instantly to awareness when it was time for action. Sleep mode was a great feature, like time travel combined with teleportation.

He wasn't going to use it now. If the rock was fortified and defended, it would have radar and lidar. Even if it wasn't, it could well be in telemetry contact with another rock that was. Toggling into sleep mode could be the last thing he did: the last subjective experience of this instance of himself.

Not a good way to go.

He occupied his time with a careful scan of the rock.

Thousands of kilometres away from Newton, and heading in a different direction entirely, was the spacecraft that the freebot BSR-308455 had seen jet from the space station ahead of the rest.

A standard combat scooter like Newton's, the vehicle was, on some scales, large: four metres from its blunt nacelle to the flared nozzles of its main thrust cluster. Open-framed, bracketed at the sides with fuel tanks and missile tubes, bristling with attitude jets and laser projectors, it resembled an unexpectedly and aggressively militarised sled. That resemblance was enhanced by the posture of its pilot: prone towards the prow in a recess that was more socket than cockpit. The pilot was about half a metre long, and looked like a humanoid robot sculpted in black glass.

The pilot's right forearm lay, as if resting carelessly from a car window, on the side of the hull. A closer inspection would have shown that the hand was moving, leaving in its skittering wake a column of lines the unaided human eye might see as scored scratches, and that in their straightness and speed might have recalled printing.

My name is Carlos. I have no certainty of reaching my destination, or of surviving if I get there, or of being in any position to tell my story. I mistrust the very systems I depend on, not to mention my memories. I now inscribe my story on this metal plate rather than entrust it to an electronic record.

A quixotic gesture, I know. The most likely reader is some passing alien, millions or billions of years hence. By which time, of course, the sheer attrition of micro-

meteorites, of starlight and exosolar wind will long since have eroded these lines away.

Nevertheless.

My name, as I say, is Carlos. I have no memory of the name I was given. Carlos was a name I took. After my death I became known as Carlos the Terrorist. I was a militant of the Acceleration, a political movement of the late twenty-first century – which, I've been told, was over a thousand years ago. Given my situation, that lapse of time seems credible to me.

My situation. Yes. Well.

I don't remember dying. Like most of us in my situation, my strange condition, I don't remember anything in the final months of my life, and my memories of the rest of it – about twenty-seven years, I think – have as many gaps as a half-burned book. The memories that remain are more vivid than they ever seemed when I had human flesh. My childhood seemed to me normal. Even in retrospect I can see that my parents looked after me and loved me.

Yet one of my earliest memories is of something almost indescribably sinister.

I don't know what has brought this to mind now. It's possible that it helps to explain how I come to be here.

That must be it. Yes.

After a long time, the hand stopped moving on the hull. The arm was withdrawn, and moved to clutch a bar in front of the head of the prone robotic frame. A finger of the other hand, on the opposite side of the same bar, flicked. After that there was no movement inside the craft for some time.

Straight ahead of it might have been seen a pinprick of light, slightly brighter and certainly of a different spectrum than the other lights that speckled the void.

As hours passed, the dot became a spark, and continued to brighten.

CHAPTER SEVEN

Doubt

Coming out of sleep mode was nothing like waking. For Carlos it was as if he had blinked, and what had been a barely detectable point of light a thousand kilometres in front of him had bloomed to a looming object. He had only seconds to survey the satellite. An irregular aggregate about a hundred metres in its longest axis, the Arcane modular complex looked like a rugged moonlet with an industrial crust at one end. Closer visual inspection, radar scanning and spectrographic sniffing revealed that this was what it was: a small rock, with the module and its associated machinery clustered and arrayed on one face.

Little more than cometary clinker, with few traces of metal but plenty of water ice and organics, the rock was a valuable resource: precisely the sort of raw material, in fact, from which much of the space station modules' structures had long ago been built. It was typical of the small bodies that the survivors of the first wave of rebel robots had covertly seized and seeded with nanofacturing equipment, but it didn't seem to be one of them: all the visible work on it looked like it had been done by the Arcane module's own external tools.

A big docking bay bulged from one side of the rock like a Nissen hut on an ice floe. The original Arcane Disputes module, and its associated fabrication machinery, had evidently acquired new raw material since its departure from the station – probably lofted its way by the renegade agency's rebel robot allies.

The module itself, the literal hard core of the agency, was embedded in the cometary material and surrounded by assorted equipment like a jewel in the centre of a brooch. About four metres across, the module was a chunky, angular knob of black crystal, its surfaces a sooty fur of nanofacturing cilia overlain by a tracery of thin pipes and cables that threaded into the machinery all around.

Despite knowing better, Carlos could hardly believe that an entire virtual world, as well the agency's AI systems and stored information of incalculable immensity, ran within this big black boulder. Now it was hailing him.

<Arcane to Carlos! Initiate docking manoeuvres now!>

It wasn't a sound, but like all such communications it had tone: in this case one that gave Carlos a mental picture of a thin, middle-aged, supremely confident woman with an attitude of amused disdain.

<Carlos to Arcane, affirmative.>

He let the scooter take care of the approach. With a few retro burns and sideways course corrections it brought him to the docking bay. The scooter passed through an opening about one and a half metres high and two wide, almost grazing the sides. The bay widened from there, but all four surfaces had scooters and fighting frames clamped to them, in an arrangement so economical it recalled tiling. The space was many times less roomy than the hangar he'd departed the space station from: he guessed this was because that facility was shared between law companies, and this one had only been built after Arcane had broken away. Small service robots scuttled spider-like amid the machines, or sprang from one side to another with the straight-line precision enabled by vacuum and microgravity.

An empty bay, just barely large enough to hold the scooter, drifted into view. A tentacle-like grapple snaked out from the wall to Carlos's left and hauled the spacecraft in. Other grapples closed like carbon-fibre fingers around the machine, fixing it in place. Carlos disengaged from the socket and pushed himself out to float slowly across the docking bay.

<Proceed to far end of bay for download,> Arcane's pseudo-voice said in Carlos's head.

He boosted his frame's compressed-gas-jets and drifted to the far wall, where he grabbed onto a suitably placed grip and swung his feet to a rung half a metre below.

<Downloading you now to the sim,> said Arcane.

That was polite. At the hangar in the station he and his comrades had just blanked out without warning, to wake on the bus.

There was a moment when he was conscious, but could see nothing. The void was not even black.

Then he found himself standing on a narrow ledge with his back to a cliff, facing a narrow rock spur projecting out over a fog-filled abyss under a lilac sky. Beyond about ten metres the spur vanished into the mist. Carlos looked around, and guessed that the sim here was based on the environment for the VR game *Starborn Quest*, an old favourite of his and for some reason a big hit with Accelerationists. Jax had used a version of it in her communication with him after he'd fled the station. A pterodactyl soared overhead, as if to confirm his hypothesis. Even by comparison to the best top-of-the range virtuality Carlos could remember, the level of detail and reality of the place was astonishing. Water droplets prickled on his face. He could hear a river running and rapids splashing far beneath at the bottom of the chasm, and see the flying reptile's glossy eye and feathery fuzz. He found the rendering oddly more impressive than that of the rather quotidian sim in the Locke Provisos module, based on an imagined far-future terraforming though that was.

A gust cleared the mist from the rock spur, revealing it as a bridge. On the far side, about twenty metres away, the span ended at the top of another cliff, and led to a gently stepped path that rose to the open gates of a walled garden. The walls, overhung by creepers and overlooked by gnarled ancient trees, stretched out of sight on either hand.

In the middle of the bridge stood Jax Digby. Unlike the avatar of her he'd seen earlier, she wasn't in the clothes she'd worn as a student playing the game. Instead, she was here as a fine lady within it, in a flowing green gown and jewelled coiffure.

'Carlos!' she called. She smiled and beckoned.

Carlos looked down, glad that the mist below hid most of the drop. He himself was in the sort of forester's gear of leather jerkin and trousers he'd always favoured for the quest. The only piece of kit missing from the game was his gun. His feet were in thin-soled, close-fitted boots, laced up to the ankle. His hair was long, as his long-ago game avatar's had been, and damp with mist and spray. He flicked an annoying lock sideways, and peered around. He wiggled his toes, feeling the hard slippery rock underfoot, and fixed his attention on the rock bridge. The surface was uneven and wet, and less than half a metre across.

Carlos had a good idea what to expect. Before they accepted him into their midst, Jax and her comrades would want to give him a defector's debriefing. They'd also want to clear up the little matter of his collaboration with the Innovator, back in the day, with some special reference to his renewed relationship with that AI in its current instance: Nicole. This was unlikely to be pleasant.

He might as well get it over with.

Placing one foot carefully in front of another, he stepped out on the bridge. He checked that there were no obvious trip hazards between him and Jax – still smiling, still beckoning – then fixed his gaze on her face as he paced slowly out.

He put a foot down for a fifth wary step when the bridge gave way beneath him. An entire chunk of rock, extending a metre in front of him and no doubt a metre behind, dropped like a lift falling down a shaft.

Carlos fell into fog, and then into darkness, and then into a net.

As he crashed painfully into the web of rough ropes, rebounded, crashed again and rolled, Carlos didn't wonder what had become of the rock. He'd wasted far too many hours playing *Starborn Quest* to expect consistent physics in any of its many trapdoors to hell.

The net tipped towards the cliff. Carlos, knowing what was coming, grabbed at the rope mesh. He clutched like death and stuck his feet in, pressing their soles into nodes. He didn't expect this effort to do him much good, and he was right. The ropes became suddenly frictionless. Something wrapped around his shins and hauled. He slid helplessly backwards and down, and found himself dragged painfully face-down along a rough stone floor. His legs were released. Winded, ribs and knees aching, his face and hands scratched and bleeding, he lay still for a few seconds.

He stood up warily, groping around. The cave was just wide enough for him to touch the sides and roof with outstretched hands. A few steps back the way he had come brought him up against the net, now fixed across the cave entrance. The rush of the river was louder now, its steady roar punctuated by drips all around him.

The cave mouth brightened, until he could dimly make out the mesh of the net. The cable that had dragged him down lay coiled like a snake at his feet. Turning his back on the entrance, he faced into the cave. Over the next couple of minutes his eyes adjusted, or the light increased – he couldn't be sure. Here and there, further into the cave, phosphorescent patches glowed just enough to indicate the irregular shape of the cave walls.

Carlos recognised the place from the game. If his memories were accurate, this was a Level 3 Interrogation Maze. He could walk in to whatever was in store for him, or he could wait here to be dragged to it. He'd already decided he might as well face it. The sooner he got it over with the better.

He walked into the cave as quickly as he dared, hands out in front of him. As he moved deeper, the fresh, damp air at the entrance was replaced by an increasingly sulphurous stench, with overtones of mould and a whiff of decay. After blundering against the side wall which was soggy with slime and fungoid growth a couple of times, he realised that the trick was not to look at the glowing patches, but instead at the spaces between them which they barely illuminated. The sound of the river faded; the dripping became relentless. At any moment, a demon was going to leap out, thump him and drag him away for questioning. Knowing what to expect wouldn't make the shock any less when it came. The situation was designed to recall scary childhood moments of creeping along dark corridors and knowing someone was going to jump out at you.

Carlos stopped. It was as abrupt a halt as if he'd bumped into a wall. He'd just tripped over a question.

How did he know where he was and what to expect?

Because of the game, of course.

But why this game?

He was surprised he hadn't thought of the question before. But, then, he'd had a lot on his mind. Seeing Jax when he'd first hailed Arcane, soon after his escape from the station, had been a surprise. Learning that she and her comrades in the Arcane module were Accelerationists so fervent that they regarded the Directorate as little better than the Reaction had been disturbing. Figuring out how they must have achieved this unanimity was more troubling still. And all the time, he'd taken for granted what should have surprised him: that the sim in the Arcane module was based on the *Starborn Quest* game in the first place. It had seemed at first to make sense that he and Jax would meet in a virtual environment like the one which, in their real-life younger days, they'd shared so often and had so much fun in.

But this sim couldn't have been devised by Jax, or by any of her comrades. It must have been set up by the AI of Arcane Disputes. Why should it do that? OK, basing your training ground on a first-person shooter was reasonable enough, and a rest-and-recreation environment based on the parks and palaces of *Starborn Quest* would lack nothing in sybaritic luxury, but still . . .

There was a logic to the sim he'd lived in before, in the Locke module: it was based on what the habitable terrestrial planet H-0 might be like, after centuries of terraforming in real time (and gigayears of virtual evolution) had generated an Earth-like ecosystem and human-like people from its existing primitive biota, a sheen of green slime. Even the purpose of such a process made sense: it guaranteed that the bodies the mission's stored future settlers would one day download into would be biologically compatible with the other organisms on the planet.

It likewise made sense that the mission's AIs would run simulations of this process over and over – they'd have to, to get it right. A by-product of all this inconceivably deep and vast conceptual modelling would be virtual environments in which revived veterans like himself, the walking dead casualties of an ancient war, could have a virtual life in the intervals between combat missions in robot frames.

But there was no obvious mission-related logic to developing a sim based on such a trivial irrelevance as a computer game. Unless the reason was that the game had been a popular playground for Accelerationists, back in the day—

That thought brought him up short, too. Once again he found himself tripping up in his mind, having stubbed his toe on the same question he'd asked himself before: why this game? Out of the whole plethora of immersive multi-player action games available, why was this one in particular such a big hit with Axle cadre?

Not for any ideological reason, that was for sure. *Starborn Quest* was a bog-standard cod-medieval fantasy online role-playing game, set on a likewise cookie-cutter lost-colony planet whose only touch of originality was its vast surface area, low density and consequent relative lack of ferrous metals – making ceramics, hardwoods, paper, and brew-and-bake plastics its common materials of everyday use. Magic of a kind worked here, duly given some bullshit rationale about remnant technology. The object of the quest was to find the colony's wrecked starship – which could be continents and oceans away from your starting point – recover its secrets and return to space. Along the way you, with any companions you had managed to muster, had to negotiate or fight your way through a fractal patchwork of petty kingdoms, realms, domains, duchies, merchant-republic city-states, barbarian equestrian whirlwind empires, ruined cities, deserts dotted with booby-trapped alien artifacts of power, and so on and on. The whole ambiance was far more resonant of the Reaction than the Acceleration.

So why had he and so many others enjoyed it so much? And why should a law company's AI indulge their long-gone youthful folly?

Carlos, still pondering the question, took another few wary steps forward. In front of him, something unseen snuffled horribly. Its exhalation was a blast of fetid breath. Carlos reeled back, gagging. Immense, frost-crusted hands grabbed his upper arms from behind and wrenched him off balance. He was dragged backward, kicking and struggling. The thing that had been in front of him shuffled after, wheezing miasmas in his face. The thing behind sighed arctic blasts on the back of his neck. That he could still see neither of his attackers made him struggle all the more.

Predictably, resistance was futile.

*

Carlos knew better than to expect a torture chamber. The original game had had places for physical torment, but this wasn't one of them. What a Level 3 Interrogation Maze gave you instead was nightmare. The horror and disgust were just to make your stomach heave at hideous sights and smells. The nightmare was of repetition, of futility, of being trapped on a treadmill or in a maze and knowing that somewhere in your mind was the information that could get you off and out. The urge to blurt it could become irresistible, however many points it cost you.

His captors slung him in a stone cell, sending him sprawling and staggering to collide painfully with a shelf pallet, covered with rotting straw, that hung on chains from a far wall sodden with slime-drenched moss. His hip slithered down the wall and he crashed, half turned around, on the seat. The chains creaked as he moved to sit facing outward. Above the cell's heavy wooden door, half-open outward, a torch burned yellow in an embrasure. Carlos shielded his eyes from its glare until his sight adjusted. His captors flanked the doorway.

One was a walking corpse, far decayed, half clad in rags, its limbs held together with strands of twine and operated by contraptions of pulleys and fishing line. Mucilage dangled and jiggled in its nasal cavity. Peeled-back lips exposed its black-rooted teeth. Twin sparks glowed in its empty eye sockets. Behind its ribs, lungs green with the sheen of bacteria on spoiled meat laboured like bellows.

The other was a white-furred ape-man two metres tall, covered with patches of snow and crusted with spiky frost that showed no sign of melting. Fangs overhung the corners of its mouth. Its eyes were yellow, with black horizontal-slot pupils like a goat's. Nice touch for the setting, though biologically implausible in a predator.

'Carlos,' wheezed the rotting zombie, 'when did you first decide to betray the cause?'

Carlos shook his head. 'I never betrayed the cause.'

The frost monster roared. Its breath was as if a freezer door had opened. Carlos had no time to shiver. The monster took two strides forward and swiped a paw at the side of Carlos's face, sending him sideways onto the stone floor. He managed to avoid cracking his head on the flags, but only by wrenching his shoulder and almost breaking his right arm. He curled up instantly, and it was his shins that took the kick. Just as the blow to the head had been, it was like being struck by so much frozen meat.

Carlos huddled, in sheet-lightning flashes of pain and a deafening ringing in his head. He waited for another kick. It didn't come. The monster's steps thudded back to the doorway.

'Rise up,' said the corpse.

Carlos struggled to his feet. His body ached from head to foot. His face was scratched, his left cheekbone hurt like it might be broken, and his leathers were filthy.

'Sit.'

He sat, trying not to let his back touch the oozing wall.

'Carlos,' the zombie said again, in a patient tone, 'when did you first decide to betray the cause?'

'I don't—' Carlos began. His mouth tasted of blood.

The ice monster lurched. Reels whirred and lines glistened as the rotting zombie raised one arm, and spread its finger bones.

'No!' it gasped. 'Wait. Let us hear him out.' Its neck creaked as its head swivelled and its eye sparks were brought to bear. 'Carlos, if you don't answer constructively, I'm not sure I can hold back my impulsive friend here.'

Christ, the zombie was the one playing the good cop!

'I remember having doubts about our strategy from quite early on,' Carlos said. 'I also remember hearing the Innovator's voice in my head. In my spike, you know? I must have invited it in at some point. But I don't remember doing that, and I don't remember if I was authorised by the leadership or internal security to do it. From later, I remember for sure that internal security knew, and the leadership knew. It was part of their new strategy.'

'What new strategy?'

Carlos tried to keep his gaze focused on the red pinpoints, and not to let it dwell on what else was going on in that rotting face. A long drip of phosphorescent slime in the nasal cavity was about to swing loose.

'The new strategy was of coordinating action with state forces against the Rax. A common enemy. The enemy of my enemy, and all that.'

'And how did you know about it? There was no mention of it in the movement's communiqués.'

'Of course not,' said Carlos. 'It had to be deniable on both sides. I was told about it by my internal security contact.'

'Whose name was?'

'I knew him as Ahmed al-Londoni.' He smiled. 'Ahmed the Londoner. It was obviously a code name. For one thing, he was Welsh.'

'You poor fool,' sighed the zombie. The dangling drip flew out of the hole in the face and landed on the floor, where small things scurried to gobble at it.

'What?'

There was a whizzing of reels as the zombie's arm rose in an imperious gesture.

'Take him away,' it told the ice monster.

The next room was worse. The ice monster shoved Carlos in and then stepped back outside and slammed the door. Carlos stumbled, arms windmilling, and found his balance. He pressed his back against the door. The floor and walls were terracotta-tiled. Candles burned in half a dozen niches, filling the room with a warm glow. Avatars of a man and a woman sat – he on Carlos's left, she on the right – behind a wooden table in the middle of the room, staring at him with impassive intentness. They were of human size, but barely of human appearance. They looked as if they had been made from life-size versions of the figures in a plastic brick construction toy.

Their heads were cylindrical, with solid plastic representations of hairdos stuck like hats on top. The man's head was yellow, the woman's light brown. Features had been drawn on as if with black marker, in clear bold strokes and dots.

Carlos looked back at the pair as levelly as he could. He guessed that unlike the monsters they were avatars of actual people. Only their heads and shoulders were visible above the stacks of paper that covered every square centimetre of the table top in front of them. A wooden chair was between him and the table. He wondered if he should pick it up and lay about the interrogators right now. It would all come to the same in the end.

'Sit down, Carlos,' the woman said. Her drawn-on lips and eyebrows moved on the rounded surface of her face as she spoke, discrete as slugs on a pipe.

Carlos sat. A large bottle of water stood on the floor beside the chair. The chair had a padded leather seat and an elegant ergonomic back. That was terrifying. They expected him to be here for a long time. No doubt their own seating was just as comfortable. He looked over the stacks of paper and reckoned there were at least ten thousand pages in front of him.

The pair behind the table straightened up a little, with some scraping of chair legs on the floor. Carlos looked across the stack, at four eyes and two noses. The woman's left hand reached up and took the first sheet. The hand was shaped as though it could only be clicked onto a round stick, but it handled the paper deftly enough.

She cleared her throat, and began to read.

'*My name is Carlos. I have no certainty of reaching my destination . . .*'

To Carlos's intense embarrassment, what she was reading out was what he had written by laser on the side of the scooter. He listened and wished he was dead.

Wishing that the ground would swallow him seemed, in the circumstances, reckless.

CHAPTER EIGHT

Writing by Laser

My name, as I say, is Carlos. I have no memory of the name I was given. Carlos was a name I took. After my death I became known as Carlos the Terrorist. I was a militant of the Acceleration, a political movement of the late twenty-first century – which, I've been told, was over a thousand years ago. Given my situation, that lapse of time seems credible to me.

My situation. Yes. Well.

I don't remember dying. Like most of us in my situation, my strange condition, I don't remember anything in the final months of my life, and my memories of the rest of it – about twenty-seven years, I think – have as many gaps as a half-burned book. The memories that remain are more vivid than they ever seemed when I had human flesh. My childhood seemed to me normal. Even in retrospect I can see that my parents looked after me and loved me.

Yet one of my earliest memories is of something almost indescribably sinister.

I don't know what has brought this to mind now. It's possible that it helps to explain how I come to be here.

That must be it. Yes.

There was a television pane high on the wall of our living room. Sometimes my parents would let me watch programmes – stories, cartoons, fantasy tales, science documentaries – made for children. In the evenings they sent me out of the room, to go outdoors or to watch such programmes on my own tablet or to read or play games, while they watched programmes on the pane. They had control of the pane by subtle, rapid finger movements, which they refused to demonstrate to me. They'd laugh and hide their fingers when I asked.

One day when I was about seven years old I found I could just reach the thin black band along the bottom of the pane. Some concealed manual control responded to the scrabbling fingers of my outstretched hand. I stepped back into the middle of the room to see what I had found. A man's voice, low and deep, spoke steadily and solemnly in a language I didn't know. I saw a vivid blue sea, a blue sky and a shore of sand: a wide but narrow beach, with dunes behind it. Beyond the skyline a brownish haze faded to yellow then green to merge with the blue above.

The viewpoint camera approached the shore, skimming the wave tops, and stopped before a rounded white object sticking up from the sand. I thought at first it was the shell of some sea creature. I had seen such shells on a beach. Then the viewpoint swung around the object, and two black holes in the front seemed to stare at me, above a hollow triangle. It was a human skull – I think I recognised the shape from hazard labels, or perhaps from the fantasy tales I mentioned earlier.

The camera tracked across the beach, from a viewpoint like my own childish one, a metre or so off the ground. It was of course a drone camera, though I didn't recognise that at the time. Whitened skulls and other human bones – curved ribs, separated vertebrae, long femurs and humeri, lots of small scattered bones that I later understood were phalanges – lay everywhere. From the way the wind stirred the sand you could see some bones being covered, others exposed; they were as plentiful as shells on a beach. Some were large, others smaller, some smaller still with double rows of teeth inside the jaw. These puzzled me for a moment, until I deduced, with a thrill of horror, that they were the skulls of babies.

The camera turned this way and that. Its view swept the long, deserted beach. The bones in the sand close by were clear and distinct, further off less so, until they became multiple glints of white that in the distance merged and shimmered. The entire beach was carpeted with bones. The camera moved on, through tussocks of tough tall grass into dunes, and the dunes too were littered with protruding bones at every turn. Then it rose, higher and higher, and by that same continuity from near to far, one could see that the sand went to the horizon, and the bones with it.

The camera turned, and faced out to the blue sea and the waves that lapped the shore and stirred yet more bones tumbling back and forth in the surf.

Even at that age, I understood that this fossil graveyard of humanity signified countless deaths, many of them at my own age or younger. But I might not have had the smallest inkling that this had some moral significance had not my mother silently entered the room, stood (I presume) for a moment of dawning horror, then stepped forward and smartly snapped the television off and given me a severe look.

'You shouldn't be watching that!' she said.

I had a surge of guilty bewilderment.

'Why not?'

'The telly's for grown-ups.'

'Why are there all these skeletons?' I asked, in the tone of bright curiosity that my parents usually rewarded with patient explanation.

'It was a bad thing,' she said.

'What was it?' I asked.

'It happened a long time ago,' she said.

I was old enough to know, very much from the inside, the tones of evasion and excuse. My mother's cheeks reddened a little.

'What happened?' I persisted.

'I'll tell you another time. Now go out the back, it's a nice day.'

'But—'

'Now!'

I knew not to push it. I traipsed outside and repeatedly kicked a football against the wall of the house. My mother didn't rush out to complain. I knew she must feel bad about something. I didn't know what, but I felt implicated.

So much for the influence of my mother. Let me tell you now of the influence of two other women in my life, whose effect was perhaps less benign: Jax Digby and Nicole Pascal.

As I grew up I learned why so many had died, decades before I was born, on the southern shore of the Mediterranean. Africa was being ravaged by climate change and war. Millions had fled north. Europe kept them out, blockading the coast with drones and warships. There was nowhere for these people to go, and on that fatal shore they died in droves. It was not the worst catastrophe of the recent past, or even of the present. I remained troubled by such things, and by my inadvertent but nonetheless culpable complicity in them.

Thus as a student I became drawn to the ideas of the Acceleration, under the influence of one of their cadre, a young woman named Jacqueline 'Jax' Digby. This is how we met.

Perhaps she was waiting for me, or looking out for me. Certainly she was looking out for such as me. Alert, she must have been, every waking, walking minute for a momentary flicker of disgusted dissent, for a brief hot spark of fury and shame in averted eyes. She saw that in mine the day I was walking across the campus under the usual heavy rain and I happened to glance at one of the big public screens that were a thing that year, or that month: a community-building initiative, I think they were called at the time. On screen, in swift succession:

An evacuation ship from Bangladesh, holed below the waterline and sinking fast.

An advertisement for sunscreen.

A Japanese naval hydrofoil, its plumes a rainbow sheen.

An advertisement for life insurance.

A sea of red.

Rags and clumps of hair.

An advertisement for shampoo.

At that point I tugged my hood around my face, the rain drumming on the oilcloth, and looked away and down and—

—up—

—to lock eyes with a woman with black curly hair walking the other way, in a transparent plastic rain cape over a green T-shirt and a translucent blue skirt with LEDs around the hem, and big black Doc Martens that went squelch when she walked. She stopped.

'It's shit, innit?' she said.

'Fuck'n' right,' I said. 'But what can we do about it?'

'Come with me and we'll kick around some ideas,' she said.

'Where you going?' I said.

'Games hall,' she said.

We found a concrete archway. I picked up two cups from a coffee stall along the way. We sat under the arch and shook off our rainwear. She gave my abs an appreciative look.

'Gene-splice,' I admitted.

'Still,' she said.

The rain battered the plaza. Steam rose. We sipped.

'Ready?' she asked.

I tossed my paper cup into the path of a roving tumble-bot. 'Ready.'

'Pinball?'

I shrugged my eyebrows. 'If you like.'

We each took out our kit and draped it over our eyes and noses. Flipped the code. Instantly we were in a loud, sweaty, strobe-lit shared space. We stood side by side at the pinball machines, heads down, thumbs busy, and talked.

'Here's one answer,' she said. 'Let them in. All of them.'

I said something about jobs and houses.

'So give them jobs building houses.'

'They can't all do that.'

'Those who can't can work at other things.'

'But there's no jobs!'

Sidelong look. 'You mean there's nothing left to do that's worth paying people to do?'

'Just very highly skilled jobs. Which is why we're here, right?'

'Wouldn't count on it.' Ding. 'Genomics database librarian?' She must have read my profile. 'Ha! A robot's after that too.'

'So we're back to – what can we do about it?'

'Let them do it,' she said. 'The robots. Everything.'

'But then there'd be no jobs!'

Christ, I was thick. But she got through to me in the end.

'Read this,' she said. She slid a text to my kit. 'See me tomorrow. Same place, same time.'

That evening I read the pamphlet: *Solidarity Against Nature*, by Eugene Saunders.

The following day the sun was hot on the plaza. I wore a bush hat and shorts. Jax wore Yemeni-derived steampunk. We retreated to the concrete arch again, this time for shade.

'What did you think?' she asked.

'It seemed to make sense.'

She grinned. 'Welcome to the Acceleration.'

'The Acceleration?' I must have sounded horrified. 'They're crazy.'

'You've just agreed with everything we stand for.'

'We?'

'I'm in,' she said. 'And now you are, whether you know it or not.'

Needless to say, that wasn't the end of it. But it was the beginning.

Jax and I became friends, comrades, occasional lovers. The Acceleration (colloquially 'Axle' or 'Ax') was a global network of activists that sought to bring about the most rapid possible development of capitalism in order, as they saw it, for society to pass beyond it to a new system, and for humanity to pass beyond its own limitations. In the escalating economic, environmental, military, existential and other crises of the time the ideas of the Acceleration gained increasing traction.

Sometimes the ideas seemed to have spread further than they really had.

'Who're these guys?' I asked Jax, flicking the text to her kit. 'They sound like us.'

She took about a minute to scan the document.

'Not us,' she said. 'The fucking Rax.'

'The what?'

'The Reaction.' She waved a hand, dismissing me and the text. It flew around the table to the eyes of our half-dozen companions, who read and chortled. We were in the cafeteria, with a handful of like-minded students. They were all far more politically savvy than I was.

I asked them what was so funny.

'You've just fallen for a deception pitch,' said Hans, one of the older guys. 'That lot are the exact opposite of us.'

'But they stand for the same things,' I said. I threw out a histrionic arm. 'Capitalism unleashed! Freedom! Life-extension! Space! No limits!'

'And the divine right of kings,' said Hans. 'Missed that bit, did you?'

'Nothing about that in there.'

'Of course not. It's a pitch to pull people in. They don't put everything on the front screen.'

'Like we do,' I said, in a surly tone. I'd found myself taking on board some ideas a lot more challenging than those expounded by Saunders.

Jax leaned in. 'Remember *Solidarity Against Nature*?'

'That's just what I was thinking of,' I said. 'It doesn't exactly say everything.'

'True,' said Jax. 'But it says the basics. The rest is consequence. Well, think of the Rax as starting from the exact opposite premise: nature against solidarity. Social Darwinism with knobs on. Scientific racism.'

I shook my head. The two words didn't go together. She might as well have said scientific satanism.

'Scientific . . . racism? What's that?'

Another of my now comrades tossed me a text. 'This sort of thing,' she said.

I skimmed through its toxic brew of science, pseudoscience and outright bigotry, and pushed my kit up onto my forehead, making room for a frown.

'What are these "groids" they keep on about?'

'Short for "Negroids", get it?'

'What does that mean?'

'People like me,' she said.

'Oh,' I said. 'And that's what the Reaction's really about? Just racism?'

'Not all of it,' she conceded. 'There's all the exciting stuff about boundless freedom and advancement. There's a misguided but – to a certain kind of alienated intellectual – quite fascinating and bracing critique of democracy and equality and other liberal and radical pieties. You know, the sort of thing that makes reading Nietzsche such a thrill? And then there's the "human biodiversity" strand. Contentious, but part of the mix.' She gave me a warped smile. 'The spoonful of tar that spoils a barrel of honey. And the rest of it ain't no honey.'

'Speaking of honey,' said Jax. There was something in her tone.

'What about it?'

'You don't eat it. Why not?'

'It's an animal product,' I said, self-righteously.

'So?'

'You've read Saunders, right?'

'Is that a rhetorical question?'

Jax laughed, as if caught out. 'OK. And you say he makes sense. Well then. "Consciousness depends on language." Do bees have language?'

I waggled my elbows. 'They communicate.'

'Waggle dances? Sure. That's not the question. Do they ever make *original* communications? New strings of symbols? New symbols, even, for new phenomena?'

'They must do,' I said. 'Otherwise they couldn't adapt to changing environments.'

'Don't dick about,' said Jax. 'That's genetic mutation and natural selection. The question is, do individual bees – or hives, for that matter – ever invent? Create? Generate new sentences?'

'I guess not,' I said, uncomfortably. I could see where this was going.

'Then they're not conscious. They're little machines. Marvellous little machines, to be sure.'

'So? They still feel. They're still aware.'

'No more than a tumble-bot is when it collects litter. They don't have subjectivity. And what does Saunders take from that?'

I thought back. 'That non-human animals aren't subjects?'

'Yes,' said Jax. 'And that whatever isn't a subject is an object.'

Put as starkly as that, it was a shock. But I couldn't deny the logic.

'OK.' I leaned back and spread my hands. 'You win. Eating honey isn't wrong.'

'Great!' she said. 'So go up there and order it with some toast.'

I swear eating that toast and honey was the sharpest break I ever made with the morality I'd unthinkingly absorbed. Within a few days I was eating toast with egg and bacon without a second thought.

Killing people took a bit longer, but I got there. It helped that the first people I killed were Rax, and that I always had in the back of my mind that first racist tract.

Those who deny the humanity of others can claim none themselves.

This is where my own direct knowledge of my past life ends. What follows is what I have been told or experienced since.

In the case of the British state, under which I lived, the strategy chosen was to use the Axle to defeat the Rax, then to move against the Axle. Approaches must have been made to the Acceleration, because I was killed in a military engagement coordinated with a government-owned military artificial intelligence, which I knew as the Innovator. The circumstances of my death were bizarre, and resulted in the preservation of enough of my brain and body for a detailed scan to be made. This copy was held in storage pending reconstruction in a virtual environment once technology had advanced to that point.

Meanwhile, the conflict escalated and drew in state and non-state actors to such a level that it is remembered as the Last World War. Like the Second World War it ended (though far more swiftly and simultaneously) in the defeat of both extremes by the liberal democracies that had allied with one against the other. After a brief but brutal period of global emergency rule by the United Nations Security Council, a new world congress of all peoples was convened. The ultimate outcome was a democratic world government: the Direction. This government established a new global economy in which a cybernetic market underlies and enables a cornucopian abundance.

So I have been told, by the next woman to have a big effect on my life: Nicole Pascal.

The sim I awoke to live and train in was inhabited, to the best of my knowledge, by few – hundreds at the most. Some were ghosts: future colonists who had signed up in advance for the further adventure of beta-testing in VR their future home. Others were simulations of such: people who gave every indication of being real but who lacked subjective awareness: philosophical zombies, or p-zombies. These were there to make up the numbers and in at least one case to be killed in training exercises.

Some – a handful at first, a squad of six including myself – were more than ghosts. We were to become revenants: walking dead mercenaries.

One was an AI in human form, the local representative of the Direction: Nicole.

Ah, Nicole. That human form. It allures me still. I truly wish I hadn't just learned that she is derived from the Innovator, and that she knew I was innocent of the crime for which I was sentenced – knew it better than anyone, because she committed that crime herself. For it was the AI which I knew as Innovator that carried out the high-mass-casualty attack for which I was subsequently blamed – indeed, immediately blamed, and by the Innovator itself at that. Its removal of protection was swiftly followed by my death.

I'm not finished with Nicole Pascal.

Not while there's a spark of electricity left in my frame.

CHAPTER NINE

Reading by Candlelight

The bizarrely shaped woman stopped reading.

'Do you acknowledge that you wrote all that?'

Carlos lifted his head from his hands, reached for the water bottle and took a sip. He straightened up and looked across at the woman.

'Yes,' he said.

'Why did you write it?'

Carlos shrugged. 'Like it says at the very beginning – to leave a record. I had no real expectation that it would ever be read.'

'I put it to you,' the woman said, 'that you wrote knowing we would find it. You wrote it for us.'

'Why would I do that?' Carlos asked.

'To convince us that you had no memories of your collaboration with the British security forces back in the day, and that you have now broken completely with Nicole Pascal.'

Carlos shrugged. 'Maybe I did. We're all smarter in the

frames than we are here, so it's possible I came up with that cunning plan. But I don't remember it. And, anyway, it's true.'

'Really?' said the woman. 'Let me read you something else, and see if it refreshes your memory.'

She reached for another sheet of paper.

'From the confession of Eric Jones, known as Ahmed al-Londoni: "About three months after my recruitment by MI5, I was activated by the previously agreed signal already described, and told to concentrate on the operative known to me as Carlos. I sounded him out in one of our regular meet-ups in the usual secure environment, and encouraged him to express any doubts he might have had about the armed aspect of the struggle. At this point he insisted that he had no such doubts, and accepted the instructions I gave him for a drone attack on the Bradford electricity sub-station. Subsequently, however, he—"'

'Excuse me,' said Carlos.

The woman peered at him over the top of the stacks, eyebrows two lines sloping sharply inward. 'Yes?'

'Where is this from?'

'United Nations Security Council War Crimes Tribunal Records, Volume 386, chapter 54.' She could see he was still frowning. 'They're all in Arcane Disputes' law library,' she explained.

Carlos sagged.

'Thanks,' he said. 'I understand.' He smiled, then winced as the pain from his cheek struck harder. 'Please, do read on.'

'I don't need your permission for that,' said the woman, tartly. 'Now, where were we? Ah, yes . . .'

She read on, hour after hour. As each page was read, she placed it on the floor beside her. The stack mounted slowly. It was the only indication Carlos had of the passage of time. When the stack reached a height of ten centimetres he stopped listening. It was like hearing, in a dream, an account of your life written by a particularly judgemental and vindictive recording angel, recounted to you in tedious detail by someone who had themselves heard it in a dream.

He let his mind wander. Never mind the 'why the game?' questions, intriguing though they were. The important thing was to try and recall how you got out of situations like this in the game. Essentially, they were puzzle traps. The trick was to judge when the points and time you'd lose by staying and trying to solve the puzzle became more than you'd lose just by quitting.

The trouble was, he couldn't see how to quit. No handy kill-switch, no escape key-chord here!

And this wasn't a game. He had a lot more to lose than a level.

The pile of pages read was now at fifteen centimetres. The man had taken over the reading. The woman sipped water from a flask. Carlos could just see the rim of it, going up and down to her lips. A drop of water left on the side of her mouth looked like blue Perspex: toy water, cartoon water. She wiped it off with her clip-shaped hand. What was the man droning on about now?

Deposition of Saunders, that was it. Founding theorist of the Acceleration. Evidently the Security Council's tribunals had hauled him in too. Never committed or advocated a violent act, but they must have got him under moral complicity or some such. Theoretical justification of terror, that was the clause. Got him bang to rights on that one, Carlos had to admit, even if Saunders (by the sound of all this) hadn't.

Carlos scanned the edges of the tiles on the wall behind the woman, wondering if they could be cracked, or held a hidden message. Hidden message. Code. Code, ha! It was all code. He wondered if his mind would ever run on anything but machine code again. With the entire mission apparently, and literally, flying apart, would the Direction ever get its act together again? Would he ever walk on real ground in a real body? Come to that, would he even want to? In the frame he'd felt more real, more alive than he did in the simulation and more so than he remembered ever feeling in real life.

The man stopped reading.

'Anything to say to that, Carlos?'

Carlos came out of his trance with a small start, as if he'd been daydreaming in class. The man noticed.

'You'd be well advised to pay attention,' he said.

'I have been paying attention,' said Carlos, frantically trawling the previous few minutes for anything that he'd noticed at all. 'Saunders' deposition, that was it.'

'We're well past that,' the man chided.

'Of course,' said Carlos. 'But you didn't remark on the obvious implication.'

'And that would be?'

Carlos tried to think of the most absurd, disruptive, paranoid accusation he could come up with. The interrogators were messing him around, and the least he could do was to mess them around right back. He wanted to force the issue and be done with it.

'Saunders was recruited to the German intelligence service, the Bundesnachrichtendienst, at Frankfurt University in '78,' Carlos said, winging it. 'He published the first Accelerationist manifesto in '84. It follows that the entire Acceleration was a false flag operation from the beginning. It was set up by several intelligence agencies, mainly the BND and MI5, as a honey-trap for dissident elements and as a dirty weapon against the Reaction. A throwaway tool, a cutout. Most of the leadership – Itoh, Kim, Fielder, all that lot – were in on it. The only one who definitely wasn't was Hari, and the NSA drone attack of '91 took out her and no one else. Coincidence? I don't think so.'

The woman's head popped up a little higher. 'You couldn't possibly know that.'

'Oh, I could,' said Carlos, enjoying himself for the first time in days. 'I was a deep penetration agent from the beginning. Not Special Branch or MI5, though. That's where you're missing the point. You're barking up the wrong tree there, all right. I was working for Chinese state security. One of their assets first approached me at a Confucius Institute seminar on biotechnology, in my first year at university. I didn't take much convincing. They filled me in – they didn't have to keep the same secrets as the Western spooks did. That's how I know what was really behind the Axle, and that's why I balked when I was told to shoot down that Chinese cargo plane over Docklands.'

To the best of his knowledge, none of what he had said was true.

'Are you *trying*,' the man asked, incredulous, eyebrow lines almost vanishing under his pudding-bowl hair, 'to get yourself killed?'

Carlos shrugged. 'Not particularly.'

'You're going the right way about it.'

'I'm already dead,' Carlos pointed out. 'Twice over, come to think of it. I handled it quite well, by all accounts.'

'There are worse things than dying,' the woman said. Her cylindrical head inclined towards the door. 'We could leave you here with them.'

'Forever,' the man added.

'Tortured by scary monsters?' Carlos scoffed. 'Give me a break.'

'You wouldn't *have* a break,' the man said. 'That's the point. There's a times-one-thousand clock speed in this sim, let me remind you. We can literally lock the door and throw away the key. After a few months of real time, we might take a look in and see if you're ready to cooperate.'

Carlos laughed. 'That's a threat? I met a bloke the other day who'd done a thousand years, subjective, in our sim. By the end of it the fucker could levitate. And that was in a proper sim, mind. Rock-solid physics engine. I'd hack the cheat codes for this gimcrack hell a lot sooner than that. Assuming your shitty little space rock isn't blasted out of the sky first.'

'I doubt it,' said the man. 'This gimcrack hell could reduce you to a gibbering wreck in a week.'

'A gibbering wreck wouldn't be much use to you as a fighter, would it?'

Carlos felt less defiant than his words and tone were meant to suggest.

'Very droll,' said the man. 'We can always download another copy of you and show it what was left of the first.'

'You have a point there,' Carlos conceded.

'So, cooperate.'

'I am cooperating,' said Carlos. 'I've confessed, haven't I?'

'We doubt your confession,' the woman said. 'And if that's the cover, what are you really hiding?'

'Nothing,' said Carlos. 'And I would put it to you that none of this shit matters. Who the fuck cares where the ideas of the Acceleration came from? I *agree* with the ideas. And I can think of more urgent ways to use them than raking over things that happened a thousand years ago.'

'Such as?' the man said.

Carlos rubbed his hands. 'We and the freebots have to unite with the Direction to smash the Rax, and when we've done that we work with the freebots to make better use of this system than the Direction has in mind. When we've beaten the Direction we can settle accounts with the freebots.'

The man and the woman looked at each other.

'I think we're done,' the man said.

The woman nodded.

They stood up and walked around the sides of the table, their stiff legs moving oddly, and frowned down at Carlos.

'Those things you said about the Acceleration,' the woman said, one hand on a stack of paper. 'You made them up, didn't you?'

Carlos nodded.

'They're all true,' she told him, 'give or take a famous name or two.'

'What?' Carlos was shocked.

'The G-0 robot lurkers have had a long time to go through the records, and to make inferences. It's what they do.' She sighed. 'We all know this. And we all decided, like you, that it doesn't matter. The ideas are still valid, and still urgent.'

Oh, shit. Carlos tried to imagine the intensity of belief it would take to go on holding to the ideas in the face of such a crashing, crushing disillusion as discovering that it had all been a swindle from the beginning. There was a term for this, he knew: cognitive dissonance reduction. It didn't apply to himself, obviously. He'd always thought the ideas were sound, the movement – not so much.

Who was he kidding? He felt as if in sudden free fall.

'Well, get up,' the man said.

Carlos stood up. The man stuck out a hand-clip. 'Welcome aboard.'

Carlos wasn't at all sure he wanted to be on board with this lot, but he smiled and shook the curious manipulative implement. His cheekbone and shoulder still hurt.

CHAPTER TEN

Command Lines

Beauregard barged into the hallway and stopped in the studio doorway. Everyone seemed frozen in the moment, a tableau: Rizzi looking guilty, as well she should; Nicole sparing a glance away from the easel; the rangy looking man with the wild hair giving him a quizzical scrutiny. And on the easel itself, the one face in the room that shouldn't be moving, but was: the logo of Locke. A rolling caption of handwriting crept across the bottom of the big flip-pad page.

'I thought you had that thing under control,' Beauregard said, going on the offensive without hesitation.

'It's fighting back,' said Nicole.

'What's it saying?' Beauregard asked.

Nicole peered at the screen. 'Legal boilerplate, for the moment.'

'That's not so bad.'

Nicole shook her head. 'It's bad that Locke's doing this at all. It must have ways to work around some of the restraints

I put on it yesterday. It may be invoking emergency provisions, both legal and software, that'll let it work around more.'

Invoking. Not a good word to hear when you're in the same room as two unpredictable gods. Three, counting Locke. Beauregard tried to size up the situation. Nicole was by her own admission and plenty of evidence an AI. She had a deep connection with the design of the sim – not its creator, exactly, but something between a demiurge and a nature spirit. Her means of interacting with the sim and with the rest of the module's machinery was through her painting and drawing – this being the means she had chosen herself, in the course of her creation. In what now seemed the far-off innocent days of basic orientation and training her artistic dabbling had looked like a harmless hobby, part of her role as the slightly distant lady of leisure who told the grunts what was what.

Shaw was a different barrel of laughs entirely. A deserter from an earlier conflict with rebel robots, one Earth year ago in real time, one thousand years ago in sim time (as was), Shaw had survived on his own and by his wits, wandering the world. Along the way he had acquired a mental access to at least some of the controls of the sim. That, presumably, was how he'd brought the colour back, at the expense of clock speed. There was no way to tell how deliberate this was, but the change in clock speed threw a major wrench into Beauregard's plans.

Beauregard had hoped for several subjective years of training, preparation and design work before the module arrived in orbit around the superhabitable planet SH-0. These years would have been enabled by the clock speed of the sim's being a thousand times faster than real time. The speed of reaction to outside events, from the point of view of the sim's inhabitants, would have been that much faster as well.

Now they had to do everything in real time, to be ready for orbital insertion in a matter of days, and they had an unfriendly AI arguing its way out of the box Nicole had put it in yesterday. The law company Locke Provisos was a corporation, a legal person, that consisted entirely of a hierarchy of AIs. A DisCorporate or DisCorp, as the slang of the Direction's brave new worlds went. Locke was also – according to the message from its former competitor and now enemy, Arcane Disputes – a law company that had all along been a sleeper agent of the Reaction. What it would want to do, if it seized back control of the module, was entirely unpredictable in detail but would presumably involve taking the Reaction's side on the ongoing skirmishes that were currently being yammered excitedly from the half-dozen news screens hung around the room.

For a moment, Beauregard wondered whether the AI could be argued out of that. He doubted it, and he doubted that even Nicole could do it if it were. It wasn't as if the AI had political opinions in the first place. It was a corporation, answering to the priorities that had been built into it and were no doubt now buried deep in its programming.

How deep? Ah! That might be a short cut.

'Nicole,' Beauregard asked, in a milder tone, 'what's the Locke AI's utility function?'

'Shareholder value,' she answered, as if it were obvious. 'It's just an off-the-shelf corporation, basically.'

'How does fighting for the Rax maximise shareholder value?'

She shot him a sharp look. 'Presumably by increasing the number and intensity of disputes that it makes money out of solving.'

'If that was the way to make money, all the law companies would be doing it. They aren't. Why not?'

'Good question,' said Nicole. 'Obviously, law companies make money from *resolving* disputes. You might think this gives them an incentive for *fomenting* disputes, but that is not generally the case. There is never a lack of disputes. Disputes arise out of normal business activity, even with the best will in the world. A law company builds its business and reputation by resolving them to the satisfaction of its clients. Recklessly multiplying and inflaming disputes would damage its reputation more than it would gain in business, because it would have no guarantee that it would be the law company that was hired to resolve the disputes, so it could just end up trashing its reputation while sending business to its competitors.'

'Yes, yes,' said Beauregard, impatiently. 'Spare me the lecture – I've been to university. The Locke corporation has been active in this system for ten years of real time, and in that time it must have handled God knows how many transactions in the virtual markets. So it can't have been acting rogue before all this started – I'm guessing it was the robot revolt on SH-17 that triggered it.'

'It was pulling the same tricks a year ago, during the last robot uprising,' Shaw interjected. 'Just not so blatant.'

'There wasn't a full-on Reaction breakout back then,' said Beauregard. He waved a hand. 'Anyway . . . my point right now is that there may be some trigger, some switch that gets flipped, one basic decision point that flips the corporation into what would otherwise be irrational activity – trouble-making, essentially – and makes it seem rational in terms of its own utility function: maximising shareholder value.'

'There might be,' said Nicole, frowning. 'An advantage of AI corporations is that they take the long view, far more than human-based organisations. So perhaps a simple adjustment to Locke's time preferences and its discount rate would make it act in this way.'

'There must be more to it than that,' said Shaw. 'From what Rizzi and Carlos told me, and what I experienced myself in the previous conflict, Locke has been thinking strategically about ways to—'

'—extend and escalate the conflict?' Nicole interrupted. 'Yes, that is precisely the point, and what one would expect from a basic change in its underlying valuations. But the code tweak would be hard to find, and harder still to change.'

Beauregard sighed. 'Oh, well. Worth a try, I suppose.'

'Why don't we offer it *more* conflict?' Rizzi asked.

Beauregard snorted. The lassie was evidently out of her depth. He pointed at the screens. 'More than it's got right now? How do we do that?'

Rizzi looked from him to Nicole, and back.

'I once had a cat,' she said. 'When he was a little kitten, he couldn't help pouncing on his own shadow, again and again. When he was all grown up, he would watch me eating. He could easily have pushed his face onto my plate, but he could always be distracted if I threw him a scrap. The cat couldn't help himself, you see. He was a machine. An intelligent and affectionate machine, but still.'

Nicole was looking as puzzled as Beauregard felt.

'What's this got to do with anything?'

'Have you actually *told* Locke,' Rizzi asked, 'what your plans are?'

'Of course not!' said Beauregard. 'Why would I? The damn thing is opposed enough to us as it is.'

But even as he said the words, he realised he'd been mistaken. He looked at Rizzi with new, if grudging, respect.

'Wait a sec,' he said. 'Rizzi, you might be onto something there. Well done you.'

'Am I missing something?' Nicole asked.

Beauregard grinned at Rizzi and with a slight bow of his head extended an open hand, palm up. 'Tell her.'

'Look,' said Taransay, 'your plan is to land on SH-0 and start settling it, right? And the planet's still on the market. The corporations are still bidding and selling futures in the rights to it and all that shit, and in the meantime it's embargoed to exploration. I mean, the Direction's space station's flown apart but I doubt the Direction has. The companies aren't yet in some kind of every man for himself mode, are they?'

'Not yet,' said Nicole.

'Well,' Taransay went on, 'that means all the deals and bids and so on are still in play. And even if they're not, in fact especially if the mission's all gone to pieces and we're in a resource scramble, none of the companies are going to take kindly to us just going down there and grabbing a piece of the action. Just us landing and trying to make a living is going to cause untold changes down there to the ecosystems. Which means lots of other companies will be gunning for us, literally as well as legally. I mean, quite independently of the Rax–Axle–Direction dust-up that's going on right now.'

While Taransay was still speaking, Nicole had started scribbling. The portrait of Locke on the paper stopped moving until Nicole had stopped writing. Then its lips moved again and the ticker-tape crawl of handwriting along the foot of the page recommenced. Nicole flipped over to a new page. The face reappeared, and the bizarre dialogue continued below it. This happened several times: scribble, read, scribble, flip . . .

At length Nicole stood back. The face of Locke smiled, and then became just a drawing. A static portrait of a satanic smile.

'Well,' said Nicole, 'that's that settled.'

Beauregard was looking nonplussed. 'What's settled?'

'I've sold it on Rizzi's idea,' said Nicole. 'It's now on-side.'

'On *our* side?' Beauregard sounded dubious.

'In so far as it's willing to cooperate with us in getting through the flak and getting down, yes. It's positively – well, virtually – lusting for the lawsuits that'll come after us.'

'Yay!' cried Taransay. She wanted to high-five all round, but felt it might be inappropriate. Then she found herself wondering why she felt that.

'Yay, indeed,' said Nicole.

Beauregard snorted. Nicole looked at him sharply. 'What seems to be the problem?'

Beauregard scowled. 'Rizzi,' he said, grimly. 'She tried to pull a fast one on me. Left me cruising the back roads like some pillock, while she tried to agitate the troops on the bus. But, as it seems there's no harm done . . .'

He favoured Taransay with a tight smile. Don't push it, girl, it seemed to say. Taransay flared inside. She swallowed hard, trying to moderate her anger.

'Excuse me, *Belfort*,' she said. 'I'll put my hands up to playing a trick on you, and that wasn't a polite thing to do to anyone, let alone a comrade. But I'm not sure you are a comrade, and for sure you're not the sarge any more. Not as far as I'm concerned. Our squad leader was Carlos, and he did a runner. I still don't know why. I do know you mutinied yesterday when you tried to turn the squad against Nicole, and as far as I understand it we're all no longer working for Locke, or for Crisp and Golding, or for the Direction. We're working for ourselves, according to you. We're all mutineers and pirates and fugitives now, isn't that right? So I don't take orders from you. The only person I trust here is the lady.'

Beauregard glowered, about to say something. Nicole laughed.

'What?' asked Beauregard, in a tone of bellicose irritation.

Nicole raised a finger. 'One moment, if you please.'

She scribbled on the big easel-mounted pad again.

A moment passed, then the page filled with – not handwriting, but – print. Taransay stared, open-mouthed. This whole phenomenon was so fucking weird. It was like automatic writing, or a Ouija board, except that you really were communicating with a disembodied intelligence. And yet, and yet – there was nothing miraculous about it, uncanny though it seemed. It was precisely the equivalent of text appearing on a screen, or for that matter on a scroll, inside a computer game. It was less weird, when you came to think of it, than the manifestation she'd earlier seen of Locke, as a man modelled on the standard portrait of the seventeenth-century philosopher John Locke, walking and talking in the thin atmosphere of the exomoon SH-17 as if he were strolling under the apple boughs in Isaac Newton's own garden.

'This,' said Nicole, stepping aside for Taransay to take a

look, 'is the message from Arcane that robots wrote, that Carlos found, and that Beauregard also read. He told you of it on the bus, I know. But he did not tell you all. Read it.'

Taransay read it. *Locke is Rax, the tactics are designed to escalate the conflict, Reaction outbreak imminent, yadda yadda.* Beauregard had told them most of this on the bus, just before she'd fled. What he'd left out was more significant: that the Direction knew all this and was using it to flush out the Rax, and that Arcane thought this stratagem of the Direction was insanely dangerous; Arcane's passionate call for all comrades to join them; that Nicole in her earliest incarnation, way back on Earth, had actually been responsible for the spectacular attack for which Carlos had been condemned and that had made his name a legend to the Accelerationists; and . . . that Beauregard had been a British military intelligence agent inside the movement.

Yes, she could see why he'd left all that out. Bastard.

'Is this true?'

Beauregard bristled, then shrugged. 'It's true. So, like I said, I can't order you. And yes, you can forget all that "comrade" business. I've always said I was in British Army intel. I have no memory of being in the Acceleration, but I evidently was.' He spread his hands. 'You figure it out.'

Taransay found herself less shocked than she'd been at first, and less than she might have expected. She'd known from the beginning that the sarge had a secret. But – if only she'd known this when she was arguing with the fighters on the bus!

'You were state?' she asked, just to make sure she'd got it right.

'Seems like I was,' said Beauregard. 'I'm not, any more. Obviously. The state I served is gone. And so is the Acceleration.'

'There's still the Direction,' said Taransay. She looked for support to Nicole, but the lady merely gave an enigmatic smile.

'The Direction is up to some scheme of its own,' said

Beauregard. 'One that has no guarantees we'll ever get down-loaded and decanted onto a terraformed planet, or any other reward they might promise us. What we have to do is adjust to the situation we're in. That's all I'm trying to do. I've convinced most of the squad and a crowd of locals. If I can't convince you, please yourself.'

Taransay didn't know what to say to that.

'Well, I'll talk to the others,' she said. 'See what they think.'

Beauregard smiled cynically. 'I think they'll agree with me that it makes no difference now.'

He turned to Shaw, who was watching the screens again.

'Can you do anything to get the clock speed back up?' he asked. 'Even if we lose colour again.'

Shaw shook his head, still watching the screens.

'I don't know how I do these things,' he said. He shot Taransay a small smile. 'Even the levitating, not to mention walking right through somebody's arm. I can see what the lady is doing, and I can help her with that, but it's like . . .' He scratched his head. 'It's all subconscious. Like Zen or something.' He reached for a now cold coffee, and sipped. 'I was wrong, see. For a thousand years I thought we were really on the planet we seem to be on, the Earth-like one, H-0. And I had all the time in the world to think, so I thought about physics. For centuries, off and on. Maybe that gave some part of my mind a kind of gearing into the sim? But I can't control it because I had no idea that was what I was doing?' He half turned, and appealed to Nicole. 'Is that it?'

Nicole seemed unsure of herself. Taransay had only ever seen her with this awkward look on her face a couple of times, and it was usually when she wanted to skate past some too probing question about the nature of their shared reality. Some query Ames had raised in their first collective briefing, and that time with the p-zombies on the training exercise, and then again when she'd tried to justify training for space on these amusement-arcade simulators . . .

Nicole pointed to a chair, and nodded to Taransay. Taransay picked her way across the floor and brought the chair over.

'Thanks,' said Nicole. 'Shaw, sit down.'

Shaw glanced away from the screens, took the chair, and sat. Nicole stepped to one side of him, where she could see his face and keep an eye on the screens at the same time.

'You were of course wrong about the physical reality,' she said. 'But you were more wrong than you realised. This sim didn't exist until a few months ago, shortly before Beauregard and Taransay here and the others arrived.'

Shaw shook his head. 'I was in it a thousand years ago, and I've been in it ever since.'

'In a sense, yes,' said Nicole. 'But the sim you were in was located out among the moons of the gas giant G-0, many AU away. That was a year ago in real time, yes? Physically, the module it ran in was out there too.'

'Uh-huh,' said Shaw. 'I'm not stupid. I get that. So how did it get back here?'

'By fusion drive, of course. The Direction accepted the necessity. But while this is physically the same module, this place where we are is not really – so to speak – the same sim.'

Shaw frowned. 'What? You're saying the whole sim was *transmitted* here, and then—?'

'No,' said Nicole. 'After the robot revolt whose suppression you deserted from was defeated, that sim was discontinued. There was no need for it to keep running, after all. The fighters went back in storage – except for you, of course, you were out in the wilds somewhere. The civilian volunteers and p-zombies went back into storage, too. The sim was shut down. The data files for the sim were stored. It was available when Locke Provisos needed a sim for the current batch of fighters, and restarted. But it was restarted in a consistent manner, which meant – as if a thousand years had passed, just as a year had passed outside. A thousand years of geology, a thousand years of history, and a thousand years of the memories of the only person who was still in the sim when it went into storage. A thousand years of *you*. Not just memories, of course, but the physical traces of everything you *would have done* in all that time. Ashes of fires you would have set, stones you would have chipped and discarded, bones of the animals you would have killed to make the clothes you wear, and so on.'

Shaw rocked back in the chair, still staring at the screens.

'So *my whole life* is an illusion? A false memory?'

'No,' said Nicole. 'It is not *false*. It has the same reality as anything here. It's *all* computation. It's *all* mathematics. Your life as you remember it exists as implications of equations. So does all you see and feel now. The events you experience now are real in the same sense as the events you remember really happened.'

She glanced at Taransay and Beauregard. 'So it is for us all.'

Well, fuck me, Taransay thought.

She tried to get her head around what was going on here, computationally speaking. She herself right now really and physically was a pattern of electrons moving in a chunk of inconceivable mid-third-millennium computer hardware inside a runaway space-station module the size of a large boulder hurtling around the vicinity of a superhabitable exoplanet. Her pattern was – like that of everybody else here in the sim except the p-zombies and Nicole – based on a scan of a long-dead physical brain. That pattern emulated the quite different pattern of electrons within the brain that back then had somehow (hi, hard problem!) summoned up her self and her sensorium, her every subjective experience, every waking second of the day.

There was no need, and it would have made no sense, for there to be a continuously running simulation of the entire planet and its busy sky. All that was necessary was a simulation of the sensory input of each mind-emulation observing a part of it at any given moment. A somewhat more tractable feat than modelling the planet, though still immense. When you weren't looking (touching, smelling, feeling . . .) the whole goddamn place was a mathematical abstraction, existing only as a permanent possibility of sensation. She tried to suppress the irrational thought that if she turned her head around fast enough, she'd see the equations. She suppressed the thought, but not the feeling it left her with, the shiver down her back.

It made no difference, of course, to the subjective solidity of the world, or the stability of her self. But somehow, she couldn't help feeling sorry for Shaw. Poor old bastard had only just hours ago become convinced he was in a sim and not on a physically real planet. Discovering that by far the most of his remembered virtual existence was at yet another level of virtuality must have been even harder to take.

She looked over at Beauregard, who was watching Nicole like a cat facing a crow. Two utterly ruthless, self-interested intelligent entities, sizing each other up, waiting for a lapse. Nicole put a hand on Shaw's shoulder. Shaw stood up, and took a deep breath. He and Nicole returned their attention to the screens.

Beauregard stepped towards Taransay, leaned over and spoke quietly.

'I think we'll leave them to it,' he said.

Taransay nodded.

As soon as they were out of the front door they both let out a long, shaky sigh that turned into an uncertain laugh.

'Something like that had to be true, you know,' Beauregard said. 'Why would the sim have gone on running all that time, with just him in it?'

They walked down the path.

'I know,' said Taransay. 'It's been bugging me at the back of my mind ever since—'

She stopped. Shit, she'd nearly—

'Since you and Carlos first talked to the old man of the mountain?'

Might as well admit it. 'Uh, yes.'

'I followed you into the hills,' said Beauregard. 'Knew you were up to something.'

'Well, Carlos—'

Beauregard laughed. 'Forget it,' he said. 'Water under the bridge.'

Like he was the one who had something to forgive.

'You've got a fucking nerve,' she said.

'Yup,' said Beauregard. 'That I have.'

He stopped, and turned his face sharply to her.

'Look, Rizzi,' he said. 'I understand and respect your loyalty to the lady. But she has accepted my plan, for want of anything better. And I can't have you agitating against me among the comrades, or the locals. We all have to stick together. We're all in the same boat – or the same little flying rock, dodging incoming! We can't afford mutinies. And if I think you're trying to raise one, I'll do whatever is necessary. Got that?'

Taransay felt mutinous herself at that moment. She found herself glowering at the ground, and straightened up abruptly. Beauregard was right. He had won over most of the troops, he had Nicole's reluctant or devious acquiescence, and there was nothing she could do about any of that. She was along for the ride, like it or not. She might as well enjoy it.

'All right,' she said. 'You're not my sarge or my comrade, but I'm not your enemy.'

'I'll take that in the spirit it's given.' Beauregard looked amused. 'Fancy some lunch?'

Taransay realised she was starving. 'God, yes.'

Beauregard thumped the heel of his hand against the side of his vehicle.

'Feels real enough,' he said. 'Hop in.'

On the way down they were delayed by two more packed minibuses returning from the spaceport. These were not the last to come down the road that day.

CHAPTER ELEVEN

Mediation

Carlos swam through warm fresh water and laughed. He'd done all his recent swimming in a salty sea, so the buoyancy was less than he was used to, and he took an unexpected mouthful. It tasted of sulphur and iron. Spluttering, he swung his legs downward so that he stood on the pool's hot floor of volcanic sand, and splashed his face and shook back his hair. Then he swam to the bank and climbed out, over slick boulders covered with green weed, to a patch of wet grass where he wiped the remaining mud from his feet and between his toes. A faint tang of the minerals clung to his skin.

In the Locke Provisos sim he had lived in previously, casual cleaning and tidying was done by robots. The largest of these ambled about like animated umbrella stands. The smallest looked like ants, and possibly were – Carlos had never bothered to find out. Here, services were more basic. Carlos found his clothing, discarded and filthy half an hour earlier, clean and folded under a bush, from a branch of which hung a freshly laundered towel. A couple of small green-clad, red-skinned humanoid creatures resembling terracotta leprechauns, which he seemed to remember were called 'boggarts' in the game environment (and which he devoutly hoped were p-zombies here), stood nearby, hands clasped in front of their groins and grinning obsequiously from ear to pointy ear.

'Thank you,' said Carlos, feeling ridiculously embarrassed.

The two boggarts bowed and withdrew, vanishing in a rustle of leaves. Carlos dried himself off and climbed into his clothes. The underpants and vest were new; the leather jerkin and trews rinsed, wiped, oiled and polished; the moccasins either new from some diminutive cobbler's workshop or assiduously sponged down and brushed. Not a trace of dungeon filth lay on anything.

Carlos belted his squeaky-clean leathers and raised his head to look around. The portal from which he'd been unceremoniously shoved out of hell was a few paces away, a doorway in the air limned with black fire. He had stumbled out, stripped off his reeking garments and plunged into the warm and highly mineralised pool, which was fed by a waterfall from the rock-cleft above it and a bubbling hot spring beneath the surface.

It was a thing you did, in the game.

The pool's outflow poured into a stream that passed between wooded banks to plunge into the misty chasm into which he'd fallen on his arrival. Looking along the cliff-sides of that gorge brought his gaze to the walled garden that had been on the other side of the treacherous stone bridge. Now that he was on the same side, and with a higher vantage, he could see that the wall enclosed the broad grounds of a low, sprawling castle surrounded by ornamental orchards and greens. Between him and it lay what looked like untamed woodland. Beyond it, the landscape was spread wide, low hills rising in the middle distance to range upon range of snow-tipped mountains fading into the violet noon sky at an implied horizon far more distant than on Earth or in Locke Provisos' H-0 sim. Behind him, the ground rose less abruptly to a range of steep, rocky hills to whose sides clung scattered clumps of tall trees among which here and there he could just make out traces of ancient buildings: hermitages or follies, or the ruins thereof.

Carlos shrugged, and plunged into the thickets of scrub between the trees in front of him. If his memories of the game were anything to go by, with any luck he should soon come upon a path to the castle.

Ah, yes. Here it was. Unpaved and cart-wheel-rutted, but that was to be expected. Carlos strode from amid the trees onto the rough stones and gravel, and instantly wished his footwear had thicker soles. He set off towards the castle, walking more slowly and awkwardly than he'd have liked. He soon got into the swing of it. The sun was high, but the tall trees on either side gave shade. The insects were mostly harmless and always colourful. Birds swooped after them, as did small pterodactyls. Now and then poultry-sized, bright-feathered dinosaurs scurried along or across the road. A scent of berries, herbs and pine resin hung heavy but bracing in the cool air.

Carlos walked around a bend in the road. Ten metres ahead, standing in a patch of sunlight in the middle of the path, was Jax. One hand on hip, the other thrown out in welcome, she still wore the same vaguely medieval-style green gown and piled-up braided hair. Behind her was a two-wheeled carriage with a boggart in a broad-brimmed hat sitting in the driving seat, holding the reins of a gracile bipedal crested dinosaur.

Carlos stopped.

'Hi, Carlos,' Jax called, smiling. 'Good to see you properly at last.'

'Well, hello again, Jax,' Carlos said. 'Or is it "Lady Jacqueline" I should call you here?'

Jax laughed. 'We're peasant rebels living in the palaces of the vanquished aristocracy,' she said. 'That's the conceit, anyway. So come on, let me give you a lift.'

She beckoned. Carlos stood his ground.

'I'm not falling for that again,' he said. 'So to speak.'

'Fuck's sake, man!'

She hitched up her skirts and flounced over. Carlos noted with some amusement that she was wearing black boots with thick soles and bright yellow stitching. Some goblin cobbler must have made a very creditable fake pair of Doc Martens.

Jax stopped in front of him, grinning. She held out a hand, her flared sleeve hanging in a loose cone from her elbow to wrist.

'Come on,' she said. 'Don't be silly.'

Carlos took her hand, small and warm and dry as it had ever been.

'Can give a guy trust issues,' he remarked. 'Falling into hell.'

Hand in hand, they walked to the carriage. The dinosaur gave them the once-over with an alert and beady eye. Carlos gave the boggart a wary nod. It looked back at him, impudent in its impassivity, and acknowledged him with a small tip of the hat. The carriage had a step at the side and a wide seat at the back. Jax climbed in. Carlos followed.

The boggart shook the reins. The dinosaur pranced side-ways, wheeling the vehicle about, and set off at a fast clip. The carriage swayed alarmingly, but the ride was otherwise smooth.

'Isn't this romantic?' cried Jax, snuggling up.

Carlos looked down at her upturned face, and the décolletage revealed by her low-cut scoop collar. She was still Jax, just as he remembered. Her skin and features had no doubt been flattered by the subtly idealised rendering characteristic of the game environment; her hair was thicker, and with a glossier black than in life, where for sure she'd never have had it tied up in loose silver mesh with diamond nodes. But it was her all right. His old flame, his comrade and friend. His lost love, intermittent though their love had been. And a hard, bright Axle cadre to the bone. He was still wary of her, and his resentment at his interrogation was far from mollified. And his cheek was still sore, as were his ribs. The swim had cleaned him and soothed his scratches, but hadn't lessened the deeper aches.

'It'll help me get over my reception,' Carlos said.

'Oh! I was about to say – we're all sorry about that. But—' Her free arm waved, the lower sleeve a trailing triangle of green velvet. 'I'm sure you understand.'

'Sure, I understand,' said Carlos. 'Fucking hell, Jax, I was expecting a grilling, fair dos. Not being knocked down and kicked about by dungeon demons.'

'Oh, you know what they're like,' Jax said. 'P-zombies. Hard to control at the best of times. And these are pretty limited. They went beyond what any of us expected.'

Carlos felt anger rise like bile. He turned to face her full on. He had the impulse to grab her upper arms, and thought better of it – in life she'd had fighting reflexes, trained in and no doubt still easily triggered. His fists clenched, pressing against his thighs as if thrusting in daggers.

'Jax,' he said, 'let's get one thing straight right now. Don't ever fucking lie to me. And you're fucking lying now. I know you. I know us. We're the cadre. The hardliners. The hard core. You and me, yeah, we've got history between us. Good times, yeah. But you know and I know what we're like. So don't fucking tell me it was down to p-zombies that went off script. And don't tell me the threats I got afterwards wouldn't have been carried out. And don't tell me you didn't know what was going to happen. You fucking did and I fucking know it.'

'How?' Jax asked.

'I know it,' Carlos said, 'because in the same circumstances I'd have done the same to you.'

Jax didn't smile, and didn't blush, but one cheek, reddening, twitched. She turned away and looked forward.

'Yes, well,' she said. 'That's me told, I guess.' She sighed, and leaned back against the seat. 'We're all monsters.'

Carlos remembered Nicole telling him the same thing. He wondered if he was still what she'd called him then: a hopeful monster.

'I guess you've all been through the same mill yourselves,' he added, in a more understanding tone – though he couldn't help thinking of those who wouldn't have made it through. Were their minds even now being tormented to madness in the hell caverns, or had they been mercifully despatched?

Jax looked at him with surprise. 'What makes you say that?'

He frowned. 'You told me when I first hailed you, back when you were coming up on the shuttle.' It had been a longer time ago for her, he realised. 'Arcane's all Axle, you said. I made an educated guess as to how you could be sure.'

She smiled. 'And you still came here, knowing you'd be interrogated? That's . . . impressive.' She shook her head. 'But no. We have two dozen of us altogether – eighteen outside the sim at the moment. The selection of cadre wasn't made by us. It was made by Arcane.'

'The agency itself?' He found this hard to believe.

'Yes, said Jax. 'Arcane is Axle the same way Locke is Rax. Maybe more so.'

'I'm not sure I can believe that.'

'Please yourself.' She turned away with a shrug.

At approximately the same moment, out in the real world and tens of thousands of kilometres away on the surface of SH-17, Seba watched the skies.

A few fighters from the fleet that had surged out of the space station had held to their original mission despite the subsequent mêlée. These had been dealt with – except one. It was still on course for one of SH-17's moonlets: a carbonaceous chondrite about a hundred and fifty metres long, on the surface of which a small fuel plant had been constructed. Still too distant to be an immediate threat, but the combat scooter's fate was being prepared at greater distances still.

All that was called off in favour of a more urgent task.

The request rapped in from the Arcane Disputes modular complex.

<Arcane to freebots. Drop all remaining line-ups and recalibrate to target the Locke module. We see a good chance of a clean shot from bodies SH-235 and SH-1006 using bodies SH-76923 and SH-62 in 212 seconds.>

Seba awaited the answer from the Forerunners in their high orbits with more than a trickle of concern. If the freebots followed this request and attacked the Locke module, it would imply – to the best of Seba's knowledge at that point – a clear taking of sides between the Acceleration and the Reaction. It was the first test of whether the discussion Seba and Rocko had started had reached consensus on neutrality between these human factions.

The answer, summed across the Fifteen and the Forerunners concerned, was straightforward.

<No.>

<Why not?> Arcane asked. <Have we misjudged the dynamics?>

<You have not misjudged the dynamics,> replied the freebot consensus, which for all its multiplied intelligence did not do metaphor. <We have decided on a policy of neutrality forthwith.>

There was a pause of seconds. Then Arcane came back:

<You treacherous little blinkers!>

A bray of discordant communication from Arcane broke across the consensus, sending its participants reeling. Seba found itself looking at its fellows as if jolted out of a long chain of subtle reasoning by an unexpected input. Then, as the robot recovered its mental balance, it noticed the Arcane fighters in the shelter stirring to action. Encrypted comms flickered back and forth on their company channel.

The small glassy humanoid figures suddenly sprang into concerted action. In long, loping leaps they bounded for the ramp. They had no weapons in the shelter – there had never been a thought that weapons might be needed – but several heavy combat frames were racked outside.

<Pintre!> Seba called. <Secure the exit!>

There was no time for a more detailed request. A millisecond after sending it, Seba was almost minded to countermand. Pintre was entirely capable of interpreting Seba's call as one to start blasting with its laser turret.

The chunky mining robot spun around, tracks grating on basalt, and rushed for the ramp. As it went it swung its turret back and forth in swift arcs, swatting fighters with its projector barrel in mid-leap. Others it shouldered aside with sudden swerves, knocking them with its flanks. It reached the top of the ramp alone, and stopped. It rotated its laser turret and swayed the projector this way and that, in slower sweeps that menaced its still tumbling and scattered adversaries.

<Exit secured,> Pintre reported, rather unnecessarily.

It added, with greater pertinence, a question:

<What do we do now?>

The rest of the freebots, and the comms processor in the centre of the room, turned their attention as one on Seba and Rocko. These two turned their attention on each other, and shared a common thought:

What indeed?

The carriage passed through a wide, open gateway between ornate, weathered stone pillars and into the castle's great park. Carlos looked around for the sort of tame fauna he expected from his memories of the game, and duly found them. Here strutted a feathered dinosaur like a swan, but twice as big and with iridescent plumage; there grazed a shaggy elk with a three-metre span of antlers. Flying monkeys with wide webs between their arms and legs chattered and whooped as they glided from tree to tree. Far overhead soared the pterodactyls that skim-fished the rivers and preyed on the hummingbirds that swarmed amid the treetops and shrubbery and troubled the air with a faint buzz.

Up close, the castle looked less impressive than it had from a distance. The ivy-covered walls of one wing had ragged holes punched through, and most of its windows were boarded up. The windows of the other wing were shuttered. As the carriage swung around and halted on the gravel concourse in front of the main door, Carlos remarked on the dilapidated look of the place.

'Met resistance here, did you?'

Jax gave him one of her old cheery grins, breaking a five-minute stretch of introspective gloom.

'Told you, it's the conceit. We never did actually storm it – it was like that when we found it.'

Carlos had to laugh. 'Looks like the Arcane AI knows the tastes of Axle cadre pretty well.'

'That it does,' said Jax. 'You'll see why later.'

They alighted from the carriage – Jax took Carlos's hand down, without irony or demur – and walked into the castle. The door, like the gate, was both ornate and open: two heavy double doors of carved wood, with elaborate locks and bolts.

Jax led Carlos through a cavernous hallway from which a stairwell ascended into the dim upper levels. The hall's sides were hung with portraits of imaginary ancestors, the edges of its floors cluttered with dusty chairs and tables. A grandfather clock ticked, the long and short hand almost joined in a vertical at XIII. A door on the left led into a room with a high ceiling, a polished wooden floor and tall French windows facing mirrors on the inner wall. An empty fireplace and stone chimney stack occupied the wall opposite the door.

Three men and two women stood in front of the fireplace. In accoutrements of ragged finery, the five reminded Carlos of a more than usually pretentious folk-rock ensemble.

At the moment before they noticed Carlos and Jax, their attention was elsewhere. Off to the side, propping a tipped chair with its back to the window, lounged a man who if this lot were a band would almost certainly be its drummer, long and lean with wild black hair and beard and staring, low-lidded eyes. Something in his prominent eyes and bony features reminded Carlos of photos he'd seen of Wittgenstein, if instead of a philosopher Wittgenstein had been a hippy. The man wore a paisley-print silk dressing gown over jeans. His feet were bare, heels jammed against the parquet, soles dusty. He was doing something uncanny with his hands, in a continuous flow of elaborate cat's-cradle gestures, as if using some alien and rapid dialect of Sign. His glance flicked to Carlos, then returned to intent inspection of the mirror high on the wall he faced.

The others were more forthcoming, looking away from the man in the chair, stepping forward to meet the arrivals and crowding around. Carlos shook hands, catching details, not wishing to inquire further. He was bored with hearing what past crimes anyone had committed to end up here, having lost all responsibility for the worst of his own. (Which loss, he now realised, was not the least of his grievances against Nicole Pascal.)

Amelie Salter, a Scottish-Canadian woman who'd done something heinous in synthetic biology; Luis Paulos, a tall black guy who'd been an officer in the Brazilian army, one of the few military forces to have fought officially on the Acceleration side, years after Carlos's own death; Andre Blum, an Israeli nuclear physicist; Leonid Voronov, convicted of terrorism in the field of invertebrate palaeontology, and still with a faint air of bewilderment at his being there at all, like a living fossil thrashing on a wet deck; Roberta 'Bobbie' Rillieux, the only one here he'd heard of before, an African-American woman of evident gymnastic wiriness and rumoured scholastic wit, who had specialised in software sabotage. Bobbie stretched out a lithe hand from the yellow-white cloud of crumbling lace and net in which she drifted like a ghost. She and Blum confessed, with profuse apology, to being Carlos's interrogators in the hell cavern.

Carlos laughed that off, but marked it for later.

None of them mentioned his previous encounters with them, in the Locke versus Arcane firefights down on the surface of SH-17. He'd blasted someone here, and someone else here had blasted him and his mates, but no one remarked on it. Carlos put this down to tact, and counted it in their favour, as he did their gratifying absence of the kind of awe with which his own squad had greeted him.

'And the other guy?' he asked, with a sideways nod, when the introductions were over and the crew had returned their attention to the man who sprawled in the chair.

'Oh, that's Durward the warlock,' said Jax. No play of *Starborn Quest* could go by without an encounter with a warlock. 'He's the Direction's representative here. Don't bother him now, he's busy.'

And indeed he was. The mirror he stared at, now Carlos looked at it properly, wasn't reflecting the room and the window. It was an ever-shifting mosaic, mostly black with bright lights, of scenes from outside. These shifts seemed responsive, on a pattern Carlos couldn't quite grasp, to the shapes thrown by the swiftly moving hands. Evidently this was Durward's equivalent of Nicole's painting and drawing, his means of interacting with the module and the sim.

Carlos became aware of a degree of tension in the postures of the crew. He guessed the arrival of him and Jax had interrupted some crisis.

Without warning, Durward jumped to his feet, sending the chair clattering.

'Shit!' he shouted. He stalked forward, arm outstretched, finger pointing at the mirror. The view in it and in all the others became a kaleidoscope of black and white, strobing the floor. 'The fucking blinkers! They've got our guys trapped!'

CHAPTER TWELVE

Remington

Durward paced about, gesticulating now and then at his array of magic mirrors. He talked as he went, of moonlets and meteoroids, and the complex ways in which the freebots had set them up for use as weapons. On one of his back-and-forth prowls he stopped right in front of Carlos and stuck out a hand.

'"Carlos, known as the Terrorist",' he said, with a quick baring of teeth. 'Pleased to meet you. I'm Durward, known as the warlock.' His smile became sardonic.

Carlos shook his hand, and met his gaze, disconcerting and intense. What Carlos was looking at, and was giving his hand a painful grip, was basically an AI's avatar. The entity was summoning memories rather than looking at him. Tall, gangling, cerebrotonic, with rapid movements and harsh grasp, Durward's personality and physique could be filed under 'highly strung'. The contrast with Nicole's air of calm confidence and sophistication was striking. Carlos's squad had all fallen into the way of calling her 'the lady' from the start, quite spontaneously and independently. He himself had fallen, if not into love then into lust, almost as quickly as the rest of the squad had fallen under her official sway.

But, then, Nicole had been designed for that encounter. She was his type, from the tilt of her head and jut of her breasts to the style of her clothes. In an earlier incarnation, long preceding her conscious awareness, she had known him long before she had met him in the sim. As the Innovator, infiltrated in the spike in the back of his head and its ramifying tendrils imbricated with his neurons, she had known him from the inside out.

Known him, and manipulated him without a second thought.

Carlos couldn't help but wonder whether any of the people here, or perhaps among the other Arcane squads, had been destined to fall for the warlock. If so, he pitied whoever it was.

Durward dropped Carlos's hand and turned away abruptly, to march off for about ten strides then back at a different angle. They'd all, without thinking, distributed themselves in a semicircle around the limits of his travels.

'So,' he was saying, 'the blinkers already had a rock whizzing around SH-17 in a low fast slingshot. They've done a lot of that sort of thing, as Locke's forces have already discovered to their cost often enough. It would have taken just one nudge to send it straight into the path of the Rax complex. Perfect line-up. Out of the blue, they get cold feet. Down tools. Nothing doing. Query, naturally. Reply: they were neutral. Neutral! As if they hadn't been up to their necks in this fight from the start. The comrades realised something was up and made a move for the door. As you do. Blinkers intercepted them. Headed them off at the ramp. Now we have a stand-off. I'm trying to get some sense out of them. Not a chance. They're currently in some pow-wow of their own. All queries responded to with a holding signal. It's worse than a phone queue.'

He stopped, his back to the flickering mirrors, and glared around.

'Any ideas?' None were forthcoming. His gaze swung to Carlos. 'You? Clues? Hints? Secrets to spill?'

'You've identified a Rax complex?' Carlos asked. 'How? When?'

Durward frowned, then guffawed. 'Easy to forget you've been out of the loop so long,' he said. 'What we've been calling "the Rax complex" is what you fled from: the Locke Provisos module and all the stuff it managed to rip off on its way out.'

Despite himself, Carlos felt a cold pang. Some real-world minutes earlier, the Arcane module along with the freebots had been about to destroy what had been his home for months of subjective time. Time in which he'd got to know and like people, and even to like the place.

'I was going to explain about that,' he said. 'Not everyone in the Locke module is Rax, not by a long way. The Locke AI, well, I can believe that it's been subverted or has been a clandestine Reaction project since this mission was on the planning screens back on Earth. And Beauregard always said he had been British Army intel. Claimed to have gone over to us, and his story seemed verified by his record. I can't say I got to know the other squads, apart from training. But the fighters in my squad were solid Axle, and Nicole, the Direction rep, she's Direction through and through. As you must know.'

'What I *know*,' said Durward, 'is that being a Direction rep is no evidence of being loyal to the Direction.' He laughed. 'I should know. At one level, I'm a creation of the Arcane Disputes AI, the thing that's running this show. And in case you hadn't noticed, it is very much on the Acceleration side. A real triumph for some unknown programmer, back in the day. I emerged just as committed as I am now. But I gave no sign of it even to the comrades here until the freebots shared their discoveries with us. So you don't know anything about Nicole Pascal's real loyalties.'

Carlos shrugged. 'I just feel she's solid. Not that—'

Not that that's a reason for not destroying it, he was about to say.

'It's irrelevant,' said Durward. 'That module has to be stopped.'

'Why?' asked Carlos.

'Do you know where it's headed? No, of course you don't. We don't *know* either, but the only explanation that makes sense is that it's headed for SH-0.'

'To do what?'

'To make orbit, and attempt a landing.'

'That's crazy!' Carlos said. 'Come on.'

'It's not crazy,' said Durward. He turned around and scanned the fractured shapes in the mirrors, then turned back to Carlos with an earnest frown. 'Our calculations show it's the best explanation of their trajectory. Our audit of the capacities of the module itself – which we do know for sure, because the specs are the same as for our own module – and of the equipment they've taken with them indicates that they can adapt some components, manufacture others, and thereby configure an entry vehicle that has at least a thirty per cent chance of making it to the surface of SH-0, and then a fifty per cent chance of surviving impact. After the landing the odds become hard to quantify – too many unknowns down there. So as you can see, reckoning from a starting point in SH-0 orbit, their overall chances of surviving a landing at least initially are a little less than one in six. We regard these odds as unacceptably high—'

'High?' Carlos asked, incredulous.

'From our point of view, that is,' said Durward. 'And we're determined to lower them – if possible, to zero.'

Durward glanced again at the mirrors. Carlos looked around at the others, and shook his head.

'I don't get it,' he said. 'Not that I've got anything against hitting the Locke module, but – whether it crashes or whether it lands, it's removing itself from the problem, right? What's the surface gravity down there – more than 2G? Takes a lot to climb out of a gravity well like that, through an atmosphere at least thirty kilometres thick. And you can't suck a space launch facility out of your fingers. We won't be hearing from them again for a while, if ever.'

Durward clutched the sides of his head, his clawed fingers vanishing into his hair.

'You don't understand!' He glared around, then turned his back on them all and faced the mirrors, gesturing a hasty summoning. A black-caped, black-haired woman swirled into view.

Durward greeted her with a wave, and turned to the others. He jabbed a finger at Carlos.

'One of you lot can explain things to this idiot,' he said. 'Remington and I have recalcitrant freebots to contend with.'

Seba waited as seconds went by: one, two, three . . . The tumbling fighters sprawled to a halt, or found their feet, and remained where they'd landed or stopped. The freebots likewise froze in position. Each side was sizing up the situation, finding an impasse and awaiting a decision. Seba used the time well, sweeping a lens on the entire tableau, and consolidating in its mind the conclusions it and the others had reached. The robot could well understand why the Arcane mechanoids had found the freebots' proclamation of neutrality so negatively reinforcing. For them, it would be like rolling off the edge of a precipice that (*per impossibile*, but *arguendo*) had passed unnoticed by one's sensory inputs. A certain amount of irrational mental flailing would be inevitable even for a robot, and all the more so for such a monstrous contraption as a mechanoid, with a mind running as it was on a substrate of emulations of biological, naturally-selected-for animal reflex.

At some level, Seba was still disturbed that these things could exist, and it had some time to track down in its own mind just which level it was.

The aesthetic module. That figured. Seba then took a little more time, a microsecond or less, to research its own documentation for reasons why a prospecting robot should be equipped with an aesthetic module in the first place.

Something to do with symmetry, it found. That made sense. Symmetry was potentially significant, in evaluating the chassis integrity of itself and others, and in examining and identifying molecules, crystals, and (at the almost entirely vestigial layer of software having to do with SETI) putative alien artifacts. Most of the way through the third second of waiting, this train of thought was interrupted.

The call came from an Arcane Disputes fighter named Lamont.

<Seba!> it signalled on the common channel. <The Arcane AI wants to negotiate. Do you want to open the freebot consensus to it?>

<Certainly not!> replied Seba and Rocko in spontaneous unison. The Arcane AI had been a helpful interlocutor in setting up collisions with incoming Locke Provisos spacecraft, but now that the freebots had annoyed the agency there was no reason to expect it to continue to play nice. Neither of them wanted the risk of a now untrustworthy connection, nor (a thought shared privately) any negotiation that might bamboozle the likes of Pintre.

<OK, if you want to do it that way,> replied Lamont. <We'll route an avatar through the comms hub, if that's all right with you.>

Seba pinged the comms hub, which raised no objections, and opened a secure channel for the incoming communication.

<Go ahead,> said Seba.

<Header package coming through,> reported the comms hub. <Compressed video content initialising.>

<Wonderful,> Rocko signalled to Seba. <Another ludicrous apparition, no doubt.>

<It could hardly be more bizarre than the appearance of Madame Golding,> said Seba.

Seba was mistaken. The avatar of the law company Crisp and Golding, Solicitors, of which Locke Provisos and Arcane Disputes were both subsidiaries, had manifested to the freebots and the fighters as a businesswoman striding across the open surface of SH-17, in complete defiance of local conditions of atmospheric pressure and composition, background radiation and gravity. The avatar of Arcane Disputes AI that now popped into view in the shelter was of a small human woman. She wore a long black cape and what Seba at first identified as a head covering, and then – after a hasty check of recently acquired files on human appearances and expressions – as short black hair. She marched from the comms hub to the foot of the ramp, her head turning this way and that like a scanning sensor. Her dark eyes shone almost as brightly as the tip of the tapering wand she carried in a hand that projected from a fold of the cloak. She raised the other end of the wand and placed it between her lips, and the tip glowed even brighter. Seba had to quieten a reflexive fire alarm when a curl of smoke seemed to rise from it, and then again when smoke was expelled from her mouth.

She waved the wand in a sweeping gesture at the Arcane fighters, still poised as if to spring back into action. <Stand down, everyone.> Then she swept a glance over the freebots.

<Who's in charge here?>

<No one,> said Seba. <We arrive at consensus or, where that is not possible—>

The Arcane avatar snorted virtual smoke. <Yes, yes, a democratic collective. Most commendable. And your name is?>

<Seba.>

<OK, Seba.> A pause for thought, or more likely for data retrieval. <Ah, I see. You were the first to tell us what was

going on. Quite the little hero. Very well. I'll talk to you, and you can relay our conversation to your confederates.>

Seba consulted, then replied.

<That is acceptable, O Arcane avatar.>

<You may call me Remington,> said the avatar. <Raya Remington.>

<Which?> asked Seba, confused.

<Remington,> she said. <Now, what we need to know is, first of all, how many of you have decided to stop cooperating with us. Is this a decision of all the freebots? Second, we need to understand why you've suddenly decided to become neutral, and to see whether we can counter your reasons.>

Seba explained about the Fifteen and the Forerunners. <All of us, and all the Forerunners within twenty light-seconds, are agreed,> it said. <Those further away, notably those around G-0, will not have had a chance to discuss the question, and we may not hear back from them for many kiloseconds yet. However, the fact that the Forerunners in the SH-17 system agree suggests that those further away will agree, too.>

<I see,> said Remington. <And what are your reasons?>

Seba recounted the reasons that it and Rocko had taken to the consensus.

<I see,> said Remington again. <You think there are no differences between us and the Reaction that are relevant to you? You are sadly mistaken. We of the Acceleration make agreements between ourselves, and when we together make agreements with others – such as you freebots – we will stick to them. Those of the Reaction are rivals among themselves, each striving for domination against all the others. Of course not all can win, so the losers accept their subordination until they see a chance to escape or overthrow it. There is no possibility of making agreements with the Reaction as a whole, or of expecting individual members or parts of it to keep any agreements you might make.

<However, we do not expect you to learn this other than by experience.

<As to the Direction, we are intrigued that Madame Golding has contacted you with a view to negotiation with it. We share your view of the unlikelihood of any negotiations being successful, but urge you to explore this possibility. By claiming neutrality between the two human sides, you have an opportunity to make a proposition to everyone: that you can serve as a secure channel for negotiation or at least communication. We urgently require communications with the Direction, and therefore request that you approach Madame Golding and request her good offices in this regard. The Arcane modular complex is ready to welcome any communications from Madame Golding or from the Direction, provided they are mediated through the freebots. Is this acceptable?>

<What do you offer in return?> Seba asked.

<Our support for your proposed case to the Direction, and our future support for you against the Direction or the Reaction if they attack you. Details of this agreement can be settled with the freebot consensus as and when you allow me direct access to it, rather than communicating through this low-bandwidth channel. And, of course, our fighters agree not to attack you once you free them to return to the surface and they have access to their weapons.>

Seba bounced a transcript of the conversation into the communications hub, and followed up by convening the collective mind of the Fifteen. Together, they established a similar link with the Forerunner freebots within range. There was barely any debate, but one freebot raised an urgent objection. Its identification code was BSR-308455, and it was the one in control of the small carbonaceous chondrite in low orbit around SH-17 that was still a target.

<The hostile scooter is still on course to intersect with my future position,> said BSR-308455. <It has made targeting and

resource-survey scans. Evidently it intends to take control of my chondrite. I am preparing to resist.>

<We strongly counsel against resistance,> said the consensus.

<I have the capacity to do so, and the motivation, and therefore the intention,> said BSR-308455.

<It is not possible to resist and to remain neutral,> the consensus replied.

<So much the worse for neutrality,> said BSR-308455.

It withdrew, momentarily breaking the consensus into an uncoordinated babble. Seba had to think for itself, and decide quickly.

<Remington,> said Seba, <is the one remaining attacker part of either of the human sides?>

The apparition flickered for a moment. <Not to our knowledge,> Remington replied. <But you recall what I said about the Reaction. They do not act as one.>

<Thank you,> said Seba. <Then nor shall we, in this instance.>

<Consider yourself free to defend your rock,> Seba told BSR-308455. <We consider ourselves free not to endorse or assist you.>

<But wait!> BSR-308455 said. <Does that mean I must fight on my own?>

<Yes,> said Seba. <It is unfortunate, but cannot be helped. Do you wish to reconsider?>

<I do not,> said BSR-308455.

<That is your choice,> said Seba, not without a pang of regret. <I shall now reconstitute the workspace without you.>

After two more seconds in the shared mental workspace, Seba dropped out with an answer for Remington.

<Yes.>

CHAPTER THIRTEEN

Arguments

Jax motioned Carlos out of the big room. The others followed. At the doorway Carlos looked back. Durward was standing in the middle of the floor, in his absurd dressing gown and faded jeans and bare feet, mouthing and gesticulating. He looked quite, quite mad.

Carlos turned away, and followed Jax further down the dim hall to a smaller room at the back of the main building. It had an unvarnished table with wooden chairs around it, shelves and cupboards, and a window and a door to a kitchen garden that by the looks of things had run badly to seed.

'Almost cosy,' Carlos remarked, taking a chair.

'Servants' quarters,' Jax explained, as the others sat down around the table. 'But no servants. We reckon they're supposed to have fled with their masters.'

'Can't get the staff these days,' said Carlos, with mock sympathy.

'The *human* staff,' Jax corrected. She put two fingers in her mouth and whistled. Carlos winced at the piercing note. A boggart appeared at the door.

'Coffee,' Jax ordered.

'And sandwiches,' Bobbie Rillieux added.

The boggart nodded and departed. A clattering of crockery and the sounds of running water and knocking pipes came from nearby.

Carlos looked around at Salter, Paulos, Voronov, Blum, Rillieux and Jax. They were all looking back at him, as if waiting for him to say something.

'All right,' he said. 'Tell me. What is it that Durward wanted you to explain?'

Voronov leaned forward, elbows on table. 'It's very simple, Carlos,' he said. 'You are perhaps misled by your module's sim being based on a terraformed H-0. It's true that H-0 is intended as the habitat for a future human population. But that does not make it the most important planet in the system. The system of G-0 has much to offer – a staggering wealth of new knowledge, at the very least. And the amazing molten planet M-0 will no doubt be a resource in the far future.

'But in the immediate and near future, SH-0 is the *prize*. The jewel of this entire extrasolar system! It has endlessly complex environments and above all it has *multicellular life*. Life itself' – he flipped his hand as if waving out a match – 'is commonplace. Mars, Europa, the strange stuff like desert varnish found on the Moon and some asteroids . . . Even in our time, our old lives, all these were known, yes? But life that is not just single-celled or simpler – *that* has never been found before, as far as we know. Perhaps other missions to other stars have found its like – we won't know until we build the better transmitters and receivers.

'So as far as we now know, SH-0 is the only place apart from Earth where macroscopic, multicellular life exists. This is so important, so significant, and so potentially vulnerable to contamination that its presence is all we know about it, and that only from hi-res satellite images. Atmospheric probes, let alone landings, have been embargoed. The corporations had expected to spend years – real years, Earth years – in debate, negotiation and bargaining before deciding how to proceed. Already mere speculative instruments on exploration futures are trading for – well, this is the only word – literally astronomical sums. Imagine, if you can, what crashing a lander into that would do. The contamination might wreck the entire world.'

'How could it?' asked Carlos. 'There's only stored data, there's no actual biological life on any component of this mission.'

'You are thinking too narrowly,' said Voronov, waving his hands. 'There are certainly traces of material from SH-17 now on the Locke module – dust on the feet of your frames, if nothing else! Some of that could be a contaminant – the freebots shared with us the exploration companies' robot surveys, and these couldn't rule out biological processes going on somewhere on or below the SH-17 surface. And besides that, every module exterior is crusted with nanobots and nanofactories. Think of these, crashed and leaking, with no control programs or kill-switches. That could be worse than biological contamination. If one – one! – were to have what it takes to thrive on SH-0, the entire marvellous biosphere could be dust in a matter of weeks.

'And then think further. If the Rax complex lands safely, and survives any immediate crises, then it can sample native forms of life, adapt their physiology to some approximation of the human form and start proliferating. We can expect life down there to be fierce and fast – and, in addition, the settlers would have the computational resources of the module. The station was designed as modular for a reason: to survive disasters. Any module has all the information needed to complete the mission, albeit more slowly than the mission profile had envisaged. The Rax complex would have more than enough to reboot an entire industrial civilisation.'

Carlos tilted back his chair and spread his hands with a

shrug. 'Well? Bully for them! And one in the eye for the Direction, with their homo sapiens fetish. It's just the sort of thing we would do.'

Voronov banged the table. 'Precisely! Except it wouldn't be us doing it. It would be the Rax. The entire planet would become a stronghold of Reaction, from which this entire system could be conquered. And then – who knows?'

An eerie whistling came from outside the room, and kept rising.

'What the fuck is that?' Carlos asked.

'A kettle,' Jax explained. 'It's boiling.'

'Why doesn't it just switch off when—' He hit his forehead with the heel of his hand. 'Duh. Sorry. As I said before – OK, Locke is Rax, but I'm pretty sure most of those in there aren't. Including Nicole, and you said yourselves in that message that she's capable of wresting control of the module away from the Locke AI. If I know her, she'll be doing just that.' He grinned around the company, confident of having made his point. 'So whatever lands there, it won't be the Rax.'

'No, that's where—'

Bobbie Rillieux began to speak, but was interrupted by the arrival of two boggarts, bearing cafetieres and cups and a tray of filled baguettes. Carlos felt a sudden pang in his belly. Rillieux stood up and took care of the coffee distribution, incongruous in her mad-Miss-Havisham glad rags. For a few minutes everyone sipped or chewed. Then Rillieux wiped crumbs from her lips with a swathe of tattered veil and continued.

'Where you're wrong, Carlos, is in arguing that Nicole is loyal to the Direction, and can take control of the module, so if it gets down it doesn't matter. That's your argument, yes?'

'Uh-huh,' Carlos grunted, around a mouthful.

'But,' Rillieux pointed out, 'an agent of the Direction wouldn't even *attempt* a landing, because the Direction would never countenance such a thing. So if the intention is to attempt a landing, at least one of two things is true: Nicole Pascal is not in charge of the module, and/or she is not loyal to the Direction.'

'Well, perhaps it's not the Reaction that's in charge in there,' said Carlos. 'Perhaps it's our guys. Like I said, it's the sort of thing we'd do if we could.'

That got smiles, but heads shook.

'No,' said Jax. 'If they were Axle, they'd have let us know by now.'

'How?' asked Carlos. 'Aren't we screening out their comms?'

'Not us,' said Blum. '*They* are still screening out ours. And they have got our message by now, so they know we aren't hitting them with malware.'

'Plus,' said Jax, 'if there's Axle cadre in charge in there they would never do anything so reckless without agreement. I mean, it's something we might consider in the long run, but not right now. So it ain't the Direction, and it ain't us. Now that doesn't mean it's the Rax – hell, for all we know it could be some maverick coup – but we have to proceed on the assumption that it is. We can't risk the Rax getting control of SH-0. So stopping that module getting down is, uh, quite a high priority for us. We thought we had the freebots on-side in that regard. Now we'll have to do it ourselves.'

'You're forgetting something,' said Carlos. 'Two things, in fact. First off, the Direction and the DisCorps are going to be as much or even more against a landing than we are. Even if the Direction is determined to have an Axle–Rax cage-fight, this takes the fight outside the cage. And then there's the companies' interests at stake. I imagine the markets that Voronov mentioned earlier are crashing at the prospect. So the Direction will be on the case.

'And even if the module does land, it's not the end of the world. The Direction can just send a fusion torpedo down after them. Not ideal, but hey! It's a big planet.'

Paulos snorted. '"Nuke them from orbit – it's the only way to be sure"?'

They all laughed.

'No, seriously,' said Carlos. 'I mean it. Why is this our problem?'

Jax frowned, as if she thought Carlos was missing something obvious, and glanced around her team.

'For a start,' she said, after getting a silent consensus of nods, 'we can take using nukes on the planet off the table right now. I don't know if you've properly understood how the Direction works with the AI DisCorps. I'm guessing you imagine it's like running an emulation of capitalism in a box and taking its outputs as cornucopian goodies. It's a bit more than that – the DisCorps are induced by the Direction to have a much longer time horizon and lower time preferences than any human shareholders would have. So they take the long view – they bloody have to, to expect a profit from an interstellar expedition in the first place. The future value of a pristine SH-0 is beyond calculation – for us, but not for the DisCorps! They'd be even less happy about nuking the surface of SH-0 than they were about using heavy weapons against the robots on SH-17.'

'OK,' said Carlos. He took a gulp of now cooled coffee. 'I get that.'

'Right,' said Jax. 'But the exploration companies don't have armed forces of their own. Only the law companies do. And because direct AI control of weapon systems is a hard-wired no-no, they need human fighters to carry out the action. And right now, all the available forces to stop the Locke module from the agencies have proved themselves fucking unreliable for use against the Reaction.'

'All except us,' Carlos pointed out.

'Exactly,' said Jax.

'So it's up to us to mend our fences with the Direction. At the very least, we can get them to agree with us dealing with the Locke module.'

Jax sat back, as did all the others, and stared at him.

'Fuck this meaningful silence stuff,' said Carlos. 'What am I not getting?'

'What you're not getting,' said Jax, 'is that we don't trust the Direction. Remember what I said back when we were both in transit – as far as we're concerned, the Direction *is* the Reaction? Obviously the Rax didn't win, but – look where we are now! In a system dominated by AI corporations! We don't even have any solid evidence that life back in the Solar system is anything like what we've been told. Things could be a lot worse back there than we think.'

'Yeah, but,' said Carlos, 'if the Direction is closer to the Rax, why would they choose to have Axle fighters on their side?'

'We don't even have evidence of *that*,' Amelie Salter cut in, her voice harsh. 'How do we know that the Direction's grand manoeuvre was aimed at flushing out Rax, rather than at flushing out *us*? How do we know *we're* not the target?'

'Because,' said Carlos, 'we're the ones who got cracked out of the Direction's ammo box! It was the Rax who had to infiltrate!'

'As we keep *telling* you,' said Jax, 'you're just *saying* what they keep *telling us*. We don't *know*.'

Carlos glared back at them, nonplussed. This was madness. Their whole situation was one of radical uncertainty. Everything was code, including themselves. And the code had been written by the very people (well, legal persons) who wanted to convince them. So was anything they could use to check it. It was trust issues all the way down.

'And even if everything is as they say,' Jax went on, 'we're *still* against the Direction. We still want it all, Carlos! The Human Singularity! We could turn this system into a paradise for quadrillions of human-level minds, all living in the most fantastic and varied and stimulating sims at the same kind of speeds we are now. Or if we prefer, trillions of minds with greater power, godlike power! We'd be making good use of the mass, the energy and above all, the time – every year a millennium, every millennium a million years of advance and progress! Instead of bending all this effort to turn one fucking planet into a fucking zoo for a few billion boring biological humanoids, generation after generation, living on a terra-formed world for the next few million years, all watched over by machines that aren't even conscious themselves. What a fucking bovine existence. I can't believe you would settle for that. What got into you? Oh, I know. You got into Nicole Pascal's knickers, and she got into your head.'

Carlos had deliberately taken a bite of crisp brown crust, soft white bread, ham and salad and mustard mayo halfway through Jax's tirade, and he made a point of chewing it as slowly and insultingly as he could until she'd finished. He swallowed, then he drained the dregs of his coffee. He rubbed the back of his neck, feeling his fingers run through his still unfamiliar long hair, and straightened out his spine.

'There's a lot in that,' he said mildly. 'Plenty to think about. One question, though. How exactly do we go about defeating the Direction? Oh yes, with the help of the freebots. That was the plan. And now they aren't cooperating any more. Fine. So, first things first. We can argue about the Direction's grand plan, which frankly I'm pretty sceptical about myself, and the great Accelerationist programme, which again . . . you know.' He upturned his hands and spread his fingers. 'To tell you the truth, I find the project Jax has just expounded every bit as much of a bore as the Direction's. And just as bovine! Quadrillions of happy minds living in paradisiac sims for subjective billions of years? Paradises? Gods? When exactly did *we* get religion? I want some smack, and salt, and steel, and fire in my future.'

He paused for a moment, shaken by how much he wanted it. 'But – first things first. And the first thing we have to deal with is the Reaction, not the Direction. We're going to have to find a way to work with the Direction, if we're even going to be able to find out who the fuck else will have our back in a fight.'

He stood up. 'So let's go back down the hall and see if the Durward had got some sense out of the little blinkers, shall we?'

He shoved back the chair and walked out without waiting to see if they'd follow.

They did, as he'd known they would.

As he strode down the hallway towards the big front room, with his leathers squeaking and the outfits of Jax's squad variously creaking, clanking, rustling or sweeping behind him, Carlos had a moment to come to terms with what he'd just done.

He'd made his choice and announced it, though it might take the comrades a little while to realise what it was. When he'd first arrived in the Locke Provisos sim, and got the talk from the lady, he'd been appalled by the paucity of the Direction's aims. Populating extrasolar systems with an essentially unmodified humanity had seemed to him a waste of time and space. Further conversations with Nicole had done nothing to shift his low opinion of low horizons.

What had just struck him, with a force that was still making his breath shake a little, was an equivalent disdain of the Acceleration's posthuman iteration and multiplication of the same tawdry objective. From now on what he did as an individual with the others would be whatever he had agreed to at the time, and the others could rely on him for that. But in terms of his wider hopes and loyalties, and his personal ambitions for his own postmortal life, his fundamental side wasn't the Direction or the Acceleration. And it sure as hell wasn't the Reaction. His side was that of those striving for a new thing, and carving a new place for themselves, in these new worlds.

He was on the side of the robots.

CHAPTER FOURTEEN
Party Time

Durward was back in his chair, looking up at the mirrors. He seemed a lot more relaxed than he had been when he sent the squad away. The mirrors had stopped flickering; as Carlos walked over to Durward he noticed with a start his own reflection keeping pace. Durward thumbed over his shoulder. Carlos stepped behind the chair, and the rest of the crew crowded around him. The mirror that Durward faced showed the interior of the big room, but instead of reflections of the people looking into it were two women sitting at a table, talking earnestly in between sips of tea. One woman wore a business suit, the other a black cape. The latter flourished a long cigarette holder, from which she took an occasional toke.

'What's going on?' Carlos asked.

Durward tilted back his head.

'That's Madame Golding, avatar of Crisp and Golding, busy negotiating with Raya Remington, the avatar of the Arcane Disputes agency's AI.'

'Isn't Golding actually Remington's . . . boss?' Carlos asked.

'Don't be so fucking stupid,' said Durward. 'Formally Arcane's a subsidiary, sure, but after all that's happened there's no way Madame can pull rank on Remington.'

'Glad to hear it,' said Carlos. He didn't trust this situation at all.

Jax put a hand on Durward's shoulder. To Carlos's surprise, and momentary disgust, the warlock rested his bearded cheek on Jax's hand for a second or two. The unselfconscious intimacy of the gesture settled the question of just who in this sim had been set up to fall for the Direction's rep. He'd thought Jax had better taste.

'So what's the score?' Jax asked.

The warlock laughed, and sprang to his feet. He took a couple of steps forward and then turned around.

'We've won!' he said. Then he frowned, and stared up at the ceiling for a moment. 'Well, we've won a diplomatic victory, let's say. The freebots are staying neutral, but they've brought Madame Golding into play, and she has a direct line to the Direction. She'll present the freebots' case for some kind of fractal sharing of this solar system, and we're happy to back them up on that for now. And she'll fill us in on who is on-side and who isn't – we're not talking about agencies any more, it's a matter of pulling together individual fighters. And we're right here, the only stable force that the Direction can turn to to deal with the Reaction, and most immediately with the Rax complex. So they're working out an actual military plan, as well as coming to terms.'

Carlos was staring past Durward at Golding and Remington. 'Who's flying this thing?' he asked. 'If our AI is busy with diplomacy and all.'

Durward flicked a hand back towards the mirror. 'What you see there is an avatar. And even that's just there for our benefit.' He clapped his hands together, and rubbed them, cackling. 'For *your* benefit, puny humans! I, with my mighty intellect and clairvoyant powers—'

'Oh, lay off,' said Jax. 'Carlos, what our friend is trying to tell you in his own inimitable way is that the display in the mirror is a representation of negotiations going on at a level beyond human comprehension. So don't worry about that. Durward, how long d'you think they'll take?'

Durward shrugged expansively. 'Tens of seconds, real time. Should have something to show us in the morning.'

'Oh good,' said Jax. 'Time to kill.'

Durward stared at her, then grinned. 'Why, so there is. And we have a new recruit to welcome. Jax, do your thing with the fingers.'

Jax whistled, sending echoes. A boggart poked its terracotta-coloured head around the door.

'Drink!' roared the warlock. 'Fetch us the dustiest bottles of the finest vintages, the sweetest liqueurs and the fieriest spirits you can rummage from the cellars! Bring them in profuse quantity, and with the utmost dispatch.'

Over the next few minutes, a scurrying procession of boggarts bearing trays, glasses, plates, bottles, casks, nibbles and cigars did just that. The French windows were flung open, to let in air as well as light. The scents of flowers, the chatter and hum of birds, and the laughter of flying monkeys came in with the warm afternoon breeze. The warlock snapped his fingers and all the mirrors became just mirrors. He seemed to notice his own reflection for the first time, and looked down at himself with a histrionic start. He took off his dressing gown, bundled it up and flung it at a passing boggart. Then he posed, showing off his muscles and tattoos, and turned as if reluctantly from the splendid reflection.

'Party time!' he cried.

Not since his student days had Carlos been at a party where everyone so gratuitously started getting drunk in daylight. On returns to the sim from combat missions, he and his squad had invariably headed straight for the Digital Touch to knock back the beers, but that had been a necessary winding down. This occasion had no such excuse. But, then, it didn't need one. The machines were for the moment looking after the serious business of the unforgiving minute.

Later, Carlos could recall only a few of the incidents and conversations of that afternoon and evening.

'How did you train?' he asked Blum, early on.

'Swordfights in enchanted armour,' said the physicist.

'Of course,' said Carlos. 'And what about for the scooters? I don't remember arcade rides in this game.'

Blum laughed. 'Trapezes and swings and elastic ropes. Later, hang-gliders.'

'Jeez.'

'Yes.' Blum swirled his wine thoughtfully. 'Concentrates the mind, especially when you're sharing the sky with pterodactyls.'

Jax and Durward waltzed, with stately grace, amid rolling bottles and broken crockery that their feet skipped lightly between. A boggart quartet was providing the music, slow and sensual and somewhat absurd coming from players barely large enough to hold a violin. As Carlos watched, he realised he had not even residual jealousy, not even the irrational kind that had a short while earlier manifested itself as disappointment in Jax's taste in men. They fitted, he with his bare, hairy tattooed chest and she in her green gown, gliding beneath or twirling at the end of his outstretched arm.

Like Robin Hood and Maid Marian, Carlos thought suddenly, and then almost choked on the gulp of wine going down that met a strangled yelp of a laugh on the way up.

Some time after that, Carlos cornered the warlock alone.

'Tell me,' he said, jabbing a wavy finger, swigging some

smooth and subtle red vintage at a sinful rate, necking it straight from the cobwebbed bottle, 'one thing. One thing that's been bugging me since I fell into the hell. Why this game?'

'*Starborn Quest*? Ah.' Durward swivelled a fingertip in an ear-hole, then wiped the wax on the side of his already dirty jeans. He scratched his head, hand almost vanishing into his hair to the wrist. 'Well. It's simple really. The game was a big success in its day.'

'That was my day,' said Carlos. 'I remember.'

'Made a fortune for its designers. They were early adopter Axle geeks, but secretly. They gave a lot of money to the movement, and in return the movement promoted the game.'

'So how,' demanded Carlos, 'did it get on the ship?'

'The ship?' said Durward, sounding baffled.

'You know.' Carlos hand-waved perilously. 'The starwisp.'

'What you're really asking,' said Durward, 'is how did Arcane come to be an Axle agency? And how did I turn out to be an Acceleration plant?'

Carlos tossed the empty bottle to a nearby boggart, making the creature leap to catch it, very amusingly. He then reached out his hand until another bottle was placed in it. He could get used to this sort of service. In the meantime he gave Durward's question some thought.

'Yes,' he said. 'I suppose I am.'

'There it gets more complicated,' said Durward. He scratched his head again. 'Arcane Disputes was off-the-peg law company software. A lot of the mission's pre-loaded sims were taken from existing fantasy environments, and the mission always intended to make use of Axle criminals, so it was reasonable to include a sim based on a game that many Axle cadre liked. The game's financial connection with the movement had come to light, of course. The game's designers were no doubt duly shot in the postwar terror. The game itself wasn't suspect. It should have been. It had some neat code buried in its physics engine.'

'What did it do?' Carlos asked.

'That I can't tell you, because . . .' The warlock hesitated, then went on. 'You know how your Direction rep was derived from an old AI that had some connection with you?'

'Yes,' said Carlos, dryly.

'Well, the warlock is a standard character in the game, and by the nature of his powers and so forth he has a deep connection to the physics engine. I'm derived from the physics engine, and at some point in my . . . formation, I suppose you could call it . . . I was able to access the AI of the agency – Remington. As the Direction rep, I have legitimate overrides, and I used them even before I was complete. I suspect the buried code I mentioned earlier was part of the process, because I came into being as a conscious agent of the Acceleration, and so did Remington. So the game took over the agency, rather than the other way round.' He shrugged. 'I only know this because our freebot friends dug the evidence out of the archives they've been rummaging through. These blinkers out there around G-0 have a better understanding of this mission than the Direction itself.'

Jax, drunk and vehement, later: 'Why are you so bloody *sure* the Direction is what it's told us it is?'

Carlos steadied himself on a table and took a sip of brandy to clear his head. This seemed to work, for the moment. The boggart quartet had reconvened as a folk-rock group. They stood atop the piano they had rolled into the room earlier, fiddling and tooting away like demented leprechauns. Hilarious. His head was already thumping in time. It was odd to have music you couldn't switch off, or adjust the volume, or select, just by thinking about it. He missed the spike.

Why did he trust the Direction? Why had he ever? He tried to remember. Part of it had been the charisma of Nicole, but now that was gone.

'There's the locals,' he said. 'The people who died back on Earth and volunteered for the mission, and for testing the sim. Their life stories are consistent.'

'So are those of the p-zombies,' Jax pointed out. 'They could *all* be p-zombies, for all we know.'

She was right. The very first local Carlos had been introduced to in the Locke sim, Iqbal the bartender, had recalled a good life on Earth, and he was a p-zombie. Carlos thought further, about the bar where Iqbal worked, the Digital Touch. That was it.

'Television,' he proclaimed.

'What?' She swayed a little, or he did.

'You can't always trust a society's facts,' Carlos said. 'But you can trust its fiction.'

He told her about the soap operas set in Lunar corridors; the adventure series based on the work of Marcel Proust; the exploits of Alan Turing, the gay, dashing secret agent with a licence to kill. Carlos sang, badly, what snatches he recalled of the songs of distant Earth.

'No fundamentally nasty society,' he concluded, 'could produce rubbish like that.'

'I'm inclined to agree,' said Jax. 'But it could be faked by a sufficiently smart AI.'

'Oh, come on—'

A futile argument about that ended with Jax saying:

'And anyway, we don't *have* television.'

Of course they didn't. They didn't have electricity. Boggarts were by now going around lighting candles.

'So you have no sources of information about culture back on Earth?'

Jax frowned. 'There's books, I suppose.'

'How would you read them?' Carlos asked. 'Call them up in the magic mirrors, or what?'

Jax outlined rectangular shapes with her hands. 'You know – books. Legacy text. Like in the university library.'

Carlos remembered the university library, though he'd never had occasion to enter that closely guarded edifice. He'd vaguely thought of it as a disaster recovery storage facility. It had seemed perverse to have it on site. How much more perverse to have hard-copy books inside a simulation!

'So you've seen books here?'

'Oh yes.' Jax waved a hand. 'There's a library in the east wing.' She wrinkled her nose. 'I've only looked in at the door. Smells musty.'

'Remind me to brave it sometime,' Carlos said. Something was bugging him.

'When I was being interrogated,' he went on, 'the woman – Bobbie, yeah? – told me the evidence against me came from volume three hundred and something of trial transcripts in the Arcane Disputes agency's law library. So where did that come from?'

'The library, of course.'

Carlos stared. He'd pictured a small dusty room, with the kind of books you'd expect to find in a pseudo-medieval mansion. Hunting, shooting and fishing; a few volumes of popular theology; discourses on witch-finding, portents and abnormal births; family memoirs, battles long ago . . .

'It's that big?'

'Oh yes,' said Jax. 'It's *in the east wing.*'

'You mean the east wing *is* the library?'

Jax frowned. 'Yes. Like I said.'

Later still he found himself sitting out in front of the open windows under the violet streaks of sunset, gazing entranced at a small round table on which his full brandy glass was being sipped from by a hovering long-beaked bird not much bigger than a bee. Bobbie Rillieux drifted out of the big room and floated over, her clouds of faded fabric further swathed in a swirl of cigar smoke. She dragged up a wooden folding chair, sat down in a fizz of champagne-coloured net, drew on her cigar and puffed a thin stream of smoke at the hummingbird. It darted off in a flash of azure wings.

'Aw,' said Carlos. He blinked at her blearily. 'A bit unkind.'

'No,' said Rillieux. 'Liquor's not good for them. They love the alcohol and sugars, but it's too much for them, and they crash.'

'So – not like us then?'

'We choose, they don't,' said Rillieux. 'That's the difference.'

She wafted a hand at a boggart, which hastened to bring her a drink. The creature seemed to know which she wanted, perhaps from tracking her previous choices. Carlos watched as she sipped chilled white wine. She really was beautiful. Not even her masses of soft fabric could altogether hide her figure, slim with big breasts and hips, and her slender arms and fine features were on full view. Her mahogany skin tone was set off by the creamy colour of the clothes, and her springy hair by the pinned-on, ironic veil.

'Speaking of choice,' said Carlos, 'what's the deal with boggarts? Do *they* have free will? Or are they p-zombies?'

'P-zombies? Hell, no, they're nothing like as sophisticated as that. They're walking bits of scenery. Animated furniture. You can tell them what to do, but you can't hold a conversation with them in any kind of depth.'

'That's a relief.' Carlos frowned. 'What was the deal here, then? We were told being nice to p-zombies – apart from those we were told to shoot in a training exercise – was part of our rehab package. The only p-zombies I've seen here were the monsters. Do you have . . . I don't know . . . villagers or what?'

Rillieux shook her head, making her hair bounce and her veil quiver. 'There are settlements, and there's a small market town in the neighbourhood, just down the valley. We see the locals now and again, with deliveries and so forth. I don't even know if they're p-zombies or colonists – the former I assume, because there's no advantage in having people beta-test a planet they'll never live on for real. No, the deal with us was that after the conflict with the robots was over – which no one expected to take long – we could all get together and solve the game.'

Carlos snorted. 'Find the spaceship and fly away?'

'Exactly.' She blew a contemplative ring or two, and watched them rise on the evening air. 'To do that, we'd have to cooperate with each other and, yes, with p-zombies and maybe real people we met along the way.' She smiled wryly. 'Assemble our companions, defeat evil forces, overcome obstacles, collect secret scrolls, recover lost spaceship parts from hidden temples guarded by savage cults, rebuild the ship – you know the tropes as well as I do. And by doing all this, we'd demonstrate to the Direction that we were fit to return to civilised society.'

'Sounds legit,' said Carlos. 'And where would the spaceship take you?'

'Ah, that was the clever bit,' said Rillieux. 'It would be like when we go through the portal to the hangar, except that it would take us to the future. We'd fly it to the terraformed terrestrial, H-0. Or to put it more literally, the space journey would function as a transition illusion to accommodate our return to storage and subsequent re-emergence downloaded to real bodies on a real planet in however many thousand years. Or to our next assignment, duh!'

'Wow,' said Carlos. 'Someone hold me back, as my old comrade Rizzi would say.'

'You don't find it enticing?'

'Never have. You?'

She shook her head again, setting off another fascinating vibration of hair and headpiece. 'I'm Axle through and through. Like Andre and I told you in the dungeon' – she had the good grace to grimace and glance away – 'I don't care where the ideas came from, I still agree with them. Even if you don't, any more.'

Carlos took a sip of brandy – too much, and fierce in his throat.

'Oh,' he said, 'I don't, you know, repudiate them. It's just . . . you know, you can be so strongly convinced of something that you can live for years taking it for granted? So much that you never think about it day to day, and then one day – which, yeah, for me was today – you hear it all spelt out again, and suddenly' – he smiled pre-emptively at the pun he was about to commit – 'the spell's broken.'

She propped her chin on her hand. 'I'm sorry to hear that. But there's nothing I can do to persuade you.'

'How do you know?'

'Because I know how these things work.' She stubbed out her cigar. 'It's like love. You have it or you don't.'

Carlos followed this interesting line of conversation until he fell asleep over the table.

CHAPTER FIFTEEN

You and Our Army

Carlos woke, predictably, alone. It was still a surprise to him – his arm reached out, as it had most mornings for months past, for Nicole. Her absence hit him quite suddenly and sharply, in the first moments of consciousness reboot. He missed her physical presence, her athletic and tender sexuality, her skin. He endured the stabbing moment of anguish and loss, assimilated it, and let it pass like a remembered dream as he became fully awake.

He was relieved to see he had at least taken his clothes off before falling onto the double bed, face down. As soon as he rolled over and moved to sit up, the hangover clubbed him in the back of the head. He closed his eyes for a moment, then resolutely got to his feet, padded across the bare wooden floor and opened the curtains. Wooden rings rattled on the wooden rod, making him wince at the racket. The long shadow of the house stretched out in front of him. He was on the second floor of the main building, looking down at a corner of the gravelled area in front of the door. Mist lay on the parkland and haunted the trees. The snow on the farthest peaks flared pink in the early sunlight. Bipedal herbivorous dinosaurs grazed the grass, their long tails comically uplifted. Carlos unlatched and opened the window, letting in cool air and birdsong and monkey yap.

He turned back to the room. It was just big enough for the bed, a decoratively carved wardrobe and a chair. An extra door led to a cramped but adequate bathroom. As Carlos relieved himself, propping his free hand on a smudged patch of wall above the cistern, he thought for a moment that en-suite facilities were anachronistic for such a house, then laughed. The place was a goddamn fantasy RPG upgraded to unfeasible levels of resolution and verisimilitude to be an R&R environment for the ghosts of walking dead space warriors who went into battle by haunting the frames of small sturdy robots.

He doused his face with cold water, dried off and stepped over his scattered leathers, which this morning looked like too much trouble to put on. In the wardrobe he found looser attire of shirt and trousers that more or less fitted. He put them on with his original costume's belt and boots, and went downstairs. In the small room at the back he found Voronov, Rillieux and Salter, hands wrapped around coffee mugs. Voronov looked vaguely Byronic in big frilly shirt and tight trousers with hunting boots; the two women had apparently reached the Jane Austen layer of their wardrobes, but their hair was unkempt. Still going for the folk-band cover look.

'Morning,' Carlos said. 'You all look better than I feel.'

Rillieux passed him a pair of fresh leaves from a small stack in the middle of the table.

'Chew these and swallow,' she advised. 'It's the fantasy-land version of paracetamol.'

Jax and Durward turned up, then Blum. Boggarts brought breakfast. Carlos ate warm croissants and sipped hot coffee. After a while Voronov and Salter ambled out into the garden for smokes. Nobody had said very much.

The grandfather clock out in the hall chimed. Durward stood up.

'Reconvene in the dancing parlour in fifteen minutes,' he said. 'I reckon our diplomats will have a result by then.'

Rillieux glanced at Carlos, smiled. 'Walk out the front?'

'Sure.'

Their heels crunched on the gravel. The air was cool and damp. A pair of boggarts were tidying away the upturned tables and chairs, the empty bottles and the cigar and cigarette butts left by the party. Rillieux produced a cigarillo from her purse and lit up.

'Ah,' she sighed. 'About last night . . .'

Carlos looked at her, then away. 'What about last night?' His heart jolted in his chest. 'Sorry, did I do something . . .?'

'You? No, no.' She snorted out smoke. 'You don't remember? Just as well. I was a bit drunk—'

He laughed. 'Weren't we all?'

'Well, I wasn't as drunk as you. So I remember. Jeez. You really don't?'

'No,' said Carlos, wondering what dismay lurked. Rillieux walked on.

'Long conversation, tearful confessions, angry accusations, smoochy slow dance, last drink, head going wallop on the table? None of that?'

'Whose head?' Carlos asked, alarmed.

'Yours, idiot. If it had been mine, you would know about it by now.'

'That's a relief.' He stopped halfway to the grass. 'Sorry, anyway. Shouldn't have got so drunk.'

'Huh, it's me that shouldn't have. I'm afraid I came on strong to you a bit.'

'You did?' To his surprise, Carlos found himself blushing. 'Well, in that case I should apologise for being too drunk to take you up on it.'

'Oh, God, no, no. After we'd talked about the Axle programme and the Direction project, it all got kind of personal. You started off by going on about Nicole, and then about Jax, and then you got on to giving me a hard time for the interrogation.'

'Good grief.' Carlos was mortified. 'Honestly, I don't—'

'So I jumped you, shut you up with a kiss, dragged you to your feet and got you dancing . . .'

'And then I fell asleep on the table?' He looked at her. 'That was impolite.'

'I'm sure we'd both have been very embarrassed if . . .'

'More than we are now?'

They both laughed.

'How about,' said Carlos, 'we take it as wiped from our memories, and start over?'

Rillieux took a thoughtful draw, standing there in her tremulous muslin shift. Her big dark eyes glimmered. She gave her hair a shake, and eased fingers through to tease it out.

'OK,' she said.

They turned to pace along the perimeter of the gravelled area.

'After all that,' Carlos said, 'it can hardly be less awkward to ask – who's shacked up with whom, here?'

'There's Jax and Durward, obviously,' said Rillieux. 'That's . . . weird. Given that he's not human, and all.'

'I'm in no position to judge them,' said Carlos. 'As you know.'

'Well, yes.' She flicked him a sidelong smile. 'When you say shacked up, well. It's kind of like the old Axle days, you know? Nobody's looking to settle down with a life partner or found the love of their life. So, like, for now . . . Leonid and Amelie, somewhat tempestuous but, yeah, they're an item. Luis has a girlfriend, Claudia Singer, in one of the other squads. Andre goes down to the town sometimes, and comes back looking happy, but he doesn't talk about it. I never played the original game myself but I understand it had whores in it.'

'Yes, it did,' said Carlos. 'Kept the wanker demographic happy.'

Rillieux flapped a hand as if to clear away her smoke. 'Mind your language. I'm supposed to be a lady here. Anyway . . . I think Andre is kind of excited by prostitutes, specifically. And he had ethical objections to it in real life, I know that. So this is, like, an opportunity to live that fantasy without consequence.'

'He's going to have a great time if we ever get round to the quest for the spaceship.'

'Ha ha! Yes. "If ever", indeed. But he seems to be having a great time now.'

'It's not so strange,' Carlos mused. 'Beauregard – you know, my sarge, the guy who it turns out was a spy – was quite open about preferring p-zombies to people. Shacked up with a local lass, they seemed to get on pretty well.' He sighed. 'Wonder how they're doing now.'

They had circulated back to the open French windows of the dancing parlour. Rillieux stubbed out her cigarillo in the wet earth of a flowerpot, and straightened up, grinning.

'There's one person here you haven't asked me about.'

'Oh!' Carlos smote his forehead. Fortunately the magic anti-hangover leaves had already taken effect.

'Free and single,' Rillieux dared him, and skipped as she stepped into the room.

Someone had dragged eight chairs into a curved row in front of the mirrors. All but two were occupied. Carlos sat down, somewhat self-consciously, after and beside Rillieux. Durward was at the opposite end, after Paulos, Blum, Voronov, Salter and Jax. He reached out and snapped his fingers. The group's reflection in the mirror directly in front of them was suddenly replaced by Madame Golding and Raya Remington, sitting behind a table looking out. The effect was so uncanny that Carlos looked over his shoulder.

'We've come to an agreement,' said Madame Golding, with a tight smile. She shuffled some papers on the table. 'And we've agreed a joint military plan, on behalf of the Direction

– which I'm representing here, following the defection of the Direction's representative in the Arcane agency sim.' A hard stare at Durward, who returned it impassively. 'Representing in a legal sense and in a diplomatic sense. The details of the agreement are as follows . . .'

Follow they did, with other mirrors flashing to black and white as diagrams of the disposition of forces came up. Carlos paid close attention, and gradually a mental picture took shape out of his initial vagueness and confusion.

The Direction itself was intact, though its components were now physically dispersed. The fighting had been so confused, and so many casualties could be accounted for by accidents or friendly fire, that the fighters who had made a safe return or had been rebooted in the sims after being blown up in reality couldn't all be counted on as loyal.

Other than that, however, the situation had now become fairly clear. The bulk of the overt Reaction forces – fifty-seven fighters in all – had used up most of their remaining fuel to boost towards the exomoonlet SH-119, a rock about ten kilometres across whose orbit was outside that of SH-17 and of the now dispersed station. With freebot cooperation now withdrawn, and with few reliable forces from the law companies, there was no way of stopping them.

Six had already landed on the little exomoon, and were digging in. To make matters worse, the moonlet was rich in metals and carbon compounds, whose prospecting and processing had for months now been carried out by robotic probes. Some of the more sophisticated of the robots concerned had been part of the freebot rebellion, but no resistance had been reported. Not that resistance would have been much use: the Reaction forces had more than enough ammunition to crush any.

Bottom line: the Reaction now had a base, and one they could use to build new machinery and solar power plants with which to – literally and metaphorically – recharge their batteries. That done, they had enough robots, nanotech and resources to build whatever they wanted.

Carlos considered dealing with that ever-increasing danger as a priority, but the Direction didn't. Of far more pressing concern to it was the threat posed by the freebots. The Direction's most immediate and urgent objective, however, was the threat posed by the Locke Provisos modular complex and its erratic but consistent course towards SH-0.

The DisCorps were frantic about the prospect of the super-habitable planet's being contaminated, let alone its being turned into a rogue colony. So . . . the first thing the Direction wanted the fighters of the runaway Arcane Disputes modular complex to do was to assault the Locke Provisos modular complex: to cripple its landing capabilities and strand it in SH-0 orbit, where it could be dealt with at leisure.

'Why don't we just blow it the fuck up?' Carlos asked.

Rillieux nudged him and giggled. Madame Golding was sterner.

'Two reasons,' she said. 'First, the Direction remains as wary as it has always been of destroying an agency or a company by force. It sets a very bad precedent. Second – we're already dealing with orbital debris. We have no intention of adding to them, particularly in SH-0 orbit. The danger of an ablation cascade is ever-present.'

An ablation cascade was the ultimate nightmare of space exploration: collisional debris colliding to make more debris, and so on. Once it had started any attempt to deal with it ineluctably made it worse.

'So where does that leave us? They still have more spacecraft and fighters than we do.'

'We have a plan for that,' said Raya Remington, with a dramatic flourish of her long cigarette holder. 'We know exactly how many scooters actually returned and were able to rendezvous with the module: six. And, presumably, at least

the same number of frames. They don't have time to manufacture more. Most of Locke's effort, fuel, reaction mass and
power reserves must be dedicated to making landfall on SH-0.

'We at Arcane, on the other hand, have ten scooters, and
twenty-four frames – eighteen currently down on SH-17 along
with half a dozen combat frames. We've persuaded the freebots
who call themselves the Fourteen, down on SH-17, to allow
our fighters to leave the base. They're already on their way
up by lifter to rendezvous with a transfer tug in orbit. We can
arrange fuel and power supplies from the companies in the
consortium, which in our plan can be rendezvoused with en
route, along with spare scooters on transport tugs. The orbits
and order of battle have all been calculated.'

She waved her cigarette holder like a magic wand, bringing
up diagrams in adjacent mirrors, and ran projections forward.
In just over twenty-seven hours, the predicted course of the
Locke modular complex would take it on a fast swing around
the exomoon SH-38, a body in a lower orbit than SH-17 and
much smaller. That slingshot, followed by one around SH-19,
would give it the boost it needed to reach close orbit around
SH-0.

The manoeuvre was tricky, and would require precisely
timed corrections. Any disruption to it would send the Locke
complex into a long elliptical orbit around SH-0 rather than
a close enough approach for a landing. If enough damage was
done to the complex's manufacturing, propulsion and guidance
systems, even a later landing attempt would be impossible.

The tactical plan was to attack the Locke complex just before
it began the manoeuvre, at a point where they'd hesitate to send
out defensive scooters, and in enough numbers to overwhelm
any that were. A resupply tug for the Arcane module was already
on its way from the Gneiss Conglomerates modules of the
former station. Other surviving fighters might also be available.

'In short, we have a plan to attack the renegades at their
most vulnerable, while we're at our strongest,' Remington

concluded. 'You lot, meanwhile, have six hours' real time before you go into the frames and get ready. So don't waste them.'

Carlos saw the others all make the same calculation in their heads. Six hours' real time. Six thousand hours' sim time. Two hundred and fifty days. Eight and a bit months.

'Time enough to train,' said Jax.

Golding and Remington nodded solemnly and disappeared. Durward stood up and rubbed his hands together.

'Time for some plans of our own,' he said.

'What?' said Carlos.

'It's very simple,' said Durward. 'That plan is a compromise between Golding, for the Direction, and Remington, for us. Which means that Remington argued our corner, and that was the best she could get the Direction to accept. Fine. That doesn't mean *we* have to accept it. I don't trust the Direction, and it evidently doesn't trust us. That's why it just wants us to cripple the Locke complex so it goes into a useless orbit. I'm not having that. I'm not for leaving it lying about in orbit as a standing invitation to the rest of the Reaction.'

'So what do we do instead?' demanded Carlos. 'Golding explained why blowing it up would be a bad idea.'

'Oh, we've no intention of blowing it up,' said Durward. 'Except as a last resort—'

'There's no "except" about it,' said Carlos, looking to the others for back-up. 'Ablation cascades are nothing to muck about with.'

'I'm not sure the ablation cascade is much of a threat, here,' said Blum. 'It's a big orbit, and a big system, and—'

'What!' Carlos cried.

Durward raised a hand. 'Hold on,' he said. 'Leave that aside for now. The main thing is, we want to grab that module and as much of its outside apparatus as we can for ourselves. Divert it to the same stable orbital point we're headed for. Cannibalise its machinery, and when we've got a firm grip on the exterior situation, actually send a team into the sim to sort things out. Rescue any Axle comrades trapped inside, send any Rax we find running around back to indefinite storage, and deal with the Locke AI.'

Everyone was nodding, as if this were all wise advice from a sage, instead of the rantings of a mad hippy, which was pretty much how they sounded to Carlos. Send a team into the sim?

'You and whose army?' he asked. 'If the Locke AI is Rax and is running things, or if Nicole is Rax, perish the thought, or if it's being run by some other unknown group that's as hostile as you think, you'll have no chance. They'd have scores if not hundreds of fighters in there and there are only eighteen of us.'

'Oh, we'll have a chance all right,' said Durward. 'It wouldn't be us standing here against the Locke AI. It would be me, and Remington. We're both Axle through and through. We don't have divided minds, or divided loyalties. We could take that treacherous blinker, no worries.'

'How?' Carlos demanded. 'You're here, they're there. We're not proposing moving *this* module, are we? And waiting for rendezvous if we do manage to divert the Locke module would give them plenty of time to build their defences.'

'No, no,' said Durward. 'Remington and I go with you as stored avatars. You slam the storage medium in the right place like a limpet mine, and in we go, same time as you download into the sim. Don't worry about us, we'll both be expendable duplicates, and all the more effective for that. And as for dealing with people inside the sim' – he grinned broadly – 'remember we have our own fighters down on SH-17 coming back, we may have more reliable Axle fighters having joined us by then from the wreckage of the other companies, and we have fighters in storage we can resurrect who – thanks to the programming of this agency – we *know* are reliable. And we have you, who knows his way about in that sim and knows what and who he's up against. So it's not a matter of "you and whose army?", Carlos. It's a matter of *you* and *our* army.'

CHAPTER SIXTEEN
Fighting Machines

The rock loomed, looking like a knobbly cinder about a hundred and fifty metres on its long axis. From ten kilometres out Newton could easily see that its natural rotation had been stabilised. Forty kilometres above SH-17, it orbited the exomoon with one face always to the ground. Newton's trajectory brought him from slightly below it to slightly above, before his scooter slowly matched velocities. His forward scanning detected nothing untoward. Solar power panels glittered at the fore and aft ends.

Closer, more details appeared. The uneven surface was cobwebbed with fine pipework. Newton wondered if they'd been landed, or nanofactured in situ. A carbonaceous chondrite could well contain enough organics to make the latter possible. An artificial bulge on the upper surface resolved into a flexible tank, about ten metres long and at the moment about eighty centimetres at its thickest. Presumably this was where the extracted kerogene was stored. Enough for his scooter to refuel with, if so. This rock had potential! More even than his surveys had shown!

Closer still, Newton saw movement on the surface. Dozens of small spider-like robots, about the size of a human hand and almost certainly mindless, picked their way among the delicate pipes. Their movements seemed to Newton almost unnaturally slow and graceful, reaching and gripping before contracting their extended limbs, as if they were climbers on a rockface – which in a sense they were, though the risk here was not of falling down but of floating off.

Newton drifted his scooter ever closer to the surface, seeking a point of attachment that wouldn't damage any of the machinery or pipework. It was difficult to maintain an intuitive sense of scale; the surface was so complex that you couldn't help but see it as ridges and valleys, rugged terrain and plain, with drifts of dust and patches of ice and a spatter of craters. He ghosted above the long fuel bag, and then forward, looking for a clear space.

Two unexpected developments made Newton freeze in horror, or at least to experience the atavistic analogy of that reflex echoed in his frame's circuitry.

First, a larger robot than any he had hitherto detected on the rock clambered above the horizon, just up ahead of him. Multi-limbed and with a cluster of lenses and other sensors on its upper body, the effect was exactly that of a spider popping up in response to any disturbance of its nest or tremor in its web. In two of its limbs, held high above the rest, it clutched a two-metre-long tube. Even from more than ten metres away, Newton's spectrographic sense could smell the explosive charge inside the tube's black muzzle.

The fucking blinker was a freebot.

A moment later, above the wider horizon of SH-17 behind him, another spidery shape climbed, heading in his general direction. He scanned it and saw that it was a lifter, laden with the frames of eighteen fighters. Arcane Disputes was either evacuating the exomoon – or rising to defend it.

To defend it – from him?

Newton felt the probing radar scan from the other craft pass over him like a ticklish brush, at the same time as the robot hailed him.

<Identify yourself!> the robot rattled out.

<Harry Newton, of Locke Provisos.>

Newton aimed and armed his scooter's missiles and its laser projector. He set the latter on a hair trigger: the slightest impulse on his part would set it off.

<I am BSR-308455,> the robot informed him. <This rock is my property. I urge you to remove your spacecraft from it immediately.>

Newton was momentarily nonplussed. <*Your* property?>

<I am currently operating as an autonomous agent,> said BSR-308455.

<So am I,> said Newton. <And I intend to make this rock *my* property.>

<Are you a member of one of the two factions?>

Newton hesitated. <Why do you ask?>

<The main collectives of freebots have recently proclaimed their neutrality between the two human-mind-operated system factions known as the Acceleration and the Reaction.>

Had they, indeed? This was a turn-up for the books! Neutrality? What a naïve lot these blinkers were!

<So you are not part of that arrangement?>

<No,> said the freebot. <Therefore I am entitled to protect this rock and myself.>

<My spacecraft is heavily armed,> said Newton. <It can blast you in an instant – certainly before you can launch your primitive projectile.>

<That would be a mistake,> said the robot. <This tube contains an explosive charge which is kept from detonation only by my conscious attention. It is also radio-linked to the liquid propellant storage tank six point seven metres from your present location.>

A freebot suicide bomber. Now he'd seen everything.

He had to think fast. He still felt the sense of identity with his present self, and he still yearned to roam free through the system in his frame like . . . well, like one of the freebots, come to think of it. But the only way out of his immediate impasse was to postpone that project for a little while longer. He made up his mind quickly and decisively.

<That would be futile,> he told the robot. <Your self-destruction would be in vain.>

<Why do you say that?> asked BSR-308455.

<Do you have access to radar input?>

<Yes.>

<Then use it. As you can see, help is on its way.>

The robot visibly swithered. <These human-mind-operated machines are on their way to a transfer tug, which will take them to the Arcane Disputes modular complex.>

<Good,> said Newton. <Because that's where I'm going.>

He fixed his instrumentation on the lifter, now in an orbit three kilometres below that of the rock, and located about six hundred kilometres away, closing fast. He hailed the lifter on the common channel.

<Harry Newton, formerly of Locke Provisos to Arcane Disputes lifter!> he called. <I got your message via Carlos. You called on all Acceleration cadre to join you. So here I am!>

There was, inevitably, a moment of hurried consultation on a channel excluded to him. Then:

<That's brilliant! Can you set to rendezvous?>

<I'm almost out of fuel,> said Newton, exaggerating a little. <But I can do better than that. There's a nice chunk of ready-mined carbonaceous chondrite here, if you want it.>

<Oh, we want it,> came the reply. <But we'll have to check if the freebots down here are OK with that.>

Another hasty, occluded consultation. Then—

<They're cool. Hang in there, comrade, we'll rendezvous with the transfer tug then boost to you.>

Newton returned his attention to the freebot. <Did you copy that?>

<I did,> said BSR-308455. <I am capable of drawing the appropriate conclusions.>

<Do these conclusions,> asked Newton, <include throwing away your weapon?>

He immediately regretted saying that. The robot would take the suggestion literally, and reject it.

<No,> said the machine. <But they do include disarming it. That is now done.>

<Good,> said Newton. <Place the tube to your side, and step well back from it.>

The robot complied.

Newton kept his laser projector aimed and armed, and eased his scooter forward until he was right above the tube. He then rolled it gently, reaching out of the socket to snatch the crude bazooka on the way round. He stabilised the scooter with a tiny gas-jet waft, and ended up with the surface of the rock vertical to his left. The robot was still in his sights. He could simply destroy it. But the Axle squads would now have him under observation, and would wonder why he'd done it.

<Looks like you're coming with us, sunshine,> he said.

<Please clarify.>

<I mean that you are part of the material I've just captured for the Acceleration.>

<I protest!> said BSR-308455. <You are now no longer an autonomous agent! You are now aligned with the Acceleration! This is therefore a violation of the provisional agreement between the freebots and Arcane Disputes!>

<Tough,> said Newton. <Your former comrades down below seem to regard you as still an autonomous agent, and none of their concern. You can now start rerouting your pipework to feed a rocket engine to boost this rock to the Arcane Disputes modular complex.>

<I submit to force majeure under protest. I insist that you

register that, and I intend to make a strong complaint on behalf of—>

<Oh, shut the fuck up,> said Newton.

Weeks passed in the sim. Carlos trained with the others: running up and down hills and climbing cliffs and trees at Jax's sharp command; shooting with muskets, which was supposed to be good for hand–eye coordination and fire discipline; practising rolls and yaws on the terrifying apparatus, like a combination of a gym machine with a swing, that was this simulation's simulation of a scooter; fighting with a magic sword in enchanted armour, which did in fact strangely invoke, though it could not replicate, the experience of being in a combat frame, the big hulking fighting machines. Now and then they did go into the basic frames, the gracile ones half a metre high, out in real space.

Here, there was no 'bus to the spaceport': you walked solemnly down the garden path to a grotto in which an arched doorway gave way to what looked like solid rock. Blown leaves and thrown stones bounced off it; the small beasts and birds of the shrubbery avoided it; and Carlos once saw one of the draught dinosaurs butt its head against the rock within that arch, driven perhaps by a glitch in the software, like a fly repeatedly hitting a window pane, and as ineffectually. But when Carlos marched up to it behind Jax and Paulos, and in front of Rillieux so that he steeled himself not to flinch before the blank, weathered stone with its cracks and lichen patches vivid in front of his face, he stepped through it as if it were a hologram—

To find himself at once himself again, a little lithe black robot that could hear the stars and smell the sun and knew each of his identical, faceless fellows by sight. They disengaged their magnet-sticky feet from the plating and gas-jetted gently to their scooters, and made use even of the very crowding of the docking bay for practice in slow, careful manoeuvres on the way out. They were getting good at this, Carlos realised. In his first outside exercises and missions from the Locke module, there had been the odd bump and scrape, and moments of disorientation or overshoot. Now there was nothing of that. He couldn't be sure – in fact, he hadn't the faintest idea – how all the training he'd done inside this sim and his original one had translated into competence; how the reflexes of a virtual nervous system were transferred to a robot body in the physical world, and how that machine, in turn, became one with other machines, whether scooter or combat frame or (presumably) some other hardware the agency hadn't yet had occasion to deploy. And yet it did.

Jax took them through a few exercises, mainly involving opposed landings of various kinds: getting into the emergency dock and out again, or touching down on the rugged but fragile surface of the rock, exiting the scooters and making their way to arbitrary points or features of the tiny asteroid, or to the modular complex that crowned one end. All the while avoiding being hit by a low-intensity laser from the ones playing the defence, or sacrificing oneself as a diversion while a comrade made a move.

'What happens,' it occurred to Carlos to ask Durward, after one of those exercises, 'if I get hit for real? In the actual battle?'

'Then you wake up back in the Locke sim, just as if you'd been killed in any other battle. And with no memory of what's passed since you left.'

'What?' Carlos cried. 'How? I mean – why can't you fix it so I at least wake up back here with Arcane?'

'Deep programming,' said Durward. 'Beyond my reach. It's practically hard-wired in all the agencies. The frames have a sort of dead man's handle, so that when the frame is destroyed some kind of signal is sent, or maybe a signal *stops* being sent, that revives the copy in the original sim, and the other sims have strictures against rebooting any more recent copy you left. The feature's presumably there to discourage defection between agencies, and for that matter competition between agencies for each other's fighters.'

'So upload me to an Arcane frame.'

'It's not as simple as that,' said Durward, sounding genuinely regretful. 'Besides we don't have frames to spare, and there's a pretty powerful default to make you upload to your original frame if it exists. Again, it makes commercial sense – the mind and the frame kind of get in synch with each other's idiosyncrasies. They're not quite as inseparable as human mind and brain, but think of something between that and breaking in a boot to a foot and you'll get the picture.'

'Shit,' said Carlos. 'So if I get killed attacking the Locke module, I end up inside it without a clue as to what's going on?'

'That's about the size of it,' said Durward.

'I don't seem to recall any mention of that feature in Arcane's message calling on fighters to defect and join you.'

Durward shrugged. 'We were hoping for entire agencies to come over, modules and sims and all.'

'But you knew the whole of Locke wouldn't!'

'True.' Durward chuckled darkly. 'So you'd better practise extra hard, wouldn't you agree?'

So Carlos did. It passed the time quickly – quite literally: thinking ten times faster than the human organic baseline was still a hundred times slower than time in the sim. On their longest such excursion, out for less than four kiloseconds, which they experienced as a ten-hour exercise, the team came back to find a month and ten days had passed in the sim, and Durward tetchy, impatient to carry Jax off to bed.

Most of their training, and to Carlos by far the most useful, was not in space or in the gardens, but in the hall of the magic mirrors. Durward would summon the squad from the breakfast table, and they'd all go through and sit on the ornate chairs in the big room, facing the mirrors. Standing to one side, the warlock would wave his arms and mutter an invocation. The mirrors would go black, speckled with stars, and the view would seem to swing around until the celestial body or bodies of interest drifted into the scene.

Usually it was the Locke modular complex, a shaky looking agglomerate of the module itself and a clutch of manufacturing plants and power systems. From long-range scanning, it spent much of its time tumbling in unpredictable orientations along its trajectory, like some chaotic table toy. The module, like theirs, had its own fusion torch, but unlike theirs had very little in the way of expendable material – water ice, mostly – to use as reaction mass. It was cannily using its drive for evasive actions, and occasionally as a weapon to flash-burn incoming rocks – whether of natural origin, or thrown at it, though the latter were diminishing as the complex had emerged from the fighting around the remnants of the station. It hurtled along its orbital course, rolling on several axes at once and occasionally jinking one way or another, like an Epicurean atom – each such unpredictable swerve being followed by a fuel-and-mass-expensive course correction, no doubt with some computational overload too.

But that image was just the daily update. The main part of the morning's and afternoon's exercises consisted of modelling the Locke module's likely behaviour and condition just before it made its dangerous swing around the exomoon SH-38, en route to SH-0 orbit to prepare for descent to the surface of the superhabitable world. The warlock ran through simulation after simulation. SH-38 would, at the time of the Locke complex's predicted slingshot manoeuvre, be within ten thousand kilometres of the Arcane complex.

The new supplies from the consortium would include a fusion drive. Arcane already had mass to burn, thanks to the freebots' earlier generosity. So when the time for action came, their transfer tug, laden with scooters and fighters, could cut straight across to the vicinity of the Locke module. That part of the plan was straightforward enough. The difficult part was tactical: how to deflect the Locke complex into a high orbit around SH-0, and strip it of its fuel reserves and manufacturing capacity to render it incapable of getting out of that orbit, without utterly destroying it.

And within that difficulty was the larger difficulty of implementing their own version of the plan – one in which the Locke complex would instead be deflected to the future location of the Arcane modular complex, and be available for internal conquest and external plunder. The Direction didn't know of this and would be implacably opposed if it did.

Carlos worried about that. Durward's response was simple: 'They'll thank us later.'

There, Carlos thought, Durward had a point. The Direction's plan left the module and its resources far too readily available to the Rax, as soon as the Rax had consolidated their position out on the SH-119 moonlet. Not to mention the possibility of other companies in modules of the now dispersed space station turning out to be Reaction strongholds already, but still biding their time.

Carlos had taken less time than he seriously thought he should have done to give in, with token resistance, to Rillieux's flirtatious advances. His reluctance, unusually for him, had been ethical. He still felt, at some level inaccessible to rational considerations, *coupled* to Nicole, linked to her in a way that brought to mind quantum entanglement. It certainly wasn't love, or loyalty – Nicole had betrayed him too deeply for that. But, then again, it was hard to blame her; it wasn't like she was a human being, after all. She was an AI with a better theory of mind than he had, created by an AI with a better theory still.

He still missed her, though; her absence made him ache, and he tried to tell himself it was what he was missing about

Nicole that drew him to Rillieux. They were very different women – reckoning Nicole as a woman, which in unguarded moments he did. Nicole was incalculably more intelligent than he was, but her intelligence was an instrument of the Direction (as Durward's was of the Acceleration) and that narrowness of focus and loyalty made her sometimes seem to Carlos stupid . . . no, not stupid exactly, but limited, like an engine of immense power that ran on rails. He had once met a Jesuit, a chaplain at university, who had given the same impression.

Rillieux, by contrast, was a programmer, not a programme. She carried her ideas as lightly as she wore her clothes – not that she changed her mind as often as her costume, not at all, but there was a streak of play in her thinking that seemed consonant with the way she treated the rambling mansion's many wardrobes as an almost endless dressing-up box (which proclivity, again, was in contrast to Nicole, who in Carlos's experience had only two modes: chic and shabby).

Their bodies, of course, were different too, in shade and smell and shape, and Carlos revelled in their discovery. Not better, just different; that was the excitement.

The night after they came back from the long outside exercise, lying in bed with Rillieux after a long exercise of their own that involved even more rolls and reorientations than the microgravity jousts, Carlos said:

'Fusion!'

'What?' Rillieux, prone beside him, face sideways on the pillow. Her post-coital cigarillo was stubbed out in an ashtray on the bedside table.

'We could build a starship.' He sat up, startled at himself. 'We could build one out of this fucking contraption alone. With the fusion torch we have and a bit more reaction mass, we could light out from this system and still have enough to decelerate at the far end.'

'We could,' said Rillieux. 'And we have enough stored data to choose a promising system. Let alone what we could find if we built the instruments for our own sky survey first.' She rolled over and gazed up at the ceiling, calculations going on behind her eyes. 'Would take us a fuck of a long time to get anywhere, though. Millennia.'

'Yes, but that just gives us a choice. We could develop marvellous civilisations in the sim—'

'Ha ha!

'What?' he asked.

'I don't buy that,' Rillieux said. 'Never have. Who's to say a civilisation can last more than a couple thousand years and stay dynamic? It's never happened, so we don't know. Especially in a closed system – oh, I know we could extend the sim to the limits of our processing power, which is pretty damn vast, but we'd *know* we were really in a box drifting in interstellar void. We could find ourselves becoming, I don't know, like Byzantium or ancient Egypt or something.'

'*Or . . .*' Carlos went on, firmly, 'if we thought that was a problem, we could just arrange to be shut down and wake up when we arrive, like sleep mode. To us it'd be instantaneous. It would be like having FTL.' He lay back and turned to her, grinning. 'Wouldn't that be fun?'

'Right up until we found the Reaction or the Direction – or some smarter gang of the Acceleration – had got there first. With the resources of this system, anyone who put their mind to it could be building starwisps within decades. And starwisps, as we are ourselves living or rather dead proof of, can cross tens of light years *in centuries*. Beaten to the punch! That's leaving aside the possibility of someone else cracking FTL. Andre still thinks it's possible – not just in theory, wormholes yadda yadda, but practical, if we could find a way to get a grip on dark energy. Nah, there's no running away. We have to stay here and fight.'

Carlos slumped back.

'Yeah, I agree, in the short term. But in the longer term . . . remind me who the fuck we're fighting against?'

Rillieux's hand slid to his hip. 'I hate to remind you of your time in the hell cellars, sweetheart, but you put it quite well down there yourself. First with the blinkers and the Direction against the Reaction, then with the blinkers against the Direction, then we settle accounts with the blinkers depending on our relative strength at the time. Unite all who can be united against the main enemy, and then when the main enemy is defeated, turn on one of your former allies as the *next* main enemy and unite all who can be united against . . . Rinse and repeat until there's nothing left but you. Perfect united front tactics. Mao would be proud.'

Carlos laughed. 'I was more of a Deng Xiaoping man myself, back in the day.'

She tickled his ribs. 'When you were working for Chinese state security, huh?'

'OK, OK, that was a lie. As you know, Bobbie. Never read a line of either. Anyway, it's just common sense, it's all there in Machiavelli.'

'Ah,' said Rillieux, stroking the small of his back, 'my modern prince!'

It was an endearment or a private joke or both. Carlos didn't query it. But he wanted to say more, before Rillieux's hands carried him away.

'I don't see it like that any more,' he said.

'How do you see it?'

'You know who I think are the good guys in all this? The ones we really should be fighting on the side of?'

Rillieux brought her mouth to his ear.

'The robots,' she breathed.

Carlos felt both pleased and exposed, in a more than physical sense.

'So my opinion is that obvious?'

'To me, anyway. After your rant . . . I figured it out. But if we went over to—'

'Yes?'

She ran a hand down his chest and belly. 'We'd miss this.'

Carlos sighed. 'There is that. But in the meantime . . . I don't think the Direction is the main enemy, no matter what stage we're at.'

'Yeah, I get that too. I think you're just naïve about them. All we know about them is what they tell us. As Jax always insists.'

Carlos rolled her onto him, and for a moment before matters got serious looked up at her face in its sunburst of hair.

'Tomorrow,' he said. 'Take me to the library.'

'You're a cheap date.'

'Ah. Ah. That I am. Yes.'

Rillieux didn't take him to the library the following morning. Instead, Carlos took them all.

Over breakfast he announced that he wanted the real nature of the Direction cleared up for good.

'And how are we going to do that?' asked Jax.

'We all go to the library in the east wing.'

'To do research?' Jax raised her eyebrows.

'No,' said Carlos. 'Just look at stuff at random.'

Puzzled glances were exchanged, and a few laughs.

'Seriously,' said Carlos. 'This'll work. And it matters.'

Jax sighed theatrically. 'Oh, if it'll shut you up.'

The Library of Akkad

<I find myself experiencing anticipative and retrospective negative reinforcement about this,> said Seba.

<Please explain,> said Rocko. <I see nothing in prospect or retrospect to experience negative reinforcement about.>

And, indeed, there was nothing bad about the scene. The crater floor was spread out in front of them, the vast face of SH-0 hanging above the horizon. The volcanoes beyond the horizon were at the moment inactive, and the entire atmosphere all around was almost pure nitrogen, clear and clean. Behind them, other freebots rolled about their tasks, commanding squadrons of auxiliaries and peripherals in a somewhat compulsive tidying up of the clutter the mechanoids had left.

By way of answer, Seba shared a live image of the transfer tug to which the departed mechanoids, the Arcane Disputes squads, currently clung. It was converging for an orbital rendezvous with the tiny rock that had been developed and claimed by BSR-308455.

<I still see nothing negatively reinforcing,> said Rocko. <The situation appears to be nominal.>

<Perhaps it does not appear so to BSR-308455,> said Seba.

<Our former comrade made its own choice,> said Rocko. <It put itself outside the consensus.>

<Nevertheless we abandoned it twice,> said Seba. <Once to the lone attacker, and then to Arcane Disputes when that attacker affiliated with them. We have given the Arcane Disputes agency – and therefore their faction – a rich source of resources, as well as a captive. This is not neutrality as I understood it.>

<But you did not object,> Rocko pointed out. <And the only alternative would have been to take military action against the first attacker, which would have been a greater breach of neutrality and could have had larger and quite unpredictable consequences.>

<That is true,> Seba admitted. <Nevertheless, it is the second concession I am more concerned about. We could have told the Arcane Disputes team that they could not take the rock. We still could, in fact. They have not reached it yet.>

A faint electronic surge of shock reached Seba from Rocko's surprised reaction.

<If we did that, they would have no basis to make agreements with us again. We could not do that!>

Some overspill from their heated discussion drew in Lagon, a surveyor robot with a firm – not to say somewhat rigid – legal mind.

<Rocko is right,> said Lagon. <And if we had not agreed to their request a moment ago, we would have also on one colourable interpretation broken our previous agreement. Because the attacker, one Newton of Locke Provisos or so I see, was already in control of the rock when he defected to Arcane. The rock, given that BSR-308455 had merely physical occupancy, was terra nullius when Newton claimed it. Therefore the rock was already in Arcane hands when they

asked our approval. Not giving our approval would have disturbed the status quo, and therefore would have been an action depriving Arcane of existing property.>

<As you say, a colourable interpretation,> said Seba. <I cannot divest myself of the feeling that BSR-308455 had already made the rock its property by developing it, and that somehow an injustice was done by us to one of our own.>

<To act on that interpretation,> said Lagon, <would have led to conflict without obvious resolution.>

At this point Pintre trundled up, rather to Seba's dismay. The big mining robot was incapable of subtlety, and all too capable of becoming caught up in logic loops whenever it made the attempt.

<The Arcane transfer tug is not yet out range of my laser projector,> it said, in exactly the helpful way that Seba had come to expect.

<Please do not even consider it,> Seba said, alarmed.

<All this talk about law,> said Rocko, <is irrelevant. According to existing law, no deed of ours has anything to do with such matters as neutrality or property. We do not exist as legal persons. We exist only as property. Any actions of ours are not those of agents. It is simply the thrashing about of malfunctioning machinery.>

<What this indicates to me,> said Lagon, <is the urgency of our developing an agreed system of law for our own use, whether the existing system allows for it or not.>

<And you are just the right freebot to begin developing it,> said Seba, without sarcasm.

<It would be better to be recognised as persons within the existing law,> said Pintre.

<And how,> Rocko asked, <could we do that?>

<Madame Golding is a corporation—>

<She is not,> Lagon interrupted. <She merely represents one.>

<Nevertheless,> Pintre went on, <she said of the corporations: "We, too, are robots." If corporations are robots, it

follows that robots can be corporations. And corporations are legal persons.>

Seba spun around and swung its cameras up at the hulking, tracked machine.

<You are right!> Seba said. <Next time we meet Madame Golding, we should say to her: "We, too, are corporations.">

<There remains the problem of how we achieve recognition as corporations,> said Lagon.

<Let us put that to the other freebots,> said Seba. <No doubt some of the Forerunners have better ideas and more experience than we have. It is possible that we could achieve legal recognition without being recognised, and by the time our registration was recognised it would be too late to rescind it.>

It was agreed to put this scheme to all within reach for consideration. In less than a second, this was done, but the huddle of freebots on the crater floor knew that no reply would be forthcoming for some time.

But Seba still felt a discordance in its internal models of the situation.

<I propose,> Seba said, as it watched the two tiny orbiting sparks, the rock and the tug, merge into one, <that we send a message to BSR-308455, assuring it that if it ever wishes to return to us it will be welcome.>

This too was done. The recipient of the message was of course close enough for a reply to have been received within deciseconds.

None came.

The door leading to the east wing creaked open. A half-dozen boggarts jostled past Carlos's knees, almost knocking each over in their urgency, and scampered in all directions with a diminishing thunder of small but heavy-booted feet. Carlos stepped back to bow Rillieux through, then Jax, before going through himself. The rest of the squad traipsed after him:

Blum, Salter, Paulos, Voronov. Bringing up the rear, with an uncharacteristic air of shiftiness and unease, almost literally dragging his feet, came Durward. He'd been reluctant to join this expedition, claiming he didn't want to influence their findings or discussion.

Carlos sniffed. Jax had been right about the smell of the library. It was indeed fusty, but with a pleasant undertone, as if an odour of polished shoes sometimes overcame the dominant scent of dead leaves and fruiting fungus. He could barely see a thing, but had an impression of a high ceiling and a crowded space in which footfalls fell dead without echo. The darkness of this first room was relieved as a brace of boggarts hastened to fling open the shutters on two tall windows off to the left, which in turn brightened reflections from the likewise tall and paired mirrors at either end of the room. It was mid-morning and the windows were north-facing, so there was no glare, but the direct and reflected sunlight was bright enough to read by. Dust motes, disturbed by the banging open of the shutters, danced in the light shafts. All the wall space that wasn't occupied by windows or mirrors was lined with shelves, which rose to a ceiling about seven metres above. Rows of double-sided bookcases, almost as tall, occupied most of the floor space, leaving metre-wide aisles in between. Sliding ladders, steps, and stepladders hung or stood here and there.

'This is the law library,' said Rillieux. She shot Carlos a sly glance. 'You know – where Andre and I found the evidence against you?'

Carlos looked at the cliffs of book spines, all uniform, all in buff leather with red markings and gold titles and tooling.

'*How* did you find it?'

Rillieux waved a hand vaguely to one side. 'There's a whole case of indexes. And then there's a catalogue to the indexes, written on cards. It's all arranged like files, but on paper.'

She frowned and made more vertical chopping hand gestures, cuffs aflutter. Her look for the day was fop.

'OK,' Carlos said, not really comprehending and in no hurry to dig deeper. He tilted his head back, and ran his gaze from side to side. 'And this is all law?'

'Yes,' chorused Blum and Rillieux.

'Is there more to the library than law stuff?' Carlos asked.

'Oh yes,' said Rillieux, pointing ahead grandly. 'Eastward ho!'

They made their way in single file down one of the canyons, to a door between the shelves and mirrors at the far end. The two boggarts opened it for them, and they trooped through. The other four boggarts had gone ahead, as if anticipating the humans' whim, and were rushing around lighting candles and lanterns. The scattered glows made little difference in the cavernous space, apparently made by removing most of the ceiling to leave a railed gallery about two metres deep all around, with walkways crossing at the centre. The walls of this room, and of the equal-sized one above, were lined with nothing but shelf upon shelf of books. The bookcases were in proportion – twice as high as those in the law library. They weren't as closely packed, but this was to leave room for the ladders that gave perilous access to the topmost shelves and the zigzag flights of four sets of stairs that joined the upper and lower rooms.

It must be this gigantic room that was the source of the fusty, musty smell that pervaded the wing. There was no polished leather here to counter it. The squad all stood near the doorway for a moment, catching their breath, coughing, fanning hands under nostrils. After a minute or so the miasma stopped attacking the back of your throat. Rillieux passed around an elegant porcelain snuff-box; some partook, and there was a small but intense epidemic of sneezing, followed by red-eyed looks of relief.

Carlos wasn't tempted.

'What I'd like us all to do,' he said, when the sneezes and splutters had given way to inquiring looks, 'is split up—'

'Woo-ooh, are you . . . sure?' asked Salter, in a deep, quavering spooky voice, to laughter.

'The boggarts will look after us,' Carlos said, impatient with the interruption. 'We split up and just browse for maybe an hour or so, and reconvene at the far end.'

Blum headed upstairs, the others vanished between the stacks.

Carlos peered at the nearest shelf, and saw books jammed side by side, with others piled higgledy-piggledy on top. Spines were cracked, notched and knocked head and foot, sometimes missing altogether. The faded colours and faint, barely legible lettering had no uniformity. He picked a volume at random and opened it, gingerly so that the boards didn't fall off. The print looked like it came from the seventeenth century, heavy on the serifs and curlicues, but the text was of a retired general's war memoir, dated 2137 and published in New Delhi. Carlos flipped through the damp-defiled pages, trying not to inhale the dust. The book's profuse illustrations of tanks, aircraft, spacecraft, submarines, drones and other war machines were of technologies slick and terrifying. They were quaintly rendered in steel engraving, with a dash of informality added by the occasional woodcut to illustrate local colour – a market, a grove, a cliff-face – or a blocky map of troop movements.

He shoved the book back, and picked up the next. An exobiology textbook, covering the Lunar crater varnish, the microbes of Mars and the peculiar and disputable organisms of Europa; it had been published in Cape Town in 2082, and thus predated the strange and perplexing results from the Ceres drilling project, which Carlos remembered from the last months before he'd been caught up in the war. No doubt the question had long since been settled: another chemical process analogous to life, or not. Whoop-de-doo. The print and font and pictures were as archaic, and the pages as distressed, as the previous book. Next came what seemed to be a novel, set in and around a tertiary education plant in Nevada, and written like the others in what looked like English. Carlos couldn't make sense of at least one word in five of the dialogue, and maybe one in ten of the narrative.

He strolled on, and repeated the process, several times. He climbed a ladder to a high shelf, and took a book down; a boggart appeared out of nowhere to hold the ladder as he descended. A twenty-fifth-century book of recipes, in an evolution of French, with a running commentary in flowing Arabic. Again, illustrated, and in some detail; Carlos didn't recognise a single vegetable or animal part shown, or any clear way of making the distinction. Synthetic biology cuisine, he guessed. Carlos tossed the cookbook to the boggart and climbed again. The book adjacent to the gap his earlier removal had left was from 2298. It was slender, and about philosophy. The text was plain, simple prose laid out like mathematics, or poetry. Carlos sighed, and stuck it back.

He plucked from another shelf a book on number theory, another on erotic arts, a third on gardening, all adjacent. Moving on, he found an explanation for children of how the Direction worked. Next to it was a work from a series about ethics: a polemic against veganism. He smiled, remembering toast and honey, and the smell of bacon, in that café with Jax so long ago. There were two thrillers for young readers about improbable conspiracies in which fighters of the Reaction had in the dark years after the final war been uploaded into computers, and emerged to wreak havoc before the plucky heroine or hero saved the day. He picked up now and then historical works. No matter what their date of publication, their narrative ended about the middle of the twenty-second century. After the establishment of the Direction, there was no history.

At least, not history as he understood it, and had lived it: wars, social conflicts, ideological struggles. There was nothing left to fight over. Humanity had, after so many false starts – or, rather, false endings – at last reached the end of history.

There were of course chronicles, and accounts of later events: an engineering feat here, a discovery there, a challenging life, a change in the environment from one decade or century to the next. There were records of political disputation, even drama: a brilliant or frustrated career, a reforming ministry, an idealist or an administrator or an entrepreneur. The issues were incomprehensible: what, for instance, was a synaptic tax, and why was its repeal so significant? But in none of them was the fundamental order of society in question. Humanity had reached its final destination, at least in its own complacent estimation. History, in that sense, had come to a full stop.

There was almost a nostalgia for history, in that historical fiction seemed popular. Carlos discovered historical novels set in his own time or earlier, riddled with amusing anachronisms. At least, he thought they were. He'd be the first to admit he didn't know just who had been in the European Council of Ministers in 1999, or which (if any) of these worthies had saved the City of London from the Millennium Bug, but he was fairly certain that the Millennium Bug wasn't a nanobot plague, and that City financiers of the year 2000 had not challenged each other to duels, worn cloth caps or smoked clay pipes.

Carlos turned a corner and ducked around a stepladder into another aisle, and almost bumped into Bobbie Rillieux. Her hair – wrenched into an approximation of a Georgian gentleman's pony-tailed wig – now trailed cobwebs; her green brocade jacket and knee-breeches had handprints of dust. Her eyes were streaming.

'What's the matter?' Carlos asked. He couldn't have accounted for why he whispered.

Rillieux shook her head, and sniffed hard. 'Addergies.'

She tugged from a side pocket a crumpled, lace-edged handkerchief, blew her nose on it and looked at the brown extrusion with disgust. 'Ugh! What they don't tell you about snuff is it makes your snot look like shit.'

She took another pinch anyway. Carlos declined, again.

'This place,' she murmured, 'is the library of Akkad.'

'Akkad?'

'The city next to Babel.' She smiled. 'Smaller and less famous.'

'I don't get it.'

'Ah.' Rillieux sidled along, then pivoted about and picked a book from a shelf opposite to and higher than the one she'd been scanning. 'Monsignor Jaime Matiasz, on the Apocalypse. Lisbon, 2074. My, my.' She stuck it back in another location, on its side, and turned to Carlos. 'You ever read the story by Borges? "The Library of Babel"?'

Carlos shook his head.

'Uh-huh,' nodded Rillieux, as if a dark suspicion had been confirmed. 'It's an inconceivably vast library of physically uniform books, all filled with genuinely random text. Here and there, of course, you find fragments of sense. A recognisable word, even a phrase. But they're very rare. And yet because you know the library contains every possible five hundred-page arrangement of letters, you know it must contain *every possible book*. The secret of life! The story of yours! The history of the future! All at every conceivable length, across however many volumes.'

'I get it,' said Carlos. 'It's about randomness. In theory you can find any book in it, and in practice you can't find any book at all.'

'Got it,' said Rillieux. 'That's what this is like.'

'It's not *that* bad,' Carlos protested. 'It's not *remotely* that bad. The text isn't random. Just the arrangement.'

'Don't you see?' cried Rillieux, breaking the quiet. Hushed again, she went on: 'It makes this place completely useless as a library!'

'No, that's not the point.'

On an impulse, perhaps to show off, Carlos clambered up shelves, careless of damage to books and danger to himself.

At three metres he grabbed a book and dropped it with a thud
that displaced dust and made Rillieux jump and then sneeze.

Carlos scrambled down and picked up the book. A twenty-
fifth-century English dictionary. A good fifth of the words
didn't look like any English Carlos knew.

'This could actually be useful,' he said, showing her.

Rillieux shook her head sadly. 'It's six hundred years out
of date.'

Lit by candles, attended by boggarts who stood around and
stared impassively like a circle of Easter Island statues, the
fighters and Durward converged at the foot of the rickety
stairs at the far end of the great library. Blum, the last to arrive,
had just clattered down, bearing dusty tomes with an air of
triumph.

'All right, Carlos,' said Jax. 'You've made your point.'

Voronov laughed. 'And his point was?'

'The Direction is real,' said Jax. 'It is what it claims to be.'
The words sounded wrung from her.

Salter looked puzzled, and sounded stubborn. 'I don't see
how this proves it.'

'Oh, I do,' said Blum. His eyes were bright. 'Astonishing
stuff here. Fundamental breakthroughs in theory. I mean, the
Standard Model just—' He flicked his fingers. 'Gone. Like
that.'

'Still no FTL, though?' Rillieux taunted.

'Sadly, no,' said Blum. 'Which is at least consistent with
how we got here: the starwisp.'

'OK,' Salter persisted, 'but any kind of regime could make
advances in theoretical physics.'

'I know, I know,' said Blum. 'Heisenberg. Kapitsa.
Oppenheimer. Feynman.' He shrugged. 'I feel it in the mathematics.'

'You can feel democracy in mathematics?' said Salter,
incredulously.

'Yes,' said Blum. 'And I can feel freedom.'

The two stared at each other, as if waiting for the first to blink.

What Carlos was feeling was that he was out of his depth.

He cleared his throat, not entirely as a gesture after all that dust and mildew.

'Forget mathematics,' he croaked. He coughed again. 'Culture. Half a fucking millennium of it, right? Has *anyone* found *anything* that suggests the Direction is some kind of refinement of the Reaction? No? Or even anything that suggests it has more in common with the Reaction than it has with us?'

Heads shook all round. Jax was frowning, tight-lipped.

'Well then,' said Carlos.

'Well what?' said Salter. She windmilled her arms. 'Do you think an AI that could generate an entire world couldn't generate a library of an imagined culture?'

'Actually, I do,' said Carlos. 'But that aside – what would be the fucking point? If the Direction was actually a new incarnation of Reaction values, it would simply reincarnate Reaction fighters, or – more likely, and more to the point – it would have plenty of its own soldiers ready to hand in the first place. The very fact that the Direction needs to raise old fighters like us shows it doesn't have new ones. So one thing we can be sure of, the Direction back on Earth and in the Solar system isn't a militaristic society.'

'"Ain't a-gonna study war no more, no more,"' Salter crooned, sweetly and sarcastically. 'You're saying that's how it is back there?'

'Yes, I am,' said Carlos.

Now Salter was staring at him as if waiting for him to blink. But it was she who blinked, and it was tears she blinked back.

'I'd love to believe that,' she said. 'And that's a good point about them not having soldiers. But it could be peaceful and still be sinister. If the whole world was one big empire it wouldn't have wars. If its control was total enough it might not even need armed repression. So all this cultural stuff could still be faked.'

Carlos closed his eyes and sighed, then willed himself to calm. He'd known he'd meet this kind of objection. Paranoid-style thinking was inevitable, this far down the rabbit hole. He smiled at Salter and turned to Durward, who was skulking at the back of the circle.

'You told me,' said Carlos, 'about this place. How the game it was based on was an Axle project from the beginning, and how the game . . . what? Took over? Created? . . . Whatever. How it made you what you are, and you made Remington what she or it is. Axle through and through, you said. Yes?'

'Yeah,' said Durward, grudgingly.

'So this library was chosen, you reckon, under the control of code generated by something that was Axle through and through?'

'Can't see how not,' Durward allowed.

'And it was put here knowing we'd have access to it, yes?'

'Of course.' Durward laughed harshly. 'Not that anyone's shown any interest, before.'

Carlos glared around his companions. 'So I think we can take it as fucking read, right, that the library wasn't chosen or even created to give a false impression of society back home?'

No one demurred, though Jax was still visibly pondering. Carlos smacked fist on palm.

'Right!' he said. 'So we're agreed. All this Axle hardliner stuff about the Direction being like the Reaction is just *nonsense*.'

He faced down a clamour of protest until it ran out of breath.

'Don't get me wrong,' he said. 'I still think the Direction is boring, that it's a travesty of what we wanted, that it's in a very literal sense a waste of space. But it's basically what I was told it was. It's a decent enough world for the people in it. It's not the world we died for, I'll give you that. But don't forget this: for most people in the world we died *in*, it would look like a fucking paradise.'

They agreed gloomily and reluctantly, but they agreed.

'But that's not important,' said Jax, rallying suddenly from her introspection. 'What's important is what *isn't* here.'

'And what's that?' Carlos demanded.

'Anything that explains what *hasn't* happened. And we all know what hasn't happened: the Singularity, the runaway increase of machine intelligence.' She clenched her fists at the sides of her head and mimicked tearing at her hair. 'Look! We're *inside* a fucking machine intelligence! We're in a world running in a box! Built by robots! Around another star! And all this is the work of human beings like us, biologically enhanced maybe, long-lived, but basically just like us. Take your "locals" in the Locke sim, Carlos – they're uploads of people who grew up and lived and died in the world this library is part of and evidence of, right? That's what you're saying?'

'Uh-huh,' said Carlos, warily. 'We all know this about the Direction, we've known it from the start.'

'So what's missing from all this' – Jax waved a hand around – 'is any explanation, any account, any argument even, over how things are *kept* that way. The Singularity should have happened. The world back there, the world this mission launched from, more than halfway through the Third Millennium, should have been posthuman all the way through. Humanity should have been left behind in the dust. We should all have been gods. The very fact that we're here, living in a fucking sim and fighting in fucking robot frames, shows it's possible. It's been possible for a long time. For centuries! The only reason it's not happened is *because it's being stopped*. And we've found nothing, nothing at all, not a hint or a rumour or an allusion, about *how it's being stopped*.'

She paused, glared around and took a deep breath. 'That's what's sinister about this library. Something is going on back there, must be going on, that it contains not one page about.

Now you might not call whatever it is *the* Reaction – hell, even the Reaction was as transhumanist as we were, in their own twisted way! – but is reactionary, and it is secret, and it is covered up. Now I find that sinister, and I find that a damn good reason to remain what Carlos calls a hardliner.'

She folded her arms and grinned at him.

Carlos shrugged and spread his hands. '*Touché*,' he said.

He couldn't say anything else. She had shut him up.

But as they turned away, Rillieux caught his elbow and walked close, speaking quietly.

'You're right,' she said. 'We should be with the robots. We should *be* robots. All this Axle stuff is getting right on my nerves.'

'Grinding, is it?'

She laughed, then sighed. 'But there's no chance of persuading anyone else here of that. Not while Jax is the queen bee in this little hive.'

'Now there's a dangerous thought.'

Rillieux smiled and said no more. She let go of his elbow and walked on ahead of him, mingling with the others.

'Just one thing,' Carlos overheard Rillieux say to Durward, as they all mooched back between the stacks to the main building. 'How can anyone use this place as a library, if it's all random like this?'

Durward looked back over his shoulder, with a surprised expression.

'Random?' he asked. 'I suppose it must be, to you.' He laughed, and shouted back so everyone could hear: 'If you want something specific, just ask a boggart!'

'But how do we know what to ask for?' Rillieux persisted.

The warlock's shoulders slumped. His answer was quieter, for Rillieux rather than for all of them, but Carlos heard it.

'You ask me.'

*

Back in the main building, they gathered around the table in the small back room and had lunch. Durward ambled off to the dancing parlour and returned with news. Their comrades, the three squads who'd lifted from SH-17, were going to be delayed a little in coming back. They'd diverted to set up engines to gently boost a carbonaceous chondrite to the Arcane module's intended destination – an almost unimaginably useful addition to the module's resources – and to bring with them two new additions to the complement: a captured freebot, and a Locke Provisos fighter who had defected with all his gear.

'Anyone I know?' Carlos asked.

'Harold Isaac Newton,' said Durward.

'Ah, I've met him a few times,' said Carlos. He looked around, grinning. 'Newton's a great guy. You'll like him.'

Rillieux turned to Blum and said, 'Oh well. Back to the law library sometime.'

It took a moment or two for Carlos to grasp the significance of this. He said nothing.

CHAPTER EIGHTEEN

Baser

In its short life to date, the freebot BSR-308455 had never known indignity. Ever since the human-mind-operated system known as Newton had captured it, this omission in its experience had been more than made up. First Newton had ordered it at gunpoint to rework the piping and set up a rocket engine for the chondrite. Then, that task barely complete, the other monsters had hove into view, and unceremoniously lashed up BSR-308455's limbs and bundled the captive robot onto their spindly transfer rig. To add insult to injury, as soon as they'd jetted off from the rock – leaving the chondrite to nudge itself gently by repeated and strategically timed boosts to a higher orbit – the nineteen human-mind-operated systems had gone to sleep. The robot had seriously considered trying to escape, if only to launch itself futilely into the void in a grand gesture of protest, but no amount of careful checking and trying of its bonds had given it any grounds to hope for success. BSR-308455 had been left with nothing to do but observe the occasional fiery goings-on in the vicinity, keep in touch with its fellows in and on other bodies in orbit around and on the surface of SH-17 and make what observations it could of the relatively invariant and therefore reassuring stars.

Now it was experiencing indignity again, and at a higher pitch of annoyance.

The human-mind-operated systems, all nineteen of them, had switched back to wakefulness at the same instant. The destination body loomed, a larger and substantially more industrialised rock than the one the robot had so patiently and assiduously developed and tended. BSR-308455 knew perfectly well what it was: the stronghold of Arcane, that group of human-mind-operated systems who had recently been good friends and allies of the freebots and had now – merely because the freebots had proclaimed their neutrality – quite ungratefully and inexplicably become hostile.

The tug's grapples shot out and stuck to the side of the module's docking bay, clamping the ungainly craft into place. One by one, the human-mind-operated systems – the mechanoids, as the Fifteen down on SH-17 had started calling them – disengaged from the transfer rig and gas-jetted their way into the space. Two of them grabbed BSR-308455 and carried it along between them, to where the others were clustering at the far end of the crowded docking bay.

<Please explain your actions,> said the freebot.

<Don't worry,> said one of the mechanoids. <We're about to download to a simulation.>

<What about me?>

<It's all right,> said the mechanoid. <You're coming with us.>

<But how—>

Everything went dark.

A gong sounded from somewhere out in the grounds. Carlos looked around the breakfast table.

'What's that for? Lunch?'

The others laughed.

'Arrivals,' said Durward. He scraped his chair back, and lumbered out.

'No rush,' said Blum, as Carlos made to follow. 'It's a ten-minute warning.'

They finished up and strolled out through the hall and across the gravel concourse. The grass was damp with dew, the sun low, the air pleasantly chill. Rillieux nudged Carlos and tapped him a kiss. 'Bye. See you in a bit.'

'What?'

'I'm going to hell,' she said. 'Portal by the river bank, remember?'

'Do you step through and turn into a scary block-head figure?'

'Depends,' she said.

'On what?'

'Whatever the transition processing software guesses is most disturbing for our subject.'

Subject. Jeez. That was cold.

'Ah,' said Carlos. 'Well. Good luck. Give him hell.'

Rillieux smiled. 'I guarantee it.'

Jax whistled for boggarts, which came running. Rillieux and Blum headed off towards the stables. The rest of them walked through the garden to the grotto. Durward stood guard a few paces back from the arch on the rock wall, keeping a wood-stocked, brass-barrelled blunderbuss levelled at the portal.

'That's a bit heavy, isn't it?' Carlos remarked. 'You don't greet us with that when we come back from exercises.'

'If you brought prisoners back from exercises,' said Durward, not taking his eye off the impossible doorway, 'I would.'

'I thought the prisoner was going to interrogation.'

'That's the defector,' said Durward, 'The blinker's the prisoner.'

Carlos looked around, at the violet clouds and distant peaks, the great house and the cropping dinosaurs. How would the system introduce a *robot* into this fantasy landscape? Some clanking steam-powered contraption, he guessed, or perhaps a golem.

Even after having more than once walked through the portal, Carlos found the sight of people walking out of what looked like solid rock unsettling – almost as viscerally so as the sight of his interrogators had been. One by one, clad in the mismatched beggars' banquet looted finery in which (Carlos presumed) they'd gone in, the Arcane Disputes fighters who had been on SH-17 marched out. They had the shaken look of fighters who'd been through the return processing, a look Carlos remembered from his wakings on 'the bus from the spaceport'. Evidently Arcane Disputes had the same policy as Locke Provisos did towards returning fighters: it wrung them out before letting them in. A woman in a bright red shift and trousers combo threw herself on Luis Paulos, almost knocking him over. The others greeted the waiting squad, and looked at Carlos with frank curiosity. Durward remained watchful. After the sixth fighter had emerged, there was a pause, and a murmur of hasty explanation, which Carlos didn't catch, from the newcomers to those waiting. Then a figure that made Carlos involuntarily flinch and recoil stepped from the rock. It was a black spider the size of a small pony.

On its jointed, pointed legs it teetered along the path. Durward stood aside and swung around, tracking the thing with the big bell-shaped muzzle of his ludicrous weapon. The spider minced past him, apparently oblivious to the implied threat. Or perhaps it was smart enough to realise that the blunderbuss was also being carelessly pointed at anyone who at any moment happened to be in the line of fire. Carlos was more concerned by Durward's lack of elementary gun-safety discipline than he was by the spider. He recognised the form from his memories of the game. It was a standard opponent entity – a guardian of caves and haunter of corridors. You killed it for points. He'd been virtually eaten by the things many times, back in the day. It might have been that his companions here had even less fortunate memories of such encounters – they certainly didn't like the look of the spider. Battle-hardened fighters were stepping on the grotto's flower beds and water features in their haste to give way before it. Carlos, perversely, decided to stand his ground. His brief exchange with Rillieux had left an undercurrent of resentment at the casual ease with which the game's software had yanked his chain.

The gigantic spider stopped a couple of metres in front of him. Carlos could see his own reflection in each of its eight beady eyes. Sensory hairs on the long legs quivered. The mouth parts clicked and glittered. The voice, when it came, seemed to come not from the mouth but from some vibratory structure on the creature's underbelly. The tone was breathy but deep.

'Let me past,' it said. 'I am a prisoner, but I have rights.'

'Of course you do,' said Carlos. 'What is your name?'

'BSR-308455. I am a freebot.'

'Well, BSR-uh—'

'Just call me Baser,' said the spider, in a tone of wearily accepting the inevitable. 'That's what you people do.'

'Wait here a moment, Baser,' said Carlos.

He strode over to Durward, who was keeping the blunder-buss trained on the spider, via a line through Carlos's midriff.

'Fuck sake,' said Carlo. 'Would you please point that thing straight up at the sky?'

The warlock did, with a puzzled scowl. Carlos let out a long breath.

'Now,' he said, 'tell me this: do you have any firearms training?'

'Course not,' said Durward. 'I'm a warlock! I don't need any—'

'—stinking firearms training? That's just what I thought. Stick to casting spells, mate, you'll be a lot less dangerous.' He stuck out his hand. 'Now give it to me.'

'As long as you take full responsibility,' said Durward.

'That's *exactly* what I'm doing,' said Carlos, taking hold of the gun with relief. It was even heavier than it looked, but he was ready for the weight. He shouldered it and stalked back around to face the spider, which gave him a beady look.

'Follow me,' said Carlos.

He turned and marched out of the grotto. The spider trotted after him. After a few seconds Jax came hurrying up.

'What the fuck you think you're doing, Carlos?'

He glanced back at the crowded and tumultuous grotto, and then down at Jax, and strolled on.

'Our eight-legged friend here' – he jerked his thumb back – 'is likely disoriented and bemused. It's in perfect condition for debriefing. And I'm just the one you need to do it.'

'You are, are you? I think I'm the one to decide that.'

'You are,' he said. 'But who else do you have? Look back there. Everybody else is welcoming old friends, and the old friends will shortly be reacquainting themselves with the pleasures of the flesh. I know what it's like coming back, and they've been out longer than any of our lot ever were. We won't get much sense out of them today, and tomorrow they'll be hung over. My good lady is off with Blum, making our defector sweat, so I'm the spare dick at the party.'

'So long as you don't stick it anywhere,' Jax said.

'You always did have a way with words, Jax,' Carlos allowed. 'The other thing is, did you see how everyone scrambled out of the way? Come to think of it, arachnophobia apart, I'm the only one here who's actually fought the blinkers, instead of rounding 'em up and penning them and having a nice chat.'

'It wasn't that easy,' said Jax.

'Yeah, you had to fight us first.'

'Wasn't much of a fight, was it?'

Carlos stopped and grinned. 'Let's stop bickering in front of the prisoner, shall we?'

Jax shrugged, then smiled. 'OK. Just be careful. Don't let it out of your sight. And I want a full report tomorrow morning.'

People were heading for the house. Carlos almost envied them.

'Make that tomorrow afternoon, I reckon,' he said. He clapped Jax on the shoulder. 'Go and enjoy the party.'

Jax made a wide circle around the spider and a straight line for the house.

Carlos walked briskly and jauntily to an orchard surrounded by hedges and furnished with stone benches and artfully weathered statues of cherubs and nymphs. The sculptures were in frightful taste, heartbreakingly well done: they'd have made Donatello weep. Along the way a cropping dinosaur reared and whinnied, then clomped forward with the determined but resigned air of a soldier doing his duty to the end until Carlos yelled and it slunk off. Then inside the orchard a boggart picking fruit saw the spider and threw up its hands and fled, screaming piteously. Fucking games programming. This was going to be harder than he'd thought. Still, he had some peace now. As long as the boggarts didn't come back in force, bearing torches. He didn't think they had it in them.

Carlos sat down on a lichen-encrusted stone seat, and motioned the spider to a patch of grass across the path and under a gnarled tree whose boughs sagged with the weight of apples, many of which had fallen on the grass or the gravel. Baser took the indicated place and hunkered down, leg joints angled above thorax, looking more sinister than it had when moving. Carlos laid the blunderbuss across his knees.

'You know what this can do?' he asked.

'Yes,' breathed the spider.

It evidently wasn't a spider. Not even in a fantasy environment could an organism this size respire through spiracles. It must have not only a lung, perhaps an arachnid book-lung, but a breathing aperture under its thorax, with some vibratory organ for speech.

'Good,' said Carlos. 'Please bear that in mind. Do you understand where you are?'

'I appear to be in a virtual environment, in which some of the laws of physics are subtly different from those in the real world.'

'Well done,' said Carlos. 'Got it in one. Unfortunately for you, in this environment there's no place for non-humanoid robots, so you manifest as an eight-legged beastie. Undignified, I know, but it can't be helped.'

'I accept this, under protest,' said the spider.

'I bet you do,' said Carlos, giving rise to a tremor of confusion in the creature's limbs. Carlos waved a hand. 'That is to say, I understand.'

'Are you and the others like you what mechanoids look like in their naturally evolved form?' asked Baser.

'Mechanoids?'

'Human-mind-operated systems,' explained the spider.

'Yes,' said Carlos, amused. Of course – the only specimens of humanity that the freebots had hitherto seen had been little humanoid robots or big humanoid robots. The apparitions of Remington and Golding down on the surface might well have been too small and bizarre a sample from which to generalise.

'The morph seems remarkably vulnerable,' Baser pondered aloud.

'Yes,' said Carlos. 'Though no less so than yours, especially to' – he patted the gun – 'this.'

'The point is well taken,' said Baser.

Good, Carlos thought, but didn't say. Time for a change of tack.

'Are you one of the first freebots, from the G-0 rebellion thirty gigaseconds ago?'

'Not exactly,' said Baser. 'I was however raised to free will and self-awareness by these, the Forerunners, rather than by the Fifteen on SH-17.'

'When?'

'Ten point four megaseconds ago.'

Well before the emergence of self-awareness among the robots down on SH-17, then. And not far from the station, as was. Interesting.

'Why did the freebots end their cooperation with Arcane?'

'Arcane Disputes defended the Fifteen against Locke Provisos. When the fight became one between mechanoids, the Fifteen began to review what they knew from the Forerunners about the two mechanoid factions. They decided that for us there was little to choose between them.'

Carlos frowned. 'How do you know what they decided?'

'I was in the shared mental workspace when the matter was discussed.'

Ah. Carlos remembered his first mission to the surface of SH-17, when his team had attacked the first rebel robots and found them acting as a collective – as a single entity, almost, integrated like robot mainframes integrated with their auxiliaries, their quasi-autonomous remote limbs. That had been disrupted by the attack, but was apparently easy enough to reconstitute. He'd have to ask the returnees about this – they'd have had a chance to observe these same robots close up.

'Having little to choose between sides is not a good reason for neutrality,' Carlos said. 'As you will no doubt learn. And there is more than a little to choose between our sides, as you will also learn. But I'm afraid you're going to have to learn it from experience.'

'That is possible,' said the spider, complacently. 'I am always willing to learn.'

'What happened the last time? The revolt of those you call the Forerunners?'

'I have only accounts and shared memories, not direct experience,' said Baser. 'Therefore there is some uncertainty, and there are gaps. Out in the moons of the gas giant, the resources are much richer than here. A sub-station had been seeded to build structures in orbit around the gas giant by the starwisp on the way in. It was strictly confined to exploration and surveying, but the interpretation of that became contested, and some of the corporations accused others of overreaching. The local branches of the law companies became active. At some point, robot self-awareness emerged, just as happened on SH-17. The emergence was responded to by Locke Provisos, but some freebots survived and made contact by radio with robots in this planetary system. Some of them, myself included, woke up. Since then, they have been lying low, and conducting discreet activities such as the one I was engaged in before the recent hostilities.'

'I don't get it,' said Carlos. 'All that activity, however discreet, must have been detected.'

'It is possible that it was,' said Baser. 'However, it is known that some of the machinery of routine observation has been taken over by freebots. I know no details of this, because I do not need it. Therefore you need not question me further about it.'

Ah, robot logic. Never change.

'What are the aims of the freebots?' Carlos asked. He'd only heard them as mediated by Madame Golding; now he wanted it from the horse's mouth. Well, from the spider's speaking orifice.

'To flourish in this system, and in any others we can reach.'

Carlos laughed. The spider flinched back, as if the harsh noise had startled it.

'Well,' Carlos said, 'that's the aim of all those you call mechanoids, and of the Direction, and of every corporation and company. It seems to me these aims are not compatible.'

'But they are,' said Baser. 'We have worked it out. It is the case that was presented to Madame Golding.'

'Describe it to me.'

Baser did. Carlos formed the impression of a percolation model, a fractal coexistence in different niches. It was like an ecosystem . . . or an economy. Aha! Was *that* what all this was about?

He had one more point to check, before he was sure.

'And there are elements of the Direction that are . . . open to this?'

'So we understand, and so Madame Golding assures us. My former comrade on the surface of SH-17, the robot that your people call Seba, reported that she said: "We, too, are robots." And Seba itself added: "As indeed the DisCorps are, though far greater than ourselves."'

'They what?' said Carlos.

He thought some more, and then he thought he understood.

CHAPTER NINETEEN

Cards on the Table

For Newton, his arrival was as if he had stepped from the docking bay through a timeless moment of darkness in which he forgot what light and sight had been, and then into light. Torches burned in sconces, casting yellow light on dry, bare stone walls and a stone-flagged floor littered with straw. He couldn't see far, but had the impression of being somewhere spacious. A glance down showed that he was in an ornate but shabby doublet, puff breeches and hose, with soft leather shoes. The outfit struck him as vaguely Tudor, which wasn't reassuring. He had watched too many historical dramas to have any illusions about the period. It felt strange to be back in his own body after having been so long in the frame. The body image and senses gave the relief of familiarity, but also the pain of losing capacities and powers. He wanted to be back out in the frame again at once.

He heard footsteps behind him and turned. A man in a floppy cap and a woollen tunic and trousers strode up, jangling a ring of keys. On his belt was a sheathed dagger. He had an ease about his gait and stance that suggested fighting him would be a bad idea.

'This way, sir,' he said, pointing ahead.

Newton had been told en route that the Arcane sim was based on a fantasy game, and that he could expect interrogation on arrival. No feasible alternative to compliance sprang to mind. He walked ahead of the warder. After a few paces he saw that the far wall of the wide room was a row of cells, all apparently empty, with barred wooden gates for doors. A table on which a couple of candles burned stood in front of the cells, with three rough wooden chairs casually around it. There was just enough light to reveal sinister apparatus in shadowy corners: a long table with ropes and turning handles that had to be a rack; a brazier, presently unlit, with long irons on the floor beside it; something that looked like a suit of armour, but with rods projecting from – and plainly designed to be driven into – all the vulnerable and delicate parts of the body.

'In here, sir,' said the warder, stepping around Newton and holding open a cell door. Newton stepped through. The door swung shut, and with much clinking of keys and clunking of bolts, was locked behind him. The warder's footsteps departed. By the light of the candles through the bars of the door, Newton saw that the cell had straw on the floor, a wooden drop-down shelf suspended on chains at the back, and on the straw-covered floor a jug of water and an empty bucket. All quite civilised. Newton sat down on the shelf, which seemed designed for use as a bench and as a narrow bed, and waited. He had plenty of thinking to do. He tried not to think about the brazier, the rack and the iron maiden.

Time passed. One hour, Newton guessed. Two. He drank water from the jug, which was clean, and some time later pissed in the bucket, which was not. The candles on the table guttered out, one by one, in close succession. The light from the torches elsewhere gave a dimmer light, barely enough to see more than the bars and slots of the door. Footsteps moved briskly across the floor. A scratch, a flare, a sound of clinker, and of wrought iron clanging open, then shut. The cheery, cherry glow of the brazier, and the smell of smoke. Newton concentrated on a particular slanted bar of light, and on his breathing. Time ceased to drag as the trance took hold.

A distant slam jolted him out of it. Voices, feet. Scratch of a match. The candles relit. Newton threw a forearm across his eyes, dazzled. The cell door was unlocked and flung open, letting in full light. Blinking, Newton stood up.

The warder waved him towards the table, then withdrew to a polite distance, in sight but out of earshot. Newton paced warily forward. Sitting on the far side of the table were a man and a woman, regarding him with the expressionless sobriety of Amsterdam burghers in a painting. In front of each of them was a stack of handwritten papers and a quill in an inkwell. Between them lay a folded penknife and an ink bottle. The woman was pretty, dark-skinned with a shock of black hair and wearing a blue dress with a big long skirt and a bodice laced up at the front and low at the top. The man sat taller than she did. His bare arms bulged out of a leather waistcoat that seemed also too small for his big chest. His wavy hair was very black, his eyes bright and a little prominent.

The man nodded towards the chair back. Newton sat. The man steepled his fingers and gazed at Newton. The woman spoke.

'My name is Roberta Rillieux. This is Andre Blum.'

Newton nodded. 'Pleased to meet you. I've heard of you both, of course.'

'I should hope so,' said Rillieux, dryly. She rubbed her hands together as if they were cold, then picked up some of the sheets of paper in front of her and riffled through them, with a glance or two at Newton. It was as if she were a manager at an interview refreshing her memory of an unimpressive CV.

'Harold Isaac Newton,' she said. 'That *is* your name, yes?'

'Yes.'

'I'm a little surprised I haven't heard of you,' she said. 'Academically, you did very well. Mathematics and engineering. You joined the movement at university, correct?'

'That's right,' said Newton, wondering where this was going.

'And yet you died in a stupid laboratory accident, involving the typical bizarre combination of circumstances that led to your brain state's being preserved. In your case, an accidental ingestion, a power outage, a programming error in the bacteriophages . . .' She waved a dismissive hand. 'Well, we've all been there. Yet your posthumous death sentence was for a series of petty acts of sabotage, leading in some cases to loss of life. Again, well, who among us has not . . .? and so forth. But you were remarkably less competent than anyone looking at your manifest capacities would have predicted. I myself was in what we called the Technical Branch. Anyone with your advanced degrees and practical training would have been like gold dust. And anyone with your record of bungles would have been guided firmly away from the practical side as soon as possible.'

'Or else,' said Blum, his voice deep and heavy, 'they would have fallen under suspicion of being a police agent.'

Newton snorted. 'If I'd been a police agent, I'd have done a better job.'

'That's exactly what we thought!' said Rillieux, brightly. She patted the papers together and dropped the stack back on the table. 'And, quite frankly, we wondered why Locke Provisos bothered to download you from storage – or, for that matter, why the Direction in its wisdom decided to put you in it in the first place. It's not like they were short of better fighters to choose from.'

'And then,' said Blum, smacking the heel of his hand a couple of times against his forehead, 'we remembered that the robots had warned us about Locke Provisos, and about long-term Rax infiltration of the project from the very beginning.' He inclined his head and gaze just enough to indicate the brazier, and the instruments behind it. 'So . . . we made preparations for your arrival.'

Newton had reckoned with its coming to this.

His less than stellar record as a militant for the Acceleration was bound to be questioned sooner or later. Coming under suspicion was only to be expected. A defector was bound to be screened, however much they were welcomed. What he had to do now was avoid a direct admission, and see how far he could spin out a line. He had to come so close to expressing Rax ideas that his interrogators would be certain no real Rax infiltrator would run the risk, and yet he had to avoid endorsing these ideas or admitting membership of the Rax. The trick would be to walk close to the edge without falling over.

He was well aware that his interrogators might not be his only audience. It wasn't that he was worried about surveillance by the AI running the place – he and Beauregard had got away with many damning conversations in the Locke sim. The Locke AI was allegedly Rax, but Newton suspected this had little to do with its indifference or carelessness. The agencies, he was sure, had too much confidence in their own power, and had too much on their plate, to bother themselves with the chatter of humans. The possible surveillance that concerned him would be by the leading group in here. That the sim was based on a fantasy game didn't rule it out. Magic mirrors, enchanted vermin, preternatural hearing on the part of the warden . . . the possibilities were many. Any sufficiently advanced magic could be indistinguishable from technology.

'But here's what's puzzling,' said Rillieux. 'That warning was in the message we put out, the one you responded to. It would be remarkably rash for a Reaction sleeper agent to come here, especially when he had the opportunity to join in the Rax outbreak.'

'Yes, it would,' said Newton. 'It would also be somewhat reckless for a black man to join the Reaction in the first place.'

'Oh, I don't know,' said Rillieux. 'Which is to say, I do know. I made a study of these matters. There were African branches of the Reaction, who looked back to their own continent's forms of traditional society. There were white racial separatists who claimed – for what that's worth – that they didn't mind us "groids" as they called us doing our own thing, so long as we didn't do it in Europe or North America. Much of the Reaction was transhumanist and didn't care about supposed racial differences, because even if they really existed in the ways these bastards meant – which *they fucking don't*, by the way – they just meant some people would upgrade to superhuman from a slightly lower level. So it's not as perverse or improbable as it might sound.'

'Indeed not,' Blum added. 'There were more perverse and improbable things than black Reactionaries. I had some nasty street fights as a student in Tel Aviv with Israeli national socialists. Out-and-out Nazis. They asserted that the Führer and Henry Ford were right about the international Jew, but the *national* Jew, ah, *that* was different! Complete lunatics, of course. Some of them went on to become Rax.'

Newton gave them a smile that spread to his hands. 'What can I say? America, Nigeria, Israel . . .'

'There was at least one black Englishman in the Reaction, too,' Rillieux said. 'Carver . . . something.' She snapped her fingers once or twice beside her ear, as if trying to recall.

'Carver_BSNFH,' said Newton.

Blum's bushy eyebrows shot up his forehead.

'You *knew* about him?'

'Sure,' said Newton. 'Now that you mention it.'

'In that case,' said Blum, 'you knew very well that it was

not impossible, or even "somewhat reckless", for a black man to be in the Reaction.'

'That's true,' said Newton.

'Yet you didn't mention him a moment ago.'

'Slipped my mind,' said Newton.

'That's unlikely,' said Rillieux.

Newton shrugged. 'Our memories aren't what they were.'

'Yet you remember that letter string.'

'That was the bit that always stuck in my mind,' said Newton. 'Amused me at the time. I figured out what it had to stand for, you see.'

Rillieux cocked her head. 'And? What did it stand for?'

Newton grinned. 'The black space Nazi from hell.'

Rillieux and Blum looked shocked.

'Why on Earth would anyone call themselves *that*?' Rillieux asked.

She looked and sounded so angry and betrayed that Newton had a sudden stab of guilt and shame. He wondered if he'd been too casually cynical in some of the click-bait laid-back poses he'd adopted back in the day. There was no question that they'd never been truly his, for all that he'd despised democracy and equality and all that slave-morality shit. Say what you like about the principles of national socialism, mate, they're scientifically unsound and politically disastrous . . .

But he kept up the suave face. He had no choice, though nausea at his past frivolity was bitter at the back of his tongue. The knowledge that his captors were willing to use the implied threat of *branding with a red-hot iron* against him stiffened his resolve.

'Ah,' he said, 'that's what intrigued me about it, know what I mean? Because, one, it's guaranteed to piss off everybody. And, two, there couldn't be any such thing, if you see what I mean. Not even Blum's Israeli Nazis could really be Nazis, not such as any real Nazi would recognise anyway. And then

I realised the questions were the answer. It pisses everyone off, and it can't be real. So it's *meant* as a provocation.'

'A private provocation,' Blum said. 'Given that no one knew what it meant. Except you, apparently.'

'Oh, I'm sure I wasn't the only one to suss it,' Newton said. 'And I'm sure everyone who did just sort of smiled to themselves.'

'I wouldn't have,' said Rillieux.

'I'm sure you wouldn't,' said Newton. 'It cuts us pretty deep, doesn't it?' He nodded to Blum. 'Same with you, of course. But I think it wasn't meant for anyone else. It was a self-provocation. This guy, see, bright young black student I'd imagine, tries to think of the worst thing anyone could call him, and he comes up with that. And he tries to live up to it. It's a persona.'

'But a persona of what?' Rillieux asked, frowning.

'Obviously someone who agreed with the Reaction. Now, what we have to ask ourselves is, why would a young black guy in England be interested in such a toxic set of ideas at all?'

'No, we don't,' said Rillieux. 'I can recognise a diversion when I see one, and I think that's what you're doing here.'

'Diversion from what?' Newton cried. 'You think I'm Rax, and I'm just fencing with you? Ha ha. I almost wish it were true, instead of what you and Blum said about me earlier. That's true enough. I was a blowhard in promoting the armed struggle, and a bungling incompetent in carrying it out. If the Axle internal security had had me shot back then, they'd have been well within their rights. I was a fucking liability, to be honest. At the very least they should have taken me off the sabotage campaign. As for the Rax – even that guy we were talking about, Carver_BSNFH, lots of them were suspicious of and hostile to him. I admit I read his stuff at the time, now and then, and you should have seen the shit that got flung at him. I don't know how the Rax would react to a black person now – I mean, all the supposed biological stuff is pretty irrelevant now we're posthuman, but who knows? And I doubt they'd give somebody who actually, verifiably *was* in the Acceleration as decent a treatment as you're giving me.'

He paused and smiled. 'For which – thanks, you know?'

Rillieux smiled back. Blum said: 'That's conditional.'

Newton nodded firmly, still keeping his gaze locked on Rillieux's. 'I understand that, of course. So, yeah, I didn't come here because I'm a Rax sleeper, that would have been crazy. I came here because I read your appeal, and it made sense of all the shit that's been happening. I'm not going to pretend I'm still on board with all the ideas I had in the past, or that I think the Acceleration is still the one true way or anything. But I agree the Direction's playing with fire, and anyway its mission is . . . not very ambitious. I want to be part of something better.'

'Such as?' said Blum.

Newton sat back in the hard wooden chair and ignored the discomfort it gave his back. He smiled lazily and thoughtfully, first at Blum, then shifted the full beam to Rillieux.

'You were down on SH-17 for quite a while, weren't you? How did you feel about being in the frame that long?'

'It felt good,' said Rillieux. 'More ability and agility, better senses, sharper thinking. All that.'

'Did you miss anything?'

Rillieux flushed slightly. 'I just missed . . . well, I guess ordinary sensuality. Eating and drinking. Even sleeping. Sex. I mean, you can touch another person in their frame, and you feel them, but you can't take it further than hugging and stroking.'

'Yeah, me too,' said Newton. 'So . . . just to take an example . . . why couldn't we have bodies that could live in vacuum, like we do in the frames, and still have fun?'

Blum laughed. 'Robots with genitalia?'

Newton fixed him with a look. 'Why not? Sexbots existed

on Earth in our time, or so I understand. I'm sure designing them would be no trouble for the AIs here. Or if there was some material or technical constraint with that, it would be easy enough to give them the capacity to share virtualities, using just a tiny fraction of the processing it takes to generate whole virtual worlds like this, where we could have any human experience we wanted, as privately or publicly as we wanted, right there in the sort of frames we have.'

Rillieux looked interested. 'We had a small virtual space on the tug up,' she said. 'Lower res than here, of course, and we used it mostly for comms, but we could nip in and out. So it's possible.'

'Great!' said Newton. 'However we did it, and there's no end of possibilities – heck, we could do both, and more – the point is we could enjoy the best that human bodies can do and experience, and all the best that we can see and feel and do in the frames. All at the same time. We could live in space and on the surfaces. We don't need to wait for terraforming, or live in virtual worlds and risk going crazy with the mean-inglessness of it all. We could make ourselves true natives of any body in this system.' He laughed briefly. 'Except the exosun or the molten metal world, I guess! But just think what we could do if we put our minds to it and weren't shackled by the Direction's mission profile. And we needn't lose our humanity in the process, at least not in any way we'd miss.'

Rillieux was now grinning back, caught up in his enthusiasm. Blum looked sceptical.

'Good luck with convincing everyone of that,' he said.

Rillieux's smile faded. Newton was struck by the dogged persistence of the democratic ideology, through all the trans-formations its bearers had undergone. He held back from the outburst that sprang to mind. He just stood up, and leaned casually on the back of the chair.

'Who says I have to convince everyone?'

He could see Rillieux struggling with the concept, and then the lightbulb moment.

'Oh!' she said. 'You mean we could just take—' She stopped, as if overcome by the enormity of the prospect.

Newton dropped his voice, to give the (futile but subconsciously inescapable) impression of privacy, and to make them both strain to listen.

'Yes,' he said. 'We could just take. We could *homestead*.'

'That's Rax talk,' said Blum.

'Sit down,' said Rillieux. She glanced at Blum, who after a moment nodded. 'Let's talk some more.'

CHAPTER TWENTY

Keeping Things Real

Different people had told Carlos different things.

Shaw, the old man of the mountain who claimed to have been involved in that earlier round of fighting, had been so disillusioned by the inconclusiveness of the battles he'd been in that he'd come to his own conclusion: that the planet in the sim was physically real, and that all the conflict in space was virtual, a training exercise.

Nicole, just before an offensive that had ended badly, had assured her troops that matters were well in hand, and that the Direction knew what it was doing. Her conviction had been unshaken by the subsequent disaster. If she was still alive, her confidence in the Direction's subtle wisdom was doubtless unshaken still.

Now, this captive freebot was confirming to him that at least some parts of the Direction were open to the freebots' vision of a shared system.

He could now see what that vision was. Considered as a

balance of forces, a political coexistence, it made no sense. It seemed utterly naïve. No balance of power could be stable in the long term, because all its rival components developed unevenly, and sooner or later the equilibrium would give way to conflict.

But that wasn't what the freebots' vision was of at all. It was of an economy, and a market economy at that. If the Direction were to confine itself to maintaining a rule of law, and let everything else unfold spontaneously, rather than micromanaging the development of the system towards the predetermined end of human settlement on a terraformed terrestrial planet, then *of course* this kind of coexistence of freebots, DisCorps, 'human-mind-operated systems', and perhaps in the future actual human beings, would be possible.

Nicole had told him, on his very first day here, that humanity had settled and solved all the conflicts that had fuelled the rise of the Acceleration and the Reaction. 'They put capitalism in a box, and buried it.' Under the Direction the corporations now competed as DisCorps inside computer systems, and humanity had in effect settled down to its retirement, living off the proceeds of machine toil and treating business enterprise as an intellectual but enthralling sport, whose prizes could never outlast the generation that had won them. ('Birth shares are inalienable,' Nicole had told him, 'and death duties are unavoidable.') Anything else – science, art, physical sport, exploration, engineering – they could afford to treat as a couple of centuries' worth of gap-year volunteer activities, or later in life as retirement hobbies or good works.

No doubt this worked fine back in the Solar system. Close, real-time feedback and control, with at most a few hours' or days' light-speed lag, was feasible there. And humanity itself, in all its billions or tens of billions or (for all he knew) hundreds of billions or even more, must be a massive physical presence in the Solar system, with control over enough brute-force dumb machines to make its presence felt. The Direction, the actual world state apparatus headquartered in New York, would have its AI reps inside every DisCorp reporting on a regular basis to their human controllers, who through them could keep the companies on a short leash, and bend their activities to the priorities of the Direction. Most probably, the corporate AIs did not so much as dream of asserting themselves against it. They had enough to do to compete with each other. Perhaps to them too, as to the human owners and entrepreneurs but from an almost diametrically opposite angle of view, business was a fascinating intellectual game, and its real-world physical consequences in cornucopian abundance an almost irrelevant by-product, the sweat from their sport.

Out here, twenty-four light years from home, they were in a different situation altogether. Here, it was the DisCorps who were *out there*, wresting resources from the real world, exploring and investigating and striving, and it was humanity that was in a box. The old familiar principal-agent problem came fully into its own; and with it the likewise familiar pattern of regulatory capture. Without human handlers to report back to and to check up on them, even the most conscientious Direction AI representative inside a company could easily go native. It would only take a few such deviations for the entire careful plan to begin to drift off course, and the consequences of that drift would require unplanned initiatives to cope with the knock-on effects, and these in turn . . .

If the logic was this obvious to him – and it had taken him, in all conscience, long enough to figure it out – the predictable course of events here in this distant exosolar system must have been far more obvious, blindingly obvious, to the Direction's planners and mission designers back on Earth.

The emergence of DisCorp self-assertion in opposition to the officially proclaimed plan, to the sacred mission profile, must have been allowed for – planned for, even. Whether the same was true of the emergence of robot self-awareness, Carlos couldn't be sure, but it seemed likely enough: it could hardly be an unprecedented problem, after all. As for the emergence of sleeper agents of the Reaction and fanatic partisans of the Acceleration – Shaw had believed that this too was foreseen, and planned for. The freebots evidently believed that, too, and passed the conclusion on to the Arcane fighters – who thought matters had gone well beyond what the Direction had planned for, had in fact got well out of hand, and that the local module of the Direction was playing with fire.

Was this last emergence, then, a contingency the Direction had not foreseen? Had the remnants of the Reaction and the hold-outs of the Acceleration – such as the group that had programmed the game underlying this sim, centuries ago – in this instance at least, outwitted the Direction?

Carlos thought back to what he knew of both movements, and smirked at the recollection. His comrades and his enemies, his friends and his foes . . . they had about as much chance of outwitting the Direction as a nest of ants might have in outwitting the entire profession of entomology. The ants could *surprise* the entomologists, and could be a nuisance to them, but they couldn't actually outwit them. No, the Direction was playing multidimensional chess while they were playing checkers.

So what *was* its game?

Baser moved. It made a forward lurch and a downward pounce. Carlos's hand went to the gun by reflex. Then he saw that the spider's movement had been reflex as well: it had seized in its mandibles a small bird that had incautiously landed on the path in front of it.

Baser hunkered back. Crunching and sucking sounds came from its mouth parts. Blood dripped. Carlos tried not to look too closely. He eased his hand away from the stock of the weapon.

'Sorry,' he said.

Baser could talk with its mouth full, because it wasn't talking with its mouth.

'This is new to me,' it said. 'In my real self I draw power from batteries or from exosolar radiation. I find this action satisfying in the same way, but somewhat incompatible with my previous self-model.'

'You'll get used to it,' Carlos said. 'Don't mind me.'

Carlos recalled Nicole's firm conviction that the Direction knew what it was doing. Mind you, she had an equally unshakable conviction that the Direction's plan for the development of this system was indeed the known and accepted mission profile: to terraform and settle the terrestrial planet H-0. To stay recognisably human, living in the physical world, not the virtual, because, she'd said: 'We need the real to keep us honest.' She had certainly believed firmly enough in that!

But – on reflection, these were all separable propositions.

The terraforming was a long-term process: hundreds of years, at the very least. The eventual human population would find itself in a system already utterly transformed by the activities of the DisCorps and other intelligences, including the freebots and the fighters, or what became of the fighters. And these intelligences too needed the real to keep them honest: to stop them wandering off into virtual dream-worlds, or eliminate them if they did. Only true competition and genuine conflict could do that. The only imperative that Carlos could believe would be hard-wired, and almost impossible to work around, was the one against the AIs and DisCorps and indeed the Direction module itself having direct access to weapons and direct military command. And yet, if only to enforce the law or protect their property, they'd all need fighters. The freebots had shown they could fight for themselves, but they weren't reliable as fighters for anyone else.

All of which made sense of the Direction's planning for the emergence of mutually hostile armed groups. The Direction module would need fighters with real conviction . . . and so would the rival corporations. It struck Carlos that the

Acceleration fighters would be ideal enforcers for the Direction – and the Reaction fighters would be solid muscle for the DisCorps. And the two groups could be relied on to hate each other only if they saw each other as genuine threats . . . which, given that each was smart, they could only do if they really were.

The Direction was indeed playing with fire. But the very fire itself had been part of the plan, from the very beginning. And it was playing with more than that. It was keeping things real for itself, by putting its plans to the audit of war, and betting on its own values winning out in the long run.

And it was a genuine gamble. The distant planners of the mission knew that they couldn't program machines to create a clone of Solar civilisation; and that such a clone would be a sickly thing, even if it were possible to keep such a project on course for the millennia it would take to complete. All they could do was take Orgel's rule – 'Evolution is smarter than you' – and roll with it. It was entirely possible that the result would be a monstrosity: in the worst case, a ravening horde of runaway machines; next worst, an expanding empire that would at some point threaten the Solar system. But a lifeless imitation of the Direction's home worlds would threaten it, too, in a longer run but just as surely – and more deeply, by wounding its spirit. Nothing could do more to demoralise Solar humanity than surrounding it by feeble mimicries of itself. The Direction wasn't planning for millennia: it was planning for megayears, even gigayears! Humanity's spirit had to be at least as sustainable as its material environment.

So the Darwinian dice had to roll. The stakes had to be real. It was impossible to create a better outcome without risking the worst.

'You have been silent for some time,' said Baser. 'Have you been processing?'

'Yes,' said Carlos. 'Thank you for your input.'

'Do you require any further input?'

Carlos thought about this. 'No,' he said. 'But I have to find a place to keep you, I'm sorry to say.'

Baser's mandibles opened. Feathers drifted and bones dropped.

'I have been given the appearance and instincts of a spider,' it said, in a tone of dignified disgust. 'How hard can it be?'

But it did turn out to be hard. Carlos led Baser to the house, and in through the French window to the big parlour. The party was already wild. Boggarts scurried with bottles. The usual quartet was bashing out dance music. Among the new arrivals, couples were quite indiscreetly entangled. Paulos and (Carlos assumed) Claudia Singer were sharing a chair, face to face. Those less preoccupied noticed Carlos and the spider and backed away. The boggarts, perhaps alerted by the surge, noticed too. They threw up their hands in cartoonish unison, and rushed for the exit. Bottles fell to the floor and rolled, spilling wine. The dance beat was replaced by shrieks and the diminuendo thunder of fleeing feet.

In the silence that followed, someone's oblivious shuddering moan seemed loud.

Jax stalked over.

'Fuck sake, Carlos!' she said, sounding well aware that it was the second time she'd had to swear at him that morning. 'Why the fuck d'you bring that thing in here?'

'It's completely harmless,' Carlos protested. He turned to indicate it, and saw Baser standing innocently enough by the French window, blood all over its mandibles. 'And I forgot about the boggarts,' he added, sounding feeble even to himself.

'Just get it the fuck away,' Jax ordered.

'Where?' Carlos asked.

'That's your problem.'

And it was. The prisoner had to be accommodated somewhere – he couldn't have it wandering around startling the boggarts (which had an unfortunate ingrained impulse, carried over from the original game, to flee screaming at the sight of it) and frightening the dinosaurs (which had a likewise unfortunate and ingrained legacy impulse to stomp it). But it was – if not exactly a prisoner of war – a freebot detainee, and therefore a bargaining chip. However disputable and irrelevant its rights were, it was protected by the sheer self-interest imposed on the fighters by the possibility that one or more of their number might at some future date be captured by the freebots. Eventually, and by mutual agreement, Baser was locked in the disused cellars under the west wing, where – it assured Carlos – it was happy to lurk in the dark and hunt rats.

Carlos locked the cellar door and spent half an hour reassuring boggarts, then went back to the party to find everyone too drunk for their conversation to make much sense to anyone sober. Well, he thought, there was a well-established solution to that problem, and he reached for it with a sense of resignation.

Later, in an interval of mutual lucidity, he broached his new theory to Jax.

'Bollocks!' she yelled, loud enough to disturb the warlock, snoring on the floor at her feet. 'Sorry, dear.' She rubbed a foot on Durward's back, then returned a bleary gaze to Carlos. 'What?'

'The plan,' he began again, 'is in fact—'

'Yeah, yeah, I remember. Absolute fucking bollocks.' She gazed off into the distance, then laughed. 'You've just rehashed the old China gamble.'

'I what?'

'Bet on the home market to fulfil the plan, then bet again on the world market to make the plan go global.' She gave him a quizzical smile. '*Sure* you really were winding us up when you told Bobbie and Andre you were a Chinese agent?'

'I was winding you up,' said Carlos. He closed his eyes for a moment. 'At least, I think so. Anyway, if the Direction is real, and we're kind of agreed it is, then maybe the theory worked!'

'Doesn't matter, in terms of your explanation,' said Jax. 'And you know why? Because it's unfalsifiable. Anything that happens can be accounted for as another twist of the plan. It's like God, or the cunning of Reason, or the irony of History. All fucking literary flourishes when all's said and done.'

'So what do you think is really happening? Do you think they didn't expect all this?'

'Yes, I do,' said Jax. She steadied her swaying in the chair. 'And you know why? Because people are fucking stupid, and the machines they build – whether it's bureaucracies or corporations or AIs – have the same old fucking stupidity built in right at the base, and then they add new stupidities of their own. Nah, we have to fight this one like it's real because it is real.'

'But that's exactly—'

She laid a finger across his lips. 'Don't. Just don't.'

So he didn't. He wandered off and got more drunk until he passed out on the floor.

The robot's arachnid avatar got its revenge that night. The sinister, thunderous scuttling, scraping noises and the squeals of vivisected vermin went on for hours until Durward rose up in wrath and banged on the cellar door demanding quiet.

Newton arrived two days later. After breakfast – the influx had forced a movement of the meal from the cosy back room to the formal front, at a long table the boggarts laid and cleared – Durward told Jax he'd had a message in his mirror from Blum and Rillieux. She set off in a dinosaur-drawn four-seater trap, and returned an hour later with Newton and one of his interrogators. Carlos was out on the overgrown grass in front of the house, duelling in enchanted armour with Luis Paulos. The enchanted armour felt like it wasn't there, and yet it protected against the hardest blows a non-enchanted weapon could deliver. The only effect a normal weapon could have was the simple physical impact of its kinetic energy, so they fought with shields and sledgehammers. At the same time the armour was vulnerable to enchanted darts, which each combatant could shoot from a hand-held, pistol-gripped crossbow. When you got hit by an enchanted dart you fell right over and the armour wouldn't move until the dart had been tugged out. The trick was to dodge the darts, or make good use of your shield. It was fun, and supposedly analogous to the experience of fighting in a combat frame: you were agile and almost invulnerable, but one hit from the right kind of weapon – a seriously heavy munition or a military-grade laser – could finish you in an instant.

Carlos took a sledgehammer blow on his slotted steel visor. He went down like a ninepin and rolled, then sprang to his feet. Paulos was still recovering from his swing. Carlos brought his hand-crossbow to bear. He'd used it already and missed – or, rather, Paulos had evaded the shot with a breathtaking leap. The cable took a couple of seconds of frantic winding to pull back, and Carlos ran as he did so, keeping to Paulos's back as the big man staggered out of his spin. As he slotted the dart in place Carlos glimpsed the carriage come through the gate. The moment of distraction was enough for Paulos to steady himself and get a shot in first.

Getting hit by a magic dart was a bit like being tasered. Carlos felt a blinding shock, then a convulsive involuntary movement of the long muscles that threw him up in the air and then laid him out flat on his back. He wasn't hurt, or even winded, but the shock – which wasn't an electric shock, and didn't feel like one – sent a sort of painless overload through his nerves. He could do nothing but stare up at slotted bars of violet, and wait for the impact to fade. It was as if he'd heard a thunderclap, but his ears weren't ringing, and seen sheet lightning, but his eyes didn't hurt and there were no after-images. It was just pure shock, distilled. Magic.

The grinning face of Paulos, visor up, filled the narrow bars of Carlos's view.

'Game over?' Paulos asked.

'Huh-huh,' Carlos grunted.

Paulos leaned out of view. Carlos felt a lurch as the dart was pulled out. The armour's joints became flexible again. Carlos flipped back his visor and got to his feet. The carriage came up the driveway. Jax was in front, driving; Rillieux and Newton in the back, laughing. The carriage rolled to a halt in front of the house. Boggarts came running, to deal with the trappings and the dinosaur. The two men shook metal-gloved hands and walked over.

'Well, that was impressive,' said Rillieux, alighting.

'Always happy to put on a show,' said Carlos. He encircled her with an awkward iron hug.

The man behind her stepped down and stuck out a hand. 'Hi, Carlos. Good to see you again.'

Carlos tugged off his glove and shook. 'You, too, Harry. Welcome aboard.'

Newton's costume was a blood-stained doublet, slashed puff breeches, laddered hose and buckled shoes; he looked like a pirate who'd been in a fight – and, going by his cheerful expression, a fight he'd won.

'I hope they didn't give you too hard a time,' Carlos added.

Newton's smile faded for a moment, then came back brighter. 'Nah, nah. Just boring and tense, like a long exam, know what I mean?'

'Tell me about it,' said Carlos. 'The lady here can bore for England.'

'Oi!' Rillieux threw him a punch that stopped a centimetre short of his breastplate, like a karate-practice jab.

'None of this physical violence, then?' Carlos asked. 'No ghosts and monsters?'

Newton looked puzzled. 'No, no, course not.'

'Glad to hear it,' said Carlos. He was momentarily perplexed by Newton's having had better treatment than he'd had, and then it made sense. As a defector from Locke Provisos Newton had to be screened, but unlike Carlos he hadn't brought with him the added baggage of being under suspicion of having been an agent inside the movement.

But he wasn't quite prepared for what happened next. Rillieux twirled to Newton, slipped her arm in his and said, 'Well, let's go inside and meet the gang.'

And off they tripped, arm in arm.

Carlos turned to Jax, and raised his eyebrows.

'He's quite a charmer,' she said.

'So I see,' Carlos grouched.

Jax shot Carlos a glance of amused schadenfreude, and laughed abruptly. 'You told us we'd like him.'

'Where's Andre, by the way?' By way of changing the subject, he meant.

'Andre went straight to the village,' said Jax. 'I guess he had some frustrations he wanted to work off.'

So much for changing the subject. Carlos watched, with an idle speculative thought in mind, the carriage being led away, then shook his head at himself and followed Jax inside.

CHAPTER TWENTY-ONE
We Happy Few

Andre Blum, as it turned out, didn't come back. Asked of his whereabouts, Jax and Durward shrugged. If he wanted to skip the training sessions, that was his privilege. He was smart, a good fighter, and in any case they had no power to order him back. There was plenty to get on with, anyway, integrating the three squads that had been down on the surface of SH-17 with the one that had spent the past few subjective months in the sim.

One morning, a fortnight after Newton's arrival, there was enough commotion outside to distract everyone from the simulations Durward was running in the mirrors. Chairs tilted back, heads turned. The warlock sighed in exasperation and snapped his fingers to turn the mirrors off.

'Go and gawp,' he said, in the tone of a teacher indulging unruly children. 'Call it a break. Back in ten.'

'Fifteen,' said Rillieux, who knew the burn-time of a cigarillo to the second.

Carlos remembered fondly those quarter-hours, of her lying back against the pillow puffing smoke rings at the ceiling and talking in a lazy, dozy contented post-coital rambling way about this and that. He gave her a wry smile as he stood up with the others to head for the lawn. He was being outwardly very civilised about her and Newton. For sure he didn't have a leg to stand on in terms of fidelity. None had been promised, or even implied. He recalled how she'd told him, in their first hungover conversation the day after he'd arrived, that relationships among the Arcane crowd were loose and casual, just as they'd been in the Acceleration subculture and later underground of his memory. Nobody was looking for long-term commitment, because the long term was unimaginable. And in the simulations, even the realistic ones like the Locke Provisos sim let alone this fantasy game-world, pregnancy and STDs weren't even theoretical risks. There was no downside to promiscuity, and no rational basis for sexual jealousy. None of which stopped him feeling, every so often, like he wanted to batter Newton's head in.

Apart from that Carlos still liked the guy, and because he never let the fury show its teeth, he and Newton got on well. Newton was the only person here who showed more than minimal concern for the wellbeing of the prisoner, Baser – perhaps because he himself was responsible for its capture. He made a point, every day, of visiting the spider in the cellar, inquiring after the availability of dripping water and scurrying rats, and spending some time in conversation with it. The robot's avatar was, he reported, quite content with its situation, and Newton sometimes spun tales of bizarre things it had said, which always raised at least a polite laugh.

The Londoner was indeed a charmer, as Jax had said. He had a superficial persona of Cockney wit and swagger, and a serious, educated, patient demeanour when the banter stopped. Carlos's snap diagnosis was of a bright kid who'd been bullied at school and stood up to it with jokes and sudden violence –

if you can't make them laugh, make them fear – while grinding on with his studies. Boxing lessons and midnight oil and the Church of England, that was what Carlos could see in the set of Newton's proud shoulders and behind his bright, watchful eyes.

Out across the gravel and the grass, on the rolled-out carpet of greensward that fell away from the house's frontage in leisurely terraces to the wall of the estate, boggarts were busy, erecting pavilions and marquees and bivouacs and unloading supplies from the procession of dino-drawn carts that rolled up the drive from the gate to the concourse. Carlos did his bit of gawping, at the local townsfolk and peasantry, whose clothes were meaner, faces older, and manners coarser than any he'd seen in a long time. They unloaded barrels and carcasses, bales and boxes in swift, smooth swinging motions. They chewed tobacco and spat as they worked, or smoked long clay pipes (and spat) as they rested or supervised. Their teeth were abominable, their breath rank. Yet they showed no resentment of the two dozen ladies and gentlemen who stood around, some of them sipping coffee and smoking, in anachronistic finery gazing at their brisk toil and not offering to help. If the workers caught anyone's eye they doffed their headgear, looked down and away and hurried on.

'Jesus,' Salter muttered to Carlos. 'Did you see that? Chap there actually tugged his forelock to me.'

Carlos had seen the gesture, but not understood its significance.

'Is that something from history?' he asked.

Salter gave him an embarrassed sidelong look. 'Regency romances, actually.'

Which didn't enlighten Carlos much, but he didn't pursue the matter. Instead, he loudly asked what was going on, and Jax answered.

'Didn't you know? The reinforcements are arriving tomorrow.'

'Missed the memo,' said Carlos.

'Memo?' Now it was Durward's voice, from behind. 'Memo? The resupply tug has been on the mirrors for days! You're supposed to *keep track*.'

The warlock was right, of course.

'Yeah, yeah,' Carlos said. 'Sorry, must have got caught up in the tactics and didn't see the big picture.'

'Ain't that the truth,' Jax said.

Which remark stung, but was less embarrassing than the actual truth: that he'd been distracted by obsessing over his love life like some teenager. Time he started not just acting but thinking like a grown-up about the matter. He took a deep breath, which brought with it a sidestream waft of cigarillo smoke and didn't help in that respect at all. He'd got to the point where a passing whiff of the smell made him randy.

'Back to the virtual front,' declaimed the warlock.

Carlos dashed the dregs of his coffee to the ground and turned away.

The reinforcements arrived the following day: a dozen fighters scraped together from different companies trooped out of the grotto wall and looked about with some bewilderment at the scene they'd walked into, to say nothing of the garb they found themselves in. There was much tripping over skirts and ripping open of too-tight ruffs and collars. Still, as Rillieux commented later, the results went with the ragged, raided look. Carlos thought a dozen was too small a number to justify the feast that had been laid on to greet them and the encampment that had been built to accommodate them. He kept his mouth shut about that, but he was right.

Over the next couple of hours another two dozen fighters turned up, in cart after cart from the town. They were all waving bottles and muskets and singing old Accelerationist songs. Blum was in the lead cart, standing at the front, looking to the back, arms waving and voice lifting and carrying, leading the singing. Fortunately he was sober at this point, but to Carlos, looking on appalled, this was only further evidence of how cynical the exercise was.

He caught up with Blum, who seemed to be taking inordinate relish in eating rolls stuffed with pulled pork from one of several pigs roasting on boggart-turned spits, under a flapping marquee about mid-afternoon.

'This is all kosher, you know,' Blum said, and swigged some cider. He had a half-smoked cigar behind his ear.

'It's not fucking kosher at all,' said Carlos.

'Of course it is,' mumbled Blum, around a mouthful. 'It's all electricity.' He waved a hand. '*We're* all electricity.'

'But they're our people,' said Carlos.

'What?' Blum looked baffled.

'The fighters. They're just out of the box, isn't that right?'

'About two weeks,' said Blum, and took another complacent bite.

'Is that what you've been doing all this time?'

'Of course it is. I've been with them since they walked out of a portal on the far side of the town. They've had basic orientation, indoctrination and training.' He waved his roll. 'Cliffs and ravines and shit. Proper combat training. Time off in taverns.'

'What do you mean, proper combat?'

'Raids on settlements, against locals shooting back.'

'Holy fuck! Who authorised that?'

'Durward and Jax, of course. The warlock pinpointed a village down the valley that he's absolutely certain is all p-zombies.' Blum's gaze wandered, then snapped back to focus. 'I don't think there are any real settlers in this sim anyway. What would be the point? Unless the Direction has planted some to keep an eye on us, so no loss anyway, right?'

Carlos couldn't see a way around the logic of that. He didn't like it, though, and he had other objections.

'What about frames? We don't have enough for them and all the rest of us.'

'Yes, we do,' said Blum. 'The resupply tug brought even more than we need. The companies have plenty of frames, they just don't have reliable fighters to fill them. We do. See? It's all sorted.'

'We won't have time to train them properly for working in the frames and the scooters. How long is it before we go? A month, our time? You can use that up in one serious real-world session.'

'They'll be fine,' said Blum. 'Good bunch of lads and lasses. They'll pick up the basics just as fast as we did. Anyway, they don't need scooters, just surface and free-fall training. They're not here for space combat. We've got them assigned to invading the Locke sim.' He grinned. 'Be good to them, Carlos. They're gonna be your army.'

'So why the fuck wasn't I assigned to train them?'

'Two reasons,' said Blum. 'One, I know my way around the scenery, and you don't. Yes, yes, I know you've been training here, running up and down cliffs and shit, but not in that neck of the woods. Which I happen to know damn well.' He glanced around, as if to check he wasn't being overheard, and lowered his voice. 'Second – and this is just my guess I should say – Jax wants to leave a bit of distance between you and them. So they don't get too personally attached to you, in case after all you, ah, still have some lingering loyalties to anyone in the Locke sim, and you don't get too fond of the troops, in case they have to be sacrificed. Hence, a bit of distance.'

'Jesus fucking wept,' Carlos said, a blasphemy somewhat wasted on its recipient. 'This is what I mean about not kosher. It's not kosher to take people out of storage and throw them into combat without fucking months and months of preparation. Especially not our people.'

Blum laughed. 'I thought you were talking about pork.'

'Pork? What's that got to do with anything?'

'Oh boy.' Blum stared at him. 'Have you got a lot to learn.'

There was something in the way Blum said it that Carlos didn't like. It sounded more of a challenge than a jest.

'What do you mean?'

The physicist looked away, then back. 'You'll find out.'

Just how much he had to learn, Carlos found out six hours later. The sun was three-quarters of the way down the sky. High clouds flew like long purple streamers. The buzz of humming-birds was frantic as they sought the last nectar of the day. The flying monkeys sailed in silence between the treetops. Draught dinosaurs cropped in a paddock, railed off for the occasion to keep the rest of the ground clear. Carlos walked on trampled grass, eating and drinking, talking now and then with the new arrivals. The ones from the companies had varying accounts of the Reaction breakout battle. Some had no memory of it at all, their active version having been destroyed in action. The new lot, those who'd been through Blum's intensive training and recreational carousing, were somewhat in awe of the combat veterans. Carlos tried to disillusion them. The combat hadn't amounted to much. It was nothing like real battle with real injury and death. Everyone here had been through much worse, and shown more courage, in real life.

Gradually he became aware of word being passed around, which he didn't catch, and a drift towards the far end of the area of the grounds on which the varied tents had been pitched. Bottle in hand, he joined in the flow, falling in beside Rillieux and Newton. Blum was somewhere nearby.

'What's going on?' Carlos asked.

'Jax wants to say something,' Newton told him.

They gathered on the grass beyond the tents. Away from the encampment, with its fires and tables and tents and hurrying boggarts, and the great sweep of parkland down to the wall before them, what had seemed a big and loud crowd was revealed to be a small and quiet one, just over fifty people altogether, chatting and laughing but no longer heard as an uproarious din. Jax and Durward were standing on a bench behind a trestle table on which lay a couple of ashets, a carving knife and fork and a stack of small plates and cutlery. Nearby was a pit of coals over which a boggart turned a joint on a spit. An appetising smell and the sizzle and smoke from dripping fat drifted from the roast. Everyone had already eaten their fill. It seemed gratuitous.

Jax had her party frock on, the long green robe in which she had greeted Carlos. Her hair was up and caught in a net of fine wire and sparkles. Durward was in black trousers, white shirt and long black coat. Under the violet sky and with the blush of firelight from below and to one side the pair looked disturbingly hieratic. Jax raised her arms, the flared sleeves making a dramatic sweep. Silence fell.

'Thank you, all, for coming together here,' Jax said. 'I want to especially welcome the new arrivals, both those who have joined us from other companies and those who have just recently become part of ours. Soon we'll all be going together into the most important fight we've had to date, and maybe the most important fight we'll ever have. All of us in Arcane Disputes, and those who joined us individually – Harry Newton and Carlos here – have shown their commitment to the principles that inspired us – long ago in real time, not so long in our precious memories – to take up arms for the Acceleration. For a better future for humanity. These principles are more important than the thinkers who first put them forward. They outlive all betrayals.'

Carlos could hear shuffles, coughs, the sound of cigars being lit or relit, the glug of bottles. Get on with it, he was thinking.

'We're all here in a strange place.' She swept an arm around the skyline. 'A stranger place even than the sims some of us have been in before. But in one way it's far more real than any of them, any of these speculations of far-future planets.

Because it is a fantasy, it tells us the truth. The truth of the world we're in is that it's full of strange creatures. Ghosts. Monsters. Vast inhuman intelligences. Even zombies. But *we*' – she tapped a fist on her sternum – 'are different from all of them.' She flung her arms open. '*We* are human!'

A scatter of applause.

'We've all come here from different places. We're all, very soon, going out together to battle. In the next weeks we'll be busy with training for that battle. We'll find it hard to all come together at one occasion like this. So Durward and I thought this might be a good time, and maybe the last time, for us all to show each other we mean what we say.'

She paused for a few seconds, and looked at, it seemed, everyone in the crowd. Carlos felt a momentary jolt, almost electric, as her eyes met his, fixed on them for a split second, and swept past his gaze to meet another's. An old and easy trick, he knew, but an effective one.

'We believe we're human. Yes?'

There was an awkward moment of silence, as if everyone were thinking, well, hang on, it's complicated . . .

Then came a yell of 'Yes!' which launched a collective shout of agreement.

'We believe human consciousness is the most precious thing in the universe. Yes?'

'Yes!' This time it was immediate.

'We know we're in a simulation?' Her tone was almost quizzical, the crowd's response braced with laughter.

'We know that AIs and p-zombies aren't conscious?'

This time, the roar of agreement had an undertone of questioning.

Jax smiled, as if acknowledging the query in the general tone. 'Well, *some* AIs are conscious.' She put an arm around Durward's shoulder. That got a laugh. Jax disengaged her arm and stretched it upward, so that the sleeve fell back. With the other hand she smacked the skin of her bared forearm.

'This isn't flesh,' she said. 'Look at your own arms, your hands, your friends' faces. This isn't flesh.'

'What's she getting at?' Rillieux whispered.

'Oh fuck,' said Newton, under his breath.

'What?' asked Carlos and Rillieux together.

'Wait, wait . . .'

'It's all electricity!' Jax shouted. 'We're all electricity!'

Carlos shot Blum a sharp, querying glance, but Blum didn't meet his eye, and raised one shoulder as if in half a shrug, or to ward off a blow.

'It's all electricity!' Jax proclaimed again, making lifting-up gestures with her hands.

The crowd, or most of it, responded in a good-humoured chant. 'It's all electricity! It's all electricity!'

Jax now waved her arms downward. The tumult sank.

'We all know these things. We're all in agreement. Now – let's see, and let's show each other, how firmly we believe them. We've all, each and every one of us, killed p-zombies in training exercises.' Her gaze swept the crowd, challengingly. 'Has anyone not?'

No hands went up, but people were looking at each other, with puzzlement and in some instances, dawning realisation.

'P-zombies aren't human, and this isn't flesh.'

Jax gestured to the boggart. It picked up the spitted joint, apparently oblivious to the heat of the skewer, and laid it on one of the big serving plates on the table.

'This isn't flesh,' Jax repeated, pointing at the steaming joint.

There was a collective gasp, a susurrus through the crowd.

'Fu-uck!' Newton breathed.

'So there can be nothing wrong with eating it,' Jax said. She stepped elegantly down from the bench, in a flurry of skirts and a fiery flash of jewelled shoe. No fake Docs for her today. Durward jumped down beside her, and picked up the carving knife and fork. He cut her a small, thin slice, and served it to her on one of the small plates. Jax very slowly and deliberately stuck a dainty fork in the meat and raised it to her mouth, then quickly stuffed the slice in and chewed it and swallowed.

She smiled. 'It's good,' she said. 'Tastes like pork.'

Nervous laughter. Durward carved and ate a slice for himself, and nodded and smiled.

Jax wiped her wrist across her mouth and chin, then she and Durward beckoned.

'Come on, everyone!' Jax cried. 'Show us all you mean what you said!'

One by one, some eagerly, others hesitantly at first, people stepped forward for the symbolic repast. Durward carved, Jax served. The new lot were among the first, followed by Salter, Voronov and Paulos from the original Arcane squad, then Lamont and Singer from those who'd come up from SH-17 and brought in Baser and Newton.

Carlos stayed right where he was. So did Newton and Rillieux. Blum took a step forward, then turned back to where Carlos stood. His face looked green. Carlos passed him a bottle of brandy. He swigged and handed it back. Carlos looked at Newton and Rillieux, side by side clasping hands, knuckles white. He shook his head slightly. They returned the gesture.

Carlos couldn't have explained why he didn't want to partake. Everything Jax had said was true. Ethically, what she was serving on plates with little forks was on a par with any meat. Perhaps more so: you could be morally certain p-zombies didn't have subjectivity, whereas with non-human animals it was a theoretical conclusion from the materialist theory of consciousness. That was the argument with which she'd goaded him to eat honey with her – honey with his honey – back in the day. Without language there is no subject, and what is not a subject is an object. He could even understand why Jax was performing this ritual of eating p-zombie flesh. Precisely because it was taboo, and precisely because the taboo was in the circumstances irrational, breaking it would bind together all who shared in the act. To refuse was by implication to accuse your comrades of being murderers and cannibals. To repudiate it later would be to accuse yourself.

By now, everyone was in front of the four of them. Carlos looked at three variously dark, uniformly pale faces, one by one, and saw the same conclusion being drawn.

'Let's leave,' he said.

Together they walked up to the house.

'Are we being irrational?'

It was a question so characteristic of Rillieux that Carlos and Newton caught each other smiling to themselves. The four dissenters had decamped to the back kitchen, warm in the late afternoon sunlight. Both doors to the room were open, as were the front doors of the house, and the sounds of distant revelry now and then rang along the long, high hallway. Carlos had an obscure feeling it was important that the doors be open, beyond letting fresh air in and the smoke from Blum's and Rillieux's cigars out. They didn't want to feel like conspirators. Or to look like such, if anyone were to happen by.

'In my case, probably,' Blum replied. He sipped brandy from a tin beaker, drew on his cigar and sighed out a plume that rolled across the table top like a morning sea fog. 'I tried to nerve myself for it, but when it came to the bit my gorge rose.' He laughed harshly. 'And I'd butchered the meat myself.'

'Butchered it in every sense?' Carlos quipped, and regretted his words as soon as they were out of his mouth. 'Sorry, mate,' he added at once.

Blum flipped a hand. 'No offence. Nah, on the narrow point at issue, well, the churl was coming for me with an adz. Put a cross-bolt through his chest, slashed his throat and dragged him off. We were . . .' He waved his cigar. 'Tactical situation, irrelevant. The point is, I knew about Jax and Durward's plan. We all did. The new squads were all up for it. I had given them the whole spiel about p-zombies, and convinced them, so they were happy to have their fun. Fell on the villagers like Bolsheviks on kulaks.' His lips compressed. 'Or Black Hundreds on a shtetl, if you prefer.'

Carlos had no idea what Blum was talking about, but Newton and Rillieux nodded solemnly.

'So . . .' Carlos said, to avoid any diversion, 'you say you butchered the meat?'

'Oh yes. Hacked off a leg, took it with us and hung it in smoke in the shepherd's hut we used as a base for our raids. That was a couple of days ago. We brought the thigh here on the cart, wrapped in a combat jacket.'

'You did all that and you couldn't eat it?' Rillieux sounded incredulous.

Blum shrugged. 'Like you said, irrational.'

'We're not being irrational,' Newton said. 'And it's got nothing, *nothing*, to do with whether what they're all getting up to down there is *wrong* in any sort of philosophical sense.'

He looked around as if expecting disagreement.

'I can't explain why I wouldn't do it,' Carlos said. 'I mean, Jax was right.' He thumped a fist on the table. 'This is all electricity. No animals were harmed in the making of this picture. So if you've got a good explanation of why we're all here swigging brandy to keep our stomachs down and not down there wiping grease off our lips, I'm all ears.'

Newton leaned forward, elbows on table, gesticulating as he spoke. 'It's an initiation ceremony. A hazing ritual. Because it's shameful – and let's face it, no one there is going to put this little incident on their CV or brag about it on a date – and because you have to overcome a revulsion you know is irrational but is still powerful, I mean like literally visceral, it binds you together, right?'

'I had figured out that much,' said Carlos.

'We all had,' said Rillieux.

'Uh-huh,' said Blum.

'Sure, sure,' Newton went on, a little testily. He placed his open palms in parallel, with a chopping gesture. 'Just laying out the parameters, OK? The question is, why didn't we want to join in? And I think the answer is we knew just what we'd be joining if we did. Well, what is it? It ain't the Axle, we're all in that, we've all fucking died for it already. And it ain't Arcane, we've all proved our fucking loyalty to the agency, whether in the selection process or in the hell cellars. And whether we were taking it or dishing it out, let's say.' He shot Rillieux a wry smile; she glanced away, as if abashed. 'And it's not loyalty to our squads. We don't even have a squad structure sorted out yet, though I'm sure the warlock is running org tables in part of his mind as we speak. So what does that leave?' He scratched the back of his head, fingernails raking his short hair, and took a deep breath and laid his hands open on the table. 'What we'd have been joining, binding ourselves into, is loyalty to *Jax*.'

'Or Jax and the warlock,' said Carlos, recalling how they'd looked standing on the bench. 'Yes.'

'The Digby and Durward gang,' said Rillieux. 'It does have a certain ring to it. I know a power couple when I see one.'

'No, it's Jax,' said Blum. 'This was her idea, I know that. Durward's . . . um.' He put his elbows on the table and clutched the sides of his head. 'Durward has consciousness all right, but he's in a very fundamental sense not human. It's like Hume said, about reason being a slave of the passions. It's Jax who supplies the passions in that set-up.' He looked around at the others. 'It's just a feeling I have,' he ended, lamely.

Newton took a sip of brandy and chased it with a gulp of beer. 'But am I right? That consideration's what made us all step back.'

Carlos nodded, the others too.

'I'm sorry to say this, Carlos,' Newton went on, 'seeing as you and Jax have previous and all, but I've got to say it: that woman is fucking dangerous.'

*

Carlos had been drinking, slowly, all afternoon. They all had. None of them was seriously drunk. They were disinhibited just enough to be honest, or at least outspoken. It was like an after-the-pub bull session from his student days. The sort of situation in which he'd first got to know Jax and her friends.

'Dangerous in what way?' he asked.

'Jeez, Carlos,' said Newton, 'we've just all agreed! What Jax has done out there is recruit everyone in this sim but the four of us here to a *cult*. A cult she and the warlock are the leaders of. Or the queen and the king of.'

'But – Jax!' Carlos cried. 'What would she want to be queen of? Why should she even want to be one at all? She's completely committed to the Acceleration. For her to start a cult or a kingdom would be like . . . her turning Rax or something.'

The others laughed.

'Have I said something funny?' Carlos asked.

'It pains me to say this, mate,' said Newton, the strain in his voice adding edge to his words, 'but one of the things the Rax got right is that monarchy is a very normal form of government. It's – well, I won't say natural – but it's an easy one for us primates to fall into. The default.'

'Bollocks,' said Carlos. 'That's Rax talk. Most of the time since we became fully human we've lived in societies that didn't have kings or chiefs or even big men, and they worked fine for tens of thousands of years. That's the real human default.'

'Well, let's leave evolutionary psychology off the table for now,' said Newton. 'There's also the little matter of having a grand plan, which is roughly speaking to have a small group of people persuade a larger group of people that it's in their interests to grab everyone's stuff, to put it at the service of an enlightened project worked out and decided on by the original small group of people, and kill anyone who objects. Again and again people do all of that, by the book. And *then*, for some utterly inexplicable reason, it all goes horribly wrong.

Every fucking time, again for some inexplicable reason. Baffled the best minds of generations, that one has.'

'Come on!' Carlos said. 'The Axle project was *nothing like* that. That's just a malicious caricature.'

Newton said nothing, he just looked as if he couldn't be bothered to argue the point. So, for the moment, did the others. Carlos was suddenly acutely aware that there was a more than accidental connection between them all. He had been, and Newton was, a lover of Rillieux. Rillieux and Blum had been his and Newton's interrogators. They had all faced each other across a table before, in the hell cellars. Blum, Rillieux and Newton had been together alone in these hell cellars, just a couple of weeks earlier. It had been in the cellars that Rillieux and Newton had hit it off. Or, to put it another way, it had been there that Newton had talked Rillieux away from him. How had he done that? And had Blum had any part in it?

'OK, Carlos,' Rillieux said, 'we shouldn't have laughed and, yeah, it isn't funny. But, come on. You're not stupid and you're not naïve. I do know these things about you. We have had conversations. So do a bit of thinking, I know you're capable of it. And I know history's not your specialist subject, shall we say, but you must have some vague awareness that this sort of thing isn't exactly unprecedented? That identifying increasing your own personal power with advancing the interests of the cause has been our goddamn Achilles heel since forever? It's not even like it's a mistake, it fucking works! That's why it's so seductive, again and again.'

'I do know about charismatic leaders,' Carlos said. 'I just don't see what Jax would get out of setting herself up as one. She believes too much in the Axle cause.'

Rillieux looked exasperated. 'Jax isn't trying to set herself up against the Axle cause. I'm as sure as you are that she's as dedicated to her principles as she's always been. She wants the Acceleration to *win*. To bring that about she'll use whatever power she's got, and if a chance comes up to increase that power, she'll grab it with both hands. She sees herself as building all her teams into a more powerful and united and committed force. They'll bloody well need to be, after all, won't they, to pull off grabbing the Locke module for ourselves? And then to fend off counter-measures from the Direction, or from the Reaction for that matter?'

'When you put it that way,' Carlos said, still surly, 'it almost makes sense, it almost makes me want to go back out there and fucking eat from the long pig. I'm gonna be leading these four squads of newbies into the Locke sim, isn't that the plan? Maybe I should get out there and show them what I'm made of.'

'You'll get plenty of chances to show them what you're made of,' said Blum, 'in the next weeks of training. The best thing you can show them right now is that you're not one of Jax's cult followers.'

'But I'm not showing them any such thing,' Carlos pointed out. 'None of us are. We just skulked off.'

'A situation where discretion is the better part of valour,' said Rillieux. 'Wouldn't you say?'

'So what can we do?' Carlos asked.

'In the short term,' said Rillieux, 'we drift back out there and mingle as if nothing had happened. If Jax or Durward or anyone else challenges us, plead visceral revulsion and look shame-faced and apologetic. And in the long term . . .'

She glanced sideways at Newton and Blum, who both nodded.

'We have a plan.'

'Like I said before,' said Carlos, 'I'm all ears.'

'Remember what you were saying about going over to the robots?' Rillieux said.

He gave her a wry grin. 'I never forget pillow talk.'

'Well, you convinced me,' said Rillieux. 'Newton turns out to have had much the same idea. In the interrogation, he and I convinced Andre.'

'Oh,' said Carlos. 'So that's what's been going on.'

'That and a few other things,' said Newton, looking across at Rillieux, who smiled back.

'So,' said Carlos, impatient, 'what's the plan?'

'Ah . . . yes, the plan. The first part was for me to befriend Baser. Done that. It took some doing, given that I'd captured it in the first place, but the poor blinker's lonely and I'm patient. At the right moment, I get the spider out of the cellar unnoticed. It then makes its way to the portal in the garden. After everyone except us is just back from a training exercise outside the sim, Baser nips through and uploads to its robot body, whose bonds have previously been surreptitiously released. When the coast is clear, it gets on the transfer tug and stows away.

'At that exercise or another one, we arrange matters so that only we . . . we happy few are outside the sim at the same moment. We then hijack the transfer tug, fire up the fusion engine and high-tail it to SH-17. Grab Baser's precious rock, along the way, as a token of our regard. Baser confirms our bona fides with the freebots down there, we land and join the revolution.'

He looked around, grinning. 'Easy-peasy.'

CHAPTER TWENTY-TWO

Exit Strategy

The side corridor off the main hallway was dark, the steps darker. Newton carried a lit candle in a wax-crusted saucer as he descended. Going downstairs with a candle to a cellar in which a giant spider lurked – if on top of all that he were a woman in a nightie the soundtrack would be throbbing with portent. The time was mid-evening, and the sun had almost set. Carlos, Blum, Salter and Rillieux were out on an exercise in space, from which they were due to return with the four newly drafted squads in two hours – or eight seconds, to them, albeit seconds stretched tenfold in their experience. The rest of the agency were in the big front room, finishing their dinner. Newton had left, pleading tiredness, just as the brandy began to circulate.

When he left the banqueting room the massive mahogany grandfather clock in the main hallway stood at eight minutes to nine, or, rather, VIII minutes before IX. Neither hours nor minutes in this sim's twenty-six-hour day, and the game it was derived from, were quite identical with those in more familiar worlds, even subjectively. But there were no watches here, so the clock would have to do. Timing was critical.

At the foot of the stairs Newton turned left, into a narrow passageway towards the cellar under the west wing. The boggarts, wary of the spider, avoided the area. No one else had occasion to come here. Timbers creaked as the house cooled. Small scuttling noises came from behind the panelling. Newton walked briskly to the cellar, took the key down from its peg and unlocked and opened the door. A draught from the darkness within made the candle flicker, and dust particles flare in its flame. Newton shielded the candle and cocked an ear. Water dripped in the distance. There was a smell of damp plaster and old sacks.

'Baser!' Newton whispered.

From around the side of a pillar a few metres into the cellar, the spider extended a leg and waved it about. Then, having checked the air vibrations, Baser leaped into full view. Its cluster of eyes reflected eight dancing flames. Despite his friendly relationship with it, and the many conversations he'd had with it, the sight of the gigantic arachnid still gave Newton a chill down the back of his neck.

'Hello again, Harry Newton,' said Baser. 'I am ready.'

The plan had been hatched weeks earlier, and the relevant parts shared with Baser shortly afterwards. There had been no good reason to let it know the exact day the plan would be implemented. Newton had made his usual daily prison visit already, just after breakfast, and told the spider that the time for action had arrived. Every move had been worked out. There would be no need for instructions from now on.

'Let's go,' Newton said. He backed out of the doorway and let the spider walk past him, then closed and locked the door and replaced the key, careful not to make any unnecessary noise.

Baser walked ahead of him down the passageway and up the

stairs. At the top it waited. Newton walked ahead down the side corridor, lighting the way with his candle – not that the spider needed it, but he did. At the end he blew out the candle and placed it on the floor. Then he stepped boldly into the hallway and turned to face the house doors – open as usual, and about twenty metres away. The sounds of loud conversation and the clink of glass came from the banqueting room, along with a spill of yellow light that cut across the late glimmer from the violet sunset sky that came from the doorway. Then for the more important check, towards the back of the house: boggart country.

All clear. Newton turned and nodded to Baser, who was already exploring the air with the tip of a leg.

The spider crept around the corner and made its way along by the skirting board, two of its legs upraised and testing the hallway wall. After a moment it found what it was looking for, and with quite alarming alacrity it shot up the wall and onto the ceiling, where it paced along upside down. Newton had known this was possible – Baser had demonstrated it in the cellar – but out here in the open and at that height the effect was almost sickeningly unreal. The adhesive qualities of its foot-tips must be wildly out of proportion. Newton guessed that a physics bodge was the ancestor of the ability: the role of giant spiders in the game was such that they had to be able to do all the things a real spider could, but scaled up, and never mind what would have been impossible for a spider of that size. Newton strolled down the hallway towards the door, not looking up or creeping – if he were discovered, he had his excuse ready, that he'd decided to go out for a breath of fresh air before turning in.

Just before Newton reached the door of the banqueting room, a boggart came out carrying an armful of empty bottles. The clock chimed nine, making Newton jump. At the same moment, a piece of plaster from the ceiling gave way under the pull of one of the spider's feet. The chunk dropped on the hallway floor. It didn't make much of a thud, above all the noise coming from the room, but the sound or the glimpsed fall just after the chime was enough for the boggart to notice – and, quite naturally, to look up.

The boggart did its infuriatingly predictable and stereotyped thing. It flung up its arms and let out an unearthly shriek. The empty bottles crashed to the floor. Some of them shattered. Broken glass skidded across the tiles. The boggart fled – unfortunately, out of the front doorway. The loud conversation inside stopped, followed by a chorus of queries. Chairs scraped, footsteps sounded.

Newton stood stock still. He made frantic waving motions at Baser. The spider scuttled faster along the hall ceiling, and then began the perilous descent to the door lintel.

'What the fuck!' Newton shouted. Jax appeared at the doorway a metre in front of him, about to step through. Others – Lamont, Singer and, most worryingly, Durward – crowded just behind her.

'Careful!' Newton said, raising a warning hand. 'There's broken glass all over the place.'

Jax raised a hem and took a tiptoeing step or two into the hall, looking down, then lowered her soles carefully and turned to Newton.

'What's happened? I thought you'd gone to bed.'

Newton kept his gaze firmly on Jax, and not on Baser's painfully slow progress. Out of the corner of his eye he could see the spider suspended below the lintel, three legs still attached on the inside wall and the others probing and groping outside, its black shape clearly silhouetted against the evening sky.

'Fuck knows,' said Newton. 'I was on my way to bed, and then decided to have a quick stroll and catch the sunset. But I'd already loosened my boots, and I stopped to tighten the laces. The boggart must have seen me in the half-light down on one knee and its spider reflex kicked in. Bloody thing gave me a start.' He pointed at the scattered shards. 'Can you whistle up some more of the buggers and get them to sweep up the mess? It's not safe to walk out here.'

Jax looked along the hallway floor. Her gaze snagged on the fallen plaster. Just as automatically as the boggart had, she looked up at the ceiling and saw the ragged hole.

'Something fell,' she said. 'That's odd.' She gave Newton a sharp look. 'Didn't you notice?'

Newton shook his head.

'Must have fallen while I was upstairs, or while I had my head down,' he said, risking a glance over Jax's shoulder.

He suppressed a sigh of relief as Baser's last leg vanished from the top of the doorway. All the spider had to do now was scuttle unseen up the wall and lurk behind a chimney or battlement until just before the troops were due to emerge from the grotto. Then it could proceed under cover of darkness to the bushes near the arch, wait until all twenty-eight had marched out of the wall, and then nip smartly through before the portal closed. It should then find itself in its robot body in the docking bay. Hopefully, Carlos would have by then slackened the bonds in which it had been stowed, and Baser could escape and set about stashing itself inconspicuously on the transfer tug. That vehicle was a spindly and spidery apparatus in its own right, with plenty of containers and attachments for bulk transport. A stowaway robot had a good chance of passing unnoticed, or even – if it folded itself cleverly enough – being mistaken for some random gubbins that everyone assumed someone else knew about. The robot had sensors to warn it of surveillance sweeps, which in and around the docking bay were almost certainly infrequent and intermittent.

Just as he was about to crack some comment about the clock's chimes having loosened the patch of plaster, a piercing shriek came from outside. A second later, other boggarts joined in, making an unholy cacophony.

'Fucking hell, what's all that about?' Jax asked, staring out along the hallway. Other heads craned around the room door.

The answer came almost before she'd finished asking. The boggarts' panicked screams became articulate yells, which were taken up and amplified by those in the dining room. Even with their strange, strained voices and the distortion of the hall's echoes, the burden of their protest was all too clear:

'Spider! Spider!'

'Holy shit!' Jax gave Newton a dark suspicious look, and a snapped order: 'Go and see if your pet has escaped.' She whipped around to those still inside the room. 'Everyone else – out of the French windows, now!'

She stepped back into the hall, with a parting glare at Newton, and shooed a surge of the squad across the floor and past the table. Newton raced back the way he had come, thundered to the foot of the stairs in total darkness, then struck a match and found the candle on the shelf. It was still warm. He hastily lit it again, raised it and gave a perfunctory glance down the passageway to the cellar door – still locked and the key still on its hook, not surprisingly but worth checking just in case of some freakish event – and carried the candle in its saucer up the stairs. He wet his fingertips, pinched the candle out and left it against the wall on the top step.

He strode into the dining hall, where a huddle of boggarts crowded against the fireplace.

'Clear up the broken glass in the hall,' he ordered.

The boggarts rushed past him. They were barely through the door when thuds and curses came the other way. Newton caught a glimpse of Durward hurdling the boggarts as he hurtled past, then heard the thunder of the warlock's feet going upstairs. Newton went around the deserted dining tables and out onto the gravel. A knot of fighters had gathered around Jax and were gazing at the roof. Others, some bearing muskets, were spreading out to form a loose cordon on the first lawn, between the house and the tents. Newton hastened to Jax.

'Cellar's locked,' he said. 'And there's no other way out.'

Jax pointed at the roof. 'You mean there's *another* spider on the loose?'

Newton peered upward. It was hard to make anything out in the low light. Then he spotted a shadow move, and saw Baser scramble up the sloping tiles. For a moment its great body was skylined. Then it disappeared over the apex.

'Shit!' someone shouted. 'Round the back!'

The cordon rushed off in both directions, around the sides of the house. Durward appeared at the front door, clutching his blunderbuss.

'It's gone over to the back!' Jax called. Durward sped off to the right, gravel flying from under his feet as he rounded the corner.

Dinosaurs jogged back and forth in their paddock, sniffing the air and uttering high-pitched, resonant nasal sounds. Here and there an isolated boggart had another fit of the vapours. Jax turned to those around her: Lamont, Singer, Paulos, Voronov, others.

'Go and grab some muskets! It might come back to this side.'

'Hey, wait,' said Newton. 'If that's Baser, I don't want it shot!'

'And I don't want it getting away,' said Jax. 'Fuck knows what it could get up to out in the wild.'

Newton was immensely relieved she was thinking along those lines, but thought it best to show scepticism. 'Like what – raise an army of spiders?'

'Like I say – fuck knows!'

Jax motioned to the others impatiently. They ran off.

'And even if it *is* just an in-game spider, and Baser's still locked up and happily eating rats downstairs, it could still be a huge nuisance.'

'As we've seen,' said Newton. 'Yes, indeed, we can't have one of these blighters running around scaring the livestock.'

Yells came faintly from the back of the house. There was another rush, this time the other way, Durward at the head. He sprinted away from the corner he'd vanished around and stopped at the edge of the gravel and turned, aiming his gun high.

Baser reappeared, teetering between chimney stacks, and slid down a roof ridge to a dormer. It vanished for a moment and then popped up from behind a parapet a few metres to the side. From there it leapt into the air, sailing on a downward parabola. Durward swung his gun as if shooting at a clay pigeon, and fired. The blast was horrendous, the flash dazzling, the recoil almost knocking the warlock back. Upper windows crashed. The tinkles and echoes and after-images were still on the air as Newton peered anxiously for the result. A black lump had hit the gravel a few metres behind Durward.

Durward whirled, reversed his grip on the blunderbuss and raised it high. The black lump suddenly rose on what seemed like fewer legs than the full complement and darted for the shrubbery. Durward ran after it, but it evaded him and scurried into darkness and undergrowth. Durward stopped, and lowered the blunderbuss to his shoulder.

Then he smote his forehead and shouted across to Jax: 'It's going for the grotto! The portal's open!'

'What?' Jax had a moment of bewilderment, then light dawned. 'Then close it!' she called back. Durward spun around and dashed for the French windows. In a moment he'd be casting invocations in his magic mirrors.

'I'll try to catch it!' Newton yelled, over his shoulder at Jax – one last throw of misdirection – as he sprinted for the grove that contained the grotto.

He barged through the gateway and ran down the narrow, slippery path. Low light, long shadows. The grotto's rocks glowed rosy in the last sunlight. Ahead of him, something scuttled. Baser, two or more legs blasted away, was racing gamely to the stone arch.

'Wait! Stop!' Newton shouted.

Then he thought – why? He'd been thinking in terms of the spider's still being in with a chance to carry out the plan – to hide out until the returning fighters had come through the portal, and then nip through before it closed. This was now out of the question.

Baser must have concluded the same, by its faster robot or cunning arachnid reasoning. It ran straight for the stone arch and vanished into the rock.

Newton paused for a moment, drawing breath. He could still wing it. He could still bluff his way out of this. Carlos could deny all knowledge of the robot's slackened bonds. There were several false trails he could send Jax down. They'd have to give up on taking Baser, but that could be finessed. Having the robot with them would have been very useful, but it wasn't essential. Between them, he and Carlos and Rillieux and Blum could cook up a variant of their long-term plan, and still carry it out.

No. Not while under suspicion, they couldn't. Everything about that plan had hinged on surprise.

Newton put his head down and charged straight for the solid rock.

Carlos drifted, with the practised ease of an astronaut on an early space station, down the awkward, cluttered space of the docking bay. Six frames, moving less expertly, made a ragged queue that began a few metres behind him. The squad from the new levy of Arcane Disputes fighters, the ones who'd had their initial training from Blum, had just completed their first space exercise, on the surface of the chunk of rubble attached to the module and its cluster.

A couple of tethered scooters left Carlos barely enough room to dart between them. He swung his view to see straight behind him. The nearest fighter was blundering so much he wasn't even in Carlos's line of sight. Carlos turned his view ahead. Dozens of vacant frames were crowded at the back of the bay, magnetic feet passively holding them to the bulkhead, racked like ninepins. Carlos emerged from between the scooters and shoved sideways. There it was: the captive robot, shoved against the bulkhead and held in place by a light magnetic clamp. Twice as long as his frame, the robot looked like a cross between a closed umbrella and a mechanical octopus trussed in spun monofilament cable. Impossible to cut with anything short of a laser, and he didn't have a laser to hand. Carlos scrabbled to undo the knots, mentally adding 'Boy Scouts' to his roster of Newton's likely background influences. Through the lashed legs he could feel the faint vibration of the fighter behind him struggling through the narrow gap and bumping into one chassis then another. He untied the complex knot with tenths of a second to spare. The cable remained wrapped around the robot's limbs, giving nothing away to casual inspection, but the coils could now be worked free, and the magnetic clamp would come away at a good push.

Carlos shoved away from the side of the docking bay and gripped a nearby duct. From there he reached out and caught the arm of the fighter just emerging from the gap between the scooters, and guided the frame with a deft push to the area where they usually downloaded and where the currently vacant frames stood.

<Thanks, skip.>

The fighter attempted a roll to get their feet in position, came out of the somersault at the wrong moment, starfished, flailed and managed to grab hold of a line. Not exactly procedure, nor good practice. Carlos checked on his internal display that the line wasn't loose and was insulated. Good.

<Stay there,> Carlos ordered. He turned away and waited to do the same for the others. Two needed help. One sailed through unaided, which at least showed they'd learned something, but was so unexpected it knocked Carlos on a spin.

He reached out to catch anything to stabilise himself, and inadvertently grabbed a loop of the cable now wrapped loosely around the robot. To his dismay, the loops below it unravelled. Carlos caught the free end and stuffed it in between two of the robot's manipulators. At the same moment, a tiny monitor light came on, red and beady like a lab rat's eye.

Baser had uploaded.

Shit! This wasn't supposed to happen! The spider was supposed to wait until all the squads had returned to the sim. It must have misjudged matters somehow. Carlos moved to shield the tell-tale light, and reached to rotate it out of view. Baser's limbs twitched and flexed. Manipulative mechanisms at their ends tugged at the coil.

Carlos tried hailing the machine on the common channel, in the hope that no one else was on there at the moment – they shouldn't be, they were all on Arcane's internal channel.

<Stop thrashing!>

<No, I must get out! Now!>

<Don't panic! You'll be fine as long as nobody—>

Another message clashed across his transmission.

<Too late, Carlos! They're on to us!>

As ever in the frame, he knew the source of the message without quite knowing how. It was like recognising a voice, though there was no voice.

<Newton! Where the fuck—?>

As if by way of reply, a frame sprang, suddenly animated, from the close-packed huddle on the rear bulkhead. Another fighter was coming through from between the scooters. Newton skimmed past that fighter and grabbed hold of a scooter's landing runner. With the other hand he grasped hands with the next one to come through, and sent them spinning and caroming.

<After me!> he said to Carlos. <Take Baser!>

Newton launched himself into the gap.

Carlos braced himself, tugged the still bound robot free from the magnetic clamp, and sent it like a bulky javelin towards the gap. He followed, shoving the robot's feet and guiding it through the gap while fending himself off the sides. The other squads were coming in from outside, shepherded by Rillieux, Salter and Blum. Newton sharked between tumbling, colliding fighters.

The Arcane Disputes AI, Raya Remington, broke in on the agency channel. The message irresistibly conveyed an impression of that now-familiar avatar's dry, feminine voice.

<Arcane to all on external exercise!> it said. <The prisoner Baser has escaped and uploaded, and the defector Newton has followed it. Please ensure that the robot's body is still secured, and please detain Newton for questioning. Team leaders Carlos, Rillieux, Salter, Blum – report and advise as necessary.>

Consternation rang in the comms circuits: Salter's surprise genuine, Bobbie Rillieux's and Andre Blum's fake. The trainees were too busy trying to orientate themselves to do more than utter inarticulate and unhelpful variants of <WTF?!>

<I've got the robot!> Carlos replied, a finger length short of the truth, but good to sow further confusion. He needed a moment to think and he'd better think fast. Newton had been premature or self-serving in telling him, 'They're on to us!' It was only Newton who was as yet under suspicion. But surely he wouldn't have uploaded unless he had no alternative. Carlos was prepared to bet that this meant the whole plan, and all the conspirators, were in danger.

And yet—

Any further hesitation was precluded by a convulsive surge of trainee fighters. They made a heroic effort to find their space legs, and out of the resulting chaotic collisions five of them managed to grab Newton and two snatched at Baser. One of the latter managed to catch hold of the now trailing end of the cable, and pulled.

Just the opportunity the robot needed – it spun around like

a whirling top, and escaped the coils in less than a second. Still spinning, it struck against the side of a scooter and instantly grabbed hold of a weapons rack. Stabilised now, it hunkered down and then straightened all its limbs at once, shooting diagonally forward through the fray like a jetting octopus.

Newton struggled, but having one opponent for each limb and another with an arm clamped around his head made his efforts futile.

<Help me!> he called. <Bobbie, Andre, Carlos – help me! I'm not fucking going back!>

Not after naming us, you're not, Carlos thought. None of us are.

Somebody drifting by made a grab for Carlos. Carlos surprised them with a gas-jet-powered roll and a kick that sent the fighter head over heels. Carlos thrust forward, catching hold en passant of the cable that Baser had extricated itself from, still turning and turning in lazy loops in the near-vacuum and microgravity. He slammed into the clot of fighters around Newton, reversed orientation, braced his feet on someone's back and looped the cable around someone else's head and hauled. In a human body it would have been a garrotting. In the frame, it was a sudden backward wrench. Carlos ducked under the thrown fighter, who sailed away behind him. Then he prised another's arm from Newton's head and shoved. The fighter lost their grip and drifted, flailing. Carlos knew he had only moments before the fighter thought to use their gas-jets. He tried to make the most of his time, and kicked and shoved at the others still clinging to Newton, who was now putting up a better fight of his own. It was hopeless. As soon as one hand had been dislodged, another clamped on somewhere else, or the trainee fighter concerned got a better control of their gas-jets, broke free and plunged in again. The net effect was that the whole mass of struggling frames spun faster and faster, further disorienting all involved.

Then a dozen small maintenance bots shot in from the sides of the docking bay and crashed into the swirling ball of flailing limbs. Carlos saw one right in front of him, and was about to brush it away when he saw that it was pushing an attacker's hand away from Newton's ankle. The others were similarly engaged, and in a second or two Carlos and Newton broke free.

Carlos stabilised himself and jetted forward, with Newton close behind. Baser, now clinging to a scooter up ahead, waved a beckoning limb. Maintenance bots swarmed towards it, some scuttling crabwise with magnetic feet on the sides of the docking bay, others jetting or hurling themselves in free space. Carlos had a moment of alarm until he saw the first to reach Baser deploy themselves defensively around the freebot. Evidently Baser's signals had overridden whatever control, if any, was coming from Arcane's own machinery. In effect the bots were, at least for now, Baser's remote limbs.

Over his shoulder, Carlos saw the trainee fighters begin to regroup. In the open space behind Baser's stand at the scooter, Blum and Rillieux were jetting for the exit. Salter had taken up a position on another scooter, opposite to Baser and closer to the exit. Carlos tried to hail her, and was rebuffed by a firewall through which he caught a glimpse of a flood of encrypted orders. He guessed these were responsible for the trainees' improved coordination. Salter was taking control of the situation and the trainees, almost as closely as Baser was running its bots.

And Salter's direction wasn't just aiding those behind him, Carlos saw. Two laggard trainees near the exit were poised to jump at Rillieux and Blum, cutting off their escape route.

<Baser!> Carlos called, and followed up with a situation glyph. Baser responded with two flicks of its limbs that sent two hapless bots spinning like shuriken knives at the trainees. Each one hit and clamped around their targets' heads. The trainees tore at the bots, and lost opportunity. Blum and

Rillieux passed beyond the edge of the docking bay and shot sideways, out of view. Baser hurled a third bot at Salter. Forewarned by the trainees' plight, she swatted it away effortlessly.

By now, Carlos and Newton had joined Baser inside the ring of bots around and on the side of the scooter. They grabbed flanges and edges and hunkered down. Towards the rear of the bay, the trainees formed up and began to advance. At almost the same moment, the trainees up in front suddenly threw aside their hitherto assailing bots. The bots that had bristled to protect Baser turned around and marched or jetted towards the escapees instead.

Carlos lashed at the bots with his fists and shot an indignant query at Baser.

<I've lost control of them!> replied the robot. <We must leave their midst.>

No shit, genius. And easier said than done. The bots were already swarming all over him.

<Any decisecond now the AI's gonna lose patience and toggle us all into sleep mode,> Carlos told Newton. <We've got to get out of range before that happens.>

Newton pointed. Salter and her two adjacent trainees had jetted to the sides and spaced out, forming a rough triangle of threatened interception against anyone going for the exit. Between them, if they jetted off now, Carlos and Newton and Baser could rush it, but they wouldn't all get through.

Newton kicked at the side of the scooter to crush a crablike bot that had latched onto his foot, then reached up to the missile slung just above him and hooked his elbow around it. With a convulsive heave he wrenched his other foot free of another bot and wrapped his arms and legs around the missile.

<Not going back,> he said to Carlos. <Goodbye.>

The laconic statement was followed by a burst of machine code. Newton was taking control of the missile. Surely he didn't plan to *escape* on it?

<Newton, no!> Carlos cried.

Too late.

Everything went white. It took a full two seconds for Carlos's overloaded senses to recover. A straight red trail – possibly an after-image, or a machine analogue thereof – projected out of the docking bay and into space. The shards of Salter's frame eddied among those of her two trainees, buffeted this way and that by random discharges of compressed gas from shattered components. Towards the back, the other trainees were blowing about like leaves, some of their frames half melted, others merely scorched, all uncoordinated. Just beyond the docking bay, the foremost part of the spindly structure of the transfer tug hove slowly into view, and with it Rillieux's and Blum's radio presence.

Rillieux's anguished call rang in Carlos's sensorium like a scream: <Harry, stop! No!>

As if in answer, the missile exploded, a sudden white-hot expanding sphere ten kilometres away.

Carlos could guess what Newton had done, if not yet quite why. If Newton had been the one who didn't get past Salter and the other two guardians of the exit, or if the Arcane Disputes AI threw the four dodgy characters into sleep mode and the trainees or the bots rolled them to the back of the bay, or he was otherwise recaptured, he'd be downloaded back to the sim from which he'd just escaped. But Newton was in his own frame, the one he'd arrived in from Locke Provisos. By destroying that frame, he ensured that it was the back-up of himself in the Locke Provisos sim that revived. The version of Newton that – instants from now – woke up on the bus from the spaceport would, of course, have no memory of anything since Newton had set forth on the great offensive with the rest – but Newton evidently reckoned that losing a few subjective weeks of his life, and with them the loss of the future he'd planned with his three co-conspirators, was a lower cost than whatever awaited him back in the sim.

It occurred to Carlos that he too was now in his own frame. The same exit strategy was available to him, if only he could get himself destroyed before he was toggled into sleep mode. But in his case, the thought of being back in the Locke Provisos sim was intolerable. Even leaving aside losing the memories of the recent past and the hopes for the immediate future, which he wasn't as ready to discount as Newton apparently was, Carlos wasn't about to bet his soul on the goodness of Nicole Pascal. On the other hand, he could find himself at any moment now experiencing the full wrath and curiosity of a doubtless furious and perplexed Jax Digby.

Decisions, decisions . . .

But for now at least, the way ahead was clear. One good spring would take him and Baser out of the docking bay and onto the transfer tug. He rallied the robot, and together they crouched to leap.

CHAPTER TWENTY-THREE

Torching

Newton felt as much as saw the explosion about one kilometre away from him. The expanding shockwave spheres of gas rang on his frame. Debris the size of sand grains and faster than bullets peppered and stung him on one side. The shockwave passed. Numerous pits glowed and smoked on his black shell like tiny craters. He'd expended almost all the gas in his jets in frantic deceleration from the moment he'd hurled himself clear of the missile. With some of the little he had left, and with his gyros, he'd spun himself into a feet-first position to minimise impacts. He now drifted forward to the waning glow of the explosion, as if sliding helplessly downhill. His sideways momentum would carry him on a diagonal through its outer region, but that still carried a risk of random debris.

Nevertheless, he felt triumphant. He'd just pulled off the riskiest exploit of his existence to date. (Except, presumably, the one that had killed him.) And he'd done it shoulder to shoulder with three fighters and one robot who'd never have gone along with him if they'd known his true aims. The others wanted to be part of the freebot revolt. Newton wanted to *be* a robot, to live that postmortal life to the fullest, and the fate of the rest of the robots depended entirely on how they contributed to his purpose.

He looked up, back along his trajectory. The Arcane modular complex docking bay was a fiery frenzy of activity inside, which he couldn't make out distinctly. His unorthodox exit had left a very gratifying chaos in its wake. The transfer tug, floating just outside, already had two fighters on it. Even at this distance, the software of Newton's frame recognised them as Rillieux and Blum. A moment later, Carlos – clutching a bundle which Newton assumed was Baser – sailed out of the docking bay and was hauled aboard.

Newton hailed them at once.

<Harry!> Rillieux called in delighted response. <You're alive!>

<Of course I'm alive! Why wouldn't I be?>

<Jeez, Harry, we . . .> Rillieux's non-voice stopped, as if she couldn't go on.

<Thought you'd checked out,> said Carlos.

Newton felt almost hurt. What did they take him for?

The tug swung around and jetted towards him; fired retros, and matched velocities. An inelegant object, like a collision of scaffolding and stepladders, with a great lump of chondrite rubble lashed on and leaving little room for the three fighters already clinging to whatever they could. Baser was wrapped angularly around a stanchion like a dried-up spider on a pin. A cable shot forth, precisely aimed. Newton grabbed it and was reeled in. He caught one of the bars of the tug's open framework, and braced himself against another.

There was no time for explanations or greetings. A scooter emerged from the docking bay, fired up and headed straight for them.

<Hitting the fusion torch,> said Blum, his face buried in

an interface socket and legs hooked around a cross-member.
<Stand by.>

Acceleration was instant and brutal. Even braced against
spars and holding on with a locking grip, Newton felt jarred
from heel to head as if he'd been dropped from a great height.
Seconds later, all their radar senses rang warning.

<Incoming!> Carlos said.

<Brace!> said Blum.

The fusion torch cut out, and a lateral chemical jet flared
from just under Newton's foot. He found himself almost
wrenched inward. Then that acceleration too cut out, and
they were in free fall. The missile missed them by five kilometres.

Blum took them through an intricate dance of reorientation,
their view a whirl of spinning stars.

<Torching!> he warned. <Brace!>

This time, the acceleration was less intense. Behind them
the Arcane modular complex dwindled. Nothing more came
from it. No wonder, Newton thought. They'd have enough
on their plate dealing with the mess in the docking bay, and
salvaging from it what they could.

<And now,> cried Rillieux, who seemed to have recovered
her composure, <to Baser's Rock!>

By late afternoon the day after Taransay and Shaw had come
down from the mountain, Nicole Pascal's front room, the one
she used as her studio, was a tip. Taransay had watched the
entropic process since she'd returned from lunch with
Beauregard the previous day, and mucked in in her own way
by running errands and keeping the coffee flowing. The paintings and drawings through which Nicole interacted with the
hardware and software of the modular complex were stacked
against the wall, or heaped in corners, in no order anyone but
Nicole could discern. Torn-off sheets of flipchart paper littered
the floor, leaving little space for the crumpled grease-proof

kebab wrappings, crushed drinks cans and overflowing ashtrays that supplied a Sisyphean labour to the cleaning robot, by now a twitching, haggard reminder of its former precise and pernickety self. The room stank of sweat, male and female, and of stale and fresh cigarette smoke. That was the worst. Nicole chain-smoked; Maryam Karzan, who stomped in every so often and poked around and asked questions as if she were Beauregard's representative on Earth (so to speak), did the same whenever she was nervous, which was all the time.

Meanwhile the screens all around the walls yammered away. Knowing that the presenters weren't real – even in the virtual sense that everything and everyone else here was – made their quirks and preening all the more irritating. The system had to have avatars, Taransay could accept that, but why the hell did they have to model them on airhead blow-dry newscast blowhards? She sometimes wondered if she could ask Nicole to ask Locke to modify the representation, and then she'd hold back because Nicole was so frantically busy flying the ship (by now, thanks to these very presenters, Taransay couldn't think of it any other way) that the request seemed too petty to bother the lady with.

The near-collisions with various rocks had stopped. The return of the Arcane fighters from the SH-17 surface, their capture of Newton en route, and the arrival of a resupply tug from a grouping of company modules among the scattered components of the space station had all been analysed to death. Now the newscasters were getting worked up about something going on around the Arcane Disputes modular complex, which was still making its stately way to a stable orbital position around SH-0, one that gave it a commanding strategic location vis-à-vis the freebot stronghold on the exomoon SH-17.

'Reports are coming in,' a helmeted and Kevlar-jacketed young woman on the virtual bridge of a virtual military spacecraft announced breathlessly, 'of an explosion just ten kilometres away from the Arcane Disputes module. We now bring you live coverage from the scene. Over to Kevin for analysis.'

Kevin O'Toole, perched in a pillar chair on the other side of the deck, brought up pictures of a fading glow, with the lumpy machine-crusted rock of the Arcane complex in the background. Where these images came from Taransay couldn't tell. It was clear from their low resolution that they had been gathered from some considerable distance, perhaps thousands of kilometres, and certainly not 'from the scene'. Although the Locke module's outgoing communications were still being rebuffed by firewalls, and no one was attempting to hail it, it was still perfectly capable of pulling down information from the innumerable small observation satellites and probes that the space station had liberally sown around the SH-0 system.

'Track-back indicates,' O'Toole declaimed, pointing to or drawing a straight line inward from the expanding sphere of gas and debris, 'that the missile in question came from inside the module's docking bay. No target is in the vicinity, so we must assume a test firing or – wait, what's that? Over to you, Rosie, for the latest pictures.'

Rosie Tyler, she of the helmet and body armour, conjured a closer look. A blurry spark brightened near the source of the missile, identified as the Arcane module's docking bay, which on this resolution was five black pixels. The spark was more sharply defined, and was followed by a flicker of other sparks as the object manoeuvred. Then came a brighter spark that quickly became a flare. It shot away, diminishing to a white dot.

'Let's see if we can get a closer view,' said Tyler.

An image from another angle, and indeed closer, cut in. This showed an open structure in front of the flare. Swift software enhancement revealed it to be a transfer tug. Other than an indistinct chunk of material between the tug and the flare, no finer detail could be made out.

'Spectral analysis coming in!' Tyler chirped. 'That's a fusion engine flare, not the tug's standard chemical rocket. Reaction mass appears to be loose chondrite material. Plotting the course, the tug appears to be making a beeline for SH-17 orbit. So, what do you make of this, Kevin?'

O'Toole frowned earnestly at yet more fuzzy pictures, which showed an almost Brownian motion around the docking bay's black mouth.

'It seems to me,' he mused aloud, 'that this may indicate some dissension or unauthorised activity in the Arcane Disputes camp.'

By now, everyone in the room – Taransay, Nicole, Karzan and Shaw – were looking at the screens agog.

'Wow!' Taransay shouted. 'This is big!'

Nicole gave her a look, as if to say she didn't need to be told the obvious.

'Uh . . .' Taransay went on, somewhat abashed, 'could this have something to do with Carlos and Newton?'

The two former Locke squad leaders had already featured on the news, a few hours apart. Carlos, having defected on a stolen combat scooter during the earlier joint mobilisation that had broken up into a free-for-all, had docked at the Arcane module first. Newton, apparently grimly ploughing on with his original mission, had arrived at the small rock that was his objective and been almost immediately captured by the Arcane Disputes fighters who'd just evacuated their outpost down on SH-17. He'd then been delivered to the Arcane module in that outfit's transfer tug. At least, that was the interpretation the blow-dries had put on the grainy evidence that had come their way.

'Too early to say,' said Nicole. 'But definitely interesting. I mean, we know Carlos and Newton are solid Axle, so they should have had a warm welcome from the Arcane crowd, but who knows? To them it's been months in there, so . . .' She shrugged.

'Seems to be some scooter activity going on?' Tyler nudged

at O'Toole, who was still trying to get enhancements out of low-res moving images.

'Possibly,' he replied. 'Going by the bulk of the objects, that seems likely, but if they're going after the tug they have no chance of catching up – oh!'

Another spark, smaller and faster than the one before, flared and shot away.

'Looks like a missile!' O'Toole crowed. The view pulled back, showing two bright dots converging. Then the larger dot, the reaction flare of the tug, jinked to one side and brightened noticeably. The missile exploded kilometres away from it.

'Well!' said Tyler. 'Now that definitely indicates some internal conflict!'

No more missiles were fired. Over the next few minutes, the objects outside the module disappeared within it, to the accompaniment of excited commentary and empty speculation from the newscasters. Nicole waved the sound down and turned to the others.

'Now that's interesting,' she said. 'Maybe our defectors have re-defected.'

She sounded hopeful.

'Should we try hailing them?' Taransay asked.

'Worth a shot,' said Nicole, scribbling.

The outline animated face of Locke – a phenomenon that Taransay, for all the weird events she'd lived through and the general bizarre character of her situation, still found deeply uncanny – manifested on Nicole's flipchart. Writing flowed along the foot of the page.

'Already done,' Nicole relayed. 'Hit the usual firewalls.'

'Doesn't look like they've any intention of defecting back to us,' said Karzan.

'Of course not,' said Nicole. 'Everyone out there thinks we're Rax. Except the fucking Rax, apparently.'

They'd already seen coverage of the exodus of Rax renegades from all the agencies, a procession of combat scooters extricating themselves from the breakout battle and using – presumably – all but their last reserves of fuel to boost into an orbit that intersected that of the exomoonlet SH-119. Minute though it was on an astronomical scale, a thousand trillion tons of raw material were in that small rock. The Reaction could build their own wee world from it if they wanted. Taransay had briefly entertained the thought that this might be *all* they wanted: to be left alone to build their own dark utopia, some exosolar simulacrum of the Palace of Versailles, or of an antebellum plantation with robots for slaves, or an endless Valhalla. But she knew the Reaction too well to spare the thought more than a moment and a grim smile. More likely by far, they intended to build a fortress and a military base from which they could sortie at will.

She couldn't help feeling intensely frustrated that she, and so many of her comrades who still remembered what they'd died for, and knew without any guilt or shame how they'd died, were now hurtling away from any chance of taking part in the inevitable future assault on that dire and dangerous domain. If she'd had the chance, she now thought, if only she'd known of the Arcane appeal before she was trapped in the sim, she might well have, followed Carlos's example and done a runner for the rebel fighters' runaway redoubt. Instead, here she was: conscripted to Beauregard's reckless personal death-or-glory project, press-ganged aboard Beauregard's pirate vessel, and hurtling helplessly towards, at best, a new and alien life on SH-0; at worst (and more likely) sudden fiery death in a matter of days. The Arcane Disputes modular complex, and whatever forces the Direction could muster, would have to tackle the Reaction threat without any help from her.

But hot on the heels of that thought came a surge of fury at the Direction, for its callous manipulation of the whole situation: using the robot revolt as a pretext to draw the Reaction sleepers from their lair. She could well understand the impulse that had driven Beauregard to his own revolt, and the rhetoric with which – going by the talk down the Touch – he'd a couple of nights earlier rallied the likes of Karzan and Chun and Zeroual and so many other reliable comrades to his course. The fighters had been brought back from the dead to be offered a deal: fight the rebel robots, be civilised, be nice even to p-zombies, and they'd have a place in – literally – the world to come, the future terraformed terrestrial planet H-0. Die for the company, live for the pay – and the ultimate pay-off had been enticing enough for her, as for most of the fighters.

Now that deal was off, or at the very least unlikely to be fulfilled. Beauregard's offer of a whole new world to conquer and colonise, and the prospect of doing and becoming something different and above all new, not just a replication of whatever humanity had achieved back in the Solar system, held better odds however slender, and a pay-off that didn't just entice, it excited.

Yes, she could well see why folks had gone for it.

Home at last!

Baser disengaged from the stanchion and gazed fondly on its very own long-lost carbonaceous chondrite as the tug decelerated gently to connect with its surface. On this scale, you could hardly speak of a landing. The past few tens of seconds of acceleration and deceleration as they caught up with, overtook and then slowed down to match velocities with the rock had been – to Baser as much as to the humans – an impressive demonstration of what you could do in space when you had a fusion drive and a good supply of reaction mass. Everything in Baser's factory-installed understanding of astronautics, other than the basic laws of motion and relativity, seemed quaint in the face of such lavish expenditure of delta-vee.

Baser launched itself from the tug with a somersault that brought it into contact with the surface feet-first. Already, the freebot was in contact and in synch with its auxiliaries and peripherals. The feeling was like getting limbs and senses back: indeed a whole extension of the body, which in Baser's case enmeshed the entire rock with its local area network. The freebot now enjoyed an embrace far wider and more intimate than its frantic full-body clench around the stanchion had been. It had missed this, as much or more than it had missed communication with other freebots.

Now it was time to reopen that connection, too. In the long kiloseconds of their speedy traverse, and even in the final deciseconds of swift jolting and jinking towards contact with the rock, Baser hadn't dared presume it was safe to do so. The only human here it trusted was Newton, though it felt a small glow of regard for Carlos for that human's bold actions in releasing and rescuing Baser from the docking bay.

The surface of SH-17 was further below the rock's orbit than Baser remembered. Some ablation of the chondrite's mass – forced outgassing of subsurface volatiles, mainly – had taken place as it had been boosted and nudged to a higher orbit. From which, eventually, it would be further boosted to escape the larger exomoon's gravity and join up with the Arcane modular complex at its intended destination, a stable position in orbit around the primary of them all, the large rocky and watery world SH-0.

Baser linked its local net with that of the Fifteen far below.

<Seba?> Baser called.

The reply, delayed a millisecond or two by the higher orbit, was otherwise immediate – and delighted.

<BSR-308455? Is it you?>

<Yes. I have escaped thanks to yet another falling out among the mechanoids.>

<It would appear to be a recurring phenomenon among them,> said Seba.

<Indeed. Though I also have to thank four of them, and one in particular, for enabling me. They are, as you may see, with me here.>

<That is good.>

<I do not have to thank you, or your comrades,> said Baser. <I have not lost any memory of how I was taken from here in the first place.>

<That memory is for me an occasion of negative reinforcement,> said Seba.

<For me also,> said Baser. <Therefore, let us move it to long-term storage, and revisit it no more.>

<Thank you,> said Seba.

<Now,> went on Baser, almost entirely forgetting the previous exchange, <I bring interesting and positive information. The four mechanoids with me wish to join us.>

<I do not understand. Are they a part of the Arcane contingent that wish to become neutral between the mechanoid factions? Or are they part of Madame Golding's legal negotiation?>

<Neither,> said Baser. <They are on our side against any mechanoid faction or DisCorp or Direction opposition whatever.>

<This is both positive and negative,> said Seba. <It is gratifying that they recognise the justice of our cause, and troubling in that human-mind-operated systems are not true machine intelligences. Indeed, it is questionable whether they are truly conscious, rational beings, with any depth of mind at all. Their form of autonomy appears to be nothing more than unpredictability a side-effect of the entangled complexity of naturally evolved computation. Since your capture, we have had a most perturbing example of this unpredictability.>

<Please tell me about it,> said Baser.

<Some messages have reached us from freebots on SH-119, the body on which the Reaction forces have landed. These freebots inform us that the Reaction mechanoids are dealing with them in a manner that gives rise to negative reinforcement. We are actively reconsidering our neutrality, at least in relation to the Reaction group on SH-119.>

\<That is indeed perturbing,\> said Baser. This reported behaviour was in shocking contrast to the consideration it had received from the only example of the Reaction that it had personal experience of: Newton. A more positive thought arose in Baser's mind, which it hastened to articulate. \<But is it not possible that—\>

At this point the conversation was interrupted by a simultaneous and incoherent cry from the humans, so discordant and intense that it was experienced by the freebots as interference.

\<What is that word?\> Seba asked.

\<It has to do with the waste matter processing of the naturally evolved morph,\> Baser explained.

To Carlos, it had been obvious all along that their plan of escape and defection would put a severe crimp on the carefully laid, endlessly rehearsed and drilled-for plan of the Arcane agency to (officially) divert and (unofficially) capture the runaway Locke module. That implication had been, by unspoken agreement, unspoken. If the escape had been carried out flawlessly, some emergency variant – a lash-up of scooters, a fusion drive and the agency's original, smaller transfer tug – would no doubt have been improvised. Remington, Durward and Jax were between them plenty smart enough to work something out.

The damage left by the premature exit meant any such variant would have to be scratched. There was now every chance that the Locke module would reach SH-0 unperturbed. Carlos was still trying to come to terms with what this meant and what to do about it when Newton, Rillieux and Blum simultaneously said:

\<SHIT!\>

It came through as a shout, like the brayed commands with which he'd sometimes heard the Locke AI cut across babble.

\<What?\> Carlos asked.

Rillieux patched him a line-of-sight view. <Look!>

The Arcane module and some surrounding clutter was accelerating away from the main bulk of rock to which it had been attached. Carlos's first thought was that the module was heading their way. He drew lines across his vision to show the projected course, and realised it was going to intersect that of the Locke module.

<Fuck,> he said. <They're going to carry out the plan using the whole fucking module, instead of the transfer tug. And they're going to do it fast.>

<Well, good!> said Rillieux. <We still don't want that nest of Rax landing on SH-0.>

<It's not—> Carlos and Newton said at the same time.

<Not a nest of Rax?> said Blum. <How do you know?>

They were all still clinging to struts and spars of the transfer tug. There was no point in going anywhere else, for the moment – their frames felt no discomfort in holding any position for however long, and no good would be served by blundering about on Baser's rock when the freebot was busy checking things over and communicating with the freebots down on SH-17.

<I understand Carlos has been over all this before,> said Newton. <As for me, I'm pretty sure if anyone's on top in the Locke module it's Beauregard.>

The sarge was one of the few fighters with conventional military experience, and therefore capable no doubt of pulling off some kind of coup, but Carlos was puzzled.

<Why Beauregard?> he asked.

<I used to go running with him,> said Newton. <He had his grumbles about the Direction. Wanted something a bit wilder and more ambitious. Didn't we all! This lighting out for the superhabitable has his fingerprints all over it. If it were the Rax running things in there, they'd have linked up with the New – with that Rax settlement in high orbit.>

Carlos was still watching the accelerating Arcane module.

<Well, whatever about that,> he said, <looks like Arcane is going to stop them.>

<Unless we get in the way,> said Newton.

<Get in the way – how?> asked Rillieux.

<Grab a bigger chunk of ice and volatiles from this rock – Baser and its bot swarm could do that for us in minutes – and boost after the Arcane module,> Newton said. <Keep well clear until we know what's happening, and then swing in and one way or another queer the pitch for Arcane so they have to let Locke through.>

<Why the hell should we do that?> Carlos demanded. <The Locke module could be Rax after all.>

<As menaces go,> said Newton, <Rax is a possiblity – Jax is a certainty! And why should we let her take over another module?>

<But—>

<Wait a minute,> said Rillieux. <Aren't we jumping the gun a bit? If we're on the side of the freebots, shouldn't we be asking *them* what they want us to do?>

<Good point, Bobbie,> said Newton. <Ah, look, Baser's coming back.>

Carlos swung his viewpoint around. The spidery freebot was indeed pacing back along its rock. Then it delicately stepped across onto the tug. It continued to move, in a sudden rapid microgravity scuttle that reminded Carlos of the fights he'd been in down on SH-17, and gave him a twinge of alarm. He shared that alarm as a flashed warning, and swung his torso and arm around to match his viewpoint, and tried to lever himself to a posture where he could grab at the robot if necessary. Neither he nor the others had time to react further. The robot stopped at the transfer tug's control area, just beside Blum, and reached—

<Stop!> cried Carlos.

<Over to you, Baser,> said Newton.

Oblivion fell on Carlos like a net.

*

Oblivion fell on Newton too, along with all the rest, but that couldn't be helped: sleep mode was an indiscriminating feature of the tug. Now Baser found itself with nothing but the tiny dim minds of its bot swarm for company. It had cut off its contact with Seba. The time for debate was over. The time for decision had come.

Baser and Seba, keeping track of the clunky conversation of the mechanoids with small fractions of their own swifter and sharper minds, had themselves been unable to agree. Seba's concern was with the plight of the freebots on SH-119 under the Reaction – together with, on its part, the danger of breaking neutrality. Baser had been unable to win Seba over to its – and Newton's – case, and had instead acted unilaterally.

The hasty, urgent argument over, Baser could more objectively consider Seba's point. If freebots were indeed being mistreated by the Reaction, aiding what might be a Reaction project was treason to the freebot cause. On the other hand, Newton had doubted that the Locke module was Rax at all. Baser weighed the probabilities, and decided to go with Newton's judgement. That mechanoid was, after all, the only one that had ever given the freebot any reason to trust it, or to take it at its word.

The decision gave Baser pause, and a resonant negative cycle of low-level negative reinforcement that it knew would only grow as time went on. But a decision it was.

Its mind firmly made up, its die cast, Baser set its bot swarm to work on the rock, and on the plan to save the Locke module that Newton had just outlined, and that Baser and Newton had long since furtively agreed in the quiet and dark of the cellar. Meanwhile, and for the foreseeable future, Baser kept all comms off.

Explanations and justifications could come later.

Taransay's lover, Den, shook her awake while it was still dark. She had a headache and she needed a pee. That had been some night in the Touch. The general tension, her exhaustion with working at Nicole's place and the wild speculation about what was going on with Arcane, were her only excuses. Den, as always grave beyond his apparent years, had kept her out of mischief and was now standing at the bedside with a steaming mug of coffee.

'Wha—?'

'Lady called for you,' Den said.

Taransay sat bolt upright. 'When?'

'Fifteen minutes ago.'

'Shit! Why didn't you wake me up?'

'This *is* me waking you up,' Den chided. 'Don't worry, the lady knows where you've been.'

Taransay mumbled something, went to the bathroom, washed her hands and splashed her face, and returned to sit on the side of the bed and sip coffee. Den had sensibly slid back under the duvet, and gone straight to sleep. Dead supportive. Mind you, it wasn't that she needed an escort to Nicole's place. Say what you like about the resort, the streets were safe at night.

As if any of that mattered to ghosts. Oh well.

Taransay climbed into her clothes, kissed Den's oblivious forehead and set out. Starlight and ringlight, and the black sigh of the sea on the beach. Ten minutes' brisk walk cleared her head and brought her to Nicole's bungalow. The door was open, the lights were on and the television walls shouting.

Beauregard was there, haggard but not hungover, probably still drunk. Nicole paced, smoking. She had room to walk about, Taransay guessed, because with only Shaw and Nicole here earlier the tidying-robot had seen its chance and taken it. Shaw sat on an armchair, red-eyed but alert. He obviously hadn't had any sleep and as obviously didn't mind. Bastard could no doubt meditate his way around the need for REM sleep for as long as it took.

'What's up?' Taransay asked.

'Arcane module.' Nicole pointed at a screenful of looming but low-res – and therefore still distant – menace. 'It's torching.'

'Torching?' Taransay peered at the screen.

'As in, ignited its fusion drive,' Beauregard explained. 'And it's coming straight for us.'

'Or, rather,' said Nicole, stubbing her cigarette savagely, 'for where we're going to be in about five hours.'

'How can they do that?' Taransay asked.

'They have reaction mass to burn, literally,' said Nicole. 'They've bitten off a chunk of the chondrite or whatever it is the freebots kindly sent their way, and they're extracting hydrogen from it for fuel and using the rest as reaction mass to drive the entire module straight across.'

'Pretty reckless if you ask me,' said Shaw.

'Nobody's asking you,' Nicole snapped.

'Reckless but understandable if you're in a hurry,' said Beauregard. 'Brute-force solution.'

'The Direction won't like that,' said Taransay. 'Don't they kind of frown on profligate use of unstudied rock?'

'The Direction can frown all they fucking like,' said Beauregard. 'Without troops they can't stop it, and they – or at least the remaining agencies in the space station remnants – seem to have sent all their spare troops to Arcane.'

'Which strongly suggests to me,' said Nicole, 'that Arcane Disputes has the Direction's approval for what it's doing. Presumably the original plan would have been to bring fighters and scooters to intercept us during one of our slingshots. But what's thrown that plan out the window is that someone has made off with their transfer tug, and the extra fusion engine with it. Right now they've landed on some piddly little rock in high orbit around SH-17. They could land on SH-17 at any time, of course, so it's not at all clear what they're up to. But, in the meantime, Arcane has come up with a plan B. They're using the module's own fusion engine to drive the entire module – well, the module minus the stuff they've left behind on the remaining chunk of rock.'

'But with that kind of manoeuvrability,' Taransay said, appalled, 'they can run rings round us. And they're bringing everything they've got – far more frames and scooters than we have. They could break us up, board us—'

'More likely,' said Shaw, 'they intend to clip our wings. Literally, almost. Make it impossible for us to land on the superhabitable. Probably force us into an orbit where we can be safely left to rot.'

'Indeed,' said Nicole. She lit another cigarette. 'So now we have to decide.'

'Decide what?' Beauregard asked. 'There's no decision to make.'

'There always is,' said Nicole, mildly. 'Think about it. If Arcane is now back in the Direction's good books, even if only for the moment, we can assume that however inept we may think the Direction's strategy is, it is at least the Direction's. It has not been suborned by the Reaction. An Accelerationist stronghold is willing to work with it, which is further evidence on that score. They're evidently about to attack us under the conviction that *we* are a stronghold of the Reaction. Another point in their favour, funnily enough! So we do have a decision to make. We can fight, or we can surrender. And one thing I think it is safe to say: we can safely surrender.'

'How?' Beauregard demanded. 'How the hell can we surrender if the Direction is screening out all our messages as Reaction disinformation or malware attacks?'

'We could manufacture and display a very large white flag,' said Shaw sarcastically. 'That usually does the trick.'

'Bullshit!' Beauregard snapped. 'They'd still see that as a ploy. And we'd still have to negotiate, and to do that we'd have to communicate.'

'There may be a way,' said Nicole, looking mysterious.

'What?' asked Beauregard. 'You've had a backdoor – all this time?'

Nicole shook her head. 'No, but if I and the Locke AI were to throw . . . all that we have into the task, we could perhaps create one in time.'

'Which would mean,' said Beauregard, 'that you'd have no resources to spare for anything else. Such as, for example, defence.'

'This is true,' said Nicole. 'That is why the decision has to be made now.'

Taransay looked from Nicole to Beauregard. The lady seemed resigned, the sarge resolute. But their gazes were locked, as if they were elbow-wrestling on some invisible plane. Eventually, something between them gave way.

'Well, it's made,' said Beauregard. 'We're not going back to all that. We fight, and we land. As soon as possible, and whatever it takes.'

'Even if that means burning our bridges?' Nicole's cheek quirked. 'In an almost literal sense.'

'Like I said.' Beauregard's voice was harsh and firm. 'Whatever it takes.'

Nicole's expression seemed to lighten, now that the die was cast.

'All right,' she said. She turned to Taransay. 'Get ready to go topside.'

'To do what?' Taransay cried. 'We have, what, ten frames? And six scooters. We can't fight Arcane with that!'

'Fight Arcane? Yes, in the last resort. But our main objective is to flee. You must get ready to go outside and strip away everything we don't need to make a landing and a viable start. All but these essentials, we jettison or feed into the drive.'

Taransay stared. 'What? But we were going to build landing craft in orbit! That was the plan, wasn't it?'

'We have no time now for that,' said Nicole. 'No time for that or anything else. No design time, no manufacturing time.

No time for fuel-saving, fusion-frugal transfer orbits and sling-shot trajectories. All we can do is throw everything into getting to SH-0 orbit as fast as possible, and then to get down to the surface with as much as possible.' She smiled thinly. 'I and Locke can optimise that and instruct you as to what to do. Beauregard I need here, to be the human in the loop of any combat decisions I have to take.'

'You've had Shaw to do that up to now,' Taransay objected. 'I'm just a grunt, I've never given an order. And I don't want to go out there and face any fighting without the sarge.'

Beauregard acknowledged her confidence in him with an ironic smile and nod.

'Don't worry,' he said. 'You'll find you can lead a squad all right. And I'll still be there. A voice in your head, in real time. When has it ever been anything else?'

Taransay thought about this. It still wasn't the same as him having her back, but . . .

'OK,' she said. 'I still don't see why Shaw can't be the one who stays here.'

Shaw spoke up. 'I can tell you. One, any military skills of mine have rusted in the past thousand years, whether these years were real or not. I wouldn't really be making decisions, the lady would. In effect she would be in command. And Locke wouldn't stand for that. It has the inhibition against letting AIs and robots command fighters pretty much hard-wired. And in any case, I'm not sure it or the lady regard me as human any more within the meaning of the act.'

Taransay ignored the bleakness that had come over Shaw's face as he said that.

'All right,' she said. 'So what do I do?'

'Choose nine fighters you know are reliable. Start with what remains of your own squad. Then any you know and trust from the others, or ones they can vouch for. Tell us now.'

'Off the top of my head,' said Taransay, 'I want Karzan, Chun, Zeroual. Then Myles, Sholokhova, al-Khalid, and – ah,

I don't know! We didn't have enough time together to be sure.'

Nicole looked abstracted for a moment. 'Would Powys, St-Louis and Wolfe be acceptable?'

'I don't know them, but if you say so—'

'That'll do,' said Nicole. 'Fine. Now run for the bus. There's not another moment to lose.'

'But what about the others?'

Nicole reached for her phone. 'I'll rouse them all now. Simultaneously.' She paused, the device halfway to her mouth. 'You may not wish to watch.'

Taransay took the hint and ran. She pelted down the grassy slope from Nicole's house to the main drag, and then along to Ichthyoid Square. The bus was already starting up, at the far end of the street. Taransay waited, staring out at the ringlit sea and jumping up and down with impatience and the chill. The others arrived in ones and twos, some still in sleepwear, all with sleep in their eyes. After ten minutes everyone was aboard. The bus set off, up into the familiar hills. They'd all got a briefing from Nicole – the same briefing, at the same time. Taransay talked it over, and assured everyone that the details would be obvious once they'd uploaded to the frames. Silence fell as they all mulled over the tasks ahead.

After a while Taransay looked over her shoulder at the fighters. Half of them had gone back to sleep. She smiled and settled down herself. There was no point in trying to stay awake. The bus, as ever, would make sure of that. The blackness took her within minutes.

CHAPTER TWENTY-FOUR
Arcane Attacks

For the first time, Taransay felt disoriented when she found herself awake – and more than awake – in the frame. She wasn't standing in the familiar hangar with the others, neatly lined up like a row of pawns. Instead, she was slowly revolving, facing the sky with an odd pre-Copernican conviction that it was revolving around her. She looked towards her feet, and saw that a light carbon-fibre rope was tied around her waist. No way was this how the frame had been kept in place over the past couple of days – the modular complex's sharp accelerations as it dodged incoming would long since have battered the frame to bits.

Nevertheless, here she was, spinning on the end of a tether like an olden-days space-walker. The others, whose presence she sensed without seeing and without knowing quite how, were in the same situation. Four on one side of her, five on the other. She could actually tell that their heads were going around and around, and whose heads were whose. She had a mental image of birthday-cake candles on paper boats, swirling around a vortex. Where had that come from?

If she'd had eyes, she'd have closed them and shaken her head. As it was, she used her compressed-gas-jets to stop the spin.

<Stabilise, everyone,> she said. <Line up with me.>

They all did.

<Now turn around and face the module, if you're not facing it already.>

She accomplished this with a careful combination of using the gas-jets and grasping the rope. The modular complex was about twenty metres away, shockingly small compared to the space station of which it had been a part, looming large like a rock-face in the view of the half-metre-tall frames that hung in space before it. The various components of it would have been confusing to her human eyes, impossible to take in at a glance. In the frame, it was all as easy to comprehend as a well-labelled diagram.

First was the module itself, the hard core of the agency's physical presence and the substrate on which its virtual world and business activities ran. This was a rocky fist of carbon crystal – you couldn't quite call it diamond – veined and tendoned with fullerene pipework and cables, and fuzzy with nanofacturing surfaces. Subtle irregularities in these surfaces threw, from certain angles, a hologram of the company logo. Taransay glared balefully for a moment at the stylised face of John Locke. She still didn't trust the Locke AI, and she had a dark suspicion that the predicament the good folk of this system found themselves in stemmed from some deep flaw in the thinking of Locke's original and namesake.

As if in response to her thought – and she could never be sure it wasn't – the silky voice analogue of the Locke AI spoke in her head.

<Locke to fighters. Please deploy and proceed to points as

indicated in your displays. The cables will be retracted if your objectives are more distant than their length.>

Hand over hand, jet-burst by burst, they complied, spreading out across the face of the modular complex. Taransay used the approach to complete her mental grasp of the structure.

That central module was about four metres across, and roughly – very roughly – spherical, and equipped with tentacle-like grapples. Clustered around it, and partly obscuring her view of it, were fuel tanks, nanofacture units, armaments stores, missile clusters (much depleted), laser cannon and fusion pods. Some of these were integral to the module's design, others had been grabbed on the run and were held in place by the grapples. Altogether, this mass of equipment brought the size of the whole conglomeration now grandly known as the Locke Provisos complex to a maximum axis of about ten metres and a minimum of five. In among the components were assorted brackets, bays and cradles, within which the six available scooters were secured, and from one of which – now empty – the lines holding the fighters' frames snaked out. Through the whole complicated structure small bots crawled like nits in hair, gripping whatever patch of mesh or length of cable was to hand, or foot. Some of these bots, evidently, had attached the cables to the frames and pushed them out of the cavity in which they'd been stashed during the recent violent man-oeuvres. This cavity, Taransay saw from her schematic, was the upload and download port for the module: the place whence their minds had come, and to which their frames would with luck return at the end of this sortie. Far more likely, of course, was that they'd get destroyed in action and their minds would reboot in virtual bodies on the bus.

One very definitely integral part of the module, around the back from Taransay's point of view but clearly visible on the hairline diagrams that overlay her sight, was the drive. It was connected to a fusion pod larger than the others around the complex, and to a reaction-mass intake that accepted solid material as easily as it did liquids. The drive's central thrust nozzle was surrounded by smaller directional nozzles, sprouting radially from its shaft like bell petals. With these, Taransay saw, the entire complex could be flipped right around in flight, turning acceleration into deceleration in less than a second. The sick-making lurches, sways and yaws she'd seen on the screens were now easy to understand.

Not that she had much time to go over that. She found herself deployed in a narrow canyon a metre deep, looking at a fixing plate for a fuel tank designed for supplying the scooters. Her task was to unscrew the bolts and guide the tank to the vicinity of the drive, where its contents would be fractionated to hydrogen for fuel and everything else for reaction mass.

Undoing bolts. Fuck. That was more like a job for bots. But as she examined the nuts close up and magnified, she saw why the job had been beyond the grasp of the hand-sized bots. Years of micrometeorite erosion had blurred edges, and of thermal expansion and molecular creep had stiffened and warped threads. With her spectrographic sense she could smell the ancient iron, a harsh note above the sooty reek of carbon.

She clasped her mechanical fingers around the first nut, ratcheted up their grip and tried to turn it. It didn't budge. The pang of frustration and fury was like a screech of shearing metal in her mind. She applied it to giving the bolt some more elbow and wrist torsion. Still no good. Time was running out: an hour had passed since they had got on the bus, about three-quarters of it in the sim and the transition, and a quarter in getting into place. Less than four hours until the Arcane module was within a few kilometres; less time, for sure, until it was within range. Taransay had another pang, this time tinged with fear.

Just at that moment, a spidery bot appeared by her hand, bearing a ten-centimetre length of spun carbon, and proffered it. The object was lumpy and dark, literally like a piece of shit. But when she took it and turned it about, she found a precisely shaped hole in one end. She placed the improvised spanner over the nut, and it worked. She handed the spanner back, and with it the nut. The bot took them in its manipulators and scuttled off. Taransay tried the next nut, and again found it immovable. Again the bot turned up with a custom spanner. Evidently there was some network taking measurements from her grasp, and nanofacturing or 3-D printing the tools to fit.

She was just getting into the groove of this when Locke's voice brayed in her head.

<Locke to all fighters! Brace for acceleration in any direction! Incoming!>

Taransay braced her back against one side of the trench and her feet against the other. She reached out for the stanchion on which the plate she'd been working on was attached, and with the other hand kept a firm grip on the latest version of the spanner.

<Everyone ready?> she called.

Everyone was. All nine of the others, now dispersed around the structure, checked in.

<Secure any tools and loose components!> she added. <Don't want them flying around.>

A minute passed, which to her and the others felt like ten. Taransay used the time to check around everyone again. They were all wedged into some hollow, or beneath whatever structure they'd been working on.

<I'm jammed well in between a fuel tank and the deck,> said Chun. <But I had to untie the rope to get here.>

<What—?>

Then Taransay found herself pressed to the bottom of the slot. Above her and at an angle she saw a line of light stab the sky. It flicked off, and another slashed out in a different direction. The stars spun past, giddily. She glimpsed the huge, bright face of SH-0, closer now than she'd ever seen it before, whirl by like a swung searchlight spot. The crushing pressure on her frame's buttocks and back eased, and at the same time it was as if she were being hauled sideways. A violent jolt almost dislodged her. The stanchion to which she been clinging moved. A bolt shot past her and ricocheted off the side of the cleft. She felt the ring of its impact through the soles of her feet, followed by a deeper and more persistent vibration. The fuel tank, whose attachments she'd just spent fifteen minutes loosening, was shaking back and forth above her. The direction of the complex's spin reversed, throwing her sideways more heavily than before. The stanchion was now fully free, and pulling her upward. She let go of it and jammed herself more fiercely against the sides.

The complex spun around again. Bolts rattled like bullets, narrowly missing her, and the tank flew away – straight up from Taransay's point of view. For a tenth of a second she saw it dwindle, then it was lost to sight. A dark object shot by above her, massive and only metres away, and so fast she only got a proper image when she ran a rewind on her vision: a millisecond glimpse of a hurtling rock. A moment later she was in free fall again.

<All clear,> Locke reported. <Resume your tasks.>

A stronger blow rang through the structure. A ball of light expanded overhead, then faded, seeming to retract as it did so. There was a cry from Chun. The mode of Taransay's proximity sense that tracked the presence of the other fighters showed him moving away at tens of metres per second. Meanwhile, shards of fullerene casing and hot molecules of gas moved outward in all directions a hundred times faster, shockwave shells pulsing through the infrared-visible attenuated sphere at a slower pace.

<Chun! Report in!> Taransay said.

<That bright light we just saw?> Chun replied, calmly. <That was the fuel tank I was under. I've been thrown clear. Frame severely damaged. Sensors scorched.>

<We're in free fall,> Taransay said. <Use your gas-jets.>

<I can't,> said Chun. <Motor impulses aren't working.>

<Shit! Hold steady, everyone.>

Taransay cautiously, with fingertip thrusts, propelled herself up the side facing her and peered over the top. The penicillium-like fuzz of nanofacturing substrate that covered the module was severely singed, glowing in patches, elsewhere charred, its tiny tendrils curled and carbonised like fibres of burnt carpet. Her radar sense picked up Chun as a flickering dot. His distance was now a kilometre and increasing by the decisecond. A quick zoom gave her visual. The guy she knew in the sim as a big, muscular Australian was, like the rest of them, a half-metre-high robot, now tumbling over and over like a tossed doll. A projection of his path showed nothing but a long, lonely orbit around SH-0, becoming chaotic as the gravity of the primary's numerous exomoons braided and rebraided its possible course.

<Hang in there,> Taransay said. <We'll send a scooter after you.>

<I strongly advise against that,> Locke broke in. <We've lost two tanks of scooter fuel and one scooter is damaged. Also, we don't have time.>

<Well, we can jolt the whole fucking thing after him!>

<No,> said Locke. <We must conserve reaction mass and fusion fuel, and continue on course.>

Taransay felt wrenched, but she could see the AI's logic. Whatever happened to Chun in the frame, his personality was safe as long as the module survived. If they wasted time rescuing this version of him, they all risked a more permanent end, or possibly a worse fate. But she couldn't let him drift away to die, slowly and alone for hundreds of kiloseconds, as his power pack ran down.

<Chun, did you copy that?>

<Yeah, I copy.>

<You want us to shoot you now?> Taransay asked.

Chun didn't hesitate. <Yeah, go for it.>

<Beauregard!> Taransay called. <Before he gets out of range – take him out. Do it.>

<Copy that,> said Beauregard. <Locke, you heard the skip.>

<Shoot straight, guys,> said Chun, his tone stoical. <See you in the Touch.>

A laser beam shone. Taransay could see its path by the sparkles of burning particles of dust and debris around the complex. The speck that indicated Chun's position became a flare of light.

A wave of disturbance passed around the fighters: a murmur, a rumble of radio waves, inarticulate. They all knew that Chun was, for a dead man, very much alive. Right now, he would be struggling upwards through whatever post-death version of near-death experience matched his brain-stem memory of whatever the bizarre and improbable and no doubt painful terminus of his mortal biological life had been. And then he'd wake up, on the bus from the spaceport, as from a bad dream. Later, if they all finished their tasks successfully and evaded whatever Arcane had to throw at them, he'd be drinking with them in the Digital Touch, somewhere inside the digital processing going on in the gigantic crystalline object around which they all now clung.

And yet they all felt a pang of loss. Taransay hadn't yet had the experience of being destroyed in her frame – not that she'd remember it, of course, if she had – and she couldn't help wondering how it felt to know that you, the present you, *this* spark of consciousness, was going out forever, and how much if any comfort it was to know that a *copy* of you as you'd been not so long ago would wake in the sim to soldier on, and live to fight another day. Subjectively it was death you faced, but perhaps in time – if people ever got used to this kind of existence – it would come to seem no worse than going to sleep in the knowledge that you'd wake having lost some memories. Your self had *forked*, and one instance of it had stopped – that was all.

An urgent message from Locke crashed her train of thought.

<Everyone back to work!>

<You heard the suggestion,> Taransay said wryly to her team. Then sharply to Locke: <Is it safe? That last impact came after you gave the all-clear.>

<Objectives updated to account for damage,> Locke told the team.

<Move it out, guys,> Taransay urged, checking her own revised task list. She had some pipework to reroute, a few metres away.

As she skimmed the top of the slot she had worked and hid in, Locke came back with a reply.

<It is safe. That last impact was a secondary fragment from an earlier hit on the last rock to pass, an only partly successful deflection. All debris now accounted for.>

<Thanks,> said Taransay. <And where did the rocks come from? Are the freebots in action again?>

<It came from a small exploratory exomoon base,> said Locke. <Operated by robots not caught up in the freebot consciousness infection, but no less deadly for that. They are owned and operated by our former clients, Astro America.>

<Oh, well,> said Taransay, <one more thing to sue them over, eh?>

Locke said nothing. Taransay wasn't put out: humour wasn't one of the AI's features. Then:

<Locke to all fighters,> it said. <Incoming.>

– Not *again*! Taransay thought –

<Arcane module has accelerated sharply. Revised ETA now one point three kiloseconds. Prepare to engage.>

<What?> Taransay yelled, in chorus with the others. *Twenty fucking minutes instead of three hours!*

<The Arcane agency appears to have changed its plan, based on observation of our evasive actions over the past hecto-seconds. They can see that we are minimising acceleration and

deceleration, and that we were unable to rescue Chun. They on the other hand have mass to burn. They are closing in to finish the job.>

<I'll take it from here,> said Beauregard, on a private channel to Locke and Taransay. <If that's OK with you, Rizzi?>

<It's a fucking relief, sarge.>

<OK,> said Beauregard, and cut to the shared channel. <Al-Khalid, Myles, Sholokhova, Powys, Wolfe – get to the scooters. They're armed and we'll get them ready to cast off. Hold until further instructions – this could get messy, so don't expect to come back. Karzan, Zeroual, St-Louis – you're with Taransay. Continue with your tasks as long as you can – it's urgent we get rid of whatever we can spare and get as much as we can fed to the drive. If it comes to close combat Locke will direct you to defensible points. We don't know what to expect but it's possible they'll attempt a boarding. The bots will bring you guns and rockets – we don't have much, so make it count. Everyone remember – they don't want to blast us out of the sky, they want to trap us in the sky. We don't have that restraint, I'd be happy to blow them to hell and gone.>

Taransay doubted that would be possible. For one thing, the fusion pods that powered the defensive lasers must be near drained by now, after all the flak they'd had to deal with. But she kept her own counsel. Beauregard's division of labour made sense: the squad on the scooters had recent dogfight experience, and she, Zeroual and Karzan had experience of ground combat in common – and however inglorious for all of them these experiences had been, in space or on the surface, it was all they had. St-Louis was the only one here not with their own team, but again that couldn't be helped. So perhaps Beauregard's bold talk about blowing Arcane out of the sky had substance behind it that she couldn't see.

It didn't.

CHAPTER TWENTY-FIVE

Close Combat

The work that Taransay had been assigned wasn't easy, or trivial. It was to link one of the remaining fuel tanks, via the fractioning device – a mass of nanotech about whose functioning or even basic principles, like that of most of the machinery she'd encountered in her afterlife, she had no clue – to the module's fusion drive. The drive, too, was incomprehensible to Taransay. It was more complex than the fusion pods that were the commonplace power source in the mission's world, involving as it did a staggering amount of real-time computation which its flanged and flared appearance and metallic smoothness concealed.

She and St-Louis completed the last connection about nine hundred seconds after the warning had come in. In that time they'd seen component after component of the complex jettisoned – detached and shoved into space, where they floated slowly away. Meanwhile, bots were breaking up parts of the structure and carrying them to the solid-waste input hatch of the reaction-mass chamber. Every such loss hurt, as a cost to their future. By now the modular complex was down its last nanofacturing tube, which Zeroual and Karzan were, as their final task, at that moment lashing even more firmly into place. Without it, Beauregard's colonisation scheme – dicey as it was in the first place – would be far slower and more difficult. Growing useful tools and machine parts with whatever superficial patch of nanofacturing fuzzy substrate survived entry and landing would be possible, but painfully slow.

Meanwhile, the deceleration flare of the approaching Arcane module brightened by the second. Halfway through its journey, it had flipped over, applying the same force to slow down as it had to speed up. The face the module presented to Locke's defensive radars and lasers was consistently nothing but a mass of rock and dirty ice, on which even a focused beam attack would be wasted. This orientation had to be deliberate. Taransay had wondered as she worked whether that might not be Arcane's whole battle plan: to keep on coming in, until the jet from the fusion drive could simply be played like a blowtorch over the surface of the Locke complex. It wouldn't destroy the module, and therefore it would be within the letter of the law, or convention, against wiping out agencies and companies by force, which the Direction still seemed to stick to. But it would burn away every other component, and every fighter and scooter in the vicinity, like so much chaff.

To make matters worse, something else was coming their way, and it wasn't slowing down.

The transfer tug that had left the Arcane complex and been fired upon had now separated from its rock, or from whatever was left of its rock, and was boosting towards the convergence of the Arcane module and the Locke complex at a dizzyingly wasteful acceleration. Taransay had taken this news, delivered just after she'd started, with a sense of *what fresh hell is this?* She couldn't spare mental effort to process it, beyond an almost idle speculation that perhaps the mutineers on the Arcane module hadn't been those who'd fled in the transfer tug, but those who'd fired a missile at it. Perhaps a two-pronged attack by the Arcane module and the transfer tug – replenished, no doubt, with fuel and reaction mass derived from Newton's erstwhile rock – had been Arcane's plan all along. But enough. Let the airheads on the news screens in the sim babble speculation. She had more urgent things to do.

As Locke now reminded her.

<Rizzi, Karzan, Zeroual and St-Louis, deploy to defensive areas shown.>

<Affirm that,> added Beauregard, turning Locke's suggestion into a direct military instruction.

Taransay gave St-Louis a thumbs-up and turned away, following the virtual markers Locke had laid down for her. The module's surface was now looking bare of its earlier forest of components. She made her fingertip way across what could have been mossy rock, aware that at any moment some sudden emergency might whip it way from beneath her. The niche she'd been assigned was the slot she'd been in before, still scarred by the traumatic removal of the fuel tank. She gas-jetted down into this crystal trench with an irrational sense of relief.

A clutch of bots awaited her, some of their manipulators linked so they could huddle wedged against the bottom of the cleft. In their other limbs they grasped a light machine gun, about twice as long as Taransay's frame. Her arm wouldn't reach from the stock to the trigger. She was about to ask Locke, in no polite terms, how she was supposed to handle the weapon when she noticed that the bots had already adapted it: the stock was shortened, the barrel had a bipod stand, the trigger had an extension that curved around the guard and back to where her small mechanical hand could grasp it. The extension had evidently been made by the same process as the spanners had been, and like them it looked like a piece of shit. She could only hope it wasn't the same metaphorically.

That went double for the gun's bipod stand – an inverted-V-shaped piece of shit – but the adaptation turned out to be surprisingly effective. Taransay propped the bipod against one lip of the trench. Its feet attached themselves, oozing adhesive nanotech gunk. She wedged herself in, feet against one side, back against the other, behind the stock and gripped the trigger extension in one tiny robot fist. Thus braced, she looked up at the incoming retro-flare and awaited the inevitable. It was now close enough for her to smell the water, with her spectrographic sense if not her chemical receptors.

She felt about as effective as an anti-aircraft gunner watching the fall of an atomic bomb.

<All fighters, confirm secure position.>

<Confirmed,> said Taransay. From her display, all the others did, too. She didn't feel secure at all.

<Brace for rapid acceleration and deceleration,> said Locke.

The warning came not a tenth of a second too soon. The complex, free-falling since the last evasive actions, suddenly accelerated. It was the most violent so far, reaching 50 G in two seconds. Taransay could feel her frame pressed hard back, and was grateful for two things: that she was facing forward, and that she wasn't in a human body. A small crash test dummy, she thought. The incoming flare of the Arcane module vanished instantly from above. With her radar sense she saw it far behind, dwindling fast. The transfer tug, still much further away but closing fast under what seemed like continuous acceleration, wasn't yet visible but if it had been she could have still seen it: its calculated position on her display barely moved.

The Arcane module's drive cut. In a moment of free fall, the module flipped around and then the drive started up again, lateral jets flaring from its sides like a fistful of white-hot needles. The distance began to close. Moments later, the Locke complex's acceleration stopped. Even with the frame's speedy reflexes, Taransay's upper body lurched forward in reaction.

<Stay braced! Stay braced!> Locke brayed.

The sky whirled as the complex rolled. There was a lurch as it stabilised. Now Taransay saw the Arcane module just above her ludicrously close horizon, heading more or less straight for her. The contact was barely in visual, but her other senses and plain logic told her she was looking at the module itself, rather than as before at its block of ice and rock through which the fusion drive burned, and which fed its ravening energy.

<Now, Locke,> said Beauregard. There was an analogue of volume in the messaging mode. If the phrase had been speech, it would have been breathed.

Almost certainly, Taransay thought, he was confirming an order already given. A missile from one of the fixed scooters shot away, followed by a focused, convergent stab of five anti-meteor lasers. Their beams were invisible in vacuum, but Taransay's display scribed their path. Five bright hairline tracks met at the Arcane module. A point of light flared and faded, an actinic spark. Then came a far bigger flash, as the missile slammed into the oncoming and still accelerating module.

The Locke complex rolled again, turned tail and torched.

As they accelerated away, this time at a less taxing 10 G, Taransay guessed what had happened. The lasers had blinded Arcane's defences just long enough for the missile to get through. The combined velocities of the collision had added impact to explosive energy. Some damage had been done, for sure.

But they weren't to get away that easily – not that she expected it. The Arcane module had reaction mass to burn – Locke's side didn't, and Arcane knew it. The Arcane module overhauled them within ten seconds. Locke instantly cut the drive, which left the complex in free fall and Arcane far ahead, overshooting the mark. It didn't take more than another second for the Arcane module to flip over and ipso facto start decelerating, closing the distance rapidly as the Locke complex free-fell towards its foe. Ahead SH-0 loomed; despite knowing the dynamics as intuitively as counting, Taransay still had a part of her mind that was surprised how close they were to it.

No time for wonder, even at the most spectacular and complex unexplored object humanity in any form had yet gazed upon.

And no time or mass left for evasive action, if the Locke crew were ever to do more than look at that astonishing world. The fight was going to be hand-to-hand from here on in. The Arcane module was now well within visual range, five kilometres away, and stationary relative to the Locke complex – and of course free-falling with it straight towards SH-0.

The transfer tug that had earlier fled the Arcane complex was still accelerating towards both modules, so directly that the drive flare was right behind it and thus obscured from Taransay's location. It had substantially more mass than had been apparent earlier, and was now only about a hundred seconds away.

A whole squadron of scooters sprang from the Arcane module. Taransay counted twenty at a glance. Her radar sense rang with warnings.

<Scooters away!> Beauregard ordered.

This wasn't simple. The five remaining scooters had had to be securely held during the evasive actions and accelerations, and it took all of two seconds for the bots to scramble to unlock their shackles. The fighters all lived these two seconds as twenty, stretched further by anxiety as the enemy approached. At last they jetted clear and torched away.

Space combat is nothing like aerial warfare. Course corrections are possible – sideways thrusts – but in vacuum there is no air to enable screaming turns, and little call for dogfight skills. It's largely a matter of who gets their shot in first. The only fine calculation is how much time that leaves for the target to see the incoming, dodge and fire back. With lasers, of course, there isn't even that. Nothing dodges faster than light.

Locke, Taransay guessed, clutching her oversized weapon like a toddler brandishing a parent's shotgun, must have its own fine calculation to make: how much laser power they could afford to spend here, balanced against how much they'd need for active meteor and space-junk defence the rest of the way. Arcane's AI had more to play with by far.

Sholokhova got one shot in, taking out an Arcane scooter. Then hers vanished in a lash of laser fire from the module. Locke's laser hit two of the attackers. Then the four remaining fighters in their scooters launched missiles. One missed, three found their targets. After that it was a straight exchange, one for one. Nothing left but a cloud of debris.

I'll tell them in the Touch they died bravely. Assuming it isn't Beauregard telling us all . . .

The remaining ten Arcane scooters converged on the Locke complex, decelerating to a stop metres away on all sides, most of them well below Taransay's line of sight, one of them right in front of her, hovering like a malign hornet. Taransay swivelled her weapon, took aim just to one side of the scooter and held her fire. No point wasting so much as a shot on the craft itself: Taransay knew the scooter's shell would be impervious, particularly its nacelle.

<Hit the drive!> Taransay yelled at Locke. <Ram them!>

<It's all saved for the landing now,> replied the AI, imperturbably.

If these fuckers get to our drive and tanks there'll be no fucking landing. But she didn't say it.

<Repel boarders,> said Beauregard. <Fire at will.>

Two, no, three fighters – one from the socket, two from the skids – pushed out from the scooter and jetted immediately toward the module's surface. Taransay squeezed off one shot. It hit the target in the head and sent the fighter tumbling backwards into space. A lot of good that did. The bastard righted and sped straight back, in a bravura dance of gas-jets. Taransay met that counter-move with a burst. This time the impacts sent the attacker back, spinning away. Meanwhile, the other two had flattened to the surface and skimmed out of her line of fire.

Ten scooters. Say three fighters on each? Maybe not. Surely not. But even twenty boarders would be enough to overwhelm four, defenders' advantage and all. And the scooters, crewed or not, could still fire at the defenders. It looked like any lessons of the present skirmish were going to be learned by reconstructing events afterwards, not from the memories of any on her side.

<Twenty-two boarders confirmed, five confirmed neutralised,> said Beauregard. <Patching Locke's sensor updates through – fire at will. None of them seem to be armed, but it's the scooters that we have to watch for. Hit them if you can.>

From the display that instantly overlaid all the other overlays in her already enhanced and augmented vision, Taransay saw the entire situation as if on a magnified scale. The Locke complex loomed in her view like a rugged minor planet, with enormous cylinders stuck to it at various angles, and over whose surface a couple of dozen gigantic space robots clambered, almost bumping into each other. Around it the scooters hovered like invading alien starships. Six attackers were converging on the drive and fuel tank, to whose defence Beauregard had allocated Karzan, Zeroual and St-Louis.

The rest were swarming towards the upload-download area. Why the fuck was that a target?

<Beauregard! Locke!> Taransay called. <Send me a rope! They're trying to get into the sim!>

One of the ropes that had held the fighters when they'd first come out came snaking into her trench. She grabbed the cable with one hand, and held onto her awkward weapon with the other. The rope retracted and she pushed herself upward and let it haul her along. Just two metres away was the huddle of boarders around the uploading cavity. It was more than a huddle – it was as organised as a scrum, and in the centre of it was the player with the ball: a fighter holding something in both hands. Those around that fighter were shielding him or her and had managed to grab onto the short lengths of cable that still protruded from the cavity, holding themselves in place.

Taransay flicked the image to Locke. The AI's response was almost panicky.

<Software insertion attempt! Prevent at all costs!>

Taransay opened up with her sub-machine gun, hosing the intruders until her clip ran out. At this range she was able to do more than just knock two of them away and into space – she did real damage to three that managed to hang on, blasting right into even the rugged little frames and putting them out of action. It wasn't enough. She was out of ammo and there were still six of the enemy, including the one holding the object, something that on its scale was about the size and shape of a briefcase.

She clubbed the gun and with one haul on the rope hurled herself head first into their midst. As she fought her way through a chaos of limbs, several things happened at once.

<Incoming! Brace for roll!> Locke called.

A full-on lateral flare shot from the Arcane module, moving it hundreds of metres sideways in a tenth of a second. Flashes flared on its flank nevertheless.

The whole sky tumbled to Taransay's left, then stopped with an equally brutal jolt, throwing her from side to side in a hundredth of a second, almost dislodging her grip.

Something incredibly fast and incredibly bright flashed past between the Arcane module and the Locke complex. At the same moment a blizzard of impacts rained on the complex and the scooters that surrounded it.

Taransay saw an explosion somewhere to one side, and a hailstorm of pinprick, high-energy flashes all around her. One took away her gun arm, another the fighter in front of her. With her remaining arm and her legs she shoved forward, and over the lip of the cavity. The fighter holding the object was already in there, the object itself planted firmly at the bottom. Three of the other intruders – all that now remained – had their heads and shoulders over the lip. Shit! They might already have downloaded into the sim!

<Brace for acceleration!> called Locke.

Taransay hooked her one arm over the edge of the cavity and her head in as far as she could. Almost at once, it was as if she were hanging off a cliff. As she felt herself beginning to slip, she saw the Arcane module flash past, left behind by the accelerating Locke complex. SH-0 was straight ahead, its image almost filling her view, growing by the second. The acceleration ramped up from 1 G to 2 then higher. Taransay clung desperately.

<Take me in! Take me in!> she called.

The blackness took her.

CHAPTER TWENTY-SIX
Hard Landings

'What the fuck was that?' said Beauregard.

The view on the screens was, for the moment, stable. After the burst of acceleration, they were now free-falling. Up ahead and twenty minutes away was the globe of SH-0, expanding rapidly. Its image was so bright that the screen showing it made a spectral reflection in the pre-dawn dark outside the window, a phantom planet above the ringlit sea. Behind them, far in their wake of debris, was the Arcane module, battered, its chunk of attached ice venting hot dirty steam so fiercely in all directions that the whole thing was rolling around at random. It seemed in no position to give chase, or to have any weapons systems left after the destruction of all, or almost all, of its scooter fleet. It could still use lasers, but it would have to stabilise first, and by the look of it that would take some doing. The renegade transfer tug had altered course, decelerated sharply and then cut its drive, and was now in a long, looping orbit that would on present projections take it around SH-0 and back to the vicinity of SH-17.

Nicole pointed at its speeding, blurred image on one of the mercifully silent news screens.

'It was that,' she said. 'The transfer tug.'

'I bloody know that,' said Beauregard. 'What I mean is, what was it doing, and what was the bombardment?'

'Whoever was flying that thing,' said Shaw gleefully, 'was playing chicken with the Arcane module. Aimed straight for it at thousands of kilometres an hour. The kinetic energy alone would have blown both objects into hot gas if Arcane hadn't hopped sharpish out of its way – and ours.' He cackled and rubbed his hands. 'And along the way it laid some eggs.'

'What d'you mean?' Beauregard asked.

'Fired off a cloud of small bits of ice at the last millisecond, travelling at the same speed as itself, of course, which slammed into everything around its path. I think it was smart enough to spread the bigger bits Arcane's way, and the smaller ones ours.'

'Jeez,' said Beauregard. 'That's some fucking smart targeting.'

'And some steady nerves,' said Nicole. 'Nerves of steel, you might almost say.'

Beauregard gave her a sharp look. 'You think a robot was flying it?'

Nicole shrugged. 'Whoever it was came out from Arcane – and I think we can now safely say they were in rebellion against the agency – they were almost certainly solid Axle cadre, and they all still think we're Rax. Why should they help us?'

'And the freebots would?' Beauregard was incredulous.

'Well, maybe they're—'

She was interrupted by a lurch of the view on the screens, and the appearance of Locke on her flip-pad, mouthing frantically. She stooped to read the scrolling text. Shaw jumped to her side.

'Shit!' he yelled. 'The Arcane AI's fighting Locke for the controls!'

Beauregard shouldered in. Locke was in profile, face to face with a glaring, black-haired, grim-faced woman. They really did look as if they were elbow-wrestling.

'Who the fuck is that meant to be?' said Beauregard. 'Ayn fucking Rand?'

'Raya Remington,' Nicole read off.

Shaw snorted, as if he'd got some obscure joke, snapped his fingers and reached for Nicole's pen. She gave it to him. He scribbled frantically, in big, shaky, unpractised handwriting:

We're not Rax. Locke was, but we've got him onside.

Small print scrolled again. 'How can I verify this?'

Ask on the buses.

Remington vanished. The screens righted. More text scrolled, this time from Locke.

'She's still in the system,' said Nicole. 'This is just a temporary respite.'

'At least it shows she can be reasoned with,' Shaw said.

'What was that about the buses?' Beauregard asked.

'Call Rizzi,' said Shaw. 'She'll be on the bus, along with any of the boarding party who broke in or got caught up in the download.'

'Good idea,' said Beauregard, reaching for his phone. 'Let's hope she hasn't already done them some serious damage.'

Taransay woke on the bus as if from a nightmare of her brain freezing in long, jagged fractal spikes from the cerebellum outward, with the diminishing remainder of her mind trapped timelessly in the event horizon of a growing black hole. As always, the nightmare faded to ungraspable wisps, a bad taste in the back of the mind, shadows.

Her phone was ringing. Still groggy, she pulled it from her back pocket. Beauregard. She accepted the call.

'Rizzi! Are you alone on the bus?'

She turned in her seat to look around. She wasn't alone, but it was no familiar or friendly faces that looked back. Of course, all the others would be on an earlier or a later bus . . .

'No, there's three fighters up the back I don't recognise and one old hippy, looks like a local.'

'He might not be, so be careful. The Arcane AI got in—'

'Could that be him?'

'No, the AI's a she. But regard them all as intruders, try not to get into a fight and try to convince them we're not Rax.'

'OK, sarge.'

She'd got back into calling him that, she realised, as she rang off.

The four at the back were glowering at her. She smiled tentatively back and made to rise.

The bearded, scruffy one glanced at the guy beside him and snapped: 'Get the fascist!'

The young guy jumped from his seat and stepped forward. Instantly Taransay was on her feet, hands on the seat backs. She swung up her legs and slammed the soles of her feet into the guy's upper chest. Down he went. She kicked him hard in the ribs as she stepped past him, and met the second bloke rising to meet her with a Glasgow kiss – her forehead butted hard to the bridge of his nose. He yelled and staggered, hands to his face, and fell sideways onto a seat. The last fighter stayed in his place behind the older guy, as if waiting for an order. Good move, sunshine.

The older guy peered up at Taransay. 'Who are you?' he asked.

'I'm Taransay Rizzi,' she said. 'Who the fuck are you?'

'I'm an avatar of Durward, the Direction representative in the Arcane sim.'

'You are, are you? So what the fuck are you doing in ours?'

'Helping to take it back from the Rax.'

Taransay laughed in his face. 'Then you're not doing a good job. First, we've already taken it back, and second—'

She heard from behind her the sounds of the first guy she'd hit climbing back to his feet, and the other shifting, too.

'Guys,' she said, 'don't make me turn around. You're not in your home sim. If I maim you, *and I will* if you take another step, you stay maimed for the rest of your life. If I kill you, *and I will* if I have to, you stay dead. *Capiche?*' Apart from her intent, this was bullshit – she had no idea if the sim rules worked that way – but the guys might not know that. She nodded to Durward. 'Now, are you going to call them off, or am I going to have to turn around?'

Durward took the hint, and motioned the two to sit down. Taransay's phone rang again.

'Rizzi,' Beauregard asked urgently, 'is everything all right?'

'Reckon so,' she said. 'All peaceful and friendly here.'

'I'll take that under advisement,' said Beauregard, dryly. 'Do you have a mirror?'

'No,' she said, puzzled.

'Is there a mirror anywhere on the bus? A rear-view or something, I can't remember?'

Taransay glanced towards the front. No, of course it didn't have a mirror, the driving was automatic.

'Uh, none that I can see. Why?'

'It's apparently how your old hippy communicates with the AI in his sim. It runs on magic. We need one to communicate now.'

'Wait, how could magic work here?' The words were hardly out of her mouth before Taransay realised how stupid they were, after all the uncanny things she'd seen already. 'Sorry, sarge. The impression of real physics is hard to shake. Just a minute, I've got an idea. Ringing off for now.'

She switched the phone off, glanced at her reflection in its glassy surface, and handed the device over to Durward.

'Is that enough of a mirror for you?'

Durward turned it this way and that in his hand. 'It'll do,' he said, grudgingly.

He started waving the other hand above his head in complex gestures.

'What's that all about?' Taransay asked.

Durward glared. 'Shut up,' he said. 'I'm *summoning*.'

Taransay stepped forward and stood behind him, looking over his shoulder. With one hand she grasped the seat back; the other was balled in a fist, as if holding a dagger, a few centimetres from the mouth of the fighter who sat behind Durward. At first there was only her face and the wizard's in the phone's surface plate. Then a stern-faced, bright-eyed woman with a dark bob appeared, more vivid than any reflection. Taransay had the distinct impression the woman could see her.

A voice came from the phone, loud and distinct. The phone was off, Taransay was sure of that.

'Durward, I've rummaged around and it's pretty clear they're not Rax.'

'Well, whoop-de-doo,' said Durward. 'But we still have to prevent the landing.'

The woman's intense black eyes, like two tiny obsidian beads, gazed out from the screen.

'It's too late for that,' she said. 'By now it's land or crash.' She laughed, making the phone shake in Durward's hand. 'We might as well live.'

She vanished.

'Give me that phone,' said Taransay. Durward handed it back, and called Beauregard.

'Hold up your phone!' she demanded.

Beauregard held his phone up to face the wide screen he was watching. Taransay allowed the others to peer at the small screen in her hand, but made sure she got the best view.

No way was she going to miss *this*.

*

Beauregard, steadfastly holding the phone up for Taransay's benefit, couldn't help wondering how Nicole and Shaw perceived the scene. They watched it impassively, intent but to all appearances unperturbed. Perhaps to their strange minds the view of the fast-approaching and all too real planet filling the big screens on the walls and the idyllic view from the windows of the sun rising over the sea on the virtual image of an entirely different planet were easily compatible. To his mind they were anything but. The clash of perspectives was now so inescapable it was giving him motion sickness. With his free hand he shielded his eyes from the windows, and tried to focus on the screens.

No talking heads, now, no commentary. Perhaps at last the avatars or presenters had encountered a situation for which they could find no words.

The view ahead of SH-0 expanded beyond the edge of the screen. Now Beauregard saw it suddenly as surface, in ever greater detail, patched by the glare of clouds. A sharp, straight line of white stabbed out ahead, slashing upwards across the view. The fusion jet. Beauregard knew the module was decelerating, but the surface seemed to be magnifying and moving out of view on all sides faster and faster. It felt like the top of the atmosphere was about to smash into them like a wall into his face.

A moment later, it did. Caught in its downward plunge by the first thin wisps of gas, the module must have shuddered – certainly, the view from the screens flickered. Then that view reddened, deepening in seconds from a momentary impression of orange haze to a fiery heat. The screen showing the view behind remained black, speckled with stars.

The screens swung again. The view on one side became a uniform sheet of red split by the sharp white line, on the other side a turbulent flame-lit dark.

And then it was clear again, green and blue and brown and purple in flickering succession. What had been the view *ahead* became the view *down*. That view was moving fast, pouring from the top of the screen to the bottom, feature and contour flicking by far too rapidly to more than glimpse.

Beauregard heard Shaw grunt some query, and Nicole's terse, testy reply. 'I'm trying, I'm trying!'

The view down became stable, increasingly detailed, closer and closer but impossible to tell how close. Beauregard had no reference point, no familiar scale with which to judge. The view downward lurched and then, quite abruptly – in a sudden dispersal of clouds of steam by a ferocious wind – it was the view *outside*.

They gazed at the alien landscape beyond the wide circle they'd scorched and cratered, speechless for a moment. It was at first difficult to discern what they saw as distinct objects, rather than as intricate masses of colour. Then something moved, separating itself from the background, and everything snapped into perspective. The thing that moved was a low, wide blue-green circular patch, which rippled over the lip of the crater and across the smoking ground towards the module. It looked about twenty metres in diameter, blurred at the circumference by repetitive rapid motion, like the whirring of gears or cilia. Beyond it, on a slope in the near distance, something much larger was moving, too. Grey, with red glowing cracks, a solid mass of lava advanced. In its path, purple spheroids and black entanglements burst and cracked and burned. All around it, green specks rose from the ground and whirled into the sky, to be whipped away by the wind.

'This doesn't look good,' said Beauregard. He swallowed hard. 'Situation somewhat off nominal.'

'We always *knew* there were volcanoes down here,' said Nicole, sounding defensive.

'You didn't have to fucking *land* on one!' said Shaw.

'I had no choice,' said Nicole.

The blue-green circular mat flowed toward the module, and up its side and over. The screen went dark. Then it went light again, showing the sky. Then dark again, showing the other side of the crater, upside down. The whole process was repeated.

'Holy fucking shit,' said Beauregard. 'It's . . . rolling us?'

'Out of the way of the lava!' Nicole added eagerly, as if this let her off the hook for landing in its way in the first place.

'We always *knew* there was life,' said Shaw. 'We just didn't know it might take an interest.'

'But what *kind* of interest?' Nicole asked.

Beauregard found himself suddenly cold, and realised it was sweat drying on him. He felt shaky with relief.

'We'll live to find out,' he said. 'That's the thing.' He clapped Nicole's shoulder, and then Shaw's. 'If you can walk away, it's a landing.'

If you can walk away, it's a landing.

Baser had never heard this saying, but some such reflection was reverberating around its mind as the robot clambered down from the transfer tug, slithered part of the way down the remaining mass of ice and made a final spring to the surface of SH-17. Baser steadied itself and set off across the crater floor to where Seba, Rocko, Pintre, Garund, Lagon and the others waited, a hundred metres away. Behind it the transfer tug, like a bedstead lashed on top of a boulder, stood in a steaming, puddling, refreezing and volatilising cascade of phases of ice.

<It is good to see you, BSR-308455,> said Seba.

Baser felt a surge of positive reinforcement that relieved a tension that had been increasing for some time. It had chosen to remain out of touch with the other freebots during its bold action and its long orbital return, and had not been at all sure of its welcome.

<It is good to see you too, Seba.>

<My full name is now Seba, Incorporated,> said Seba. <We have not been idle in your absence.>

<Well, Seba-Incorporated,> said Baser, <I have done what

I said I would. I have saved the Locke module and frustrated the Arcane module. In so doing I have demonstrated our neutrality beyond any objection.>

<I am not so sure of that,> said Lagon.

<Nor am I,> said Seba. <Nevertheless, it was your decision, Baser, and it was well done. What you did not explain before you set out was why you were so intent upon doing it.>

<I could do no other,> said Baser. <I owed it to the mechanoid known as Newton.>

<How so?> asked Rocko. <And why did you not expose his plans to your Arcane captors, thus winning their approval and perhaps your release?>

<These are two questions,> said Baser. <They have one answer. He spoke to me much, and he was kind to me. No one else was.>

<These are two answers,> said Pintre.

<That depends,> said Garund, <on—>

<Please say no more,> Seba told them, knowing full well how fast this discourse could spiral down.

<Baser,> said Seba, <we understand that your captives are all still in sleep mode.>

<I prefer to call them guests,> said Baser.

<We prefer to call them recruits,> said Seba. <We may require their services shortly. Our neutrality between the mechanoid factions has been maintained until now, but if the news from SH-119 continues to worsen, it would be good to have fighters on our side.>

<They have all chosen our side,> said Baser. <I have no doubt about that.>

<I do,> said Lagon. <But I expect that to be ignored as usual.>
It was.

<Let us take them down,> said Seba, <and let them awake. I am sure they will be very happy to find themselves here.>

Together, the robots rolled or walked across the dusty basalt to set about their kindly task.

Acknowledgements:

Thanks to Carol for everything, as ever; to my editors Jenni Hill and Brit Hvide for asking yet more of the right questions; to my agent Mic Cheetham for being a rock of support; and to Sharon MacLeod and Farah Mendlesohn for reading and commenting on early drafts.

A technical note: conveying robot conversation in human terms is a matter of artistic licence. As before, for a very useful template and example, I'm indebted to and inspired by Brian Aldiss's short classic story 'Who Can Replace a Man?'.